I0760364

RABID

THE SAVAGE SPIRIT OF SENECA RAIN

RABID

Cover Design: Story Wrappers
Editing: Polished Perfection
Book Design and Typesetting: Enchanted Ink Publishing

ASIN: B08JPN4BMN (E-book)
ISBN: 979-8733650821 (Paperback)
ISBN: 978-1-959537-01-4 (Hardcover)

WWW.IVYASHER.COM

WWW.RAVENKENNEDYBOOKS.COM

For all the broken, shattered, *rabid ones*

who still came out on top.

IVY ASHER
RAVEN KENNEDY

RABID

THE SAVAGE SPIRIT OF SENECA RAIN

ONE

THE SMELL OF RAIN TICKLES MY SENSES AND RIDES the delicate breeze as it winds through my hair. I can almost taste the threat of moisture all around me, feel the heaviness of the storm clouds as they move sluggishly closer. The change in weather feels fitting for today. It's as though the sky is willing to open up and release its sorrow, something I still haven't been able to do.

Murmurs all around me pull my attention away from my wandering thoughts. I focus back on the shoots of greenery spilling out between the white flowers cascading over the top of my mother's casket. They really outdid themselves with the arrangement, and I'm trying to appreciate the thought and effort put into it instead of thinking about how much my mother would have hated it.

As pack healer, my mom despised premature death and useless violence in equal measure. Her feelings weren't only reserved for those of our kind or the humans we so closely resemble when not in our wolf form. They applied to *all* living things. Give my mother a plant she could nourish and encourage to grow, and she'd love you for life. Give her a bouquet of flowers doomed to die the second they were picked, bundled, and handed over like some prize to revere, and *that* would earn you a lifetime of side-eye.

She was strong in her convictions, gentle in her bedside manner, and the best mom I could have ever hoped for.

And now she's gone.

I trace the lines of her casket with eyes that still haven't cried, and I can't help but feel like none of this is real. I know I'm still in shock, probably with a little denial sprinkled in for good measure, but I just never saw the day where I would be here without her unwavering strength and guidance standing right beside me. Especially not with the Flux being only days away.

Hess, my mother's closest friend, finishes his speech and wipes at his eyes. I look around to see if any of the gathered pack are looking at his show of emotion like it's a sign of weakness, but instead of gauging how many challenges may be coming his way in the near future, my empty stare lands on a set of familiar, shifty black eyes. They watch me intensely, and a shiver of disgust licks its way up my spine. I force my grossed-out gaze away from the pack's alpha and settle on one of the betas, who rises from his seat.

His cargo khakis are wrinkled, just like his white button-down shirt. There's an unkempt brown scruff on his cheeks and neck, all of which would be okay if he were grieving, but he's not. No, his disheveled state is from the bender the pack had last night. Their antics and laughing were loud enough to reach even my house on the outskirts while I tried to prepare for today. It's as though they were celebrating the loss instead of being crippled by it like I am.

The disrespectful beta steps up to say a few words before it's time to lower the coffin, and I want to growl at the absurdity.

I can't focus on what's being said anyway, because I can still feel Alpha Burke's eyes on me, and it's making my skin crawl. I've had far too many run-ins with him since he showed up three years ago with his band of rogues and attacked us before successfully taking over the pack. He took an interest in me right away, but my mom was always there to intervene and keep things from escalating like they have with so many other females here.

Gifted healers are hard to come by, and it seemed no matter how much Burke wanted to mess with me, he wanted my mother to stay and do her job more.

But now she's gone, and I'm alone. Maybe if I had my mother's gift, I'd have room to negotiate for my safety, but sadly, that blessing skipped this generation.

Now, I find myself trapped in what could become a very volatile situation. It doesn't matter that I want to be left alone and have no interest in being claimed by the alpha or anyone else in this pack. If I survive the Flux and get my wolf, I know that I won't be given a choice. I'll be claimed by someone whether I like it or not.

I do my best to ignore the weight of Burke's unwelcome gaze as it roves over me. I try not to fidget or show any sign of weakness or discomfort. If I do, it'll invite trouble, and that's the last thing I need so close to the ceremony. I'll need to come up with a plan, figure out what I'm going to do about my place here. But right now, I just need to bury my mother and come to terms with the fact that she's no longer here.

Seamus, the mountain-sized beta pretending to give a shit about my mother and my loss, gives me a nod that tells me it's time. Pulling in a fortifying breath, I stand up slowly, walking to the head of my mother's coffin. I stand there, numb, lost, and not nearly ready to say goodbye.

Grief tightens my throat as I reach out and place my palms on the smooth shiny wood of her coffin, a hint of red in it that would have made her smile. I lean down and kiss the top of the box that will encase her until the dirt and the plants claim her for their own. My chest tightens as I step back, and then I watch as they lower her into the ground where I can't follow.

Cold anguish washes through me. My breath feels labored, my limbs exhausted, but the loss I'm drowning in still doesn't prick my eyes. I exhale through the pain, robotically moving over to the pile of dirt and palming the shovel that's been speared into the side of it. I stomp it all the way into the soil and lift out a small mound, waiting until her coffin rests solidly at the bottom of the hole the omegas dug earlier.

When the straps are pulled up, I sprinkle my dirt into the earthen tomb, wishing I could crawl in and be buried right alongside her. The dark soil spoils the pure white of the flowers, but it feels like a fitting metaphor for what my life is now.

The shovel is gently taken from my hands, and one by one, the pack lines up to help cover my mother and say their final goodbyes. I step to the side of the procession, but I can't ignore the feeling like something inside me is dying with each shovelful of dirt dropped on top of her.

Tilting my head back, I look up at the darkening sky. The vastness of it settles over me, and I try to feel less caged in, less trapped by my pain and my circumstances, but a large body steps next to mine, his heat and intention impossible to ignore. I don't need the senses of a wolf to know who it is.

I look up to find hair as dark as pitch, skin the color of warm oak, and twisted black eyes. Burke is stacked like a house with enough muscle and brains to hold tight to the reins of the Twin Rivers pack. He's gorgeous, he knows it, and he likes to act as though his looks and status entitle him to certain things. He doesn't understand in the slightest that when you're cruel and corrupt on the inside, it taints what people see on the outside. I like to call it the Gaston complex.

"You're going to be okay," he tells me, as though I'm some distraught mess in desperate need of his half-assed consoling.

"I know," I reply simply, offering a weak smile to someone who pats me on the back as they walk by.

My throat grows tighter as the grave quickly fills up, and all I want to do is wander into the woods I've spent my whole childhood in and get lost for a while. To be away from calculating eyes and the crowding grief.

"You'll have your wolf soon, and all of this will feel more bearable," Burke declares, as though he even cares or thinks the loss of my mother is something that can be replaced by a pet.

Shame instantly fills me for that thought. The wolf spirit that chooses us is not a *pet*, I inwardly chastise myself. I subtly move to put a few more inches of distance between me and my alpha. But he steps closer, as though my retreat is an invitation and not an expression of discomfort. I feel his hand land against the small of my back, and the ends of my long hair brush across his arm. He leans down, crowding my space, and as much as I want to pull away from him, I don't.

Fighting Burke's advances spurs him on almost as much as being weak and vulnerable does. He's a predator through and through. I was hoping to avoid him until I could figure out what to do, but I should have known better. Far too many females can attest that Alpha Burke doesn't back off until he gets what he wants, one way or another.

Just get through today, Seneca. After that, he and everyone else will be busy preparing for the ceremony, and then you can come up with a plan. Honor your mother, let him paw and get it out of his system, and then the Flux will be here before you know it.

I hold my breath, my body going rigid as he practically buries his face in my hair. A few of the pack members skirt by us, their eyes locked on the ground, not interested in getting involved, no matter how wrong this is or how uncomfortable I obviously am.

"*Mmmmm*," is growled into my ear sensually, and I tamp down the revulsion that crawls up my throat. "Yours might be my favorite scent ever," he declares, his chest brushing against my arm.

I roll my eyes and lean away from him as much as I can, completely disgusted. What kind of male hits on a pack member who just lost her mom?

Burke picks up a strand of my thick umber-brown hair and plays with it between his fingers before leaning back with a chuckle. Sometimes, I can't tell if he's oblivious to the nauseating effect he has on me, or if he likes it and pushes my boundaries solely because my discomfort does something for him. I look up, unable to stop the warning that fills my arctic blue eyes. It's one thing to corner me around our home and pull this shit, but this is my mother's *funeral*. I thought he'd at least pretend to care and show a little decorum. Now I see how naive and stupid that was.

His black eyes glitter with amusement as I shove my hair behind my shoulder and step away from the hand at the small of my back.

"I need to finish burying my mom, if you don't mind," I announce caustically, and his lascivious smile grows even wider.

"Sure, you do that," he tells me, his tone authoritative as though I require his permission. "But you and I need to talk about your living situation, so come find me when you're done."

Confusion moves through me, and his words cause my feet to stop in their tracks. "What's the problem with my living situation?" I ask, crossing my arms over my chest when his skeevy eyes spend too much time studying the neckline of the black dress I'm wearing.

He lifts a shoulder. "It's no big deal at all, it's just that your home belongs to the pack healer, and...well, the pack doesn't have one anymore. You have until after the Flux, but when the new healer arrives…" He doesn't finish his sentence, but he doesn't need to. Is he seriously going to kick me out of my home? My father built that house.

I clench my jaw, swallowing down the vitriol I want to spew, refusing to take the bait. This seems to amuse him even more, because he flashes a wolfish grin at me like a starved person watching a loaded dinner plate being set in front of them.

"Of course by that time, your wolf will have come, and you know what's going to happen then, Seneca."

My spine stiffens both at his insinuation and the use of *Seneca*. I don't want him to have any part of me. Nothing. Not even his mouth momentarily wrapping itself around my name for the second it takes him to speak it.

"The Flux ceremony is about honoring the wolf spirit that chooses its host," I bite back, while the rest of the black-clad and disheveled pack members trickle away.

"Sure it is," he replies with a cocky twist of his lips. "It's also about the males choosing between the she-wolves who come to play and claiming one for himself." His eyes skim over me. "I've been waiting a long time for this, and I'm going to enjoy seeing your new wolf immediately roll over to show me her belly. Once you have her, you'll be *begging* me to claim you."

Bile rises up the back of my throat, but I say nothing. What can I say? The horrible thing is…there's a very real chance it'll happen exactly like that. And there won't be a damn thing I can do about it.

No one can control the Flux. When I give myself to the ceremony and take in the wolf spirit that chooses me, it's out of my hands, and most females immediately submit to a male. It's a sacred ceremony, one that should be honored and celebrated. But all Burke cares about is dominating. Claiming. Taking what isn't offered. And the salt in the wound is…my wolf might want him to.

As if he can see the fire dim in my eyes, Burke winks, and then he leans down, fisting some loose dirt in his hand before dropping it in my mother's grave with an unceremonious toss. Then he turns and walks away with his hands in his pockets, whistling a damn tune as he goes.

I hate him.

Looking back at the freshly turned soil now covering the coffin, I swallow hard, ignoring the two gangly shifters waiting off to the side awkwardly, shovels already in their hands to finish securing my mom's body in the ground as soon as I leave.

She's gone. My father's gone. I have no other family left.

Above me, the sky finally crumples, like it's squeezing the clouds in its fist. Raindrops fall just as I turn away, unable to bear the sight of the grave turning into a muddy, puddled mess. My mom would've hated that.

I walk away, the sky's offering mocking my dry cheeks. Even knowing that I'll forever be separated from her by six feet of cruel earth, I still don't cry. Instead, the clouds mourn for me as if they're trying to show me the way.

If only I weren't too lost to follow.

THE HEALER HOUSE, *MY* HOUSE, is quiet.

It was never quiet before.

With a pack as large as Twin Rivers boasting several hundred shifters, our house *always* had someone in it being treated by my mother. That's what happens when you're the pack healer. Rain or shine, dawn or dusk, someone always needed her.

Full moons were the worst. That's when Burke runs the mandatory pack fights. *To keep a healthy hierarchy*, he always says. But really, he just likes watching pack members beat the shit out of each other. Since most of them don't actually move up, it's all for entertainment.

My mom despised the fights, of course. A lot of the pack do. But leaving isn't easy, especially for the families who've been on this land for generations upon generations. So, we all just wait and hope that the day will come when Burke is challenged and he loses.

Until then, my mother was always there, ready to set bones before they healed too quickly, to use her magic to ease their pain and calm their wolves. If Burke wants someone to patch up his pack members by the next moon, he's going to have to get a healer soon. And just the thought of someone taking her place, of living in my home...

I shake my head and walk down the light-yellow hallway that suddenly feels too narrow. Mom painted it a happy color. She said it would wrap you up in a hug when you came home. But all I feel is cold and lonely as I head for my room. I don't let myself look in the direction of hers; I don't want to see the emptiness that's a reflection of what I feel in my soul.

The smell of lavender and vetiver greets me as I open my door. I peel off my wet dress and underwear, flopping them into the sink as soon as I walk into the bathroom. It takes me fifteen minutes of just standing under the hot spray of the shower before I feel whole enough to actually wash. Another fifteen to get myself out and dressed in leggings and a long-sleeved shirt, because even though it's warm out, I feel cold to the bone.

Another fifteen minutes go by, and all I can do is sit on my bed, staring at the sunset bedsheets we picked out together on our last girls' day. My skin is crawling, the walls closing in, and I realize I can't sleep no matter how exhausted I might feel. This used to be my sanctuary, my escape from it all. The four walls of this room have watched over me since I was a kid, but now they just feel as hollow as I do.

I flee my own bedroom and head back downstairs, only to find myself standing in the doorway to my mom's supply room. It smells like sage and oleander and something unmistakably *her*. She loved this room, and even with the clouds still crying outside, I have to admit, it's calming. I especially love the dried herbs she always has hanging on the wire that runs along the length of it—a way to make the plant live on in the mixtures she made with them.

She was always in here puttering around, mixing up ointments, arranging bandages, planning for births, and making natural remedies for our pack for things that didn't need her magic. If only I'd been born with the gift too, then I would be valuable. I'd have leverage to apply to join a new pack and leave Burke and his unwanted attention behind.

Instead, I'm nothing.

I can't leave without the alpha's permission. Not unless I want to abandon the ways of my people and live as a human. Even then, I risk being discovered and returned. Pack alliances are fragile, which means even if I could find a pack that would take me in *no questions asked,* they might be at risk of attack from Twin Rivers. Who's going to do that for a nobody like me?

I sigh and reach up to gently stroke the dried petals of a hanging dog violet and glance around at all the things my mom won't be using. An abrupt knock on the door makes me flinch, and I whirl around and rush out, passing the living room and kitchen to see who it is. Swinging the front door open, I find Hess standing there soaked through, with two bottles of beer in one hand and a grim expression on his face.

I frown in confusion for a moment, but quietly stand aside while he clomps in. The old curmudgeon kicks off his wet shoes by the door so as not to track in water and mud, and we both know it's because my mom would have given him a glare otherwise.

"Did you walk all the way here from your house?" I ask, taking in the mud-stained hem of his pants, and the now see-through button-down shirt as I close the door.

"Yep." He walks straight to the kitchen where he flips on the lights and puts down the bottles on the bar before easing himself onto one of the stools.

I hesitate awkwardly in the doorway, surprised that he's here. Ever since my dad died three years ago, he's been a good friend to my mom, but he and I never really formed any sort of relationship. I've always been polite but distant, and that was fine with him. I'm glad my mom was able to get through her grief with Hess's help, but he's not my dad, and we were never close, so this impromptu visit feels awkward.

Hess tugs out a keyring from his pocket and uses a bottle opener to flip off both caps. Heartbroken gray eyes rise to meet mine, and he slides the second beer to the open seat next to him. "Sit," he says, rubbing the dark blond scruff on his jaw as water drips from his wheat-toned short hair.

I slip onto the stool, staring at the dark brown offering. "You know I'm not twenty-one quite yet."

Hess doesn't even look over at me, just takes a long gulp from his bottle. "Please, you really want me to believe you've never had a beer before? Besides it's just a month out," he grunts. "I figured if there was any time you'd need a drink, it was tonight."

He lifts his bottle, and I take mine in my hand so he can clink them together. "To Delaney."

My throat goes tight at the sound of her name, at the wetness that gathers in his eyes.

"To Mom," I repeat.

Together, we drink in silence, with just the rain and our sips to fill the air of the kitchen that's splashed with greens and yellows and somehow feels so much less cheery than it ever has before.

Hess and my mom bonded over the loss of their mates, and I thought for a while that maybe he had a thing for my mom. I even gave her my blessing one night as we made cookies and salves and lost ourselves to laughter and girl-talk. Turns out, they didn't see each other in that way, they both simply understood loneliness and loss, so they made an effort to be there for each other.

"She shouldn't have died."

Hess looks over at me from the corner of his eye, and I wait to see what he'll say.

"Terrible accident," he grunts out, but I don't miss how he gulps down the rest of his beer in one swig.

My heart drops at the way he's already given in. There's no one to challenge or question what happened to her, just me, and what can I do against so many? I feel even more alone than before. I want to be mad, but how can I really blame him? None of us are what we used to be. Burke's made sure of that, made sure to turn our pack into a distrusting, cowardly lot who turn a blind eye to everything wrong.

When his beer is gone, Hess pivots to look at me again. "You nervous?"

I don't have to ask what he's talking about. "Yeah," I reply with a nod, my fingers picking at the label on the bottle. "I mean, I obviously knew this day was coming, and I'm excited to finally get my wolf. But doing it without Mom or Dad..."

"You'll be fine."

I cut him a look. "The Flux can be agonizing. Some people *die*."

That used to be my biggest fear about the ceremony, that I wouldn't be strong enough to take on my wolf, but now, it's Burke that floods me with trepidation and dread.

Hess shrugs and scratches the stubble over his chin, wiry gray hairs starting to mix in with the dark blond. "Yeah, maybe so. But for some people, it's like being able to breathe right for the first time. Your mom for instance. When she got her wolf, she just smiled and sighed, like she finally felt at home in her own skin."

My lips tug. "That sounds like her."

The rain seems to slow its drizzle as I take another drink, the bitter bubbles pairing well with the tepid sadness inside of me. This is nice, actually. Sitting here with Hess, the one person left in this pack who'd actually talk to me about her. Maybe this is his olive leaf, maybe he's showing me that even though she's gone, I'm not alone.

"Did your mom go over what you can expect?" he asks, and I can tell the question makes him feel uncomfortable. I nearly laugh at his venture into the Totemic Wolves *birds and the bees* talk, but he's off the hook. I'm aware of how it all goes down.

"Yeah, I know about the rituals and the preparation. That the Spirit Weaver will call down the wolf spirits and then give the bite to draw the wolf inside of the person it chooses." I look down at my forearm as if I can already see the mark that will be there. "The Weaver will sing the old songs of our shifter ancestors while the pack offers fresh meat to the wolf spirits."

I purposefully leave out the rest about the pain, potential death, and the first shift if the Flux is successful. I also leave out everything my mom explained about claimings and wolf nature, and how the spirits we protect inside of us can drive us instinctually, more or less overriding logic or the human thought processes.

Hess nods, and the kitchen grows quiet again as he stares unseeing at the floor. I wonder what he's thinking about, but the look in his eyes tells me it's deep and personal, so I leave him to it. We're not close enough for me to go there.

I tip back my beer, finishing it off with a couple of deep pulls, wishing it would help make all of this go away, but Hess was right.

It's not my first beer, and I have too high a tolerance for this to do anything anyway. I suppose that's a good thing though. As much as I'd love a drunken escape, Burke is on the hunt, and I can't take the risk of being black-out vulnerable around him.

"Seneca," Hess starts, and I can tell by the way my name falls out of his mouth that whatever he's about to say is going to suck. He releases a deep breath and turns to look at me, his gray eyes filled with pain so raw it makes my breath catch. "I'm leaving the Twin Rivers pack," he announces, and it feels like a kick to the gut.

Surprise and disbelief war for my attention and my shoulders sag slightly with defeat. Just when I think I can't be any more alone and exposed, my last line of defense against the predators here announces he's leaving. Heat crawls up my throat, and I try to stomp down the hurt and betrayal I feel. He wasn't here to extend an olive branch after all. He was here to yank the roots out entirely.

"Oh," I reply, my voice rough, not sure what else to say. I'm upset, but at the same time, I get it. If I had the luxury of leaving, I'd be right there with him, but I don't. Burke will never agree to let me go.

"I'm sorry," he rushes to tell me in a rare glimpse of guilt. "I just can't stay here anymore. There's nothing for me here. My mate has been gone for a long time, and now that your mother..."

His *nothing for me here* statement stings, but I shove it away, burying it under all the hurt already weighing me down.

"Where will you go?" I ask, my voice a little smaller than it was when he first walked through the door. Even though we aren't close, I still counted him as a permanent figure in my life. To hear that he's leaving is like a hit to the jaw.

"My brother is alpha of Plummet Lake pack. But I... You should come with me," he offers, and I'm taken aback by the gesture.

Unfortunately, we both know that's all it is, a gesture.

I try to give him an understanding smile, but when he drops his eyes from mine with a gleam of guilt in them, I suspect it turned out to look more like a grimace. "I wish I could, but Alpha isn't going to let me go just like that."

"There's no guarantee that your wolf will accept him as a mate," Hess challenges, some of the sadness sloughing off of him to reveal the dominant beta that he normally is.

I raise a brow. "Do you really think Burke will care?" I counter, filling the question with more annoyance than I mean to. "I mean, if Mom was still here, he wouldn't dare, but..."

But there's nothing stopping him now.

I love what I am and where I come from, I just wish pricks like Burke didn't have to taint it all with their lust for power and control, for their dislike of the word *no*. I also wish there were more wolves out there who would put a stop to alphas like him. Unfortunately, the pack leaders only get together once a year, and there's not exactly a forum for members to attend where we can complain about the leadership or air our grievances. It's our duty as pack members to submit—that one word completely ingrained into our culture.

It doesn't help that those who get their wolf spirits in the Flux have another side to them that follows a whole different set of rules. Animalistic rules that are more about brute and brawn and the strongest genes for survival. Wolves are about pack and hierarchy. It's difficult to demand equality and rights when your animal happily submits to maintain pack balance and secure a strong mate.

Knowing my luck, the spirit I get will be an omega, and then I'll constantly be at war with my head and my soul, bowing down to anyone and everyone who demands it of me.

Ugh.

It's sacrilegious and very frowned upon in our culture to hope for one thing over another. *The wolf chooses wisely* is what I've been taught since I was in the womb, but I can't help but hope for a beta, or at worst, a delta.

A howl rends the air, echoing from the distance, calling for a gathering of some sort. I groan and rub a hand down my face. I can probably ignore it since I have a good excuse for not wanting to be social. But I should leave just in case a certain asshole comes by looking for me.

"You should go, Hess," I encourage, pushing up off my stool. "Like you said, there's nothing for you here. You deserve to be happy. Mom would want that for you, and so do I," I tell him, tossing my empty bottle into the bin and thinking through the safest places I could go right now where none of the other pack members will be.

"I didn't mean it like that," Hess interjects, but I wave his concern away.

He did, and that's okay. It's time I start figuring things out and accepting that I'm all I've got now. No point holding a grudge against Hess who's also trying to do what's best for him.

"I'll stay until after the Flux. Make sure you're okay," he tells me, and I offer him a smile that I know doesn't quite reach my eyes.

If he's leaving that soon, it means he already has permission from Burke, confirming my suspicions that his asking me to come is nothing more than a formality. I bet Burke signed that transfer order quicker than he's ever signed anything. One more wall between us is gone, and he didn't even have to kill anyone this time to make it happen.

"I gotta go, Hess," I announce thickly, and before he can object or so much as stand up, I'm out the door.

My world is falling apart, and there's nothing I can do to stop it.

Outside, I see pack members heading into the woods, jogging away from their houses, but I don't follow them. I need to be alone. I need to be safe. The problem is that I'm not safe here. My wellbeing isn't a factor in anything that's happening. My mom is barely cold in the ground and already, I'm wading through threats and thieves lying in wait to steal my choices, my freedom.

I have to leave.

The realization sinks into my spirit, dampening me more than the last of the light rain still misting from the sky. But as soon as I face the facts, I know it's the right thing to do. If I get my wolf, I lose the last barrier I have keeping back Burke.

I need to figure out how the hell I'm going to get out of here. Twin Rivers has been all I've known my entire life. I was born here, and I thought I'd die here. But as I start to run in the opposite direction of the pack gathering, the cool air doing nothing to soothe my fevered skin, I realize this place is no longer my home. It's all just a trap. A trap that Burke is waiting for me to walk into.

My hair flies behind me as I pick up my pace as though I'm running from something that I'm not sure I can escape. Alpha Burke is coming for me, but I'd sooner die than be claimed by him, the male who brought a pack war here to Twin Rivers. The male who let loose his band of rogues, killing our old alpha and countless others.

Murdering my *dad*.

If I stay here, I have a feeling it'll be me who's destroyed next. Maybe not in the *dead in a grave* kind of way, but certainly my soul will shrivel and shatter, and I'll be broken beneath the rule of a cruel male.

Somehow, that seems worse.

TWO

MY RUN LASTS WELL INTO THE NIGHT.

A *Cheshire cat grin* of a moon hangs in the sky, ringed with a nighttime rainbow, the air heavy with cloying fog. Even though I don't have my wolf spirit yet, I'm a natural-born Totemic shifter, which means I was made to share the body and soul of a sacred wolf. My senses are sharper than a human's, my body quick and limber.

Which is why it doesn't bother me in the slightest to be barefoot in the wild, my soles soaking up every damp step in the forest. The smells and sensations are a balm to my battered soul, and it all makes me feel less alone. Like I can feel the people I love still watching over me through the canopy of the trees.

My dad and I used to race each other through these woods.

We would come home with brambles in our hair and splinters in our feet, and Mom would pluck them out one by one. She would scold us and then we'd all laugh and raid the kitchen to replenish the energy we just burned off. The memory fades, and with it goes all doubt and concern over what I've decided. This run was exactly what I needed. There's a sort of clarity that comes with it, like my expanding lungs expand my thoughts too.

Things are solidified now. I'm not going to go through with the ceremony that I've been preparing for my entire life. I'm not going to be able to take in my wolf. And as much as that grieves me, I know it's my only shot at a life. A real life, minus the subjugation and threats that exist around every corner here, where I can choose for myself and be *me* without fear of being broken for it.

I'll have to live like a human. I'll have to sacrifice my heritage, my ancestors, my second *half*, but it's the only way. After the Flux, my wolf will have to answer to her alpha, whether Burke claims her for a mate or not, and I can't willingly subject myself *or* her to that life.

Bypassing the other pack houses, I skirt around the edge of the forest, my internal compass pointing me back home. The scent of pine trees fills my senses, wet needles and damp soil breathing out into the air like nature is exhaling with me.

With trudging steps, I reach my dark and quiet house and head to my room, where I pass out in bed almost as soon as my head hits the pillow. It's a choppy, troubled sleep, filled with dreams of a wolf crying at a moonless sky, lost and wandering in the spirit world.

I wake up several hours later with sore, swollen eyes, like all the pent-up emotion has clogged them with unshed tears. Guilt tugs at my chest at the dream of my wolf spirit out there somewhere knowing I'm abandoning her, knowing that she's going to come down during the ceremony and not find me there waiting for her.

I'm sorry.

I shove the regret aside and force myself to go through the motions. Showering again, I get dressed in jeans and a gray shirt, feet slipping into socks and worn-in sneakers. While my long brown hair air dries, I grab a backpack from my closet and begin to roll up carefully chosen clothes. Jeans, drab T-shirts, plenty of socks and underwear, nothing bright, everything as plain as possible so as not to draw attention.

Toiletries go in next, and in no time, my bag is near bursting. I grab a waterproof jacket and consider the phone on my nightstand but decide against it. The last thing I want to do is make it easier for Burke to track me. Besides, who do I have to call anyway?

For no other reason than it's been hammered into me since I was little, I find myself making my bed, straightening my pillows, and tucking in my sheets, just the way my mom insisted. *"Life can be messy, Seneca, so make sure the bed you lie in isn't."*

A sad smile quirks my lips as I step back, and then with my shoulder straps tugged tight around me, I walk out, forcing myself to head toward the door at the opposite end of the hallway. My fingers trail over the wainscotting, the family pictures hanging up above, covering nearly every inch of available wall. It's like walking past paused memories that were once happy but now just feel haunting. When I get to the closed door, I have to take a steadying breath before I'm able to open it and walk inside.

I'm immediately hit with my mom's scent, and it chokes me with sorrow so visceral that my hand comes up to cradle my throat. It's as though I can feel the rope of a grieving noose wrapped there. It takes me several gulps of air before I can push away from the doorway and walk to my mom's dresser.

She didn't wear jewelry or perfume or scarves or anything like that, but she did have a favorite two-piece hair pin that she always used to sweep up the front pieces of her hair when she needed it out of her way. The cuff and smooth stick are both waiting right here where I knew they would be. I grab them, fingers rubbing over the hand carved wood that's been polished from years of wear, a rose at the end of the pin stick, and delicate leaves carved into the cuff.

Reaching up, I secure the two front layers of my hair with them and pin them back, feeling stronger for it. Then I dig into her bottom dresser drawer where I know she kept some money. Not much, just a few hundred dollars, her *just in case stash*, she called it.

It's enough to get out of Twin Rivers territory. After that... Well, after that, I'll get a job, find a place to live with humans, and hope Burke doesn't ever find me.

I walk out of my mom's room, letting myself look back once, allowing myself to breathe in her scent just one more time. Then I'm down the hall and out of the house. I move casually into the surrounding trees, listening carefully for any signs that I'm being followed. I wouldn't put it past Burke to put a guard or two on me, not because he thinks I'll run, but just so that he knows where I am at all times. *Controlling bastard.*

I figure if anyone is on my tail, I can lose them in here, but as I move silently, listening to everything all around me, I don't hear anyone. It's probably all-hands-on-deck in preparation for the Flux ceremony and the Spirit Weaver that will be arriving today, which is good for me. I waste no time in taking advantage and sprint in the direction of the nearest human town, away from my pack and my home...forever.

THE TREELINE STOPS JUST A couple miles out of the town of Hillsend, and I feel like a jumpy fox as I traverse the flat land between the forest and where houses start to pop up sporadically. I pass the ranches and farms of people who have worked this land for generations, some of whom still tell stories of my people and their reclusive, secretive ways.

Most people think we're like the Amish and that's why we keep our distance. Some think we're some cult that started in Eastern Europe and migrated over here due to persecution—that rumor is a personal favorite. And then there are those who suspect we're something else but say nothing. We're the fuel for scary stories told around dimming fires or late at night amongst a group of friends. The tales of the wolves that roam these woods for hundreds of miles is the stuff of legends, but most people never even think to see the connection. There's no room for magic and mystery in their lives, so my pack exists right under their noses, exactly the way we like it.

I jog down the two-lane road that leads into town, though I slow to a walk so I can look as casual as possible whenever I hear a car approaching. Each time I hold my breath until it passes, hoping that it won't be someone from the pack. We usually only come into town to buy or sell supplies, and I'm counting on the fact that all of that was done earlier in the week.

Soon, the intermittently placed homes begin to morph into neighborhoods as I get closer to the heart of town. I wish the bus depot wasn't on the opposite side, but I'll just have to hurry and hope there's something going out within the hour. So far, this couldn't have gone any smoother than it already has, but there's no need to tempt fate. Deciding to play it safe, I skirt the center of town, even though it'll add more time getting to my destination. I work my way through the less populated areas rather than walk on the busy streets. Fingers crossed, I'll be on a bus in no time, never to look back again.

My heart aches at the thought.

I never in my life thought I'd be doing this. I've been planning for my wolf since forever, thinking I was safe in the shadow of my mother and what she meant to the pack. The weight of what I'm doing, what I'm leaving, is crushing, but I know it's what I have to do. I exhale a resigned sigh and tuck my thumbs in the straps of my bag. I round a corner, my gaze tracing the cracks in the pavement as I calibrate myself for the new life I'm walking toward, when a squealing voice calls my name.

"*Senecaaaa*! I didn't know you were coming!" Trinity White calls out, and my head snaps up to find no less than ten females spilling out of a pack van on the side of the road.

My breathing stops and my heart stutters for a beat before picking up and kicking into high gear.

Shit. What are they doing here?

I look around the neighborhood of houses, like I'm making sure I didn't circle back to pack land, because I can't for the life of me understand why they're *here* of all places.

This is what I get for thinking everything was going so smoothly. Why do I have such horrible luck?

The gaggle of females gather on the sidewalk, most of them talking excitedly, looking over at the two-story house in front of them. That is, until they spotted me. The jubilant chatter slowly dies off as looks of empathy and prudence fill their gazes.

"I am so glad you decided to come, this is exactly what you need! Get out of the house, let loose, and let go of the funk you've been in," Trinity declares, as though my funk is nothing more than an unjustified episode and she holds the cure.

I look away from her to the clear road just beyond them and try to work through a way past.

"Seneca, come on!" Trinity calls again, practically jumping up and down in excitement.

I just stand there, confused about what to do. My eyes flicker over to the van, and my stomach drops when I see Seamus in the driver's seat. The giant of a man is staring at me, his face hard as stone, like he *knows*. When I see his gaze drop down to where my hands are clutching my backpack, the blood drains from my face. It's enough to spur me into action.

I let a carefree, excited smile take over my mouth before I hurry over to the small pack of females. "Hey!" I greet them like some mindless twit, hoping against hope that I'll blend in enough for Seamus to ignore my presence.

Trinity jabs her shoulder against mine playfully, her heart-shaped face beaming as she gathers her black hair onto the top of her head in a messy bun. "I'm so excited you came! Daisy, aren't you glad Seneca came?"

Daisy is as pretty as her name, so short and petite she can probably be plucked off the ground as easily as her namesake. "You never come to our get-togethers," she says, coming up beside Trinity. Her voice is light but her eyes are slightly wary. She's right. Although we're all in the same pack, I never lived in shared housing like some of them, and like my mother, I was more of a loner. "This is going to be so much fun."

I just nod and smile, because although I have no idea what they're talking about, I can feel Seamus's stare burning a hole in my back. I clutch my bag tighter, my entire body hot with burning worry. All I can do is play this off and pretend I was meeting them all along. If I try to leave now, Seamus will know. It doesn't look like he's going anywhere, based on the way the windows are rolled down and the engine is off.

Crushing disappointment at my failure to escape floods my ears. My mind whirls, trying to spin a new plan, so I don't even hear the girls as they all continue to talk. On autopilot, I follow the group, and we make our way across the lawn until Trinity is knocking on a robin egg colored door.

It swings open within moments, and the crowd surges inside, bringing me right along with it like a leaf in a river. We fill up a decent-sized entryway where I'm swept up in the noise of happy *hellos* as we're greeted by a trio, and my nose immediately perks at an unmistakable smell.

Lycans.

I study the three people with wary curiosity. I've always felt a little sorry for our shifter cousins. It's said their bloodline was cursed centuries ago, which is why their transformation is so terrifying. Unlike my pack of Totemic shifters who can transform at will from human to animal once we have our wolf spirits, shifting is uncontrollable for Lycans. Their bodies are forced into it by the moon, and though they're practically unstoppable once they shift, they're also terrifying monsters that walk on two legs, complete with wolfish faces, hair-covered bodies, and animalistic rage.

These three are family—that much is made immediately clear by their resemblance. All of them have dusky skin and dark hair, with wide, friendly mouths made to smile, and almond-shaped eyes. You'd never know looking at them now about the *Underworld* style monsters they turn into.

There's an older woman and two younger Lycans, a male and female, who look so alike that my guess is they're fraternal twins. And based on the collar-to-knee aprons they're all wearing, I realize what this little trek is. I'm so out of the loop when it comes to the social happenings of the females my own age that I forgot I heard talk about them planning a treat yourself day before the Flux.

I just unwittingly walked into a girly bonding *thing*.

Uncomfortable is an understatement to how I feel right now. Not because the girls are bitches or anything—I don't subscribe to that generalized bullshit—it's just that I've never become friends with any of them. We're friendly sometimes, but I've never felt bonded or experienced that click you feel when someone really gets you.

I take in the comfy-looking home as our group is led further inside, to a set of stairs leading down into a finished basement with beautiful plank flooring, barber chairs, and lit up mirrors. The entire space is wide open and welcoming, the faint scent of hair dye fumes clinging to the walls.

I wait awkwardly at the base of the stairs as three of the females are immediately selected from the group and placed in the salon chairs to await their pampering.

"So, why'd you decide to come?" Trinity asks, leading me toward the couches set up on the far side of the space. The rest of the group is already over there, flipping through hairstyle magazines and watching reality television from the hanging flatscreen.

"Oh, um, I needed a break, and I figured it would be fun," I offer, hoping that doesn't sound as cringy as it felt.

But Trinity just smiles kindly at me before hip bumping another girl over so she and I can perch ourselves onto the couch. "Are you nervous about the ceremony?"

I place the backpack between my legs on the floor, fingers curling around the handle like I'm afraid someone will rip it away from me at any moment. "Definitely. You?"

"Yeah. But I'm excited too. I feel...empty lately. You know?" she asks, thick black lashes fanning across her cheeks with every blink. "Like my soul is missing that other part of me. I can't wait for my new spirit to come and fill that space."

My chest gets tight again, and I have to work to swallow down the lump that rises in my throat, because I know exactly what she means. It was easier to ignore when I was younger, but every year I've spent without gaining my wolf spirit, it's been harder to ignore that missing puzzle piece. Like I can't truly be *me* without *her*. Knowing I'm going to keep on feeling like this, knowing that I'll never get my wolf because I'm leaving, it hurts more than I can put into words.

I decide to change the subject. "How did you guys find Lycan hairdressers?" I whisper, not wanting to offend the trio behind me, and knowing that their hearing is much better than mine.

Trinity laughs and settles back on the leather couch. "We've been using them for the past couple of years. They stay off Twin Rivers territory, and since they don't belong to a bigger pack, Alpha Burke lets them be, so long as they treat the females whenever we want."

I frown a little at that. Typical of Burke to force them into working on our pack simply because they live nearby our territory.

Trinity nudges me. "You'd know that if you ever came with us."

A twinge goes through me at her words. I know she doesn't mean to sound like she's reprimanding me, but the truth is, she probably is. Out of everyone, Trinity was the one I was the closest with before Burke came along. I was always a loner, but whenever I did things with the pack when I was younger, it was with her.

But that all changed when Burke took over as alpha. It became very clear that he'd set his sights on me for whatever reason, and I wanted nothing to do with him. So I started staying home, skipping pack gatherings so I could be out of sight, out of mind. My mom helped me, kept me with her as her helper, kept me busy and as far away from Burke as possible. Unfortunately, that distance extended everywhere, until I became the pack outsider.

I clear my throat awkwardly, not really knowing what to say. "Yeah, I just started helping more with the healer side of things, and my mom just always cut my hair..." It's a lame excuse, but what more can I say?

A look of genuine sadness crosses Trinity's face. "I'm so sorry you lost her, Seneca. That we all did," she says softly. "It was such a shock."

"Yes, it was."

It's the most she dares to say, because the truth is, my mom *shouldn't* have died.

The thing about shifters with the rare magic of healing is that they're susceptible to giving too much power to help others. It's why they have to pace themselves, to train for years, and to learn how to concoct other remedies to use besides just magic. If healers push too hard, if their magic runs out, their power can start pulling on their lifeforce.

My mother knew this, worked to counter it, and never blurred the line between her gift and her life. So when Burke and the betas carried her lifeless body back to the house and told me that she had drained herself past the point of saving, I didn't buy it for one second. Neither did some of the other members of the pack.

The problem is, I couldn't prove otherwise. There wasn't a mark on her or anything else that would give me any clue about what really happened. No broken bones, no sign of poison...I looked at every possibility I could think of. It has to be something to do with magic, but I have no way of knowing for sure. And because Burke rules through fear and threats, there's no one who dares question him about it. Not even Hess.

I thought maybe the Flux would be pushed back at least, just until a new healer joined the pack—in case anything goes wrong with anyone's transformations. But Burke said he wouldn't cancel the Spirit Weaver, since he's coming down from a neighboring pack specifically to perform the ceremony. So despite the mystery surrounding the death of my mom, everything is continuing on like normal. It's like we all know that something happened, but no one is willing to stick out their neck for her. Or for me.

"Do you know what you want to do to your hair?" Daisy asks me, steering the conversation away from the heavy shit. She hands over a magazine, and I take it but don't bother opening it up. "I've always been jealous of your gorgeous hair, so please don't tell me you're chopping it all off and dyeing it blue or something."

"Hey!" Mackenzie objects from where she's leaning against the wall by the snacks the Lycans laid out for us.

Daisy looks over sheepishly and smiles at the female with the pixie cut that's currently dyed bright orange. "I didn't mean you, Mack, you totally pull it off. But can you picture Seneca with a bright blue mohawk or something?" she teases as she strokes a strand of my warm brown hair.

"Bright blue would be the wrong color with those icy blue eyes. She needs something dark, more like a navy or midnight blue. Ohhhhh, that would be pretty!" Mack declares, and the other girls all look over at me appraisingly.

"I'm just gonna trim it," I hedge, pulling my hair away from Daisy and bundling the rest of it over one shoulder protectively. Just in case anyone gets any bright ideas about pinning me down and bleaching anything.

"You should totally curl it," Trinity encourages, and Daisy starts nodding eagerly in agreement. "Lee has a technique that would make a Victoria's Secret Angel jealous, that's how gorgeous it is."

"Count me in," I concede, worried I might tip them off if I'm not more into this.

"You're already super tan, so I wouldn't recommend a spray, but mani and pedi for sure, and maybe wrangle those eyebrows," Trinity assesses, like this is makeover day on some rigged TV talent show.

My hand shoots up to cover my eyebrows. "Thick defined brows are in," I defend, but she just waves a hand at me dismissively.

"I know, but some of those hairs are trying to make friends with your eyelids and that should never be allowed, girl," she teases, making everyone around me chuckle.

"Don't worry, everyone's usually too busy staring at those eyes and the lips you've been blessed with that most women have to buy. I doubt they've ever noticed the caterpillars you're trying to grow, but this is what a pamper day is all about," she encourages, bumping my hip with hers and whooping excitedly.

The whole salon whoops in return, and I can't help but crack a small genuine smile at the antics. I drop my hand from my forehead. "Fine, turn these bitches into butterflies," I tell her, pointing at the offending strips of hair as she claps excitedly and pushes me in the direction of a salon chair.

Two hours later, after gaining firsthand knowledge of what Toula from *My Big Fat Greek Wedding* felt like on her big day, I emerge, not quite a *snow beast*, but definitely something outside of my norm. Thankfully, nothing required Windex, but I've been waxed, polished, curled, and contoured, until I look like I belong on a red carpet instead of amongst the rivers and trees that make up our pack land. This look is *definitely* not inconspicuous for riding on a bus.

The entire time I was being transformed and girl talked, I tried to think of a new plan. Maybe some errand that calls me away so I can sneak off. If I hurry, I might still be able to get away.

"May I take a couple pictures for the salon's Insta?" Lee asks me shyly, and I offer him a warm smile and nod. "Perfect! Let me grab a ring light. One sec," he says before rushing off.

I sit here in the chair and stare at the person in the mirror looking back at me. I can almost see a happy-go-lucky girl if I don't look too closely. Just like the foundation I'm wearing that hides the few freckles I have dotting my nose, my makeover is a mask, hiding what's really going on underneath. I'm not sure how to feel about that.

"Omg, who do you think will claim you?" I hear Lana ask Tiernan.

"Ugh, I'd love for Ollie to have a go, but he's been stalking Harper for a minute, so I doubt I'll get what I want."

I hold in my snort. From what I know, Harper would gladly have Ollie off her back, but stuff like that doesn't mean anything to the males in the pack.

It's shifter nature. You'll understand when you have your own wolf, is what people always say when objections to this kind of behavior come up, but it reeks of bullshit to me. Yeah, I get that there's an animal's drive to contend with, but why are the males circling someone without their wolf spirit yet? Wolves seek out wolves for mates, but some of the hierarchy tries to push a claim before the females are even full wolves. It's what Burke has been trying to do to me, and what my mother put a stop to while she was here, but not all pack members have the chance to shut it down.

"I don't care who claims me, I just hope it's good," Lana announces, a foxy gleam in her dark brown eyes, her new platinum bob bouncing around her face as she giggles impishly. All the other females laugh and encourage her.

Becca throws a towel at her teasingly. "Yeah, right. You and your wolf are going to be chasing after Alpha just like you've been since he first took over our pack." Her eyes meet mine in the mirror, and her face falls a little as though she forgot I was here.

It gets even more awkward when the girls all turn to look at me, as though I'll have something to say about Lana pursuing him. I return their stares and offer a shrug. "Take him. I have no issue or interest," I offer genuinely.

Instead of making Lana happy, her eyes narrow angrily on me. "Oh, please, Seneca. I'm so tired of you thinking you're such hot shit." The entire salon goes quiet. You could hear a worm fart from a mile away, that's how quickly her words vacuumed up all the noise.

"Lana," Trinity admonishes after a beat, shooting me an apologetic glance.

"What?" Lana clips in return. "You know you're all thinking it. She walks around the pack like she's God's gift with her long legs and pretty face, convinced that she's too good for our own alpha.

Our *alpha*!" she repeats, as though that fact needs to be emphasized. "I'm not just going to kiss her ass because her mom died and she deigned to step down from her imagined throne to slum it with us common wolves. She acts like Burke is a monster and we're all her enemy."

I bark out a hollow laugh at her words. The other females look as though they're watching a riveting tennis match and it's my turn to hit the ball. Their eyes search my face, expecting to see anger and outrage, but they won't find it. I don't care what Lana thinks about me or how I live my life. I know what she's saying is pure crap, and that's all that really matters.

"Yeaaahhh, I'm gonna go." I stand, taking this as the perfect opportunity to get away, no questions asked. *Thank you, Lana.*

"See?" Lana whines as though my lack of response is all the proof she needs. "Like mother like daughter," she lobs at me venomously as I bend to grab my bag.

I freeze, her words slicing into me despite my efforts to ignore them. "Excuse me?" I ask evenly. There's no sign of the anger now flowing through my veins in either my tone or my face, but it's there, simmering to a boil.

She looks at me with a flash of vindication. "You heard me. Your mother was a pretentious bitch. She never gave our alpha the proper amount of respect. She was barely even civil with our betas."

I look at her like she's lost her goddamn mind, because clearly, she has. "I'm going to give you the benefit of the doubt and say the nail polish fumes you've been inhaling for the last hour have fucked with your good sense," I warn her. "I'm also going to give you a pass because I'm sure the stress of the Flux is making you say stupid shit. But I suggest you shut the fuck up now."

"You're not even worthy of Burke," she spits at me as though it's some kind of insult.

I laugh. "You know what? You're right. I *do* think I'm too good for him. Even you, the nasty bitch that you are, are too good for him. At best, the asshole is unstable, and at worst, a cancer to our kind."

There's a collective intake of breath in the room. Even the Lycans look nervous. But now that I've started, I can't stop.

"My mother wasn't a pretentious bitch, she just wasn't about to roll over to a bunch of thugs who killed her husband and violated pack law. Or are you forgetting what happened that night, Lana?"

She glares at me like she wants to rip me apart, and I really wish a bitch would try.

"Let me remind you," I coo, tone saccharine but infuriated. "Burke challenged Alpha Wolcott and then didn't fight fair. Tell me, Lana, how does a male die from stab wounds when the fight is supposed to be wolf to wolf?"

She doesn't say anything, and I take the chance to look around the room at the shocked females, faces blanched and eyes filled with denial.

"And before any of you say that was just a rumor, I saw the wounds with my very own eyes. But anyone who challenged the result was killed, so the rest of the pack stayed quiet because they didn't want to die. We can all pretend the shit that happens in our pack these days is okay, but each of you knows deep down inside that it's not. Our *alpha*..." I mock, "isn't even worthy of the title, so he's sure as fuck not worthy of me, my body, or my wolf, and if you were smart, you'd stay the fuck away from that psycho."

"That's *enough*," a deep voice suddenly booms through the room, making me flinch.

I look over to find Seamus standing in the doorway, glaring at me, a phone clutched in his palm. He gives me a long, heavy look, and I swallow, palms going sweaty. Silence stretches between us as the tension peaks, so thick in the air that I have a hard time breathing through it.

None of the other females moves. I'm not sure if anyone even dares to blink with the angry beta glaring at me. Lana probably has a pleased smirk on her face, but I won't turn to look.

I wonder exactly how much he heard from my rant, but judging from the enraged look in his eyes, I'd guess he heard plenty. I have no doubt that Burke's right-hand thug will be reporting all of this back to him, but the question that makes my stomach roil is... what will Burke do? Will he order his men to rip me apart like he did my father? Will he excuse my rant because he wants to get into my pants?

I'm not sure which option is worse, and doesn't that just say everything about what I'm up against?

Finally, Seamus moves his gaze away from me to cut across the room. "Time to leave. We've been called back to the pack. The Spirit Weaver has arrived."

The other females gasp in surprise and excitement, but my breath hitches with dread.

How am I going to get away now?

I thread one arm through the strap of my bag and hang it from my shoulder. Without waiting, I stomp past the other females and squeeze past Seamus, heading upstairs and back outside for the van. No one says a thing to me as I go, but I can feel every set of eyes following me.

My plans for escape burn to nothing right before my very eyes. Like a flame to a piece of paper, one minute it's there, and the next it's charred ash floating on the wind. There's no way I'm going anywhere right now. Seamus would be on me in a second. Which means I'll have to try and run again before the ceremony. That doesn't give me a lot of time and decimates the head start I was hoping to have, but it's doable.

Until then, I'm riding shotgun, because if they put me in the back with that squawking shrew Lana, shit will get ugly.

I just need to play it cool and then run the first chance I get.

THREE

The entire ride back to pack land, I sit ramrod straight, with a white-knuckled grip on my bag. Seamus says nothing, and I don't either. Despite being overheard, I meant every word of what I said, and not one of my pack members in the car can deny that I'm right.

The females talk quietly amongst themselves in the back of the van, all the previous enthusiasm deflated out of them like an old forgotten balloon. With practiced ease, Seamus cuts through the town and into the forest area that separates the human territory from ours. A dirt road through the woods leads past the rushing twin rivers our pack is named after.

White rapids cut a path, each river at least fourteen feet across with a wide strip of land separating them. They're two sisters who refuse to see their similarities and get along enough to become one. Their water is tumultuous and punishing while also nurturing the land and our people since we first settled here.

In no time, we're pulling up to the main pack house where hundreds of shifters are already gathered. My stomach threatens to lodge itself in my throat, but I know better than to risk an elevated heart rate in front of Burke. So I take a fortifying breath, forcing myself to go numb before I step out and close the door behind me.

The other females stream toward the huge circle that the pack has formed. I glance around surreptitiously for a place to stow my bag, but there are too many people around. I consider stuffing it under the van, but when I make a move to do that, my eyes snag on Seamus, who's staring right at me.

Fuck.

I jerk my attention away and turn back to the pack, falling into the crowd. Letting myself get swallowed into the tightly packed bodies, I shove and squeeze my way forward. I need to bide my time, and curiosity has its hook in me too, pack mentality taking over the second I'm in its midst.

When I work my way to the front, I find Alpha Burke there with the person who must be the Spirit Weaver. The male has tan skin and white hair strung with wolves' teeth and rawhide ties. His lined face is pulled into a friendly smile, but the bright orange paisley shirt he's wearing mismatched with the pea-green corduroys really sets him apart.

This isn't the same Spirit Weaver who came last year to perform the Flux, but since they're so rare, even more so than healers, I'm not surprised. They're not always available to help. Apparently, this one dresses like he's ready to watch reruns of *That '70s Show*.

"Ah, I sense our hosts have arrived," the male says.

Burke raises two fingers to his mouth and releases a shrill whistle. Immediately, the crowd parts, letting the rest of the females through.

They all gather to the front together while the rest of the pack backs away to give us a respectful distance, but I'm the only one to stand alone. How fitting.

"Spirit Weaver Yaromir, these are the members of my pack who will be taking part in the ceremony," Burke announces, standing straight and tall, and behaving every bit like the proud and prudent alpha he pretends to be. I have to control my lips so they don't draw up into a sneer.

Bright, wise eyes take all of the females in as the Spirit Weaver nods at them, and then his gaze lands on me. For a second, I'm frozen beneath his scrutiny, worried that he's looking right through me and seeing *my* spirit inside. Will it show him the truth of what I have planned? Does he know my wolf is going to be doomed to walk the spirit world alone forever?

Just as nervous sweat begins to bead at the base of my neck, he looks away and offers the crowd a genial smile. "I am honored to perform the Flux with Twin Rivers pack. Should we get started?"

Burke nods, and like the pack has practiced this, they all turn and begin walking to the ceremony setup that's located behind the large home that houses the alpha and other higher up members of our people. I take advantage of the busy moment, eyes flicking left and right, but Seamus is nowhere to be found, and Burke is walking the Spirit Weaver the opposite way, their heads tilted toward each other like they're in deep discussion.

Making sure that no other betas are watching me, I spin on my heel and race to the trees just behind me that nestle against the side of the pack house. As soon as I'm beneath the shadows of their cover, I stop at the first full bush I see and then shove my bag between its thick branches.

I rip off pine needles from the tree above it, stripping the branch bare and dumping them on top. That will help disguise my black bag, but also help to cover up my smell. I check my handiwork, bending back some of the bush's leaves and branches to better cover it, and then wipe my hands on my jeans. It's the best I can do.

Hurrying back to join the others still moseying toward the ceremony grounds, I walk as fast as I dare, knowing that if I were to run, it would just draw attention. Luckily, there are a few stragglers, but I quickly pass them by with a nervous smile, catching up to where everybody else is now gathered. There are picnic tables on one side of a massive bonfire that's already being lit beneath the pre-dusk sky. The base of the converging rivers sparkles in the waning light, and just behind us is the place where the spirit ceremony will take place after the feast.

Every second is going to count.

I waste no time filling up a plate and picking a seat away from the commotion and as close to the trees as I can get without being conspicuous. I eat my mountain of food, barely even tasting it as I wolf it down, my eyes on my pack and my mind on how the hell to get away from them. I go over what I know is going to go down tonight. I've attended these every year since I can remember, but it all feels so different now. Maybe it's because there's so much riding on my getting away, or maybe my wolf spirit is close and that's what I'm reacting to, but I feel off, anxious, and desperate.

I focus on something else and tell myself I have time, that I'll figure this out. First, the Spirit Weaver will invite the spirits to dine with us, and the pack will bring all of the sacred and specially prepared dishes and set them out on a special table for them. Then all the Flux participants will be excused to go dress in their ceremonial robes and return here for the blooding, but if I'm still here by then, I'm screwed.

My best bet is to sneak off when we're supposed to get dressed. By then, a good portion of the pack will be drunk, full, and relaxed.

I'll grab my robe and then slip out of a window or something. I'll only have maybe a forty-minute head start, but I'll have to make it work.

The feasting pack starts to quiet down, and I glance around from my spot on the picnic table to see Burke and the Spirit Weaver walk into the gathering. They greet a few people as they make their way toward the front, Yaromir carrying a leather pack with him.

Part of me is saying I should run now while this man sets up and everyone is busy watching him, eagerly anticipating what's going to happen. But I worry they'll notice too quickly that I'm not here when they call all the participants together to get changed. There's also another part of me that desperately wants to see him call the spirits down.

I've never felt or seen anything at any of the other Fluxes I've attended, but I wonder if this time it will be different. Will I feel her? Will I know she's nearby? Will she understand why I can't take her on?

An ache starts in my chest, but I do my best to ignore it. One look at Burke as he fawns all over the Spirit Weaver is enough to remind me that I don't really have a choice. This is about survival, and if my wolf doesn't get that, how compatible would we have been in the first place?

Weaver Yaromir unrolls his leather pack to reveal tufts of fur, oils, and all sorts of other things he'll need for tonight's ceremony. Then he walks over to the large bonfire, stopping just in front of it, and sets down his sacred haul. Meticulously, he spreads out several small pots filled with dried herbs, powders, and other mysterious things that those with magic know about, while those that don't never question.

As quick as a stalked hare, the Weaver pulls an arm-length log from the burning fire, not even flinching as it sparks and sputters in protest. A hush further blankets the pack as he lowers the burning wood to the things he gathered and sets the contents of the pots aflame. Immediately, large plumes of white musky smoke pour out from the bowls, and the Weaver hands the torch off to Seamus.

I watch the beta, wondering if he's had a chance to tattle on me yet. When I look away from him, my gaze accidentally lands on Burke, but to my dismay, he's already watching me. I try to read what's swimming in those inky, conniving depths, but it's impossible to know the inner workings of such a tainted mind. If he knows what I was saying about him, he doesn't let on, and even though I know I should drop my gaze and not provoke him, something in me refuses to do it.

Just this once, I don't want to feign submission. I stare at him for what I hope is the last time. Soon, I'll no longer be forced to cater to his ego for the sake of flying under the radar. For whatever reason, tonight, I want him to feel the weight of my judgment and scorn, to know that I don't bow down to him and never will. I want him to see the girl I've been forced to hide, the one I decided deserves to be free.

Our eyes stay locked on each other for a long moment. I can tell he's waiting for me to avert my gaze like I always do, but it's not going to happen this time. Whether I make it out of this pack alive or dead, I'm done pretending to have any respect for this wolf and the wolves that follow him.

Weaver Yaromir starts to chant the magical words of the wolf spirits, and Burke is forced to break my gaze when he's handed something. I quickly get to my feet while his back is turned and slip amidst the group of people who have already gotten up from their tables to gather around. As soon as his attention comes back, he'll be searching me out instead of paying attention to the ceremony. Good. Maybe then the Spirit Weaver will start to see the cracks in the *perfect alpha* facade.

Several older members of the pack start to hum in harmony, lending their voices to the steady chant spilling from Yaromir's mouth. The eerie wolfish music mixes with the magic smoke that carries the smell of bay leaves, angelica, and calendula. The Weaver picks up an apparatus that looks very similar to a priest's aspergillum, but instead of sprinkling holy water, he whirls it around his head, spilling blessed and secretly curated oil out in arced circles around him. Then he raises a small ball and chain and whips it expertly around his head, creating an unearthly whistle to aid the call of the spirits. If I listen closely, it's almost as though I can hear the lonely note of a single wolf calling to the moon.

The melodic words of shifter magic take on a more urgent note, and chills crawl up my arms as a wind whips around the pack playfully, like the spirits are here to cavort. People hoot and children laugh while they start to chase the unseen and howl into the darkening night, dreaming of the day it will be their turn.

Excitement ripples through the crowd in a wave, and awe fills the faces of so many in the pack as Weaver Yaromir's piercing voice starts to call out the invitation to the spirits that belong to those of us participating tonight.

He's speaking in a language I don't know, one I'm not even sure is really used anymore other than for the spirits. But regardless of my inability to understand what's being said word for word, it's impossible not to see the beauty and raw power in what's happening. The Spirit Weaver then starts to do exactly what his title suggests and lifts his hands as he begins to weave two planes together for the night. His fingers move like he's plaiting invisible strands together that represent our world and the world of the spirit wolves we're meant to harbor and protect.

I can't say that I feel any different right now than from previous Fluxes during the spirit calling, but I have a deeper appreciation for the Totemic shifter culture and the beliefs of my people tonight, because it was supposed to be *my* night. The night I finally inherited my wolf.

I close my eyes and sway to the gentle beat of the Weaver's feet as they start to dance across the hard-packed dirt. I invite his song to move through me and tilt my head back, feeling the blessing of the rising moon. Everyone else sways with the chanting and the rhythm of heavy footfall, bodies moving with the wind.

I rock back and forth in place, wishing that my mom were here and that everything hadn't gone to shit. I feel the loss of her so deeply in this moment that it tightens my lungs and makes it hard to breathe. She always loved nights like this. The magic always renewed her in a way that nothing else could. Right now, she should be dancing alongside me in the moonlight, beautiful and strong, everything I've always wanted to be.

I think of my dad, of my parents slow dancing in the kitchen late at night and sneaking kisses and winks whenever they got the chance. I think of his hugs and the way he always saw *me*, all of me, all the parts I tried to tuck deep and hide. He always understood and nurtured those bits, and I was lucky for that. This place holds so many beautiful memories and yet so much tragedy all at the same time. I can feel the love here, but I can also smell the blood. Too much blood. It's old and stale and stains the grounds of this pack like a warning.

I tear my eyes open, ripping myself from the moment. The Weaver is calling to the sky, arms outstretched, and a stream of omega females file past the congregation in a line. They're wearing revealing dresses as a mark of their fertility, and a line of blood is drawn down their foreheads. They all carry heavy platters of food together, at least two omegas per tray. The kappas were obviously hard at work this year, because the offering is impressive. Fresh kills still bloody from the woods have been prepared in true Twin Rivers custom, the scent of the slain prey permeating the air.

There are skinned rabbits and muskrats delicately arranged on a platter topped with fresh sage. Then a deer, its removed antlers set above its butchered meat like a cake topper. But then more omega females stream past with the meat of an entire elk. All of it is placed around the bonfire in a perfect circle, arranged accordingly, the raw meat an offering to the wolf spirits.

With their hands now free, the omegas start to dance. Sheer dresses sway with their movements, their bodies undulating in a practiced performance of sensual virility. While they twirl around the bonfire, the Weaver sprinkles some sort of powder over the food, grunting and growling and chanting too low beneath his breath for me to hear.

Pack members begin to line up, eager to lay the gifts they've brought at the base of the spirits' feast. I can almost smell the competition in the air as wrapped packages are set down, the givers wearing smug looks as they go, certain that they've brought the best prize. I try not to roll my eyes at the display. As if *this* crap will make the spirits look more favorably down on this pack. Not with an alpha like Burke, he just claims every single present for himself.

The growls, yips, and barks of wolf-speak grow louder, Weaver Yaromir's sounds so steady they're almost a thrum, one that feels like it's controlling the beat of my heart. The omegas dance like they feel the frenzied pull of music, and the crowd feels it too. There's a vibration in the air, and I'm all too aware of how my feet are planted on the ground, of the press of my pack members' bodies around me. So much smoke rises into the darkening sky that it consumes my senses. The Weaver pulls at the air, hands moving through the smoke like he's arranging the wisps, intertwining some invisible force with the work of his bony fingers.

I don't know if it's just the intensity of the moment, but when he shouts out a wordless noise of supplication, eyes on the rising moon, I feel...*something*.

Gasps ring out through the crowd when the bonfire hisses, sparks flying, charred pieces landing on the meat and making it sizzle. The omegas still dance, not hitching a step, and everything seems to come to a head before it all just...stops.

While the pack collectively holds its breath, the flames flare, so bright I have to squeeze my eyes tightly shut. Exclamations sound off throughout the pack, and then everything falls silent, and a stillness slams around us so loud it seems to crack the air, making bumps rise along my skin.

They're here.

It's the only coherent thought that blasts through my mind, and I know I'm right. I can feel it with every inch of my essence. The hairs on the back of my neck lift, and I find myself searching around desperately as if I'll be able to see my wolf even though the spirits are invisible to the eye. But I have my other senses, and they confirm that she's near. Just knowing that, just *feeling* it, makes joy unlike any other surge through my chest. The ceremony has always been impactful, but this is different.

A howling wind cuts through the stillness, blowing through the bonfire and kicking up dirt like the race of dozens of paws. The crowd cheers, clapping and crying out, and I feel so charged with the energy that I'm practically shaking.

But just as quickly as the happiness comes, it gets cut off at the knees with devastating loss. Because...I'm abandoning her. I'm leaving my wolf behind.

"The wolf spirits have blessed us with their presence!" Weaver Yaromir cries out, earning even more celebratory noises from the pack. "They are pleased with Twin Rivers' offering!"

The crowd surges, forcing me to stand on my tiptoes and peer over shoulders. I see Burke's smug face as he nods respectfully to the Weaver. "Time for the hosts to prepare!" he calls out, and my stomach twists. "Everyone else, continue to celebrate with our fellow spirits."

The pack cheers, everyone going back for more food and drink, pack males wasting no time in grabbing the dancing omegas, dragging them onto laps. I turn around numbly, following the other hosts as we all head for the pack house. Just before I enter through the back door, I look behind me at the wolf spirit I can feel is watching me, and at the alpha just behind her.

I wonder which of them will hate me more when they realize I've fled.

FOUR

EXCITED CHATTER EXPLODES ALL AROUND ME AS EACH OF the participants is shown to a room to change. My heart hammers harder than the ceremonial stomps that just rang out in honor of the spirits, and I move robotically to the robes that have my name written on a white piece of deer hide that's pinned to them so that there'd be no confusion.

I run my hand down the smooth fabric, the wool of the robe feeling heavier than I realized it would. The wide stitching on the sides is to allow the fabric to tear apart easily so that our new wolves don't get stuck in it when we change for the first time. It leaves small gaps between the pieces of fabric that show off hints of skin and peeks of the body. I've always wondered what I would look like draped in the black fabric. I guess I'll never know.

I grab my hanger and the beautiful belt that's laid out separately. I run my eyes over the fine stitching on the belt, an image of a howling wolf appearing through the various colors of thread that have been sewn together masterfully. I'm curious who made it for me. Usually, it's your family that creates the special sash and it's the only thing we're allowed to keep from tonight other than the spirit of the wolf that chooses us. But I found my mother's half-finished efforts in her room after she died, so I know this belt isn't her handy work.

I run my thumb across the beautiful gray furred image and look around to see other participants still laughing and teasing each other and just now starting to undress. I fold everything over my arm and leave in search of a bathroom. No one says anything to me as I go. The awkwardness of our exchange earlier in the salon still hangs heavy in the air between us, and I get the impression they don't care that I don't want to change in here with them. They're just happy I'm gone so I don't continue to dampen their moods.

A delta waiting outside starts in surprise as I open the door and walk out. Straightening up, he looks over at me with confusion when he sees my robes draped over my arm instead of being on my body like they're supposed to be.

I shut down any nervousness and fix a sheepish smile on my face. "Is there a bathroom I can change in?" I ask awkwardly.

"Four doors down on the right," he answers, an understanding look in his eyes.

Luckily, my request doesn't seem to be all that strange. Yes, once we start shifting, regular nudity isn't taboo at all. But none of us have shifted yet, so I was hoping the shy card wouldn't be all that unusual.

"Thanks. It's just so loud in there, and I really want to take my time and mentally prepare," I explain, hoping the lie helps to buy me just a little more of a head start.

The delta offers a grunt and nod as I walk past and hurry to where he said the bathroom was. I open the door, locking it behind me, and flick on the light. I shove my robes in the sink and quietly move to the window on the back wall just left of the toilet. Biting my lip, I turn and shove my robes aside before turning on the water to help drown out any sounds that could give away what I'm really doing in here.

Adrenaline spikes through me as I pull the lever that locks the window. A small click sounds off when I flick it open, and then slowly, I start to push the pane up. The smell of trees, sap, and soil greets me, and I quickly bend to the side and flush the toilet so I can knock the screen out undetected. The delta isn't standing right outside the bathroom door, but I can't dismiss his shifter hearing.

As soon as the toilet whooshes with a loud flush, I jam my elbow into the screen as hard as I can, inwardly celebrating when it pops right off and falls outside. I stick my head out of the window and listen for a beat, waiting to hear any indication that anyone has heard or noticed what I'm doing, but nothing happens.

I pull my head back in, grab onto the upper sill of the window and kick my legs out into the open space, swinging my body out. I drop to the ground with an audible thud on the balls of my feet. Breathing hard, I stay frozen, not daring to move as I try to clear the beating of my heart in my own ears so I can hear if anyone is coming.

All that greets me are the sounds of the forest, but I don't let excitement or victory wash through me just yet. This is just the beginning of what I know is going to be a long and terrifying night.

I move stealthily away from the pack house, out into the tall trees, while working through the best option for how to get to my bag and then where to go from there. I won't go to town this time. They'll expect that. Maybe my previous trek will work in my favor and my scent from earlier will be a trail that leads a good portion of the hunting party astray.

Instead, I'll run for the rivers tonight. I'll douse my scent in their waters and ride them as far down as I can until I'm closer to a safer civilization. It's a risky plan, but the only one that will work. I won't be able to outrun the pack all night, and they won't immediately think I'm in the freezing cold water until I have a solid lead on them. There's got to be another human town I can reach, and then I'll stuff myself into a bus or cab and put as many miles between us as I can.

For a second, I consider abandoning my bag in the bushes, but it has everything; my clothes, my money, and my mom's hairpin that I stuffed in the front pocket at the salon. I can't leave that behind. It's all I kept that was hers.

Determination filling me, I know I have two options. I can pick my way through the woods and stealthily make it back to where I stashed my things, or I can make a run for it and get to it as quickly as possible. As risky as that seems, I know it's what I need to do. There aren't any betas sweeping the perimeter tonight. Burke always gives them the night off from guard duty during the Flux so they can partake. As if to prove my point, I hear cheers and clapping, the celebration growing rowdier.

I take a second to gather my bearings, eyes sweeping the dark side of the pack house, the noise and orange glow of the fire emanating from the other side. I don't have a second to waste. With one more puff of breath, I take off. My feet fly across the grass and mud, past pinecones and rocks. I think for a second that I've somehow overshot my direction, but then I spot it—the bush I hid my bag in. I rush over to it, digging my hand beneath the rough brambles, fingers closing around the strap. I yank it out, pine needles falling off it like rain.

My heart is pounding now, so hard I can practically taste my pulse in the back of my throat. Hurriedly, I sling the bag over my back, holding the straps tight as I turn and run deeper into the woods. I make it ten feet before the first shadow moves.

I skid to a grinding stop, shoes digging into the earth, eyes going wide in horror as Burke steps into view. The break in the trees above shows the glittering fury rising in his black eyes. "Going somewhere, Seneca?" The tone of his voice is filled with something dangerous, something dark.

Instead of answering, my feet back up a step and turn to the right, my body ready to tap into the flight response now surging through me, but as soon as I take a step in that direction, Seamus steps out from behind a tree. I go left instead, but another beta steps out next, blocking my path. A snapping twig makes me jerk a look over my shoulder, finding a fourth male, Conrad, behind me.

I'm surrounded.

I lick my lips, shooting another look at Seamus, who now has an ugly smirk on his face.

Burke clicks his tongue, and somehow, it sounds as loud as a cocking gun. "What's in the bag?" he asks, stepping closer.

"None of your business."

A sharp crack of a laugh comes out of him, but it's definitely not humorous. "That bitchy tone isn't going to be tolerated." His eyes flick behind me, and that's all the warning I get before Conrad is there, yanking the bag from my back. I whirl around, clawing at the straps and trying to get it back, but he's too strong. It rips out of my hold, and I go falling onto my hands and knees.

I scramble back to my feet, shoving curled hair out of my face, just to watch the bastard unzip it and dump out all the contents in a pitiful heap. "Ha! Got some cash here, Alpha," Conrad says, but when he steps forward to pick up the money, his boot lands on my mother's hairpin. I hear the snap like it's my own bone cracking, and fury floods me. One blink, I'm standing there in horror, and the next, I've rushed at him with all my might.

Because I surprise him, I'm able to push the big beta off, making him stumble back a step. I reach down and grab the snapped wooden stick and cuff, but before I can shove it into my pocket, Burke appears in front of me and tries to rip it from my grasp.

"No!" I cry, as his thick, meaty fingers pry my hand open from its protective fist. He plucks the pieces from my grasp, holding them in the moonlight for a second before his cruel black eyes fall to me. "Token from Mommy Dearest?"

"Give it to me."

I shouldn't have shown how much it meant to me, not in front of them, but it's too late. I just reacted without thinking.

My eyes track the movement as he tucks the pieces into his pants pocket. "Nah, I think I'll keep it."

"You fucking bastard," I growl, and I raise my hand to smack the look off his face, but my arms get restrained by Seamus's hold. I struggle in his grasp, but I might as well be a mouse trying to pry itself off a glue strip.

"Here's what's going to happen," Burke says, taking a step toward me, feet crunching over leaves. "You're going to walk back into that clearing, wearing your robe like a good girl, and then you're going to get your wolf."

"It's my choice," I snarl, arms bending painfully beneath Seamus's merciless hold.

"I'm your alpha, and you do what I say!" Burke snaps before he raises his hand and grips my face hard. "Once you have your wolf spirit, things will become clearer for you. You'll know your place."

I stare at him defiantly. "At your feet? No fucking thank you."

He drops my face to wave a dismissive hand. "At my feet, on your knees, bent over in front of me, your cunt ready and waiting..."

My foot shoots up to nail him in the groin, but he catches my ankle, twisting it enough to make me yelp in pain. "I see you're gonna do this the hard way. That's just fine."

Still holding my foot, I'm forced to balance on one leg as he looks over to Conrad. "Robe."

Wordlessly, the beta steps forward, somehow already holding my robe in his hands.

He and Seamus shove me into it like they're dressing a doll, and I'm in danger more than once of getting my shoulders dislocated from their manhandling treatment.

"I'm not doing the ceremony!" I spit as Burke finally drops my ankle with a heavy thud, my thigh muscles screaming from being overextended too long.

"Yes, you are. And you're going to behave yourself in front of the Spirit Weaver."

I glare at him with all the hate I can fathom in the depths of my eyes. "Fuck. You."

Quick as a flash, his fist is in my hair, yanking my head back. "I *will*. Before the night is done. I bet your wolf can't fucking wait for some alpha cock." I start trying to fight again, but he looks over to the other betas. "Bring him."

A frown mars my brow, but I can't turn my head, not with the painful hold he has on my hair. My ears twitch with the sound of a struggle, and then two new betas are dragging someone forward between them in front of my line of sight. The blood drains from my face when they toss the male to the ground, and I see it's a bloodied and beaten Hess.

"No," I whimper, my heart squeezing at the sound of his pained groan. "What did you do to him?" I demand.

Burke wrenches my head back so hard I see stars, my scalp screaming, neck bending to the point of paralyzing pain. I freeze, staring up at his hateful face. "I didn't do anything, Seneca. *You* did this. By betraying your pack. By trying to betray your wolf. Since you don't have the spirit, I can't punish you physically...yet. So that leaves your kin." A mean smirk curls his lips. "Too bad you don't have any of that either. Hess had to fill the position. You should be thanking him."

My burning stare drops down to Hess, whose swollen eyes are watching me with too many emotions to track. Sadness. Guilt. Desperation. More and more cross his features, but Burke blocks my view, hand leaving my hair to pinch my chin. My heart feels broken in my chest, shattered into sharp pieces that keep stabbing me from the inside.

"If you don't do the ceremony, Hess's life is forfeit."

Burke's words make me slump, all of the fight cut out from me like a tripped circuit. It's gone, and in its place, there's nothing but dark failure.

Vicious satisfaction crosses his face. "You're going to do what you're told tonight. Say *yes, Alpha*."

I swallow thickly, eyes trained numbly on my feet. "Yes, Alpha."

His hand drops, and so does Seamus's hold, making my body slump to the ground, palms scraping on a rock hidden beneath the brush. Burke yanks me back to my feet so fast my head swims. "We don't want to get your robe dirty, do we?" he asks with condescension, but my eyes are on Hess, who's still bleeding, still breathing heavily on the forest floor, his pained and defeated gaze still on me. I can't bear to keep eye contact, to see what they've reduced him to because of me, so I drop my stare to the ground, submitting to what's been done even though everything is screaming for me not to.

When Burke leads me away, I go without struggle. "See? Already being a good little bitch," he jokes.

Somewhere far above the treetops, I swear I hear a wolf spirit growl.

FIVE

OUTSIDE, BENEATH A GLARING MOON, I KNEEL IN THE dirt and watch as the Weaver marks Trinity's forehead with a dot of blood. Her chest rises and falls even more rapidly as her blooding gets closer and closer. Snarls, bellows, and cries fill the air all around me from the females who've been marked and bitten already. Each of them is now experiencing the bond, their bodies taking on a spirit and working to adapt and make room while they transform into so much more than they were before.

Becoming what they were always meant to be.

The Weaver growls something, but it's unintelligible because his face is half-shifted. His eyes are his own, but his mouth is more wolf than man. Trinity offers her arm to him, and I can see the tremble in it from where I am about four feet away. Burke is to my left, his arrogant and vile presence a constant reminder that there's nowhere to run.

Maybe I should have left Hess to his fate, but that thought curdles my stomach, even though the spirits know he was going to do the same to me. A part of me wishes I could be that cold-hearted. My life might've been easier if I thought and behaved like Burke, but I don't know how to turn my conscience off. Now I'm here, counting down the seconds until I'm a slave to my alpha, and he'll probably kill Hess anyway.

How could I be so stupid? I should have run before, but I thought I had time. I thought I could get away. Yet now I'm on my knees, trapped, exactly where Burke wants me. Waiting to become another she-wolf for him to dominate, a *bitch* for him to claim.

The Weaver takes Trinity's hand, and in a move so fast it would be startling if I hadn't seen him do it over and over again tonight, he bites her forearm. She flinches, face gone pale as his wolf mouth releases her flesh. Gnarled fingers curl as he cups his hand under the wound he made, collecting some of the blood now flowing freely from it. When he catches enough in his palm, he moves over to the fire and throws it into the flames with a growl.

Trinity sucks in a breath, and I watch as the blaze from the inferno flickers from orange to blue. Sparks dart out from the middle of the flames as though a sharp wind has sent them flying, and then that same rushing wind and fiery particles seem to swoop right for her.

Trinity's eyes grow wide with fear, but behind the fear is a gleam of excitement. The invisible force still carrying the glimmering sparks from the fire hits her square in the chest, and she gasps, closing her eyes against everything that slams into her. She falls backward writhing, and my heart races as I watch the physical and spiritual struggle going on.

However, my attention is pulled away from what's happening to her, because the Weaver steps in front of *me*. My heart leaps into my throat.

This is it.

I look up at him, his bright blue eyes surveying me, taking my measure. I wish I knew what he was seeing. Is it a failure? Does he see a female who tried to save herself but couldn't? Does he see a coward who's swallowed her fight and traded her tenacity for the illusion of safety?

I think he smiles at me, but it's difficult to tell with his mouth in the state that it is. I've seen others in the pack in a partial shift, and it always looks so painful, but it doesn't seem like this hurts the Spirit Weaver, or maybe he's used to it. He must've performed this ritual hundreds of times in his life.

He dips a finger into the bowl of deer blood and then starts to draw symbols on me. First, he marks lines down my arms, then taps my collarbone before parting the robe slightly and tugging down my shirt collar so he can paint blood on my chest. He speaks in that way that sounds more like growls and yips, and my entire body goes tight with tension, my skin tingling every place the blood touches.

My eyes flick to where Burke stands just off to the side with his arms crossed in front of him. I recoil at the hungry look on his face, at the way his gaze burns into the marks on my chest. When I feel a finger press against my forehead, my eyes shoot back to the Weaver as he holds his touch there, his throat working with a nearly silent wolfish rumble.

The blood is cold everywhere at first, but it seems that with each added stroke and swirl of the Weaver's design, the symbols begin to warm. By the time he draws another line down my throat, I feel like I'm glowing. Panic slams through me at the sensation. I feel like a beacon, and in my vulnerable state, it terrifies me.

I want nothing more than to turn off the light I sense radiating out of me. It's like my life is being ripped away, and with it goes my hope and the few shreds of happiness I'm desperately trying to hold on to. At the same time, I can't fight the curiosity coursing through me. I can't ignore the exhilaration I feel. I've waited so long for this. Celebrated and anticipated it, wished for it to be my turn every time I watched a Flux. I've been looking forward to it my whole life, and now it's here.

But this isn't how it was supposed to be.

It wasn't supposed to ruin me. I wish my mom were here. I wish I could welcome this spirit the way my animal deserves, and not hate her for what her presence will do to me. Receiving my wolf spirit is supposed to make me complete, but because of it, I'm going to be *less*. I'm going to be treated no better than a whipped dog, bred and dominated for Burke's pleasure.

I flinch at a clawed tap on my arm just as my alpha growls, the sound more excited than threatening, and I realize that the Weaver is waiting for me to extend my arm. It's time to be blooded. It's time to be *owned*. Dread spreads inside of me like a wildfire through dry terrain.

Hesitantly, I lift my arm, prepared for the bite that will quickly morph into a shackle, tethering me to this life whether I like it or not. I just hope my wolf accepts me after my near abandonment. I wonder if she knows, if she senses what I tried to do.

Before the Weaver grips my arm, Burke steps in front of me. "I'll be blooding this one," he announces, and the Weaver looks from him to me and back again, his heavy white eyebrows dipped with consternation. At the tense pause, Burke snarls, "Is that going to be a problem, Yaromir?"

My heart slams in my chest, and I want to shout out, *don't let him touch me*, but all I can picture is Hess's beaten and bloody face, and the words shrivel on my tongue. Eyes wide, I latch onto the Spirit

Weaver like he's my only lifeline, hoping he won't let this happen.

Yaromir stares at me for a moment, then looks over at the alpha. I follow his gaze, hoping he will protect me, but Burke stares at the Spirit Weaver with eyes that scorch with warning. The Spirit Weaver doesn't speak a word, but after an edgy moment, he gets to his feet and steps back, conceding to the alpha's request. I look to Yaromir as though he's betrayed me, but he avoids my gaze and moves on to the next host.

Burke steps forward and grips my chin, tilting my head up until my angry eyes are fixed on his. A salacious smile spreads across his face, and then I hear his jaw crack and pop as it begins to morph into the muzzle of his pitch-black wolf.

I try to yank my arm away, but his grip is too tight. *This is wrong*. He shouldn't be allowed to do this, to mark me like this. The Flux is supposed to be sacred, the blooding done by the Spirit Weaver. My whole life is going to be tainted by this piece of shit, and now he's going to be allowed to tarnish this too. I pull harder, growling with desperate fury as I try to get away, but before I can so much as push to my feet, Burke pitches forward and sinks his teeth into the meat of my forearm.

Pain explodes through me.

His bite is cruel and vicious, sinking in far deeper than the Weaver would've. My mouth opens in shock, but I fight not to let out the cry that bubbles up my throat. Black eyes stare down at me, shining with arousal and promises of pain.

My stomach rolls from the contact, from the violation, and I fight the light-headedness that hits me and muddles my mind. Burke stays there, fangs sunk into the tender flesh of my forearm, tongue slathering against my bleeding skin, and I just want him to get the fuck off me.

The Spirit Weaver suddenly steps in, practically shoving Burke out of the way. As soon as my alpha's teeth pull out, blood gushes from the holes in my arm. With a deep frown between his brows, Weaver Yaromir cups his hands below my arm, collecting my blood to complete the ritual. I watch him catch the scarlet liquid spilling down, my senses feeling fuzzy and slow. When he has enough, he straightens up and heads to the fire while Burke licks crimson from his lips mockingly, a vindictive streak spilling from his inky gaze.

Heart pounding, I watch everything happening like it's a movie skipping, the film sputtering over the reel, everything feeling disjointed and choppy. The Weaver moves to the fire, hands holding an integral part of me, and then he tosses that part straight into the flames, my blood offering complete.

One second, the pyre is burning in oranges and yellows, but then, it explodes into a blaze of effervescent violet, shifter magic thick in the air. The heat coming off of the fire magnifies, growing so hot that sweat beads against my brow. The Spirit Weaver and surrounding pack are forced to step back from the blistering intensity as it crackles and smokes. I try to shield my eyes from the brightness, but my body doesn't seem to be working right.

And then, a shadow appears.

Right there, in the middle of all that burning color, a form coalesces. I blink, squinting as a massive dark gray wolf steps out of the flames. My breath stops. My heart does too. With glowing violet eyes locked onto me, their depths soaking me in, she begins to walk forward, and I recognize her immediately.

She's mine.

I can't move as she closes the distance between us. I feel every step through the ground as I stand, and it's as though my body is moving of its own volition, bare feet sinking into the dirt. I hold my breath when she stops in front of me, unsure of what to expect. We stare at each other, and a quiet tranquility fills the air between us.

I let out a shaky breath as I take in this beautiful creature. Her fur is the color of steel and ash, her body almost as tall as I am standing up. She lets my gaze sweep over her form, and when my eyes come back to her violet ones, she lowers her head to mine. Instinctually, I press my forehead against hers, feeling the solidness of who and what she is, her soft fur against my fevered skin like a balm to my soul.

We stay like that for a beat, just breathing each other in. My eyes flutter closed as her scent surrounds me, seeming so *familiar*. Like I've scented her spirit in the air my entire life without knowing it. I *feel* her. Recognize her in a way I can't quite explain. She feels like me and yet...not. There's a primal wildness to her presence, a strength and well of potent power that charges my every nerve. We're pieces of a whole who finally fit together, and for the first time in a long time, peace washes over me.

Instinct takes over, and I open my arms and tip my head back, inviting her blessing into my body. Without hesitation, she leaps into me, and the force is so strong that I fall back, my body hitting the ground hard.

The world around me disappears in a clap of thunder that only I can hear. I'm lost to the crash of sensations suddenly erupting through me. Pain. Serenity. Disarray. Battle. Movement.

My thoughts and body are a mess of primal needs and innate understanding. My insides feel too small, and it's as though the seams of who I am are bursting, ripping apart to make room for her. I ache as I adjust to the fullness of our souls, and her spirit burns through me, melding us together in a way that can never be severed. It's humbling, empowering, and so much more than I ever knew it could be.

I am hers.

She is mine.

And *we* are one.

I want to throw my head back and howl with happiness, to shed the confines of my skin and feel the world through our wolf body. It's time for us to run together, to bond in every possible way that we can, but...something holds us back.

Something is *wrong*.

I'm stuck inside the merging, unable to use my body, while she's unable to use hers. A prickling sensation thrashes through us, so we reach out with our other senses, past our paralyzed form. The smells of the woods surround us, which should be a good thing, yet for some reason, alarm pumps through our veins. Something sickly sweet with an undertone of rot clings to our nose, making us agitated, like the scent of fruit on the cusp of going bad.

My wolf and I are stuck in some weird state of limbo, where we need to choose who takes control. And although I can't move, I have the strangest impression that I'm being carried. I don't know if that's just the sensation of the wolf taking over, but that doesn't seem right. I know she needs to run, that we need to shift and solidify our joining, but when I encourage her to do just that, she answers by shoving herself at me hard, almost combative like she wants to fight me.

Her mind feels like a mess of panic as it meshes with mine. I'm lost to all the confusing images, smells, and sensations. Wet ground presses against my back, and for some reason, the distinct feel of it stokes complete rage in my wolf. She slams against me again, ripping us away from this beautiful spiritual exchange, and ramming us brutally back to reality.

I come to as though I'm breaching the surface of a still lake. One second, everything is blurry and muffled, and then the next, I come up gasping from a daze as the world around me slams back into focus.

A snarl is already building in my chest as I get my bearings. I'm no longer in front of the fire as the pack watches me receive my wolf spirit. Somehow, I'm deep in the forest, lying on the damp floor, the cold and wet seeping into my clothing and leeching me of all warmth.

I feel a tug at my feet, and horror rockets through me as I look down and find Burke pulling my jeans off. Inside of me, my wolf snarls again, and I immediately skitter back away from him. My hands and legs rush to put as much distance between us as they can. Burke's head snaps up, and the smile he gives me makes my skin crawl.

"What the fuck are you doing?" I demand, feeling disoriented, adrenaline pumping through my veins and making the world tip and teeter.

Sticks and rocks dig into the bare skin of my legs as I move. I look down, realizing that my ceremonial robe is gone and my shirt has been ripped open from the front, exposing my bra. I pull the two pieces of fabric back together and try to scramble to my feet, but Burke is on me in a flash.

One moment, he's feet away from me, tossing my pants into a bush, and the next, he's pinning me down. I try to scream, but his massive hand slams over my mouth, trapping my call for help as I'm held against the wet earth. Terrified and driven by raw panic, I struggle, flailing and kicking, trying to get him off of me.

"Fight me, Seneca," he growls in my ear, grinding against me as I try to get out from underneath him.

I feel his hardness dig into my stomach like the threat it's meant to be, and I hate the whimper of fear that's smothered by the hand he has pressed bruisingly against my mouth.

"Fight me until you realize that you're not going to win," he grunts, shoving his knee roughly between my thighs.

I twist my body to keep him from angling my legs apart and scream against his hand. His evil eyes light up with excitement at the muffled noise before he licks up my neck and nips at my jaw. I battle and try to get him off of me, but he's too big, too heavy, too powerful.

Anger and fear war inside my body. He couldn't even let me settle. Couldn't even let me enjoy the sacred moment of joining with my wolf before he pounced.

Hate consumes me.

"You thought you could run from me, that I wouldn't hunt you down and take what's mine. Don't you get it by now? I *own* you. I've owned your sweet little cunt since the minute I strolled into this pack. I've waited patiently, put up with your bitch of a mother long enough, but I will not be denied a second longer. You are *mine*, Seneca Rain. You always have been, and now I'm going to make sure you always will be."

He leans down and nips hard at my breast, making me jolt. His canines start to elongate, and I know this is a prequel to the claiming bite he's about to give me against my will. I whimper against the uninvited touch and try to wiggle out from under him, but he just moans, like my every movement is turning him on more, like it's going to get him off.

No.

The word snarls through me, more animal than human.

My vision bleeds red, and I can feel the wolf in me pushing to take over. I try to stop her from gaining control, terrified that if she does, Burke will call his own wolf and I'll be forced to submit. I get one of my arms free from his hold and drag my nails down his face. I try to shove my fingers into his eyes, but he bellows in pain and turns his head, keeping me from doing the kind of damage I want.

Pain explodes in my cheek when he cocks back a fist and punches me. A ringing starts in my ear, and I'm momentarily stunned by the hit. Burke takes advantage by tearing off my underwear, but my lapse in conscious control also lets my wolf surge to the forefront. I scream as she fights her way through, clawing at my mind, my body, my spirit. My vision fractures when Burke forces my thighs apart, the colors around me becoming muted while the detail of everything sharpens.

Fingers dig into my flesh, trying to take what doesn't belong to them, and all at once, I rip apart. All control is fully relinquished in a split second that seems to split *me*. Agony is all I know as my bones splinter and my skin stretches, fur erupting over my body as sharp teeth punch through my gums.

A fury-filled snarl explodes out of my throat, and in a flash, clawed paws are raking against him. Strong limbs shove him away as I shift into my wolf, and she starts fighting tooth and claw. Burke falls backward from her sudden appearance, and my wolf lunges, snapping at him, sinking sharp teeth into the arm he raises to keep her from catching him in the throat. He might be bigger than us, but my wolf is *savage*.

"You fucking bitch!" he screams, but my wolf doesn't back off. Instead, she bears down, shaking her head hard as she tries to rip his arm from his body. She tosses the bastard around like a fucking rag doll, but then there's the sound of his splintering bones as he calls on his wolf and starts to shift.

Fear strikes through me as I wait for my wolf to react to his, but she's too busy mauling him to care. Blood coats my beast's tongue, and the taste spurs her on. She abandons her hold on his arm mid-shift and flings herself at him, but he pivots just enough that she tears into his shoulder instead of his face. Fur explodes through his skin, and Burke's yelling morphs into a deep, vicious growl as he completes his transformation.

As soon as his hands turn into paws, my wolf surges for his neck, shoving the massive black wolf onto its back with immense strength. I'm shocked that she doesn't submit to him, even though we can feel him try to push at us with alpha power. Burke yelps, but there's no hesitation, no submission, not even any mercy from her. She wants to rip his throat out and shred his body, and I can see the surprise flash through his wolf.

Teeth sink into my foreleg, making pain shoot through me as Burke thrashes underneath me. A menacing growl rips from my wolf's throat as she snaps at his face, swiping at him with her front paws at the same time. Then it becomes a blur of fangs, fur, and fury as the wolves bite and tear into one another. Burke keeps trying to force me to submit, snarling at me and trying to put me on my back, but my wolf is not fucking having it.

It's as though she's lost to the bloodlust, broken with her need to destroy this male wolf and anyone else who would think to harm us. Her furor is a sight to behold, a visceral feeling pumping through our veins. It makes me feel both unhinged and unstoppable. It doesn't matter what injuries Burke inflicts, my wolf isn't stopping until the ground is bathed in his blood and his throat's been torn open, his life crushed between her teeth.

Together, we are not timid. We are not submissive. We are not omega. And we will *not* let him claim us.

My wolf surges with a strength that matches Burke's, flooding our spirits with vicious enmity. He will take his last breath with us standing victoriously over his body, and then he'll know he should have never fucked with me.

Burke tries to throw my wolf off-balance, but she clamps onto his ear for his efforts. He yelps and yanks his head away, leaving part of his ear in her mouth. She spits it out, just as he raises his head and lets out a deafening howl.

Outrage courses through us. My wolf is furious by this weak alpha's call for help, at his inability to face her, and then even more disgusted when Burke tries to turn away and run.

Fucking coward.

She pounces on him, clamping onto the back of his neck in an unforgiving bite. Her hind paws do their best to shred the skin and muscle of his back, loin, and flanks, while her forepaws dig into his shoulders and withers. When he yelps, she sinks her teeth deeper and deeper into his neck. It's not a killing bite, but it's a good hold, and he's tiring. The sharp scent of fear has entered these woods, and it doesn't belong to us.

But before she can maneuver into a killing blow, the distinct sound of our pack members on both paws and feet are rushing our way. My wolf snarls and shakes Burke by the back of the neck, and he growls, trying to throw us off of him. It doesn't work. Wrath pumps through our veins, and my wolf is pissed that dishonorable mongrels are running to stop a fight their alpha started. *Where the hell were they when this piece of shit dragged me off and tried to rape me?*

I know I'll be outnumbered soon, and maybe a normal wolf would run, but my wolf doesn't feel *normal*, and she has no intention of giving up this fight.

Burke rolls us into a tree, and even though it hurts her, she refuses to let go. It's like the pain parts of her mind are shut off, because all she can focus on is the kill. Wolves howl in the distance, closing in on us, and she tries to muscle Burke into a better position so she can kill him before they arrive. He fights her, but inch by inch, she's getting closer to the upper hand, and the whimper he releases says he knows it.

Need for his blood surges through us as she gets closer to that sweet spot of his throat. But there's an odd pop that echoes around the forest all around us, and then something pierces my flank. She ignores the stinging sensation, keeping her focus on Burke's wolf as paws run for us. She lets out a snarl with a mouthful of fur, muscles tensing in preparation to be attacked, just as another wolf hurtles into view.

The mongrel is smaller than Burke's animal with a light gray coat and hints of red around his muzzle. Recognition fires through me, and my wolf releases Burke's throat at the last second as Seamus barrels into her. She turns and sinks her canines into his shoulder, forcing him back into a tree, overpowering him so easily that it sends a shockwave through me.

He throws his head back to yelp in pain, and she pounces on the opportunity. Salty blood tries to drown me as she tears into him. Seamus doesn't even have time to yip and squeal in pain before she rips the front of his throat from his body.

Just like that, he's dead.

She drops the meat of his neck and then picks up his body, tossing it away like the garbage it is. She turns to find Burke again. He's hurt and unmoving, but the second she takes a step, she stumbles. My beast's body is suddenly heavy and uncoordinated, and she shakes her head to clear the daze filling our vision while trying to stay upright. In my head, I know that someone shot us. I can feel the tranquilizer coursing through our adrenaline-fueled veins, but we're only focused on the threats.

Shadowy figures surround us, and my wolf bares her teeth in a livid growl. She leaps at one of them, teeth sinking into skin with no fur. The man screams, but we're hit from the side by a different pack monster in fur. We go down, but when my beast tries to get up, her legs no longer work. She rages, growling and snapping at anything that gets too close.

A completely feral sensation overtakes us, tainted with helplessness. No one tries to get close as the man and wolf scramble away. Everyone just stands around like weaklings with their tails tucked between their legs as they wait for the drugs they darted us with to render us unconscious.

My wolf and I try to fight it, but our vision tunnels and everything inside of us goes numb. We bite back a whimper that wants to escape, refusing to show any sign of weakness, even though fear spikes in us. I don't know if we'll wake up or if they'll kill us in our forced sleep, but I feel sick satisfaction that she at least took one of them with us and fucked up Burke.

My vision splinters, everything around me doubling. My wolf and I both look out at the pack that failed us, at the alpha somewhere in the shadows who betrayed us.

And then, everything around us blurs and blinks to nothing.

SIX

I WAKE UP WITH CLAWS AND FANGS.

My dry eyes peel open and focus on a cold, concrete floor. There is no forgetfulness, no struggle to remember what happened. I wake up as though I'd only just blinked, my consciousness snapping to immediate awareness.

I take stock of my sore and chilled body, trying to let my senses tell me where we are. I smell blood and dirt and bleach. Gooseflesh covers my body nearly as much as bruises do. I try to look around, but my vision bends, nauseatingly so, and I realize that my wolf is *right here* with me. I'm not shifted into my wolf, but when I look down at my naked body, I see hooked claws in place of my human fingers and feel elongated canines in my copper-tasting mouth.

The rest of me feels normal, but when I attempt to pick up my head, my vision roils again, like I'm standing on a boat in the middle of a storm. Realization strikes me that we're both looking out of my eyes, trying to claim control over my sight. She grapples with one eye while I hook onto the other, and it's so disorienting that I have to squeeze them shut, have to breathe out a shaken breath as a wash of seasickness sways me.

"She's awake!"

The shout has us springing our eyes open, which only pitches us into horrible dizziness. It doesn't pass until a pair of feet are standing in front of us, and the scent of that overly ripe, rotten fruit invades the air.

"Shift."

The alpha order washes over me. I can feel the potency of it as it licks across my skin, but shockingly, the power doesn't sink into me and force me to follow it. I try to look up at Burke, but this double spirit vision that's happening is disorienting. I reach out to my anxious wolf, soothing her and reassuring her that we're one. I ask her to give me control, but she's wary. I make it clear that if she senses anything and needs to step forward to protect us, I won't fight her, not like I did before.

Burke snarls above me, bellowing, "*Shift*," with even more authority than before. My wolf and I ignore the command, which is something we shouldn't even be able to do, but with a warm sensation and a small nip of warning, she backs off and gives me control.

In a painful yank, my half-shifted state retreats inside of me, my animal crouching down in wait. My claws disappear and my fangs recede, and luckily, my vision settles back to normal as she pulls away from my eyes too. I roll my sore body up to a sitting position, wrapping my arms around my knees protectively to shield my naked body as I look up at the malignant alpha.

I want to kill him, I want to taste his blood on my lips and teeth as it rushes out of him and cools on the ground. I look from him to his back up, incensed that they would lend their muscle to execute this weakling's orders. My wolf and I can't beat them all, but maybe if we time this just right, we won't have to.

My glare finds Burke's cruel black eyes, and he stares down at me with venom dripping from every plane of his face. Dark satisfaction spills through me as I take in the face Burke is so proud of and the claw marks now running down it. His neck is also bandaged, and I suspect that's not the only wound that had to be dressed, based on the lumpy bits beneath his T-shirt. "You are going to regret attacking me," he promises, standing over me like some angry god with little man syndrome.

My wolf paces inside me, but I work to calm her, asking that she trust me. As much as I'd love to give her control, we need to be smart about this. We're only going to get so many chances to rip out this fucker's throat, and we need to make it count. They didn't kill us, so there must be some form of a plan happening, and I need to be lucid enough to know what it is so we can make it work for us. Thankfully, she backs off, and I send her my gratitude as I focus back on Burke with every ounce of hate I possess.

"You're going to regret killing my mother and not finishing me when you had the chance," I bite back, working hard to tamp down on the almost overwhelming desire to paint the room with the blood of every wolf standing in here.

For a second, he just stares at me, and then quicker than I can stop, he sends a kick into my ribs.

I cry out in both fury and pain as my body slams to the side, falling into a concrete block wall that I realize makes up the entirety of this ten-by-ten room. He steps on my hand, pressing my splayed fingers against the hard floor, putting all his weight on it until I'm sure every bone is going to snap.

"Watch your fucking mouth. I am your *alpha*!"

"You're a fucking coward," I toss back, yanking my hand away and cradling it against my chest. "A male with no honor. You killed my old alpha with trickery, and you tucked tail and ran from a fight with me."

He kneels down in front of me and clutches the hair at my left temple, yanking my head to the side so far I worry he'll snap my neck right here and now.

My wolf surges, and this time I don't stop her. We snap for Burke's neck, faster than a bolt of lightning, teeth sinking into cotton as a ferocious snarl tears from our throat. Just as fast, wolves are ripping us away from him. The smell of blood fills the room as they punch, stomp, and kick us until all we can do is cover our head and take it.

Slowly, like the trickle of an ending storm, the attack stops. The smell of testosterone and rage is an acrid tang now mixing with the tinge of my blood that coats not only me, but spatters the floor, walls, and wolves all around me.

Burke's angry steps sound like cannon fire as he leers over me, more gauze pressed to his neck. Once again he bends down, but I'm too battered to take advantage of his closeness this time.

"You will fucking submit!" he yells into my face, but this time it's not power he's radiating as he bellows the command. It's *fear*. I can smell it leaching out of him, and it's cloying. So potent I can taste it.

And that taste, that response from this joke of an alpha, it sinks into me, charging me with a burst of power. I spit the blood in my mouth at his feet and lock eyes with him.

"*No*."

My response is more growl than word, more wolf than woman. A flip has switched, pure animal instinct overtaking my humanity, fed by the weakness of his fear.

My vision breaks, sways, fractures. Fur begins to sprout over my body, and my mouth begins to froth. Eyes burn with a glow that blazes hotter than that violet flame during the Flux, so searing that it feels like I'm seeing through the heated fires of hell. My chest pants, my throat roars, all consideration of pain and injury shoved aside as the need for blood, the need to *kill*, is suddenly the only coherent thought I have.

Burke backs up so fast it's like he's a car hydroplaning over a wet road. Wide black eyes stare at me. "Impossible..." he whispers, but I barely hear him over the snarls in my burning throat. I feel wild, untethered, like something in me is spinning out of control, and yet, I'm so damn *strong*.

It's almost laughable that this stupid shit, Burke, thinks he has any power over us. *Try again, little alpha wolf.*

"Y-your eyes..." he stutters, shaking his head like he can't believe what he's seeing.

"Alpha?" Conrad calls, standing just outside the open door leading into this bare, frigid cell.

"Look at her eyes," Burke hisses, expression turning to one of such disdain, if only to hide his panic. "Her transformation fucked up. She's gone rabid."

The male at the door blanches, eyes swinging to me.

The word bounces in my skull too loudly for me to grasp. But in this moment, I *feel* rabid. I feel irrational. Extreme. *Savage*.

"Hold your form!" Burke cries as more fur begins to erupt from my skin. He still doesn't get that my shift was *my* choice, not his, so when nothing happens, understanding dawns in his heartless black eyes.

I'm stronger than him.

I leap to my feet, watching in satisfaction as my fingers curl into razor-sharp claws. He must anticipate I'm going to lunge for him, because he and Conrad are out the door and it's slammed shut against me by the time my body hits it, teeth snapping at the place he just was.

There's a small square of reinforced glass cut into the steel door, just big enough for Burke's face to fill, to have me clawing at it as if I can drag my nails down his face instead.

"What are you going to do with her?" Conrad asks, his voice muffled behind the thick door, but not enough with my new wolf's superior hearing. "Are you still going to claim her?"

"Claim *that*?" Burke snaps, like the very idea is appalling. "Fuck no. She's not worthy of me and my wolf. Not like this. She's useless now."

My nails dig into the glass with even more force, etching divots into it with every screeching scrape as I imagine gutting the male deigning to look at me like that when *he's* the one that forced me to snap.

"Should we put her down?"

That question sends me into a rage. I start snarling and clawing at the door harder. There's no handle to grapple with on this side of the cell, so I start punching it instead. My half-shifted fists slam against the steel so hard that the metal starts to bend and dent.

"No," Burke says, and I snap my teeth so close to the glass near his face that he flinches back. I give him a cruel, fanged sneer. Fury flashes through his eyes, and he glares me down. "No, I'm going to make sure she suffers."

I hear him, but I *don't* hear him at the same time. I'm too busy tossing my shoulder into the door, trying to break it down, too busy being completely overcome with this all-consuming animal hostility. I want to get lost in it, fall deeper, because there is power in this unhinged ferociousness.

Glittering, vindictive eyes hold mine, making me pause, and I watch the wheels turning in his mind. The smile that curves his lips is so cold that the temperature around me seems to drop. "I know *exactly* what to do with a rabid bitch."

He's gone before I can snarl again, and someone flips off the light, trapping me in the concrete cage as the darkness swallows me whole. The lack of light is so encompassing that even my heightened sight can't pick up anything.

And that vicious, burning part of me explodes with a terrifying howl that rattles the window and cracks the air. My savage fury is so loud that there's no way the members of the Twin Rivers pack can run from it.

I SLEEP.

I wake.

I claw at the concrete all around me and fight to break down the door.

I don't know how much time has passed. It's impossible to know when all there seems to be is darkness. Well, that and the rage festering inside of me. My wolf and I take turns expressing it and then we sleep and wait for the next bout to hit. It's cold and we call on our fur to warm us in between the purging of our ire. Our stomach is long past hungry, the pains now quiet from being ignored for so long. Our throat no longer craves water, and our body, in both forms, is growing weaker with every bout of snarling fury we discharge.

I've heard people watching me from the other side of the door. They seem to only come so that they can set me off again. But my wolf and I caught on. We realized quickly that they might be trying to wear us down on purpose, so we started to steep in our vengeance, waiting to react until it's the right time.

Burke's words splash around in my mind, *shattered, useless, rabid*. I chew on some of them, slowly growing accustomed to the truth of their taste. But I also know there's more to it. He thought he'd rule over me, and now he knows that will never happen.

And yet, here I am, still alive.

I've wracked my mind, trying to anticipate what he's going to do to me. I think it will be something public and obviously painful in front of the pack. He'll use my current state to his advantage and try to teach the others a lesson. For some reason, I feel oddly okay about that. Probably because it will be an opportunity to break free and slaughter anyone who's stood by and allowed this monster to run our pack.

That'll be fun.

A distant clang has my wolf and me perking our ears and listening to the heavy footsteps that cautiously approach our cell. I chuckle inside at the smell of their trepidation wafting beneath the crack of the door. Satisfaction moves through me at how easy it is to make these big strong wolves so uneasy. I hear one of them messing with something, chains maybe, or some other kind of equipment. I refuse to react, not wanting to take the bait to rage and weaken ourselves any more than we already are.

A latch on the door slides open, but it doesn't allow any light in, and I can't see what's going on. Every muscle in my body tenses as silence once again envelops the space, and we lie in wait to see what they're going to do. A familiar *pop* fills the cell, followed by a rush of air, and then a dart sinks into my shoulder. I snarl, fangs jutting out from my gums as I reach up and yank the needle out of my arm.

The drug starts to work immediately. The concoction makes me feel both heavy and weightless while my senses dull and everything around me becomes muted. I work to calm my wolf and to try and steady my heart rate, stopping the shift. Getting angry and losing it now will only help to spread whatever they just shot us with faster. I want them to have a false sense of security. I want them to open that door so we can rip their heads from their fucking bodies.

My wolf warms to that idea and stops pacing inside of me. I sag against the cinderblock wall as my limbs go numb, and I pull back on the change, keeping control of my body. I try not to worry about where we'll wake up next, confident that we will at least wake up.

After all, Burke has to save face. He has to reinforce his weak control over the pack by picking on the girl that almost tore him apart. I wonder if anyone knows the truth of how he got his injuries. I wonder if any of the betas will get together behind closed doors and discuss when and where to challenge the alpha who's so clearly unworthy of the title. I know some of them must be itching for more power. Their wolves have to be clawing their insides, just begging for an opportunity to lead.

I wait for unconsciousness to creep over me, but it doesn't. The door to my cell opens, but by the time it does, I can't move a limb, no matter how much I want to. I close my eyes against the light that floods my dark prison, but I can't turn my head away from it. Male pack members in their human form pour into the cell, tense and ready. Someone holding chains approaches me, the links of the metal clinking from the shaking hands holding them. I'd smirk if I could move my lips.

A deep warning growl resonates in my chest as Conrad comes forward and binds my ankles and then clamps chains around my wrists. I bark out a snarl when he moves to fix a muzzle around my face, and it makes him jump back, while another beta in the cell yelps in fear.

Conrad watches me warily, brown eyes thick as mud. "You try biting me, and you're gonna catch my fist in your fucking teeth," he threatens.

"She's drugged," someone behind him drawls. "She can't move."

Conrad glares over his shoulder. "She shouldn't have been able to resist Alpha's shift command either, but Nico said she did."

"Nico's probably full of shit."

Conrad thrusts the muzzle at him. "Oh, yeah? If you're so cocky about it, why don't *you* put the muzzle on her?" The argumentative beta goes silent at that. Conrad turns back to me, grumbling under his breath. "That's what I fucking thought. This bitch killed Seamus. Just tore his damn throat out as easy as ripping a piece of paper. If it were up to me, she'd be fucking dead already."

"Come on," the yelping beta says, kneeling down next to me. Saul, I think his name is. Not very high up, but a beta who's used to doing plenty of grunt work. "Let's just get this over with."

Conrad nods. "Hold her head."

Try as I might to thrash my head, I can't. The medicine has a grip on my nerves, my muscles, even my damn bones. Saul squats at my side and grips my head, his fingers digging into my skin. When Conrad lifts the gag in front of my face, a wash of panicked hysteria overcomes my wolf and me. Through my gritted teeth, bloodthirsty growls cut through the air, so vicious that I can practically feel the wolves inside of them tucking their tails.

Conrad wastes no time in shoving it against my mouth, a thick leather strap driving between my teeth. I try to snap at him, try to tear through the leather, but my jaw won't work. All I can manage is a weak press of my tongue against the foul-tasting band. Saul and Conrad work together to fasten the two other straps on either side of my head, the leather tightened against my skin, ensuring that I can't spit the strap out, can't bite or talk, even muffling my snarls.

I start to breathe heavy, true panic setting in when the two other betas yank on the chain attached to the metal cuffs on my ankles and then check the one on my wrists next. The feeling of utter helplessness bleeds through my mind, my vision, my throat.

That wild part of me begins to hammer against the glass of my control, and froth bubbles up, coating the barbaric strap I'm forced to bite down on. But the last of my resolve cracks when Conrad grabs my naked body and tosses me over his shoulder, and the air is stolen from my lungs, ripping away all my snarling with it.

Flopped over him, his bones digging into my stomach, I internally scream, willing my head to lift, my hands to move, my legs to do something...anything.

But the tranquilizer did its job all too well, keeping me on the cusp of consciousness, not letting me tip over, while stealing every ability to move other than breathe and blink.

The lather in my mouth drips down uncontrollably, and I stare at the bobbing floor as Conrad's footsteps take me out of the cell and into a cold, dark hallway. My chained wrists clank together, hanging impotently against his back, and I wish I could drag my nails down his shirt and shred his skin into ribbons. Someone smacks my bare ass hard when I'm carried up a set of steep stairs, tearing a yelp from me that ends in my eyes tunneling with their heated glow, my snarls coming back full force.

I can't look in any direction other than down, and I'm carried out of wherever they've been keeping me. The floors are bare concrete, and smells hit me of several pack members as I'm taken up a set of stairs and then outside, where it's still dark. Or...dark again. I have no idea what day it is or how long I've been down in that cell. This dark smells like the dark of a pre-dawn. A broody prequel to an angry coming morning.

I black in and out of consciousness as I'm carried, but suddenly the familiar scents of the pack house wash over me, including dozens upon dozens of my pack members. I can't see them, but I can smell them, and as we get nearer, I can hear them too. Some of them are whispering, some gasp at the sight of my manhandled and shackled body, and all I can do is continue to watch the ground, head bobbing against Conrad's back with every step, growling out a warning that my body can't mete out.

There must be another bonfire tonight, because smoke is thick and acrid, but it doesn't overpower the rage pouring off of me, or the anger I scent coming from my pack members. For a second, my stomach leaps, because I think that this might be it—they might turn against Burke. They might—

"Traitor!" someone yells.

"Coward!"

"Bitch!" is snarled too close to my ear, and then I'm pelted in the back with something hard and sharp—a rock maybe—and realization dawns. They're not angry on my behalf. This anger is directed *at* me. As if I deserve this.

I seethe as the pack all around me shows they're more sheep than wolves. With each vitriolic word spit at me or projectile that connects with my body, they prove just how stupid and weak they all truly are. I snarl and bellow out my rage, wishing I could tear each and every one of them apart, but all I can do is foam and drool and make myself look like the monster they all think I am. I thought Burke was the blight tainting this pack, but it's clear his poison has destroyed any good that was ever here. These fuckers deserve him.

The dam seems to break within the pack, because more insults and threats hurl my way.

"Rabid!"

"Put her down!"

"Her wolf can't be trusted!"

"Yank out her teeth!"

As if my wolf's fangs heard that one, my gums begin to throb, fangs wanting to punch through and sink into whoever called out that threat. I froth and growl so loud it shakes through my entire body, fighting off the drug gumming up my system, my blood feeling thick, muscles encased in stiffening plaster.

Incomprehensible shouting pounds in the air, the voices of too many packmates turning on me while I'm naked, drugged, and bound. The reek of anger is sharp in my nostrils, but my wolf's hate is even sharper as her nails seem to drag against my skin.

"She's ready, Alpha," Conrad says, coming to a stop.

Steps march over to me, and then Burke is there, with his disgusting arrogant scent surrounding me as much as the smoke.

"Good. Let's go."

My mind spins, wondering what the hell they're going to do to me, and my anxiety spikes. If only I could just *move*. I wouldn't feel so vulnerable, so trapped. But I can't. I can do nothing as I'm taken to a van and tossed mercilessly into the back. The bench seats have been removed, so I get tossed onto the hard, bare metal floor. Instinctually, I try to brace my body as it goes down, but I can't even manage that, and I know my entire side will be black and blue from the impact. I'm sure the bruises will fit in nicely with all my others.

As soon as the back doors slam shut, my chest restricts, sweat gathering on my skin.

Where the fuck are they taking me?

My wolf hates this, her entire spirit shaking inside of my skin as I lie here in an uncomfortable heap, unable to even lift a finger.

Two people get into the front seats, car doors slamming, and I immediately smell Conrad and Burke. The van takes off with a sudden speed, making my useless body go rolling, which only makes the males laugh. Tires go over bumpy terrain, and I'm jerked around by Conrad driving like a shithead on purpose, just to jostle me. I scream and try to bite against the leather ties, but all I can manage is the barest clamp of my teeth, not even hard enough to depress the leather.

Maybe they'll drive long enough that some of this drug will wear off. It's a long shot, but it's the only string of hope that I have, so I hold onto it as hard as I can.

I have no choice but to wait until whatever is in my blood releases my limbs. So that's what I concentrate on. Because whatever Burke has planned for me, wherever they're taking me, it will be nowhere good. Patience and preserving my strength, that's what I need to focus on, not the rabid panic spiking through my veins.

I tell my wolf and myself this over and over and over again until I fall into a fitful sleep, with shackles digging into my skin and fangs throbbing beneath my gums.

Patience.

SEVEN

MY HEAD IS SLAMMED AGAINST SOMETHING HARD, waking me with a shock.

I hiss and clench my teeth against the pain as I look around, fighting off the white spots now speckling my vision. I can tell the van has stopped, but there aren't any windows back here for me to get an idea of where we are. My body aches from being bound and battered by the drive, and I scoot away from the metal wall my head just rammed into as I take stock. All of my limbs are still slow and heavy, but at least I can feel them now.

Burke and Conrad are talking, but I can't hear what they're saying over the ringing in my ears. Two car doors open and then shut, and a spike of panic tries to push away the pain and disorientation muddling my mind. With great effort, I manage to pull my feet underneath me as footsteps move from the front of the van to the back, and I brace myself in a crouch, begging my body to cooperate.

The second the doors screech open, flooding in afternoon daylight, I clumsily leap from the back of the van at whoever just cleared the path to freedom. My stomach roils angrily thanks to the drugs they shot me up with, but it doesn't keep me from clotheslining Conrad with the chain connecting my wrists. He shouts with surprise as we both go down, but I'm barely able to bruise his skin, let alone pop his head off like I want to, because Burke grabs me by the waist and tosses me away.

Dry, dirt-packed earth breaks my fall, dust rising up from the force of my landing and clogging my airway. I rip the muzzled gag off my face, coughing and hacking to clear my throat. I toss it away with a snarl and push myself to my feet, body swaying with the effort to stand, ankle chains pulled taut.

"Where's Hess?" I demand, spitting out a glob of dirt.

"Hess is dead."

The cold declaration staggers me where I stand in a cloud of dust and dread.

No.

I feel the blood drain from my face right before a rush of anger overwhelms it. My hands curl into fists, and I tense, ready to attack him for all I'm worth, but when the haze of wrath and dust clears, I find myself staring into the barrel of a gun. I have no idea if it's what they use to tranquilize me or if it's the bullet-shooting kind, but the sight makes me freeze in place.

My wolf howls inside of me, insisting that we can get to his throat before he can so much as pull the trigger, but I'm not so sure. The dart's effects are still weighing down my blood and my body, and as much as I want to get to him, I want to make sure I can rip him apart when I do.

I glare at the weak alpha, my stare furious and filled with disdain. He wouldn't know a fair fight if it bit his dick off. Looking around, I see tall grass and foreign trees. I don't smell anything other than nature, maybe a hint of water nearby, and a fox den over the hill the van just drove down. I have no idea where we are or why he's brought me here. My foot shifts, and Burke's gun-arm springs up higher, just an inch of movement making him trigger happy.

"If you come any closer, I'll put you down like the pack was begging me to," he threatens, his unwelcome gaze dropping to my bare body.

A warning growl crawls up my throat, and his black stare flashes to mine. Disgust fills him as he looks at my eyes as though something has changed about me, though I don't feel anything is different. Cheekbones, lips, nose, they're all the same. Maybe he just sees the red-hot rage he sparked to life as it burns through my gaze. My wolf and I want to claw his fucking eyes out and drown in his screams as I slowly rip him to pieces.

"Not impressed?" I seethe, gesturing to my face. Regardless of what he sees when he looks at me, it's made him want to tuck tail and run.

Good.

He made me snap, attacked me, threatened me, tried to claim me against my will. And now, a fissure has opened inside of me like the cracked earth after an apocalyptic quake.

Rabid, he called me, expelling it like a repulsive curse. Am I rabid? Is there something wrong with me and my wolf? Maybe, but I'll take it if it keeps him the fuck away from me.

I shake with the effort not to shift as my wolf surges forward, demanding Burke's blood. I remind her of the gun and the chains on our limbs and beg her to bide her time. *Not yet.*

"You're a fucking *stain*," he snarls, spitting on the ground like he's purging his mouth of the foul words, as though they might be catching. "A malignancy to our kind. You and your wolf are defective—a disgrace to Totemic shifters everywhere."

Conrad crosses his arms next to Burke and nods in agreement, though his eyes keep straying to my breasts and to the juncture between my thighs.

My legs are shaking with the effort it's taking to stand, but I lock my knees and keep my spine snapped straight, refusing to let myself fall. "Then shoot me," I challenge, wondering what the hell he's brought me out here for. "Be the spineless piece of shit that everyone knows you are."

Our kind doesn't use guns against each other. Doing so is considered the epitome of weak. We use teeth, brute force, and instincts, not bullets. The fact that he uses darts is bad enough, but if he kills me here today, at least my death will show him for what he is. A feeble alpha who could only win by cheating, and there'd be no denying it this time. The pattern would be clear, and no pack would ever let him live that down.

Burke smiles, and I reassure my wolf that one way or another, we'll wipe that arrogant grin off his face, even if we have to do it without teeth. Slowly, he backs away from me, moving closer to the van. "You think I'd kill you, make things easy for you after what you've done?" he taunts, just as Conrad gets into the driver's seat and starts the engine, a door slamming shut in his wake.

"After what *I've* done?" I hiss, hands curling into fists, making the shackles around my wrists bite into my skin.

Burke jerks the barrel of the gun at me as though he's telling me to stay put. I glare at him but don't press my luck. If they think dumping me in the wild is going to get rid of me, then they're dumber than I thought. I'll hunt, I'll heal, and then I'll come for them.

As though my thoughts are written plain as day across my face, Burke's smile grows even wider, and the sight makes an uneasy trickle drip down the back of my neck. He backs up all the way to the passenger side and gets in, shutting the door behind him, gun still pointed at me out the open window.

I take a step forward just as Conrad slams on the gas and jerks the van forward, but Burke's shouted words stop me in my tracks. "Say hello to Ruin Falls." A horrible gleam in his eyes freezes the air in my lungs. "I'd start running if I were you."

Kicking up dirt and dust, the van speeds away down the narrow dirt path, and all the blood drains from my face.

No.

The name Ruin Falls pounds in my ears in time with my galloping heart. I spin around frantically as though wolves are sneaking up on me at this very moment, but there's nothing there. Only trees and grass and the cloud of dust left in the wake of another cowardly move. I immediately hurry toward the tall grass and crouch down in it. I wince at the soreness in my muscles and at the suddenly too loud clinking of my chains, wishing I didn't feel so exposed.

Ruin Falls.

I try to listen for the sounds of predators stalking me through the tall grass, but all I hear is the wind as it tickles the tall light-green blades, bending them to its will, the same way this savage pack will if they get their hands on me.

I pull in deep lungfuls of air, but I don't smell any wolves on the gentle breeze. There's no hint of territory markings or indication that the pack is nearby, but that doesn't make me feel better. Sweat starts to kiss my skin, and my leg muscles tighten with the urge to run. Holding my breath, I try to think through what the hell I should do.

I thought the Twin Rivers pack was bad, that staying there was the end of everything for me. But the Ruin Falls pack is the stuff of nightmares. Everyone knows the stories. The warnings. There isn't a pack as vicious or more feral than that one. Their alpha has never lost a challenge, and everyone knows better than to mess with them.

These wolves are the definition of barbaric and ruthless, so wild that they aren't allowed near humans, and I've just been dropped somewhere in their territory, naked, chained, and weak—the very definition of easy prey.

My wolf whines inside of me, picking up on my fear, and as much as I want to keep her calm and reassured, I can't. I crawl forward on my hands and knees, ignoring every bite that digs into my bare skin. The chains make it difficult to move and impossible to shift. I can't risk our bones snapping beneath their hold, but I need them off if I have any hope of getting the fuck out of here.

If Burke truly dumped me in Ruin Falls territory, then I need to get away fast before I'm detected and ripped apart. I might be rabid, but they're *monsters*.

I start looking for a rock or something I can wedge into the keyhole of the manacles. I stay low, using the long grass as cover, more or less frog walking my way to the treeline while looking for something I can use to break my chains.

The sound of a twig breaking in the distance might as well be cannon fire.

I freeze in my reach for a palm-sized rock and try to listen to my surroundings over the pounding of my own heart.

Dread hammers through me, but I can't smell or hear anything. The little hairs rise on the back of my neck, and my wolf paces nervously inside of me. Out of nowhere, a massive crow lands to my left, making me nearly jump out of my skin. It blinks, shouting an ominous croak at me. I snarl at it and skitter away, fur exploding all over me as my hands morph into paws. I try not to give in to the panic, yet my vision once again breaks into that disorienting double sight.

A fiery rage builds in my chest as though it's a forge. I spin wildly again to keep anything from sneaking up on me because I feel *stalked*. I try to take deep, measured breaths in an effort to calm the frantic and turbulent emotions coursing through me, telling myself that everything's okay. No one knows I'm here. Burke probably dropped me off on the outskirts of their territory. I doubt that chicken shit would have had the balls to set one paw on their land.

I move closer to the trees, instinctively drawn to their cover and protection. At least from the forest, I can see what's around me, because this grass is starting to feel like hundreds of grasping hands against my half-shifted skin.

My wolf calms slightly as we pull in the soothing scent of the pines, firs, and cedars. The dirt smells different here, richer, more uncultivated, and I'm surrounded by rolling hills with larger snow-capped peaks in the far distance.

Cautiously, I stand, hiding my body behind a tree, pressing my furred back against its rough bark. After a moment of nothing happening, I begin to shuffle from tree to tree, my eyes peeled for something that will help me get the chains off. My gaze surveys my surroundings in a constant sweep, while my ears strain to hear the slightest hint of anything amiss. I can still feel the effects of the dart making me lethargic, but I keep going, scenting everything around me for hints of wolf-claimed territory.

Soil sticks to the clammy soles of my feet, but I make steady progress. A deer rounds a bend in the distance, but one quick flare of its nostrils in my direction and it goes leaping away. My wolf perks up, wanting to chase it, and I'm reminded of just how empty and silent my stomach is. I need to get food, maybe find water, and—

Snap.

In a flash, I'm whipped off my feet and thrust into the air. I shout, panicked, as a snare wraps painfully around my ankle and yanks me upside down until I'm dangling from a large branch of a tall tree.

"No no no no no..." I cry, panic flooding my trembling voice as my body sways in the air, hair hanging like the sweep of a broom.

Frantically, I try to bend to reach my ankle and the tight cord biting into it, but my body has been pushed so hard since the night of the Flux, and right now, I just don't have the strength.

Instead of reaching my foot, after a few shaking tries, I manage to hook the chain tethering my wrist around a different branch to take some of the weight off my poor ensnared limb. Now I'm hanging from my foot and my wrists and bent awkwardly, but at least my shackled ankle doesn't feel like it's about to be yanked out of its socket. I fight with everything I have to pull myself up and try to get the snare off, but the few times I manage to reach it, I can't loosen it enough to rip the damn thing off.

After who knows how long of snarling, grunting, and pulling, my energy is spent. Gone. I hang from the tree like a lamb on a spit. My eyes dart around frantically as though some fanged beast is going to burst from the bushes at any moment and tear us apart. Fear and distress stew my insides. My wolf whimpers and flails inside of me, but we can't break free.

With drugs still pumping molasses through my veins, I'm starving, thirsty, tired, aching, cold, naked, chained, and strung up. All of this compounds into utter helplessness that crashes into me like the brutal crest of a storming sea. A pitiful whimper escapes me, and dread pools in my soul.

I can't believe that this is how I'm going to die.

I'll either hang here until I starve and my body shuts down, or until the Ruin Falls pack finds me. I am painfully aware of which option is worse.

Please let me starve.

MY ENTIRE EXISTENCE IS JUST one blur after another of lost time, confusion, and horrible mind-wandering dreams. I have no idea how long I've been hanging in this trap, could be ten minutes, could be days. My head has long since stopped pounding from the blood rush pooling in my skull, and I slip in and out of awareness often, making it impossible to gauge anything.

When the white wolf first appears upside down in my line of sight, I don't even register that it's not a figment of my imagination. I don't feel fear as I blink heavy lids, my chest struggling to pull breath into my weighed-down lungs.

But then a gray and white wolf lopes over the hill behind it, and somehow, despite my position and utter exhaustion, a warning growl seeps low and menacing from my lips as my wolf grasps at our flayed consciousness.

The wolves inch cautiously closer, ears perked, noses pulling in deep breaths of my scent. My eyes connect with a pair of golden orbs and white fur, while a deep rumbling growl resonates all around me. My wolf struggles to stir, weary and depleted, but she musters the strength to flash fangs at the strangers nearing us, and the significance of their presence hits me.

The two wolves circle beneath me as though they're working out how to snap me from the air and devour me whole. I'm under no illusions that a pair of native gray wolves have stumbled upon me. No, these two have the size and cunning eyes that my kind has.

This is the Ruin Falls pack.

Terror strikes hard enough through my debilitated mind that my body jerks into movement just as a man crests the hill. Somehow, seeing him is even scarier than seeing the two shifted wolves. I scramble and pull at my bindings, struggling again to get free, as though there's still some possibility that I might escape, and these three won't just hunt me down if I do.

By the time the man gets closer, surveying the trap that I've sprung, I'm panting, muscles screaming, and once again hanging limp. The last of my reserves are gone.

The shifter in man form is older. His hair is more white than gray, half covering a face that's battle-scarred, and even in my upside-down perusal, I immediately note that he's missing an eye. The look of him has my hackles rising, while his one light hazel eye takes me in as though I'm no better than a next meal. The white wolf whines and scratches at the base of my tree, and the man stops beneath me to survey my situation.

"What do we have here, boys?" he grumbles, as though he's disappointed he didn't catch something better.

With half-shifted claws, he slashes out at the taut line of the snare holding me hostage, and I immediately begin to drop. The sudden change in my falling weight snaps the branch that my chained wrists were hanging from, and I go crashing to the ground. I hit the unforgiving earth hard, my bones rattling with the collision, my body destined to become a walking, snarling bruise.

I try to flip to my front, the itch of my wolf's shift just beneath my skin, but the two massive wolves are in my face instantly, growling their threats before I can so much as blink. I cough through the pain, vision swimming as my blood tries to get back to where it belongs in my body. Through the dizziness, I flick my gaze back and forth between the predators, while my wolf tells me to fight. She might have a point. We're going to die, there's no doubt about that, but at least we'll go down with our fangs in someone's fur.

"If you know what's good for you, you'll talk yourself down, mutt," the old man warns with a growl, his one eye narrowed on me, while the empty socket of the other is wrinkled with the lines of an old, mangled wound. "I can smell yer desperation right alongside that fury, but neither will serve you well. Shut that shit down." Without warning, he reaches down and grabs the chain at my ankles and yanks. Rocks, pine needles, and sticks dig into my back as he starts dragging me away, the wolves walking threateningly on either side of me.

I scream at him to let me go, but I can do nothing to stop him. Not with this battered body. I need sleep and food and water. I need to heal, and then maybe I could go down in a blaze of glory against these three—a proper fight to the death. But right now, I'm no better than the deer carcass the man just drug me past, the scent of its blood clinging to the air.

Stopping, he drops the chains, and my legs fall uselessly to the ground. He stands over me, irritation emanating through him. "Listen here, mutt, I don't know how you got here, and I don't care. Yer pack owned now."

Pack owned.

I stare at him with a mix of fear and hate in my glare, wishing I had the strength to kick his knee from its socket.

If he can sense the vicious want in me, he doesn't let on. "You got two choices. You come quietly, or we tear you apart now," he offers, as though either option is just fine with him.

He gestures to a sling-type litter on the ground, made with heavy canvas stretched between two carrying poles. The dead deer is on it, along with a decent-sized pile of hares and pheasant. These shifters have obviously been busy in their hunt. "You can ride on that, or we can keep dragging ya across the ground, but I can't promise you'll still have all yer skin by the time we stop," he tells me. The two wolves watch me like they enjoy the option involving flayed skin and are hoping I choose the hard way.

With shaky arms, exhausted grunts, and heavy effort, I begrudgingly scoot myself right next to the carcasses. Sweat spills down my back, and I pant like I just ran a marathon instead of pushing my sore body onto the fabric that's stained with animal blood. Once I'm settled, he nods in approval. The white wolf huffs, but both of the shifters slink forward and take position between the poles, teeth biting down on the strap tied between them before they start dragging the litter forward through the forest.

My body bumps and falls, the fabric cinching tighter around me as the pole smacks my face. It's not the best mode of transportation, especially when a string of dead rabbits fall onto my lap, but it's marginally better than being dragged on the ground.

The man walks beside me, his good eye cutting over. "Oh, and if yer thinking of running, *don't.* You'll be fair game for claiming if you do."

My blood runs colder than the dead deer's.

What the hell does that mean?

EIGHT

I'M NOT SURE HOW THE HELL IT'S POSSIBLE, BUT I somehow doze off.

That reprieve is cut short when the litter is abruptly dropped, and I go pitching forward. My bound wrists catch my fall before I faceplant, and I feel the canvas drop flat on the ground, no longer curled around me or the rest of the caught prey.

"What the hell is *that*?" The voice isn't what I'd call feminine, but it's certainly female.

I look up and sit back on my bare ass, taking in the female standing over me with her hands on her hips, while the one-eyed male who caught me comes up to her side.

The woman looks...well, *rough*. There's no softness to her whatsoever. As if she's spent every single day with bare skin baking beneath the sun or rolling around in the dirt. Her gray hair is pulled back in a harsh tie secured at the base of her neck, and frown lines bracket her downturned mouth. Her clothes are strange, but now that I have a moment, I notice the male is dressed the same way. He's in a pair of dirt-colored pants, the hems stained all the way up his calves. As if he ran through mud puddles every day for a month and never bothered to change. She's in the same crude fabric, in a shapeless smock.

"Caught her in a snare," he says with a shrug.

She cuts him a look. "She best not have tainted the meat, Terris. Get her off of there and go tie her up in the back."

My eyes widen at the *tie her up in the back* threat, but just as I start to scramble backward, her hand shoots out lightning-fast and grips my hair. "Don't you fucking move," she growls, and I freeze beneath the sudden presence of her wolf pressing just beneath her skin.

In response, my wolf rises up, fangs popping through my gums, an answering growl ripping from my own throat. I'm not sure how I forgot about them, but a sharp pain appears on my hip as the white wolf from earlier nips at me, pinching the skin in an obvious warning.

My growl tapers off to a grumbling wariness, heated eyes flying between the woman, the two wolves, and the hunter who caught me—Terris.

"We don't play like that here, girl. You try to flash fang, and we'll tear into you so fast your head will spin," she promises. I'm outnumbered and incredibly weakened, so I force my wolf back inside me, and my fangs disappear. With a brutal shove, the woman releases me before hauling up the string of hares and walking off. "Boys, get the deer. And *don't* rip off any of it, or I'll rip off a piece of you."

The wolves rush to comply, teeth yanking the heavy carcass forward and leaving a trail in the dirt in its wake. I take the moment to look around, my nude body prickling with the cool air, but what I see makes even more chills scatter over me. This place looks like something right off the horror set for *The Cabin in the Woods*. A sagging, dilapidated two-story cabin bears down on me, set between the trees like it shoved its way between them and decided to grow roots.

A crude washing line is erected on the side of the house, full of bloodstained rags that no amount of scrubbing can clean, along with more handmade clothing flapping around in the breeze like hands shooing me away. Somewhere far off, the sound of snarling wolves travels through the woods, making my blood run cold at the ferocity of it.

This pack is exactly like the rumors made it out to be.

Terris looks down at me with zero expression on his scarred face. "Get up."

When I don't move, he rolls his one eye before latching onto my ankle chain again. He drags me off the litter and across the ground, and I cry out from the immediate road rash. "Okay, okay, I'll walk!" I try to yell as I kick out, but my voice is as dry and brittle as sun bleached bones.

He drops the chains, and I roll over, pushing to my feet. I almost fall again in the process while Terris looks on, noting every weakness I display. My wolf nudges me with an internal nip like she's shoring me up, reminding me we can't appear frail and vulnerable in front of these shifters, even in our human form. Every muscle burns and shakes with the effort it takes to walk, but my anger and her ferocity keep me from collapsing.

He grabs hold of the chain between my aching wrists and tugs me forward. I'm led around the side of the slipshod house, its plank siding made from the same wood as the trees surrounding it, aged from years of wear. In the back, there's a fire pit, cold and unlit, composed of kindling found in the woods and a circle of rocks surrounding it. Terris leads me past, but when my eyes swing to the shed he's aiming for, my heels dig in.

It doesn't matter. Not that I stop walking, not that I pull back, not that I start to kick and scream and try to claw him. He still drags me into that wooden shed. Still tosses me inside of it.

My wolf bays and shoves, wanting to tear into him as he wraps a rope through an iron hoop in the wall and ties it in a tight loop around my forearm. I have to shove her down, all effort going to stopping the shift as my body shakes all over with the force of the resistance. Unfortunately, that internal struggle exhausts me, and I fall to my knees.

Terris looks down at me, unimpressed. "Stay here," he grumbles, scratching a hand down the puckered flesh cut into his cheek. "You get caught out in them woods tonight, and you'll be sorry." With that threat, he walks out, the shed door slamming behind him as loud as the heartbeat that slams against the bones of my ribs.

The shed smells like fear. Piss, dirt, and fear. The smell is sticky and nauseating, and I can only wonder how many people have ended up in here just like me. It looks on the verge of collapse, like it's just waiting for some big bad wolf to come blow it down. As much as I want to curl into a ball and drift away to the nothingness of rest, I need to get the fuck out of here.

A screen door slams closed somewhere on the house next to me, and I peer out between the cracks of the shrunken wood beams of the shed. When it seems as though the coast is clear, I turn away from my slivered view of outside and begin pulling on the knots in the rope with my teeth. I drag it down my forearm, closer to my wrist where I can reach.

Focusing, I try to call on my wolf to get her fangs to drop again, but she doesn't listen. She's too tired and still fighting with the remains of the drug. But I can't give up, so I focus all my strength and efforts on getting loose with my own teeth, hoping I can find some tools under the tarps in the corner to relieve me of my chains. Chomping ruthlessly, I gnaw on it, ignoring the pricks of pain as the rough material of the rope scrapes my skin off every time it moves. I just start to get through one twisting cluster of knots when the door to the shed flies open, and I jump in surprise.

I yank the rope from my mouth and drop my wrists, looking up to see a man carrying two dog bowls in his hands and some kind of clippers tucked under one armpit. He's dressed in similar hand sewn clothes as the couple, his pants made of some kind of hide and the shirt a rough-looking linen or itchy cotton.

A golden gaze fixes on me, and he brushes long strands of dark blond hair from his eyes with his bicep. I wait for his gaze to dip down my nude body, a ready snarl tickling my lips, but to my surprise, his eyes never leave mine until he looks at the rope I tried to chew through.

"If I make things more comfortable for you, will you be good?" he asks me with a scratchy voice, the tone thick and slightly dull as though he doesn't speak much.

I don't answer. My wolf and I just watch him, not trusting him for a second, but he still doesn't leer at my breasts. He doesn't seem to be bothered by my lack of response either, but his stare never leaves mine as he bends and puts a bowl of water on the ground and another stainless-steel bowl next to it that has cut up chunks of raw meat. My wolf wants to dive for the offerings, but I stay back. Warily, we watch him, not willing to take our focus off the stranger for anything.

A small smile pulls at the corner of his mouth, my lack of reaction clearly amusing to him, and he pulls the tool out from under his arm. It looks like a rounded pair of hedge trimmers, and I really hope he's brought them in here to deal with my chains and not anything else actually attached to my body.

With the Ruin Falls pack, I'm thinking it could go either way.

He pulls apart the arms, opening the mouth of sharp clippers, and then waits.

"Well? What's it gonna be?"

I stare at him, wondering why he'd be removing one of the obstacles that's keeping me here. I study his face and then the tool, trying to see the catch. My wolf gives me an irritable nudge, so I tentatively stretch my clinking chains forward. Maybe she's right and it doesn't matter why they're doing it. Getting these chains off is vital.

Instead of snapping the chains, the golden-eyed stranger moves the tool to my wrist, and I automatically yank back in horror.

He clicks his tongue. "Relax."

Opening the blades wide, he slips the mouth of the cutters between the inch-thick cuff around my wrist. I tense, but with strong muscles and precise movement, he snaps the metal clean off me. I try hard not to sigh in relief or rub at the raw skin and sore joint that's now free of the imprisoning metal. He doesn't say a word as he snips the cuff off my other wrist and then lowers the mouth of the curved blades to my ankles.

I smell the air for any hint of lust or interest, any sign that this is about to take a turn for the worse for me, but the male is focused on severing the metal and is even careful not to cut my skin.

"You smell like you could be from Twin Rivers, is that who left you here?" he asks, his nostrils flaring as though he's confirming his suspicion.

I don't say anything, not sure if confirming or denying or even speaking to this shifter is a good idea.

"I'll bring a bath in for you," he announces, as he stands up, clearly not bothered by my silence. He kicks the food a little closer and then turns around and leaves, just like that. The door snaps shut behind him, and I hear the telltale click of a lock being put in place on the other side. I stare with a frown of confusion for a moment as

I gently rub my wrists and ankles. The rope is still tied around my arm, but the chains are blessedly gone.

Why did he just do that? Why would this pack care if I'm more comfortable?

Is it a trick?

Leaning forward to peek through the slats, I stare at the rickety old cabin of a house as though the answers are written in the sun-bleached siding. My wolf gives me another nudge though, and the smell of fresh meat hits me. I turn back to the food and shuffle over to both bowls, trying to scent if anything is off. Burke was a fan of drugs, so maybe this pack is too. Yet all I smell is fresh meat and clean water.

Picking up the bowl of water, I tip it back, my body waking up with desperation as soon as the first drop hits my tongue. I gulp down half the contents of the refreshing liquid before my stomach demands more. I set it down and look at the bowl of food, and my mouth waters. I've never had raw meat before, and the sight should turn my stomach, but I'm salivating as much as my wolf is.

I dig into the meat like I'm the feral beast my pack accused me of being. Growing up, I've watched other spirit-bound pack members prefer their meat raw. I never thought I'd be one of them, but it tastes like heaven. I swallow down huge mouthfuls, and I can practically taste the mountain grass and fresh springs that clearly sustained the venison in my mouth. I moan around a bite, and maybe I'm just starving, but this just might be the best damn thing I've ever eaten.

I debate saving some food for later, because who knows if this will be a regular thing, but my wolf and body are desperate for nutrients and fuel for healing. I don't stop myself from eating every single scrap and then licking the bowl clean.

Oh, if Burke could see me now, acting like the flea-bitten mongrel he's reduced me to.

I shake off the thought of him and what he's done to me as I slurp down the rest of the water. My concave stomach is now pooched with sustenance, and my body begs me to rest so it can heal. But I don't answer the call of sleep even as my eyelids grow heavy and my mind slows. I ignore the deep, jaw-cracking yawns that overtake me and start on the rope again with my teeth.

I'm not sure how much time has passed as I work to unthread and loosen my ties, but true to his word, the golden-eyed male returns, carrying in a long and narrow oval bucket that's big enough to fit a person. Another unfamiliar male is holding the other end, and they set it down with a thud. Pulling a hose into the shack, they slowly start filling the metal container. I watch like a cornered dog, just hoping they ignore me and don't send a kick my way.

"Terris isn't going to like this, Warrik," the new male with the ash brown hair says.

"Terris doesn't like anything, and he's not in charge, so what does it matter? Tyran will order it eventually. I'm just moving things along," Warrik—my blond-haired shackle cutter—answers with a casual shrug.

The other male looks over at me and then back to his friend. "You know Tyran would only order it after she's been tested and proven. You're letting your cock do your thinking again."

"Fuck off, Reap," Warrik barks, but I don't miss that he doesn't deny the accusation.

Reap shoots me a scathing glare and then exits the shed, waiting just outside of it as though I'm contagious and Warrik can't be trusted.

"You should clean up as much as you can," Warrik tells me, his eyes fixed intensely on mine. "And then you should run. Run as hard and fast as you can."

With that ominous warning, Warrik leaves, taking the hose with him, and I can hear the two males start to argue as they once again lock me in.

"What the fuck are you doing, War? You know tonight—"

"I know exactly what tonight is. And you and I both know she's fair game for the pack. She was on our land in one of our traps. You saw the state of her. She didn't get there by accident," Warrik argues. "If she can run, she'll have a fighting chance," he adds, and then they move further away, making it harder to hear the back and forth over the pounding pulse in my ears.

If she can run, she'll have a fighting chance.

Goose bumps crawl up my arms at the foreboding words. I need to get the hell out of here before whatever they're talking about goes down tonight. The name Tyran sends dread hammering through me. He's the Ruin Falls alpha, and I am not even slightly interested in what he considers *tested and proven*.

I stare at the rudimentary bath, debating if it's better to clean up or stay filthy. After a couple of minutes, I decide that the buildup of sweat and filth might make me more potent than I want to be when trying to run and hide from the ruthless brutes of this pack. I walk over to it, rope plenty long enough for me to get there unhindered. I step into the lukewarm water, dipping my hair under and scrubbing the strands and my scalp as best I can without the aid of products. I wash my face next and then slowly start to scrub my body down.

I'm gentle at first, careful to work around sore spots and deep purple bruises. But as the dirt and grime slough off into the water, I suddenly find myself scrubbing frantically at every inch of me. I bite back a whimper as I rabidly work to clean away every unwanted touch, every kick, or hit, or lascivious stare from my body. Savagely, I wash and scour my skin, scraping it free of Burke, his bite, his hands, his violation.

I'm pink and raw and on the verge of screaming by the time I stop. It feels like my pack and the horrors of the past days, weeks, and months are sinking to the bottom of this now filthy water.

What would my mom think if she saw me right now?

I step out of the sludge, air drying in the cooling, dusky air as I renew my efforts with the rope still keeping me here. I get one knot loose and swallow down the elation that strikes through me, looking around as though someone might be watching and will come in at any moment to destroy the progress I'm making.

Yet nothing happens, so I keep working, wishing again that my wolf's fangs would drop to help me tear through this thick binding. But no matter how much I plead, I can't get her to half-shift. My eyes bounce around the waning light, the oppressive night closing in. Shadows and darkness will help my wolf and me as we run for our lives, but that ominous warning the males were talking about still blares through my head.

If she can run, she'll have a fighting chance.

My wolf and I can do this. We will run and we will escape. We *have* to, because I don't want to find out what happens tonight if we don't.

NINE

It's amazing what my newly shifted body can do.

Now that I have my wolf, so much is different. My heightened senses, the overall feeling that I'm *complete*, my ability to shift... and how quickly I can heal.

The spots of skin that were raw and bruised from the snare and the chained cuffs are nearly cleared up. My joints no longer ache or sport rings of scraped off skin. The food and water replenished me too. By the time the sun dips down, leaving me bathed in shadows, my teeth finally saw through the last of the thick rope, lips rubbed raw, gums aching.

I yank free with an internal whoop of victory and then press my face against the slats of the shed, watching. Everything outside is already pressed with darkness, even the windows of the cabin lack any light shining through. *They probably don't even have electricity*, I think to myself. When I've ensured that all is still and quiet, I straighten up and pull on the door, already knowing it won't open. I test its strength anyway, but considering the state of this place, the lock and door are both shockingly sturdy.

"Dammit," I whisper beneath my breath, head whipping around the shed. No window or hanging tools are in here, but my steps hurry toward the tarps bunched up in the corner. All I find is an empty paint can, a plastic dustpan, and a bag of soil. Hissing beneath my breath, I drop to my knees and yank the tarps away in frustration. "No, no, there's gotta be something else..."

Frantically, I search every corner, and I'm just about to grab the paint can and start slamming it into the walls when a glint of silver catches my eye. Rushing over, I grab the screwdriver out of the edges of the folded tarp where it was hiding and hold it up like I've just managed to yank Excalibur free from its rock.

I waste no time, because I ran out of that as soon as the sun went down. Using my wolf's superior sight, I whirl around, searching for the weakest-looking wooden plank in this place. They're wide and rough, and if I can just get one loose...

Spotting a round hole in the natural wood, I bustle over to it, kneeling down. Shoving the screwdriver into the weak spot, the metal end wedging against the hole in the plank, I pull with all my might, using it like a crowbar to yank the piece free.

With every inch that the wood loosens, I tug the screwdriver out before thrusting it right back in and doing it again and again and again. I manage to pry it away from the rest of the wall enough to get a grip on it, and I drop my tool, curling my fingers around the side of the plank to pull as hard as I can.

Splinters of dry wood cut into my skin, but I ignore the pricks of pain. I thank the wolf spirits that this shed was built so rudimentary and that no other layers are in my way. With gritted teeth and planted feet, I use all of my body strength instead of just relying on my arms. Holding my breath, I pull as hard as I can, cursing the wood in my head with silent threats if it doesn't fucking *give*—

With a snap, the board flies free, rusted nails nearly catching me in the face. My fingertips throb as I scrabble for the plank next to it, but it's already weakened, already lost its support, and it comes free with an angry squeak of a nail.

Yes!

Dropping to my hands and knees, I squeeze my body through the narrow space, biting back the hiss of pain as my hips and shoulders scrape against the old boards on either side of the hole. Tiny beads of blood rise along the drag marks, but the moment I tumble out of the shed and onto the hard ground behind it, I forget all about the scratches.

I'm out, and now I need to fucking *run*.

Head thrown back, my body is already shifting before I've even fully formed the thought. My wolf shoves her way up as though she were just lying in wait, ready to pounce. I fall on all fours as bones begin to shift and grow, break and realign.

Fur bursts from my skin, while thick pads form on my palms and the soles of my feet. A mouthful of sharp teeth lengthens my jaw, lips already pulling back into a wolfish sneer. My vision sharpens, nose poised to scent the air, and the moment our shift is complete, my wolf takes over.

She doesn't just run toward the trees, she practically *flies*.

The speed of her, the precision...I wish I could just enjoy this, but the fact that we're running for our lives taints the moment. Still, I'm in complete awe of her as she moves, her dark gray body as fast as a bullet. She follows pure instinct as we race away, her head constantly lifting to take in the scents in the air.

Unfamiliar wolves pollute every inch of this place, and their aroma makes her uneasy. She doesn't like the assault of their fragrance. But we stop mid-stride as something rises on the wind and practically slaps us across the muzzle. There, woven deeply within the smell of foreign and threatening wolves, there's...something. Something that speaks to my wolf on a visceral level. She drops her nose to the ground, pulling the smell deep into her lungs, trying to decipher what it is.

It's a musk of wild *maleness* that's so strong she can taste it. The heaviness of the scent is so powerful that it lingers even though the source hasn't tread through this area in a very long time. My wolf abruptly veers off, her nose searching, hunting, following a trail. Panic explodes through me, and I shout out at her to focus, to get us out of here. But she doesn't listen. To my horror, she's so in control, so deeply driven by her animal instincts, that it even bleeds into *me*.

It's dizzying and addictive, this sense of feral power that radiates through her, and I fall within its temptation, sinking beneath her consciousness as her compulsions and urges snap free and wrap around us.

Instincts take over completely.

It's all that we are. Just running and scenting, driven by the need to hunt, to dominate, to kill, to fall into every animal urge, including finding the source of this potent bouquet.

When the sound of baying wolves erupts beneath the half moon, we both turn toward it, ears pricking. They're calling to us, and we want to answer.

Somewhere in the back corner of my mind, I know that's wrong, that we need to escape, to run from whatever is stoking our instincts like this. But that corner gets silenced with a snap of my wolf's sharp teeth, and then she betrays us completely by throwing her head back and howling. It's a haunting, singular lament to the sky. The stars blink down at us as though they're watching with bated breath as my wolf announces to the Ruin Falls pack exactly where we are.

Then she turns and *runs*.

Excitement pumps through our veins as we weave our way through the night-kissed trees. Bracken and soil kick up in our wake as we push our wolf body to move as fast as it possibly can. I try to make sense of the idiotic wolf logic of announcing that we've escaped and *then* trying to get away, but it all feels so good to her, so right, that I can't seem to shove the emotions away from me. I'm enjoying this as much as she is, every single one of my senses in tune with hers, and those senses tell us one thing.

They're coming.

We both know it, and I'm trying to figure out why this now feels like a game to my wolf, instead of the life or death situation it is. Faster and faster we fly, and then we catch the telltale sound of a snarl somewhere behind us. My fear spikes and tries to battle my wolf's exhilaration, but she bats my apprehension away.

She takes in the new wolf with curiosity instead of terror, but her nose wrinkles, because the smell of it is wrong. Yet that doesn't keep her from radiating eagerness for the fight we feel nipping at our heels. She pushes harder, and in a burst of incredible speed, she quickly leaves our pursuer in her dust. I find myself whooping in celebration, and her own pride lifts with it. She's focused, ready for whoever is going to come next, but I wonder how we're going to get out of here. Are we even going the right way?

A red and gray wolf leaps at us from the side, and we snarl at the charge. We turn and bite into him, while simultaneously pushing him in the path of a massive bush. Wolf number two is picked off by nature, and I can practically feel the spring in my wolf's step at besting another one.

We blaze through the forest of the Ruin Falls pack, but that niggling part of my conscience works to piece the puzzle together, to make sense of her being dead set on playing cat and mouse instead of stealthily getting us away. I wrack my brain for any stories of similar experiences from my pack growing up, but I can't pinpoint the cause of this weird dominant *catch me if you can* behavior.

The slope beneath our feet changes, and she begins to run hard uphill. We hear heavy paws just behind us, and I scream for my wolf to hurry. Her tongue lolls out of the side of her muzzle, and she starts to pant against the exertion. Determination strikes through our veins as my wolf digs in even harder, loving the push of her body and the embrace of what it was built for.

We just crest the peak of the steep hill when the wolf behind us bats a paw at our hind legs and sweeps them out from under us. My wolf snarls her objection as we go tumbling, but quick as a flash of lightning, she spins and rounds on the massive white wolf on our tail. Gleaming golden eyes take us in, and the air is suddenly saturated with dominance, purpose, and need.

Warrik.

My wolf growls at the big wolf, ready to fight, when suddenly, what's happening hits me across the face like it's a two by four.

A warning voice fills my mind, but this time it isn't my liberator Warrik telling me to run. It's Terris's gruff words I hear, something he said when he first found me that I didn't think was important... until now.

Oh, and if yer thinking of running, don't. You'll be fair game for claiming if you do.

A claiming. This is a damn *claiming hunt.*

That's what's thrown my wolf for a loop and has her acting as though this is all some big game. She's daring a wolf to claim her. She's marked a certain essence from the woods, hoping whoever that scent belongs to is wolf enough to show up and let us see what he's working with.

Fuck!

Warrik, the white wolf, attacks us again, clearly hellbent on putting his paw in the claiming ring. I want to scream, to shout at my wolf that this is a horrible idea. Claiming anyone in this pack is a recipe for misery worse than the likes of Burke, and I suddenly find myself beyond pissed that she's not listening.

Teeth snap at us, and our shared irritation meets Warrik's wolf head-on and with zero fear. Golden eyes glow with the challenge we're presenting, and I want to kick my own ass for being so stupid. Warrik wasn't helping us escape or making us more comfortable. He was sizing us up as a mate and making sure I'd let my wolf out, knowing I wouldn't be able to override her instincts once they were at play.

This motherfucker set us up.

Rip his throat out! I shout at my wolf as we slam into Warrik again, neither one of us showing any mercy as our wolves tear into each other. He works hard, pushing to dominate us and get us to submit. In answer, my wolf demands that he be powerful enough to make us. *Only the strongest will do*, my wolf's instincts drive through us. And even though Warrik is strong and formidable, we're stronger.

My wolf surges against the white wolf, knocking him off-balance enough that we can sink our teeth into the base of his neck. It's not an angle that will deliver a killing blow, but it will allow us to get the golden-eyed male on his back and make it clear to him that he's not worthy, not dominant enough to control our wild spirit.

We move to flip him, but out of nowhere, a gargantuan deep brown wolf comes charging toward us. I manage to leap out of the way the second before he slams into Warrik. The brown wolf attacks him mercilessly, and in less than a minute, the golden-eyed male is slinking off with his tail between his legs. A feverish thrill rockets through my wolf, excitement spiking when she pulls in the deep musky aroma of the male she scent marked before.

Finally, he's here.

A vicious growl resonates in the brown wolf's chest, but instead of evoking trepidation or making my wolf think twice about taking him on, it drives her wild. She releases a challenging snarl of her own, and the need now permeating the air isn't Warrik's. It's coming from *us*.

The brown wolf lifts his nose and stares us down.

He's big. So much bigger than the others that tried to catch us. So much bigger than us. With his deep brown fur and coppery-brown eyes, he'd be able to blend into the bark of the trees and mulch of the ground if it weren't for the glowing orbs locked on us with unblinking intensity.

He growls again, low, and the noise vibrates through the air. Our lips peel back, feet braced, anticipation pulled as tight as a leash.

And then my wolf bolts, as fast as a flash of lightning.

A furious howl rends the space behind us, but that only adds to the exhilaration, the sound feeding into us through our ears.

I thought she was flying before, but this time, my wolf's feet move so fast she's a blur. Paws race across the forest floor, body weaving between trees. One, two, three, four... Five seconds, that's the only head start we get before the male is racing after us.

My wolf yips, leaping over a bush before taking a sharp ninety-degree turn. She makes him work for it. She makes his huge body put every single one of those muscles to good use, because she won't be caught by anyone unworthy.

I shriek for her to stop, raging at her for falling into this game of claiming instead of escaping, but she bats away my human proclivities like a pesky fly. The chase is all she knows, all she wants, all she feels.

I'm not sure how long we run.

He nips at our hind legs, she leaps. He cuts her off, she turns. He races alongside her, she shoulders him into a tree before sprinting in the other direction. It's a game, a dance, but it's also a *hunt*, and in a hunt, you either get away...or you get caught. For whatever reason, my wolf has decided she wants to get caught by him—but only if he earns it.

She manages to lose him near the stream. Paws splash through the frozen water running off from the mountains, and she muddies up her trail by making a giant figure eight loop to keep him going in circles. After that, she doubles back to the water and races down a small mountain. It's pure luck that we happen to spot a cave halfway down.

Panting, she zips just inside its shadowed mouth, spins to face the outside, and drops down on her belly. Then we wait.

Because the male can chase, but can he seek?

My wolf rests her overworked muscles, hiding in the crescent of darkness that the shallow cave provides, while the waxing quarter moon glows in the sky above us, its face cut in half by darkness. Tongue hanging out of the side of her mouth, she catches her breath, though her attention never strays from the small clearing in front of us, from the shadows that move with every swaying branch or flutter of grass.

The forest is suddenly too quiet, too still, and her hackles rise, eyes locked onto the space between the trees directly in front of us.

Without warning, without even his scent betraying him, the dark brown wolf bursts from the spot in a powerful leap as if he ripped himself from the very shadows surrounding us. He's on top of us in an instant, but my wolf is ready for it.

She flips over onto her back and shoves all four paws into his belly, knocking him off. They begin to grapple, with careful bites and the swipe of paws. Her deflection is meant to shove him away, while his every move is with the intent to pin us down.

The more we fight, the more we're able to evade his maneuverings, the more excited he becomes. His brown eyes flash, his delicious scent plugging our nose, and then as quick as a whip, he uses his bigger body to his advantage by sideswiping us and trapping us against the rocky cave wall. She snaps at him, going for his shoulder, but he knocks her head away with a swipe of his paw.

My wolf is panting even harder now, and he watches her, lips pulling back in a wolfish grin. It's the fanged smile of a predator turned victor. He fought and ran hard, proved himself to my wolf that he's strong and quick and cunning enough.

A worthy mate. Our mate.

That thought blares from her mind to mine, and then she shifts her hips with a whine, a clear invitation for him to mount her. The brown wolf reeks of smug satisfaction, while my female practically purrs, ready to move onto the *claiming* part of this claiming hunt as our pheromones hit the air in a seductive call.

He moves around, sniffing down her back, tongue dragging against fur, but then, without warning, or perhaps because we're both too distracted to have noticed, two gray and white wolves crash into us.

The force of the hit sends me flying back, head smacking against the hard cave wall.

I hear ferocious snarls and snapping teeth in a vicious fight, but I can't look to see how the brown wolf is handling the unwelcome male, because the other unfamiliar wolf springs on top of me in an instant. His body immediately responds to pheromones that weren't meant for him as his teeth go for my wolf's neck. He aims to bite us, to pin us between his jaws while he claims something he didn't earn.

Flashes of Burke trying to do the same thing slash through our mind, his revolting scent filling our senses as though he's the taker on top of us and not some strange unknown gray and white wolf. Rage shuts down the feelings of helplessness that try to swell in our chest. Everything around us shifts, all playfulness gone.

We snap.

My human consciousness bows and breaks, and those melded, savage, fractured parts of our spirits take over. We will never let another Burke break us even more or take what wasn't offered. We were dumped here because we became rabid, because our beautiful joining was forced to embrace raw ferociousness in order to survive. Burke and my old pack want us to feel wrong about what we are now, like it makes us less than or damaged. But right now, my wolf and I welcome our mercilessly wild ways, happily give ourselves over to its tainted call.

Violet eyes burn crazed and bright, teeth sharpen like razors as our mouth froths with frenzied fury. Our vision, our need, all tunnels down to one repeated mantra—*kill, maim, destroy*. The only anecdote is to bleed this wolf until there's not a drop in him and then offer his body to the earth in pieces.

We tear into him. He's not prepared for the strength of our attack or our level of violence. My vision bubbles and dots with the surge of adrenaline and single-minded viciousness, and then all we know is his flesh in our mouth, the taste of his blood on our tongue. We kick and shake and bite and claw until his whines and yelps pour out of him, his pain bouncing around the cave and feeding our demand for vengeance.

The gray and white wolf is knocked beneath us, and we stand over him, teeth bared in a growl, eyes glowing as a drip of bloody foam falls from our mouth to his face. He flinches and whimpers, showing us his neck, submitting to our dominance, but we're too caught up in the rabid bloodlust to let him off the hook.

We don't realize that the brown furred wolf has already finished fighting the other attacker until he slams into us, knocking us off our prey and keeping us from executing a fatal strike. We counteract the big brown wolf's charge, staying on our feet and fixing him with an enraged gaze and a snarl. Why would the male we chose deny us our rightful kill?

We drop our head threateningly, fangs bared and dripping with wrath and blood as we unleash the full extent of our spirits' ruination. The brown wolf stills as though he's just now understanding what he's up against. As though our shattered, jagged pieces are on full display.

You're a fucking stain.

A malignancy of our kind.

A disgrace to Totemic shifters everywhere.

An intensity enters his bright tawny eyes, and we glare at him, chest heaving, ready for him to deny us, to put us down now that he's seen what we really are. It should hurt, the way he's looking at us. The way his gaze confirms the horrible things spat at us by lesser wolves. But right then, there's too much hate in our hearts to care. Too much violence. If he tries to kill us instead of claim us, we will go down in a fury of teeth and claws.

He stares at us, those bright brown eyes looking like they're staring straight through our soul. Instead of going for my throat, he makes a noise low in his. With a clear order, the wolf I dominated and almost killed whines, crawling with his belly scraping the rock of the cave, ears pressed back and tail tucked as he slinks away slowly. We try to snap at him, to still go for that killing blow, and he yelps when we lunge, but we're once again thwarted by the huge brown wolf.

The other one turns and races away as fast as his limp and trodden pride can carry him, and then it's just the two of us again.

We snarl at the male my wolf thought was worthy of us, furious that he let those males get away, but he just watches us as though he's puzzling things out. We snap at him, and he gives a warning growl, daring us to take our anger out on him. But instead of the warning putting my reactions in check, it drives my wolf harder to do just that.

Someone has to pay. It may as well be him.

TEN

IN A SPLIT SECOND, EVERYTHING CHANGES FOR ME AND MY wolf. We stop pulling in the tantalizing scent of this male, stop looking at him as though there's a future there, and instead, we view him as the enemy.

My wolf studies him, quickly assessing the best way to take him on. The tension in the cave rises, and the hair on our spine rises with it. There's an electric charge all around us as though lightning is threatening to strike at any moment. And just when my wolf is ready to charge, to attack, to *maim* him in an unleashing of our savage ire, the brown wolf does something that makes us pause.

In a shift so fluid and seamless, he rises from four legs to two. His skin absorbs his fur, muzzle reduces until his jaw is squared and chiseled, his fangs now a row of straight white teeth. Eyes the color of tanned leather stare me down, and shoulder length carob-brown hair frames his magnificent face. He's solid muscle, pure dominance, and sex on a fucking stick.

"Shift," he commands, his voice deep, powerful, and undeniable.

The order washes through us, demanding that we bend to its will. My wolf and I are all rage, wrath, and fury. We're lost to the rabid call of our broken nature, but dominance rolls off this male in waves, and for some reason, my wolf *wants* to answer it. It's not that we have to, but something in his command and his presence makes us feel as though it's safe to.

Shock slams through me as my wolf submits. One minute she's there, driving us to attack, to force this wolf to pay the price of his betrayal with his own blood. Then the next thing I know, she's retreating inside of me as though this male's order is the voice of reason she's been so desperate for. That he might just be the glue that could pull us back together.

My bones crack and fur recedes as my wolf abandons me. No longer cloaked in her protection, I rise shakily on two feet, all the emotions and savage struggle still boiling my blood. My wolf has heeded his command, submitted to his dominance, and left me feeling crazed and fuming, still needing to rampage. I eye the stranger under my lashes with a fierce glare, resentment crawling under my skin for what he just did. He might've won over my wolf, but I'm full of so much vehement violence that I'm trembling with it.

He studies me with interest, and the distinct smell of lust wafts through the cave. My eyes harden even more, and the reaction sends a flicker of heat through his gaze. "She's still riding you," he states evenly, his eyes studying mine as though the answers are all written right there.

I'm getting really tired of people doing that to me. What the fuck is wrong with my eyes that others now look at me like that? A snarl builds in my chest, and I start to pace, unable to stand still. The need to act, to hurt something, is the only thing I can seem to focus on. I feel too full of anger, too wild, the rabid switch still flipped inside of me, even though my wolf retreated.

"Want me to help you?" his deep voice asks, but somehow, it feels less like a question and more a declaration of intention.

A growl of frustration clacks against the cave walls like tossed rocks. "And just what the hell are you going to do? Bring more wolves in for me to fight and just let them go after they've attacked me?" I taunt, pissed that he's the reason I even feel like this. If he had just let me handle things like I wanted to, I'd be rolling in the blood of my enemy right now, exactly like I need.

Kill, kill, kill...

I close my eyes, bracing my body against the rough wall as I try to fight the rampant need, my mouth salivating at the want for blood.

"I'll give you an outlet."

My head turns toward him, attention latching onto all of those chiseled muscles cut in his skin as he stands unashamedly in front of me. The idea of the two of us fighting, of skin hitting skin, of rushing through this near-bursting adrenaline with unrestrained movement while I punish him...it fills me with excitement.

Yes.

That's exactly what I need. An outlet.

I don't bother answering. The offer to battle these cloying feelings out of my system is the exact salvation that I'm craving.

Without warning, I launch myself at him.

His eyes light up with excitement just as I slam into him, but before I can so much as land a punch, my hands are cinched in a tight grip and he's twisted us, pinning my back mercilessly between the wall of the cave and his hard body.

I snarl at him, but infuriatingly, he lifts his lips into a cocky smirk. Enraged, I try wiggling my hands free so I can claw his face off, but his hold is firm. I shout at my wolf to come help me fight, to give me a burst of extra strength, but she just pants and watches from the sidelines, like she's suddenly a golden retriever and not the rabid beast responsible for the state that I'm in.

The male drops his head to my shoulder and breathes me in deeply. I go still, my heart suddenly beating fast for an entirely different reason. Instead of fighting me like I expected, he runs the tip of his nose up the side of my neck, his plush lips a hair's breadth from my ear. I can't suppress the shiver that travels down the edge of my too-tight skin.

"Come on, Vicious. Show me what you've got." It's not a taunt or a jeer, it's a genuine invitation.

My blood burns with unspent rage, but suddenly his musk, his need, is all I can smell. His hard body pressing against mine is all I can feel, and a new wave of sensation moves through me, stoking a different need. My nipples harden as interest pools between my thighs, and I stop struggling against his hold.

I'll give you an outlet.

I start to pant as the outlet I want shifts into something else. My eyes lock onto his, my stare suddenly banked with heat, as though the claiming drive that my wolf was feeling before is back in full force. Desire mixes with my rabid acrimony, and together, they create a volatile cocktail of savage need and barbaric ablution.

I don't need to kill, don't need blood to coat my tongue. I need...

I need.

His nostrils flare and his eyes brighten as though he knows what we're on the cusp of, and without warning, I drop my head to his shoulder and bite down...*hard*. He wants to see how vicious I can be, wants to give me a place to ride out the caustic tangle of emotions slamming through me? Then I'll give it to him.

His blood seasons my mouth, tasting of moonlit runs, power, and untamable wildness. His growl vibrates through me, but instead of jerking me away, he presses against me harder. His hard cock digs into my belly, the heat of it making my entire body flush. My hips jerk forward, grinding into him, and he drops my wrists to reach down and cup my ass instead. Releasing his skin from my teeth, I snarl at him as he pulls me up and settles himself between my thighs, demanding I wrap my legs around his taut torso.

He answers my half-assed objection with a nip to the neck as his other hand pinches my nipple hard, as though he expects it to bring me to heel. My moan turns into a growl, and I try to push him away from me, needing more fight with the fucking. I need so much more if I'm going to purge myself of the onslaught of anger still pumping through my veins.

"Mmmmm," he rumbles with approval, and then his hand is on my throat, pinning me to the rock wall of the cave, a silent promise in his eyes that he can handle whatever I'm going to throw his way.

Good. Because I can't hold back. I don't want to.

I whimper with need as his hold tightens around my neck, and I reach down and fist his cock, squeezing as hard as I can. My eyes light up when he groans, the noise traveling from his chest to mine. But it's not enough. I want to feel that groan with his cock buried deep inside of me.

Needy and impatient, I line him up and grind against him, working the tip of his dick shallowly in and out of me, fueling both of our desires. He keeps his hips back, watching me work over his length, not driving into me the way I'm practically begging for. But the growl of irritation I let out is suddenly swallowed when his mouth crashes against mine. His kiss is bruising and punishing in all the right ways. His full lips consume me, his tongue searching and plundering just like I wish his fat cock would right now.

I roll my body against him, arms locking around his neck, each movement a silent plea for more. If we were in wolf form right now,

I'd be licking his muzzle and offering him a ready cunt, whining and arching until the brute took me the way his animal instincts would be driving him to. I bite his lip, drawing blood as I rake my nails up his back, needing him closer. He doesn't so much as flinch at the brutal contact, just simply smiles and deepens the kiss even more. His blood, lips, and tongue are like a heady aphrodisiac that has me panting, my entire body thrumming with lust.

His voice rumbles. "What do you want? Tell me."

I thread my fingers into his long dark brown hair, pulling his head back viciously and scraping my teeth up the line of his neck. I nip at his chin, and then I stare him right in the eyes. "Fuck me!" I command, teeth snapping. "Fuck the rage out of me. Make me scream until I can see past the need for blood. Make it hard. Make it fast. Make me not think about killing anything."

Raw lust flashes in his tawny gaze, and then without a word, he slams into me. My scream of relief and desire crashes around us. He grinds deeply just once, and then holds himself there, as though this is all the time he's going to give me to adjust to his size. Then slowly, deliciously, *maddeningly*, he pulls out, just to shove roughly back inside of me again.

My head falls back in bliss as all pretense of teasing and languid passion goes right out the window. He thrusts into me so hard, with piston-like strength slamming in and out of me. I'm fucked so roughly and thoroughly, that all I can think about and feel is what he's doing to my body.

With his blood still on my tongue, I nip at his ear, moaning as he rides me hard, exactly like I need. The rock of the wall he's fucking me against bruises the very bones of my back, but I need the pain and the passion to drown out the heat of my rage. I close my eyes, lost to the sensations of his cock as it moves in and out of me, our skin slapping and pounding against one another while our moans and growls paint the walls of the cave.

"Harder," I demand, nails digging into his back. Just when I think his pace can't get any more barbarous and perfect, he kicks it into a whole other gear.

"Look at me."

My eyes immediately snap open and fix on his as he shows me just what he's capable of. He's strong and fast and drives all thoughts of fury and vengeance right out of my head, my rabid need replaced with pure, dirty, rough fucking.

I moan in vicious satisfaction, his eyes filled with fire and the promise of so much more. It's as though his gaze is burying itself as deep inside of me as his cock is, tearing away my wild.

When I stare at him as though he's some sort of lifeline, he doesn't shy away from the raw connection. I open up my own expression, showing him just how good he feels, how badly I needed this. The muscles in his neck tighten, and I know, just like me, he's on the verge of crashing into a massive and all-consuming orgasm. I pull his lips to mine, wanting to drink down his moans and taste the pleasure of his release on my tongue.

Tingles wash through my every limb, heat coalescing at my core, and I yank at his hair, suck on his tongue, taking him—taking it all. Our heady pheromones fill the air, only accompanied by the dirty noises our bodies work in tandem to create. Rocks cut into my back, my nails draw new bloodied lines down him, and I *need*...

He breaks our kiss, pounding into me with such force I'm sure he just might break me in half.

Once.

Twice.

Three times, before he roars his release and buries himself as deeply inside of me as he can go. My orgasm rips through me just as unforgiving and unrestrained. I throw my head back to ride the delicious warmth and pleasure that pulses through me, and he pins me in place with his sharp teeth against my shoulder, and then bites. *Hard*.

I scream, reveling in the pain that heightens my pleasure, and look over to see his mouth is half-shifted. Sharp wolf canines pierce my flesh, blood dripping down from the wounds. I watch, vision steeped in lust, as he licks the crimson trails from my skin, his cock still seated deep inside of me.

For one prolonged moment, he stays there, until his mouth morphs back into full lips and gleaming teeth. He licks at the place he ravaged, and even though I hiss in pain, a shock of heat emanates from the move too, lining it with an edge of exquisite, sharp pleasure.

He kisses up my neck and nips at my lobe, and a full-body shudder travels through me, my core clamping down on his still hard length. He groans at the sensation, and my own body responds in kind, but then...

Reality starts to set in. And all of that delicious satisfaction, the carnal bliss, it just freezes up inside of me, turning my languid heat into ice.

Oh, shit...

"You claimed me." It's a whisper spoken against his ear, but I'm looking into the darkness of the cave, feeling that same darkness begin to yawn open in me. *What the hell did I just do?*

"Yep."

My attention jerks to his cocky expression. "You were just supposed to fuck me, not *claim* me!" Panic seeps through me, stemming from the wound now throbbing in my shoulder.

Brown eyes harden, as abrasive as the wall I'm still pinned to. "It's the claiming hunt, and you ran," he says with zero sympathy. "I proved myself and won over your wolf. She submitted to me, and so did you." He thrusts his hips forward, making me gasp as he seems to grow, to harden. "You were fucking begging for it."

It wouldn't matter if I didn't hear the arrogance in his tone, because I can *feel* it, pulling from those horrible punctures in my shoulder, tiny strands of thread that seem to lead from me to him.

Claimed. Claimed by a male whose name I don't even know. Shoved into a ruthless, backwoods pack.

"I don't want to be claimed by you. I don't want to have anything to do with Ruin Falls."

He locks me with a menacing stare. "Too fucking bad, and way too late for objections."

Denial curdles my stomach like sour milk. I know what a claiming bite means, what it entails, but I still feel myself shaking my head. My wolf is giddy, basking in the new mating connection. There's an underlying eagerness for her to mark him back, to seal us together mind, body, and soul, but I cringe away from just the thought of it.

"The hell it is." My hands brace against his chest and shove, but he doesn't move. Not even an inch. My teeth bare at him. "Get off me."

"Can't."

The prick— "Get your dick out of me right this second!" Hysteria tinges my tone as the panic sets in. My wolf...I was so in tune with her, and she was so unbridled, so wild. Even now, she's smug, happy with the way things have turned out, with gaining a male of her choosing, one who's worthy. But all I can think of is that woodshed they shoved me in, the cabin in the middle of nowhere, the bloodstained rags. My stomach drops. I don't even know the name of the male who's still impaling me.

The rush of anger makes my throat tighten, solidifying my panic. "Get. Off. Me." I snarl at him and begin to shove and kick and scrabble, scraping my back up in the process, but that hardness buried in me doesn't move, doesn't even slip an inch, and when I try to reach down to yank him the fuck out, he hisses and slaps my ass so hard it sounds like a crack of thunder.

"Stop that. You know we're stuck together."

"The *fuck* we are!"

"I'm not talking about the claiming mark, though it's true for that as well." When I say nothing, his expression turns from one of irritation to confusion as he cocks his head. "Wait...you *have* fucked a shifter before, haven't you?"

"Of course I've had sex before," I snap. My hand runs over the bite on my shoulder, fingers pressing, nails digging, as if I can scoop out the connection binding us together.

His hand slaps mine away. "Stop it and hold still. You're just hurting yourself."

"The only one hurting me is you. Your dick is starting to hurt."

He gives me a strange look. "You've fucked shifters?" he asks again. "Full-spirited shifters?"

"No," I hiss. "But what the hell does that have to do with anything?"

A chuckle comes out of him, and I hate that it makes my nipples pebble against his hard chest. "You've never been knotted."

My eyes widen as my stupidity sinks in. Of course, I knew about full-spirited wolves knotting during sex, but I've never had a shifted partner before, and hearing about it versus experiencing it are two *very* different things. At the look on my face, his chuckle deepens until he thrusts his hips up again, making me hiss in pain. "Ouch! Get that thing out of me. It's getting too big." I fidget, trying to crawl my body up the wall to get out, but that just hurts more.

"That *thing* is my knot stretching your tight pussy. And you're gonna learn to love it."

Challenge blazes in my face. "I will not. And I'm never letting you fuck me again."

His mouth drops to my neck, lips skimming down until he licks the wound in my shoulder. "It's pretty fucking sexy that mine is the only knot you've ever taken," he says, ignoring my declaration completely. "Right now, it's stretching you to your limits, trapping my cum inside of you, while your sweet little cunt milks me again and again and again."

His words are filthy. The heat of his mouth more so as he licks against my sweat-slicked skin, and my clit starts to throb, heat flourishing in my core.

"By the time my knot deflates and I slip out of you, you're going to be gushing with my seed, drenched in my scent, and want nothing more than for me to bend you over and fuck you again. Because you're mine—wolf, spirits, and *body*."

My tongue is thick, coherent though hazy with the lust he's coaxing with his dirty words. And then he shoves in, knot stretching, feeling like he's going to rip me right in half, and I howl in pain.

"Shh, stop fighting, Vicious. Let me make you feel good."

A rough hand curls between us to press against my clit, and I buck against him at the electricity that sparks from that single touch. That small movement has my pussy protesting, and I go still, panting through the pain.

"Relax," he murmurs.

"Why don't you try to relax with a baseball bat shoved up your ass?"

He laughs, and I have to tell myself that I don't like the sound, that I don't like the flex of his muscles as he uses one arm beneath my ass to carry me away from the wall and place me down on the cave floor. It's not exactly soft, but the dirt and leaves are better than the rock I was pinned against.

"The more you come, the faster my knot will deflate," he says, bracing himself over me, his body so much bigger than mine as I lie beneath him.

And then he thrusts his hips in again, fingers circling my clit, and my body betrays me just like my wolf did. A moan slips from between my lips as my eyes flutter closed. Just like that, the pain has been replaced with pleasure, and it's so intense, so *deep*, that I'm already rising up, climbing another peak. I come with my back arching up, shoulder throbbing from the mate mark.

"That's it. Let that pussy come on your mate's knotted cock."

My eyes spring open, but my voice is far too husky. "You're not my mate."

"Wrong."

As if he's punishing me, he starts fucking into me with hard, shallow thrusts, dick barely able to move because of the knot tying us together. But he fucks me into the ground regardless, while I claw at him, pulling his ass closer, demanding, growling unintelligible words for him to keep touching my clit, harder, faster, more, more, more...

I come again with a scream, clamping down so hard on him that I feel it force another spurt of release from his cock, his red-hot seed bathing my insides.

And still, he fucks me. Still, I growl and writhe for more, demand he make me come, to keep the pleasure riding high so the pain doesn't drag me under.

He rolls us over, his back now pressed against the ground. At this angle, he's so gorgeously chiseled, so masculine and strong, his tanned skin bared in the moonlight. Brown hair disheveled, tawny eyes scouring me. Even in this position, he's so utterly in control of my body, and it makes me clench around him as my gaze skates over every dip and angle of his muscles. Without hesitation, I ride him, his hands coming up to grip my breasts as I grind back and forth, finding the perfect pressure for my clit and riding the delicious line between pain and pleasure as his knot stretches me even tighter.

"Come again," he demands, jutting upward with gritted teeth, while I rake my nails down his hard chest.

"Don't tell me what to fucking do," I growl back, even as my body follows his command, the walls of my pussy clamping down on him like a fist.

"Christ..."

I scream out my bliss before collapsing on top of him, my body going jellied with exhaustion. I press against his heat, and even though he's pure muscle, his firm form is deliciously comfortable, and I find myself just wanting to get closer, to have more of him. He curls us over to our sides and bends my knee up, and then he's still grinding, still forcing me to come.

"I can't..." It's an out-of-breath plea, because I don't have it in me to come again.

But the infuriating male doesn't stop. Instead, his hand curves around my hip, and he slaps my clit, making me squeal with a jump. "You can. Now come for me again."

That order shouldn't turn me on. His arrogant dominance shouldn't make my core flood with wetness, but it does. It does, and I hate it. I want to fight, to make him suffer for my body making a liar out of me. But a punishing spank against my pussy turns to more pleasurable abuse as he pinches and flicks and then rubs it like he knows my cunt better than I do.

He pulls his cock out as far as it will go, eliciting a scream from me, the pain of being so horribly *stretched* all-consuming. Just when it starts to be too much, he shoves back in, and I see stars, the forced orgasm exploding a thousand of them into existence.

A roar in my ear accompanies the crash of our collision, as my body gives the last it can. The orgasm to end all orgasms finally fists the last of his release from his body in a squeeze of merciless demand before I crumple.

A blanket of sleep wraps itself around me, its weight pulling me under instantly, my entire body wrung out. The last thing I feel before I slip into the sweet lure of dark unconsciousness is his seed shooting inside me and his mouth clamping down again on the mark he already made. As if he's showing me, without a shadow of a doubt, just how thoroughly I've been claimed.

ELEVEN

BIRDSONG DANCES ON THE AIR ALL AROUND ME AS A cool breeze coaxes goose bumps to crawl lazily up my thigh. I roll onto my back, a delectable soreness having settled into my muscles and limbs. I stretch, fighting off the ache in my body and ignoring the twinges between my thighs.

Images of what happened last night flit in and out of my mind, reminding me of what it felt like to have the mystery male moving in and out of my body, working me over in ways I never knew I needed and am now worried I'll crave.

Anxiety crawls up my throat, and I crack open my lids, intent on sneaking a peek at this male and trying to determine what to do about him. Except when my eyes adjust to the daylight now penetrating the cave, I discover that I'm alone. Annoyance settles in my chest that he's not here, and then I get irritated with myself for that thought.

I don't want this.

I fought against Burke's threats to claim me, to take what he wanted. I tried to run from my pack, from the only home I've ever known, fully intending to abandon my wolf spirit just so I could avoid being forced into a mating I didn't want. And yet here I am. Dried cum on my inner thigh, a fresh bite on my shoulder, and a body that's begging for more despite my feelings on the matter.

My wolf growls inside of me, and I huff out my irritation. No, this male didn't take me against my will like Burke tried to do. Yes, I did practically beg him to fuck me. But I didn't ask to be marked, to be tied to a wolf I don't know in a pack that's known for its barbaric cruelty and backward, feral ways. No, this forced connection is what I tried to run from. *This* is what I fought against and what made my home pack abandon me to a bunch of savages. This is exactly what I didn't want to happen, despite the way my wolf lost her mind last night.

I pull in a deep inhale. The scent of the male mixing with mine is an undertone to the smell of lust and aggression that was expressed in this cave last night. I look around me, no hint of the male anywhere or sign as to where he went, and I debate what I should do.

Technically, our bond isn't complete. My wolf needs to bite him back to finish the claiming. Which means maybe I can still run. If I could get far enough away, the pull to him could weaken and fade. I could build a life. I'd still have to stay away from other shifters and constantly watch my back, but I could do that. I was prepared for that exact outcome before.

I feel my wolf's hackles rise and release a frustrated sigh. The only problem with that plan is that I have my wolf spirit to contend with now. And if what's happened to me since our souls merged has taught me anything, it's that there's something wrong with us, and that fighting against my baser wolf instincts is easier said than done.

I really was going to kill that other unknown wolf last night. The image of me attacking him flashes in my mind, and I thread my fingers through my tangled and dirty hair before dropping my head in defeat. The brown-eyed male stepped in, fucked me, claimed me, and now my wolf wants to stay. Yeah, I could run, but how long would it be before my wolf forced me to come back? And worse, what would this pack do to me when that happened? What would *he* do to me?

"Fuck!" I shout out. The shock of sound sends a flock of birds up into the air, abandoning their safety in the canopy of trees.

The bright blue sky looks down on me without a care in the world, and as though I find *that* a personal affront, a burning anger starts to build in my gut. I recognize the now broken parts of myself and my wolf, rearing up to drive us into a fit of rabid fury. I fight it, trying to breathe deeply and measuredly through the sensation instead of letting it take root in my chest and drive my actions to madness. I need to figure out how to combat this, to shut down the wild insanity of it if I'm ever going to hope for some semblance of a life that I can live with.

My wolf is ready to dive into the anger as though nice weather is a worthy foe for us, but I know logically that makes no sense. Her instincts are riding me hard, but I'm still in here too, and I need to learn to fight it off.

I focus on the weird chirp of insects, a sound and creature we don't have back home at Twin Rivers. I try to let its music pull me from the madness and focus on the fact that I'm alive. That I survived Burke. I run through the good things that have occurred in my current state instead of focusing on the bad, in hopes it calms my jagged soul. I need to be strong.

I get tossed a vision of the brown wolf as if in response. I grudgingly give my wolf that one, because he *was* strong. He did win the chase and the fights. And mate or not, that was the best fuck of my life. I'm never going to do it again, but at least I'll have the memories. My wolf growls at me, but the menace that was filling my veins is suddenly calmer. I dismiss her protest and push to my feet, because whatever it is I'm doing, it's time to get going.

My stomach growls and gurgles, voicing its opinion on the matter of what my priorities should be. I also feel sticky and disgusting. I need to find a way to scrub the male from my body. I turn my head, eyes landing on the bite puncturing my shoulder.

You're going to be gushing with my seed, drenched in my scent.

Swallowing hard, I yank my eyes away from the spot before I march out of the cave and start down the small mountain. I go in search of food and some form of water, while also keeping an eye on the ground for snares and traps. I don't need Ruin Falls to catch me twice, and after my unknowing join-in of their claiming hunt last night, I have no idea how they're going to react to me.

As a stranger, I posed a threat. But now, thanks to Warrik and my fuck buddy last night, I have no idea where I stand. Am I now pack? Will my half claim offer any protection? Or will I still need to be tested and proven like that other wolf in the shed said?

I growl at the uncertainty of it all. I don't even want to be part of this damn pack, but for some reason, the potential for rejection feels smothering and sour. I'm such an idiot. I don't know my half-mate's name, his position in the pack, where he lives, or what the hell I'm supposed to do now.

He just left me behind in the dirt, with his cum on my legs and blood on my shoulder. The asshole left me to wander around naked, in a territory I don't know, and on top of that, I'm thirsty, dirty, starving, and pissed. Some fucking mate.

After just a few minutes of walking in the forest with my skin getting scratched up, my feet stepping on sharp sticks and rocks every few seconds, I decide I've had enough. "You got us into this mess," I snap to my wolf, hands placed on my hips. "So *you* can come out here and help. Find us water and a damn bunny to eat for all I care, but I'm done walking around and getting messed up."

I realize I probably look like a crazy person standing here talking to myself, but my wolf rolls her eyes and stretches to a stand inside of me. Then, she lunges up, and our body shifts as she takes over.

It's not as painful this time. Hopefully, the more I do it, the sooner it will become as easy as breathing. When my mom shifted, she always did it happily, like she was simply stretching out her limbs, the other part of her spirit rising up.

Right now, I can't even fathom that sort of harmony with my wolf. So far, we haven't had the chance to just...*be*. To learn each other. To get settled.

No, Burke ensured that, from the moment I got her, we were being pushed and pulled and forced to fight. I worry that if our switch keeps getting flipped, this rabid piece of us will only get worse. Which is why I have to figure out how to control it, and why I need to learn her better so that we're on the same page.

The moment our shift is complete, my wolf yawns and yips, waking up as she takes in a thousand scents mixed with the crisp morning air. For a moment, she just walks around, stopping every few seconds to smell something, letting herself enjoy this like it's a meandering Sunday stroll. But soon, she starts walking determinedly, paws never straying from the direction she's set her sights on. I sure hope it's a stream where I can shift and clean up.

I expect to feel tension, all senses on high alert as we pad through this unfamiliar forest that reeks of unfamiliar wolves. Anxiety hammers through me as we go, but my wolf doesn't seem to feel any of that. She's calm and confident as she picks her way through the bracken and underbrush. Her gait is determined, and she moves as though there's something about this place that she knows and I don't.

The more she walks, the more relaxed I start to feel. Her certitude is catching, and I let go of the worry nipping at my neck. I'm able to take a breather. And this forest, even though it's the territory of some fucked up shifters, it's almost...peaceful. Serene. I always loved walking with my dad through our woods, but here, everything is so much rawer. Like no part has been touched by humans. It's just the sunlight filtering through the trees and a refreshing breeze that seems to ground us both.

My wolf picks up her nose, her steps quickening, and I perk up at her enthusiasm. Please be a river... Except when my wolf walks us out of the clearing, it's definitely *not* a river. It's the damn Ruin Falls pack houses.

Motherfu—

It's strange to glare inside her body, but I manage it. "This is *not* water or food! You weren't supposed to take us to their damn homestead!"

My wolf chuffs at me but is otherwise completely shameless. She stops right beside the last tree, like she wants to creep on the houses first, and together, we both take stock.

She notes the collection of wolf scents soaked into the air. I note the collection of hand-built cabins seeded around, every rough-paneled face matching the bark of the surrounding trees. These ones aren't dilapidated like the first cabin I saw, but they're still raw and boasting of imperfections.

She takes in the scuff marks on the ground, while I take in the outdoor sitting area smack in the middle of the clearing. She sees the meat dripping over a spit; I see the carefully fed fires speckled around the open space.

With a snap of her teeth, she jerks her attention to the largest house, and just behind it, I see a huge glittering lake that's fed from the mountains just beyond. My wolf swings her head back and forth between that and the cooking food, chest puffing with a rush of arrogance as she seems to say, "*Food. Water. Shelter. Happy, bitch?*"

I open my mouth to argue with her, but the scent of that cooking meat floods her senses, which floods *mine*, and then we're both salivating. I try to tell her that we can't get to their food without someone spotting us. I don't care if she doesn't currently see anyone around. Someone is feeding those fires, and a lot of someones are cooking that meat, based on the quantities of it.

All these smells, all these threats permeating the air should alarm her. We're the lone wolf surrounded by an unknown pack. There's nothing about this situation that should have my wolf feeling as calm and entitled as she's feeling. I study her lack of reaction to the threat all around us and worry that the anger and fight isn't the only thing about us that's broken. Maybe all her natural instincts have been shattered beyond repair with what was done to us?

Let's just double back, I say inside our shared minds. *Find a private lake, and then you can hunt, and we—*

My wolf trots out into the clearing.

Trots. Out.

Fear percusses through me like thunder rumbling through a storm that's dangerously too close. Alarm bells clang in my head, and trouble crawls up my back and perches heavily on my shoulders.

What the fuck are you doing?

No matter how much I urgently demand that she turn the fuck around before someone spots us, she ignores me completely. Walking right over to the nearest fire like she owns it, her front paws step onto old charred rocks, and she reaches up, not paying any heed to the flames licking beneath our stretched body. With a single snap of her teeth, she yanks off something the size of a goat on a spit, and then lies down next to the fire and starts digging into it like the feral beast she is. The satisfaction of the fat dripping down the half-cooked meat is so delicious that I stop yelling at her for a second and just enjoy the meal with her.

That is, until we get caught.

"What the hell?"

My wolf's eyes roll up at the intruder who's threatening her meal, and her stance instantly changes. She tenses over the food that she's deemed is hers, even though it's nothing more than bones now, and her lips peel back at the females striding forward. One has strawberry blonde hair, like it can't decide if it wants to be pink or orange in the sunlight. With a round face, tinged lips, and high cheekbones, she's pretty, and clearly pretty *pissed*.

My wolf feels like she could take her, and maybe she's right, but what she doesn't seem to understand is we can't take them all—and where you find one angry wolf, there's always more.

"Is this the new one everybody's talking about?" the other female says. She has dark skin and short straight hair pulled back tight against her scalp. Both of them are dressed in sewn scraps of animal hide, with straps around their chests and knee-length skirts hanging from their hips.

"Who are you, bitch?" Strawberry demands.

My wolf peels back her lips and growls low in warning. This sets the females off, who both immediately go tense, their own wolves sending out answering snarls from their throats.

"You think you can come here on *our* land and steal *my* fucking kill?" Strawberry shakes her head, eyes gone dark with threat. "I will mangle you worse than that stolen meat at your paws."

The menace that's crawling out from the female's rough voice doesn't impress my wolf. I know without a shadow of a doubt that if I don't stop this, she'll attack, and our unhinged state will take over. Regardless of how ready my wolf is to tear into this female, I know better. Which is why, with everything I have, I shove my beast down and force back control.

With loud pops, I yank her inside of me, my bones twinging, skin stretching as I take over. Breathing hard from the shift, I manage to stand tall in front of the females. "I'm sorry, I was starving," I explain. "We haven't eaten regularly in...well, in a while, and I couldn't get her to stop."

My stomach rumbles loudly as though everything I just ate wasn't nearly enough. Growing up, my old alpha would wait to eat if there were wolves around that were in more desperate need of food. All of that changed when Burke showed up, but I remember the way it used to be. Judging by the look on Strawberry's face, this ruthless pack also has no place for empathy or understanding.

"I'm Seneca," I offer, in hopes this female sees me as a person and not some outside enemy that needs to be immediately reported to their heinous alpha. I don't even want to know what punishments are standard in a place like this. "I'll talk to my wolf about—"

"I don't give two fucks who you are," Strawberry snaps. "There are rules about stealing food. Do you want what I lost to come out of your hide?" she threatens, not an ounce of compassion in her eyes or her tone as she rakes her dark green eyes over my naked body as though she's repulsed.

"Presley, chill. You can have some of mine. You heard Terris talking about where they found her and how. I mean, look at her, she clearly needs it," the other female declares dismissively.

"I don't want yours, Vera. I want what's rightfully *mine*," Presley snarls as though I've caused her some greater injury beyond stealing a little food. "I don't give a crap how fucked up she is. It's the way of the pack, and you know it."

Vera shoots Strawberry a glare and shakes her head. "She's not even pack yet, Pres. You know she's not held accountable until she is."

Presley's eyes fix on the bite on my shoulder, and it's all I can do not to cover it up with my hand and fidget guiltily. I know I can't show any doubt or shame, despite how much I might be feeling it.

She sneers at me as she cocks a hip. "From the look of her, she's *something*. If she can spread her thighs for pack, then she can learn some damn manners," Presley growls out, and I work to shut down my wolf as she tries to rise and answer the challenge in Strawberry's cold gaze.

"Then take it up with whoever claimed her," a tall, rail-thin woman declares as she walks up. Her hair and eyes are the exact same shade of wet oak, and there's a vicious scar displayed on her neck. I stare at it for a beat, unable to stop myself. It looks as though she's had her throat ripped out and survived it.

I stave off a shudder as I take in the healed injury, and then I snap myself out of the rude perusal and look up at her eyes. The female's brown gaze widens slightly as it lands on my surveying stare. Confusion once again trickles through me, wondering what it is that she's seeing in my eyes that's set her off. I look over at Vera, and although her gaze isn't fixed on the ground, she's sure as hell not looking right at me. If I were actually part of their pack, I would take the lack of eye contact as respect and submission, but I'm not, and this feels... off. Like they're too uneasy to look me in the eye.

Presley, on the other hand, doesn't seem to have any issue staring me down, although her annoyed glare is now fixed on the thin newcomer.

"She's fresh meat, and the pack says whatever she screws up in the first month is the responsibility of whoever claimed her. Go whine to them," the new female states as she meets Presley's glare with one of her own.

"Who is your mate?" Vera asks me, her face kind, even though her eyes won't meet mine.

A tic starts in my jaw as I battle the embarrassment and frustration that wants to climb up my neck and settle in my cheeks. Presley starts to laugh, the sound mean and callous. My eyes harden despite the humiliation falling like a stone in my stomach.

"Look at her, the bitch doesn't even know who claimed her!" she taunts maliciously, eyes flicking away. "You know what that's like, don't you, Harlan?" she jibes, her spiteful gaze once again settling on the lean, brown-haired woman.

Harlan's lips peel back as a snarl bleeds out of her, but a loud howl interrupts whatever it is she's about to say, and I go rigid at the noise. All at once, the open space starts to fill with members of the Ruin Falls pack. I have no idea where they all flood in from, but suddenly, there are people and wolves alike all trickling in from the surrounding homes and bounding out from the bordering treeline.

At first, I think it's the call of the dinner bell so to speak, but the bodies ignore the food roasting around the fires and start moving as a whole toward the large house bordering the lake. The females who caught me stealing are bickering, and I take the opportunity to try and disappear into the gathering crowd.

I'm acutely aware of my bare body as I weave through the pack. I feel eyes on me, drinking their fill, and I hate it. On the fringes of the gathering, I see other wolves shifting and joining in on whatever is going on, and although they're sans clothes too, it doesn't make me feel any better.

I still feel vulnerable, exposed.

The number of wolves around me grows denser, and panic claws through me, driving me to get out from the center. How long will it take for them to notice I'm not one of them? What will they do to a stranger in their midst?

I push my way to the outskirts, but I'm only able to make it to the side with the pack houses behind it. I lope with the crowd, looking between the cabins for any path that leads to freedom.

Unfortunately, they all back up to a decent-sized mountain, so unless I'm going hiking naked again, there's no getting away in that direction. I know my wolf could probably make quick work of that incline, her color would even make the climb inconspicuous, but she's proven she can't be trusted.

If I'm going to get away, it's going to be up to me.

Behind one small cabin, there's a taut line stretching from the house to a pole full of clothing dangling in the breeze. They're practically waving at me, just asking me to take them. I look around, but thankfully, no one seems to be paying me much attention.

There has to be at least one hundred wolves now gathered in the center of what is definitely pack communal space. Some of them are on two legs and fully dressed, some nude and fresh out of a shift, and some trotting along as wolves.

As inconspicuously as possible, I veer away from the main group, slipping into the shadows to the side of a rudimentary looking home. My eyes are fixed on the fluttering fabric just ripe for the picking. I mean, if they're going to punish me for stealing food, I might as well be dressed when it happens. I try to tap into my wolf's give-no-fucks attitude as I reach up to unclip what looks like a shapeless wool dress from the line.

"You know, Vicious, this pack has very strict rules about wolves taking things that don't belong to them," a deep rumbling voice declares.

My heart tries to jump out of my chest. I barely bite down on the squeak of alarm that wants to fly out of my mouth as I whirl to find *him* casually leaning against the house opposite me as though he hasn't a care in the world.

Well, fuck.

TWELVE

MY BODY REACTS INSTANTLY TO HIS PRESENCE.

Fire ignites through me, and my wolf wags her tail and yips with excitement.

My clit starts to pulse with desire, and my nipples harden as brown eyes move salaciously over me before settling on my face.

"My name is not Vicious," I practically growl at the stranger who somehow has dominion over parts of me he shouldn't.

He smiles, flicking imaginary lint from his leather pants before his heated gaze returns to me. His back is pressed against the house behind him, one leg stretched out to support his weight and the other is cocked at the knee and resting against the log siding. The male tilts his head and takes me in, and instead of being bothered by the fact that I'm still naked and standing here, I suddenly want to own it.

"Well, now that you've bagged the coveted prize, maybe you can tell me who you are and just what the hell you're doing here on Ruin Falls land?" he demands silkily, and I have to stop myself from rolling my eyes.

Full of himself much?

"*Prize* is questionable, and if I could be anywhere else in the world, trust me, I would be," I snark, and his eyes harden ever so slightly.

"Who sent you?" he demands, his tone just a hint sharper under the languid confidence.

"If by *sent me* you mean *dumped* me here against my will, then you have Alpha Burke from Twin Rivers to thank."

"And what did you do to Alpha Burke to warrant exile, *Vicious*?" he asks me tauntingly as he casually cleans dirt from under a fingernail.

I pull in an even breath, trying to rein in the heat of temper that warms through me. If this pack doesn't tolerate stealing, they sure as hell aren't going to be a fan of me mauling one of them in the middle of whatever gathering is going down.

"The name is Seneca, and it wasn't what I *did* that landed me here, it's what I didn't do. That, and almost killing him for trying to force himself on me," I reply saccharinely, a glare punctuating my words.

The male's body tightens almost imperceptibly, and I swear I see a shudder of a shift move through him so fast that makes me question if it was ever even there. The hairs on the back of my neck stand up as though they're warning me of a threat, but in the blink of an eye, his relaxed, nonchalant mien is back in place.

"Shame you only *almost* killed him then. Someone like that should be put down painfully," he tells me, his eyes far away and his tone crawling with savage promise that makes me think he's considering doing just that.

I snort incredulously. "As if you're one to talk," I challenge, and he steadies a stony, incredulous gaze on me. "Do you often hunt and claim unwilling females here in Ruin Falls?" I lob, watching as the accusation hits its mark and his brown eyes harden with insult.

"There was nothing *unwilling* about it," he counters sharply, his eyes dropping slowly down my body before rising back up.

I feel his gaze like it's his hands moving down my suddenly heated flesh before they rise back up, leaving goose bumps in their wake. I stifle a shiver and feel my pupils suddenly dilate with need.

I shoot him a glare as a knowing smile tilts one corner of his luscious lips up as though he's replaying a visual of what we did together last night in the heart of the cave.

"Tell that to my shoulder," I bite back. "I don't recall agreeing to *that* before it happened," I add, gesturing to the bite that's on its way to becoming a prominent scar. "You have strict rules here about wolves taking things that don't belong to them, so what's the rule about mating someone without their permission?" I counter, and his eyes flash with savage anger.

He pushes off the wall and stalks toward me, his muscles tight and tense as though he's ready for a fight. I can't help but notice that he's just as stunning in the light of day as he was by the light of the moon. He has a thicker shadow of stubble on his cheeks than the night before, and I have to force myself from wondering what it would feel like between my thighs.

"We're still on that one, are we, Vicious?" he asks, a hint of menace underlying his tone. "I seem to recall you telling me to fuck you. I believe you asked me to make you scream until you and your wolf could see past the bloodlust. Correct me if I'm wrong, but didn't you demand that I be hard and fast?" he asks me, closing the distance between us until the thin linen of his shirt tickles my nipples and his heat washes over me like warm steam on a cold day.

I want to back up, to create space between us, but my wolf is having none of it. She roots our legs to the ground, breathing him in greedily, trying to pull us under with the weight of his dominant pheromones. I growl at him, but it isn't backed up by the ire of my wolf. It's all me, and the pitiful sound seems to amuse him.

"I did all of those things," I admit, hating the heat that I know is gleaming in my gaze. "But I'd love for you to point out where I begged you to *claim* me. Where I demanded that you mark me hard and fast while you made me scream?" My blood is starting to boil, my tone seething with it.

I can feel I'm close. Close to that side of me that shuns logic and instead lives for the fight, for the blood, for the kill. Yet just like before, this male seems to eat it up, like it's his favorite dessert instead of a sign of a severely unhealthy wolf.

"You didn't need to ask for those things, and I didn't need to ask to take them. You were out running during a claiming hunt. That's all the permission I need."

His stare is a molten challenge, and I press into him even closer, outraged. "I'm not in your pack. I was trying to get away, not join in on some fucked up past time."

His pupils dilate as his eyes drop to my lips, like he wants to lean in and lick up the heated vitriol flying out of my mouth. "Tell yourself whatever you want. Your wolf wasn't trying to go anywhere except under me. She wanted my wolf to fuck her. Needed it as badly as you needed your...*outlet.*"

With a screech of anger, I lift my hands to push him away from me. I hate that he's right, but *I'm* right too. *I* am not my wolf. I didn't understand until it was too late, and I couldn't grapple back control. Despite the hit I try to land, my angry palms never meet his chest. The force I fill my arms with is never released, because as fast as a snake bite, I'm shoved between him and the wood of the cabin behind me. He has my arms pinned behind my back with a punishing grip as a deep growl vibrates through me, moving from his chest into mine.

He leans in close, the stubble I was curious about a hair's breadth away from my cheek. "Listen closely, *Vicious*, because it's the only time I'm going to tell you this before I start showing you what happens if you try to fight me." His tone is screaming that he's not fucking around anymore as he presses harder into me. "You can hide from the truth all you want, bury yourself in whatever delusions that make you feel better, but you're *marked*, and you're *mine*, and there's not shit you can do to change that."

Rage engulfs me at his words. My wounded glare doesn't stray from the hard conviction I see in his face. I hate how trapped I feel, but even more, I hate how a part of me *loves* it.

I'm being destroyed by the baser nature of my wolf. Her needs are chipping away at who I am at my core, and I feel fragmented in a terrifying way. How can I ever be at peace when the very pieces of my soul are at war?

A large, calloused hand traces softly down my side, and he drops his nose to my shoulder, pulling my scent deeply into his lungs as if he's savoring it. His fingers skim a path across my stomach before dropping lower and lower, until he's playing with the short hair at the apex of my thighs.

Need pools low in my stomach, and a satisfied growl rumbles through him as though he can smell my pussy growing wet for him. I close my eyes, trying not to like the way his body feels against mine, trying not to beg for his hand to drop lower so he can dip his large fingers inside of me. Like he's determined to make me give in to my lust, he nips at my jaw and runs his fingers over the seam between my thighs, making a noise get caught in my throat.

Both of us start to breathe heavy as desire fills the almost nonexistent space between us. I tip my head back, scolding myself for my reactions and demanding that my body doesn't play into this. I will not roll my hips against his featherlight touch. I will not bite his shoulder, no matter how much my wolf is riding me to. I refuse to rub my cheek against his so I can feel what his stubble is like against my skin.

I gasp as his mouth drops to his bite, and he sucks on the tender skin there. To my horrifying embarrassment, I feel an orgasm starting to build in me from just these simple touches. Try as I might to suppress it, a small moan works its way from my parted lips.

But my small, sensual noise is drowned out by a long haunting howl that bursts through the air all around us. He growls frustratedly, pulling his mouth from his mark, clear irritation at being interrupted shining in his gaze. He nips at the side of my neck once more and then drops his forehead to my other shoulder as though the mark on the opposite side is more temptation than he can bear.

With great effort, I try to calm my breathing, thankful that this was cut short before I caved and jumped him. Out of nowhere, his fangs sink into my skin, and I jump, whimpering at the pain that suddenly consumes me. He releases me as fast as he bit me, hips grinding against me once before he backs up, putting distance between us.

I look at my other shoulder to see the bite he's left there too, and I shut down my wolf's smug satisfaction and focus only on my resentment. Warm blood trickles from the new mark, but before I can so much as push off the wall with a snarl, he's whipping his shirt over his head and shoving it over mine.

He tugs at the hem until it's pulled down all the way, dressing me like a child who couldn't manage the task myself. My relief at being covered again battles with my need to want to rip this male open and tear his scent-soaked shirt from my body. But I also can't help from running my greedy eyes over his shirtless form. I knew he was hot last night, but in the day? He's even *better*. Tanned skin like he lives and breathes the outdoors, sculpted muscles that curve over every glorious inch of him. This asshole is fuck-me candy that I have the sudden urge to suck on.

One side of his mouth twitches as if he knows what I'm thinking, and I glower at him to keep the blush from my cheeks. "Come on, the alpha has called a meeting," he declares before grabbing my hand and pulling me behind him. His deceptively soft shirt hangs mid-thigh, and the blood from my bite is already dotting the fabric.

I'm dragged behind him as we pass the back of cabins with gardens and playhouses for pups. It's all so quaint and normal looking and doesn't fit at all with the image I've always had of the Ruin Falls pack. I try to dig my heels in and stop his forward momentum, but he's too strong. Even with my wolf's help, I don't stand a chance. Nerves and worry flash through me as it looks as though this male is aiming for the front of the pack like he's eager for a good seat, or maybe to turn me in.

I'm glad to be covered, but not stoked about the fact that I'm bleeding, especially not right now when I'll be seeing the alpha for the first time. I know he's ruthless and formidable, as savage as they come. The last thing I want when the alpha sees me for the first time is to be bleeding like I'm prey he should take interest in.

I'm tugged to a stop just as we reach the front of the pack, and I almost let out an anxious sigh but stop myself. I don't know what's going on or what my place in all of it is, but as I look around me, I don't see any worry or tension in the faces or body language of the surrounding wolves. Next to me, the infuriating male who was just playing my body like his favorite game drops my hand. I'm both relieved by it and equally annoyed, which just serves to anger me even more at the divide happening inside of me.

I keep my eyes diverted from him, focusing instead on the front of the pack house we're all gathered around. It's elevated slightly, a deck and wood balcony positioned perfectly for the alpha to stand above the gathered wolves in a position of power, making whatever decrees he sees fit.

Everyone seems to quiet just before the pack house door opens, and out walks a large man with blond hair and brown eyes. He strides confidently down the flight of stairs that leads from the front door to the deck. He's younger than I thought he'd be, and his face is kinder than I expected. As feral and vicious as this pack's reputation has grown to be, it's only been that way since this new alpha took power about ten years ago.

Alpha Tyran was young when he bested this pack's former alpha, which marked the beginning of his legendary notoriety. It didn't take him long to become the most feared and despised alpha in power, and that's saying a lot when so many packs are led by wolves like Burke and worse.

The blond male grows more and more somber as he closes the distance, and even though I do get a sense of power radiating off of him, it's nowhere near what I thought it would be, given his renown. Out of the corner of my eye, I see someone start to climb the stairs that lead up to the deck. I pull my eyes from the alpha and look over to see that it's my male, his coppery brown eyes fixed on the blond guy as they both reach the deck landing at the same time.

I look to my right as though I expect the male who was just standing next to me to still be there. Sure enough though, I've been abandoned once again, because he's standing up there with Tyran.

Heat fills my face as I realize he must be a high standing beta. Worry fills me that he's up there to announce our mating, and apprehension moves through me at the thought of the whole pack's eyes turning to take me in. I'm a mess. I'm also still divided on how I feel about all of this, and I don't know what happens to me if that's written all over my face when he announces it. I shift my weight anxiously. For fuck's sake, I still have his dried cum on my thigh.

I look up as the two males nod at one another, and then the blond moves to the side as my male steps forward. His dark brown hair dusts his squared shoulders, and his head is held high as he places his hands on the railing.

"Ruin Falls," he calls out, his voice booming, and the wolves all around me are dead silent as though they're hanging on his every word. "I've called you here today because the way of our pack has been violated. As your alpha, I call for a reckoning."

Tawny brown eyes drop to mine, and horror rushes through me like a tsunami. My heart goes wild inside my chest as though it too is nothing more than a rabid being raging and rioting until it can escape its confines. Dread consumes my every cell as understanding rips through me like a first shift.

The blond male isn't Tyran, the tyrannical alpha of the Ruin Falls pack. The male who *claimed* me is. I don't just belong to this barbaric group of wolves. I've been mated by the male who leads them.

Fuck. My. Life.

THERE'S A COLLECTIVE INTAKE OF breath from the pack as I reel with understanding and shock. My feet are backing up before I even realize I'm doing it, but as soon as I do, I force myself to stand still again. The second I'm rooted in place, his eyes move away from me. "Warrik and Reap, step forward."

My head snaps to the right as I watch the two wolves who filled the bath in the shed come forward. Warrik looks rough, as though he didn't sleep last night after my run-in with him in the woods. Tyran's eyes stay locked on the two males as they stop in front of the deck, heads tipped up to look at their alpha. If they had tails right now, they'd be tucked under them as tightly as they could be.

Beneath the sun, the tanned skin of Tyran's muscled chest makes my mouth water. Right now, with his hands braced on the railing as he looks down at the two wolves beneath him, he looks every bit the formidable alpha leader. I kick myself for not realizing it sooner. He's strong. So much stronger than anything I've ever experienced. No wonder he was able to handle me and my wolf at our most rabid.

"Beta Warrik, you are accused of giving an outsider access to the pack and our territory on the night of our sacred claiming hunt." Tyran's grip tightens on the railing, and my stomach tightens right along with it. "Do you deny it?"

Warrik stands tall and proud, hands clasped in front of him as he looks up at Tyran. "No."

At his answer, voices murmur through the gathered group.

"What was your reasoning?" Tyran asks, his face a stony mask, expression unreadable.

For a split second, Warrik turns, his eyes finding me in the crowd. "She was captured on our land, which means she belonged to our pack the moment we found her. It was moon-blessed that she arrived here on the night of our claiming hunt," he argues. "She's wild, and there are males here who deserve a claim. All females in our pack participate in the hunt."

"She was not yet part of our pack," Tyran snaps out, voice cracking like a whip. "You could have loosed a spy. A saboteur. Or an even greater threat. But more than that, you acted without your alpha's permission and without thought for your fellow pack members."

It's almost imperceptible, but the shifters standing around me seem to inch away from me at Tyran's words, distrustful gazes falling on me, though every time I try to meet their eyes, they've already turned away.

Tyran moves his attention to the second male. "Delta Reap. You are facing the same reckoning."

The second male's eyes widen, and he tears a hand through his ashy brown hair, yanking on it in frustration. "I told him it was a bad idea!" he calls up, shooting an angry look at Warrik that's filled with blame and accusation.

"But you did nothing to stop it from happening," Tyran bites out. "You did not report Warrik's behavior to your superiors."

At that, Reap goes silent, head hanging down as he stares at the ground. Warrik continues to look straight ahead, though I don't miss the way his face has seemed to pale. I have no idea what a *reckoning* involves here, but it's put fear and dread into these males, and tension is pulsating out of the rest of the gathered pack.

Tyran lifts his gaze to the crowd. "At the moon's first light, the reckoning begins," he announces, and the pack nods almost in unison. "May it be a good reminder for everyone that your alpha does not tolerate disobedience or selfish acts that could put the pack in jeopardy."

Without another word, he turns and walks into the large house with the blond male, door slamming shut behind them. And I...I just stand there, gaping, blinking, a hundred thoughts swarming in my mind. But one blares louder than the other. He didn't announce me. He didn't announce that my escaping the shed and running in the hunt has resulted in *him* claiming me. And for some reason, that bothers me. Much more than it should. Yet when I look around, I find every single pack member is still standing in place, staring at me, and my wolf and I bristle.

A nervous lump gets stuck in my throat, but I meet their gazes head-on. Tipping up my chin, I pretend I'm not covered in dirt with their alpha's teeth marks in my shoulders or his release caking my thighs. I pretend I'm not completely clueless about pretty much everything when it comes to this pack or what the hell is going on.

The rankling fact of the matter though is that Tyran has left me to flounder. The prick bit me not once but *twice*, ensuring that my blood tainted the air during this announcement, making his scent mingle with mine more than it already is, and has essentially just left me to be fed on by his wolves. I'm no better than the meat roasting on spits over the spread out fires. Will someone do to me what *I* did to their food earlier? Swipe me away and gobble me down?

"Problem?" I ask testily, my gaze swinging from left to right. It might seem a little bit like poking the beast, but I'm not left with another alternative. If I drop my gaze and tuck tail, I have no doubt this pack will pick their teeth with me. No, I need to make each and every one of them think that I'm the biggest, baddest bitch they've ever seen.

Tense seconds tick by without anyone saying a damn thing. My muscles are stiff, my wolf so near the surface that I'm itchy all over, dying to scratch the fur right out of my skin. The next pass of my gaze snags on Warrik, and I'm stunned at the level of resentment I see reflected back in his golden eyes, as if he blames *me*.

The entire pack looks between us, a level of excited anticipation staining the air, and then Warrik spits on the ground and cuts through the crowd, walking in the opposite direction. As if his movement acted as the catalyst, everyone else begins to disperse too, and I'm finally able to let out the breath I was holding.

That is, until I hear Presley's voice behind me. "Did you hear him? Alpha is pissed that she got loose and that his wolf claimed her. I don't blame him, though. I mean, *look* at her. Did you see her eyes? Her wolf is bent as fuck. It's only a matter of time before she goes completely rabid."

I whirl around, catching the tail end of her biting comments. She and three other females are staring at me over their shoulders, their eyes dripping with disdain. Presley shoots me a look of contempt before turning back around, her words getting swallowed up with distance and the rest of the pack's mingling voices and sounds. My hands curl into fists, my nail beds aching with the press of sharp claws just threatening to break through.

But I can't do that.

I can't lose control and prove what Presley just so loudly said about me. I'd just be playing right into her hands, giving merit to her words, and making myself even more of a leper to a pack I might be stuck with.

"Don't worry about her." I look over to find Harlan coming up next to me. "Presley has some deep-seated bitterness against other females. She's neither a powerful alpha, a coveted omega, or an equal beta."

"She's a delta?" I ask with surprise.

"A kappa," Harlan corrects. "Just one of our hunters in charge of feeding the pack."

I wince a little. No wonder she got so pissed my wolf took part of her kill roasting over the fire. It wasn't just her food, it was her contribution to the pack.

"She's been wanting to rise in rank for years, and going about it in all the wrong ways. Your wolf is strong. She sees it as a threat."

"And you?" I ask. "Do you see me as a threat?"

Something flashes in her light-brown eyes before she shutters it closed. "All outsiders are threats."

Without saying another word, she turns and walks away, my gaze dropping to her stiff shoulder and the faded mate mark that's there, while Presley's previous words filter back through me. I find myself standing completely alone, in front of Tyran's house, while the rest of the pack lumbers off to do...whatever it is they were doing before. Everywhere I look, clusters of shifters are working together or just loitering, but all of them are ignoring me completely.

Anger bubbles up inside me, because *fuck* this. Fuck this place, fuck these wolves, and fuck *my* wolf for bringing me into this situation. All I wanted was to be left unclaimed, left to live my life the way I chose. Now, I'm in the exact situation I was trying to run from, with twin marks in my shoulders and a temper flaring in my chest.

With narrowed eyes homing in on the alpha's door, I find my feet moving, taking the stairs up the deck two at a time. I don't bother knocking, I just march straight for the door, intending to burst through it and slam it shut behind me. Except it opens a second before I get there, and I jerk to a stop in front of the blond male who was standing on the deck with Tyran earlier.

He cocks an eyebrow at me but steps aside. I falter in surprise for a second, but then manage to march my ass right past him like I have every right to be there. Anger is driving me hard, and I have every intention of laying into the male whose teeth laid into me.

The inside of the house is cozy. Rough around the edges, but even in my current state, I note the well-made furniture, the leather, woven rugs, and the wooden floors that make the large space not feel cold or lifeless. Directly in front of me is a wide staircase, each step made of a log cut in half, it's rough bark arching beneath the sanded tops. My bare feet pad up them, and I don't let myself stop, even though I feel the weight of the blond's stare on my back as I head upstairs.

I let my wolf's nose lead me, seeking out the combination of musky amber, cedar, and cashmere that are key notes in Tyran's masculine scent. We find it easily, the aroma saturated in here, but even if it weren't, I have a feeling my wolf would still be able to pick it out of a slew of other smells.

Luckily, I get my *burst through the door* moment this time, because I scent him just on the opposite side of the long hallway. I shove open the door without warning and slam it behind me, breath already panting in anger the moment I find him sitting behind his desk.

He still doesn't have a shirt on, and it pisses me off seeing him just sitting there cool as a fucking cucumber. But it's mixed with surprise, because he's sitting behind a *desk*. He's holding a pen and doing...paperwork. I have to blink for a second as I try to assimilate this vision with the famed and monstrous leader I've always heard about.

The overwhelming scent of him surrounds me as he leans back in his chair, making the wood creak. His brown eyes latch onto me as he cocks his head. "Something you need?"

The arrogant impatience of his tone snaps me back into my irritation. "You didn't tell me you were the fucking *alpha*." I practically hurl the words at his face, mine burning with anger.

He shrugs and scratches down his sharp jaw. "It's not my fault you weren't wolf enough to pick it out."

This arrogant *bastard*.

"My wolf was a little preoccupied being overrun with instincts."

Heat flares in his eyes, which just makes me want to slap him. "I'm aware. You should let her do that more often," he smirks.

"Screw. You."

Tyran scoots the chair back and pats his thigh. "The invitation is open."

A rage of noise strangles in my chest, and my vision pulses. He leans forward, bracing his elbows on the edge of the desk, watching me. "You need me to fuck that anger out of you, Seneca?" he says, his voice practically purring. I shouldn't like the way my name sounds on his lips, but I do. Dammit, I do. "I worked you up outside and now you're snarling."

"No!" I bite back, but I can't help the trickle of shame that drips down my spine, because part of me wonders if he's right. Because even now, his new bite is throbbing, and it seems to be in direct correlation with the throb between my legs. "I don't want you to touch me ever again. In fact—" I rip off his shirt and throw it in his face, flaring with satisfaction when it hits him. "I don't want any part of you to touch me, not even your scent. I want a shower to wash you off of me, and I want my own goddamn clothes. *Now.*"

He watches me.

I watch him.

I'm heaving, spitting mad, feeling like my world won't stop crumbling around me, and all I have is my teetering anger to keep me standing on two feet. I want...*fuck*. I don't even know what I want, but I *do* know that I need to stay pissed at him, need to ride on the coattails of this anger, because it's all I have that's keeping me upright.

"You need to watch your tone."

"Are you serious, asshole? I'm not a pup to be reprimanded."

"No, our pups are much more respectful," he snarks.

My eyebrows shoot up. "*Respect*? You expect me to give respect to the alpha of Ruin Falls?"

His entire countenance changes into one of deathly coldness, but I don't care.

"I've heard all about you and your pack and the savage things you've done, the punishments you mete out. You live life on four legs more often than two. You're all wild beasts who don't ever interact with humans. Which is a good thing, I guess, since you're also known for kidnapping other shifters and killing their families. I don't know which is worse though: killing strangers or leading a massacre on your own pack." My challenge is breathless, but my eyes are unforgiving.

I've heard all the rumors about him, heard all the gossip about what sort of monsters the shifters in Ruin Falls really are. I've always hated the fact that they were so close to Twin Rivers. Now I've been dumped here, only to be claimed by the greatest monster of all.

How's that for fucking luck?

His abs tighten as he leans in closer to the desk. "You're exactly right. Ruin Falls does do all of those things. So why the fuck would you run during our claiming hunt?"

"What part about *I didn't know there was a claiming hunt* do you not get?" I shout in frustration. "I was trying to run away, not run into a mate!"

His brown eyebrow arches up. "I have it on good authority that you were told to stay in the fucking shed."

"Was that before or after your people snared me like hunted prey and then tied me up like a dog?" I shoot back. "Forgive me for not wading through the cryptic mumblings of an old male or putting a lot of stock into what your crazy ass pack members said to me. If it were you, you would've tried to escape too. And Warrik made damn sure that I heard him say I needed to run if I had any chance last night. So that's what I fucking did. I ran."

"Warrik is being dealt with."

I roll my eyes. I have no interest in hearing about this alpha's need to get into a shifter brawl with Warrik so he can flex his own brutality. "I'm sure your pack of savage monsters will enjoy watching," I retort.

Something cold pierces me from the narrowing of his eyes. "You're awfully quick to judge *my* pack when Twin Rivers was the one to dump you on our land like trash."

Furious heat crawls up my chest, spreading a flush to my cheeks all the way to the tips of my ears. But the worst part of my anger is how much it's filled with crushing sadness. I can't even argue with him. Because my pack *did* let Burke throw me away. They let him attack me, dump me on a monster's territory, let him kill my mom. No one did a damn thing to stop any of it.

Everything in me crumples, like all of my hot air was just deflated with his one sharp blow. "I want clothes and food," I say thickly, my arms crossing over my breasts.

I wait on tenterhooks, expecting for him to dig further into the crack of weakness he just found, to attack it until I'm a broken mess beneath his feet. I'm already tipping to my breaking point, and we both know he won, so I ready myself for another crushing blow. Because that's what monsters do. They destroy.

But to my utter shock, Tyran's expression softens. "Okay, Vicious," he says quietly, using a tone I wouldn't have ever guessed he was even capable of. "Second door to the right will get you to a bathroom. There's clothes that should fit you in the attached bedroom."

I turn on my heel and stalk to the door, more than ready to scrub his scent from my body and get away from his domineering presence so I can steel myself once more. But just as I open the door, his hand is there, slamming it closed. I gasp, head whipping to the side, finding his face just an inch from mine. Without warning, he shoves his shirt back over my head, so hard that the collar practically chokes me.

I'm ruffled with hair in my face, cheeks hot with irritation, he gets right up close and personal, his nose nearly touching mine. "Go ahead and try to wash me off you, see how well that works out for you and your wolf," he says in a clear taunt. "But if I see you unnecessarily walking around naked in front of any of my pack members again, I will take it as a sign that you want to be fucked in front of them. To which I will happily oblige, and then I'll bend you over my knees and spank you raw."

I gape at him. "What? I'm a shifter. Shifters *shift*. It's not like my wolf can walk around wearing a damn dress!"

He's already sauntering back to his desk, sitting down again and paying me no mind whatsoever. A frustrated growl clambers from my throat, and I yank open the door, slamming it behind me as hard as I can, hoping it rattles his stupid walls.

Fucking wolves.

Fucking alpha prick.

THIRTEEN

HOT WATER RAINS DOWN ON ME AS I SIT ON THE TILE floor of the shower. My knees are to my chest, my head resting on top, my thoughts far away and overwhelming. The steady stream of scalding water has made my skin turn even pinker than it was as I scrubbed all traces of what happened last night off of me. I watched dirt, leaves, and blood wind down the drain as I scoured my skin before shampooing and conditioning my hair and scalp raw.

I should probably get out. I think I've been in here for over an hour. I'm surprised the water hasn't become ice-cold at this point, but this small, tiled space feels like the safest option for me right now, and I'm not ready to abandon it to discover what's on the other side of the connecting doors. My throat is thick with emotion, but no matter how long I sit here and think about every awful thing that's happened to me recently, I still don't cry.

My heart aches as though someone put it through a shredder and then did a shit job of trying to tape it back together. Nothing in me works the way it's supposed to. I've been sitting here trying to figure out what can be done about that, but I still have no idea. All I want is to talk to my mom. She would know exactly what to say, know exactly how to help me fix my broken. But she's not here. And the wrongness of that feels like a grater against my insides.

I've never felt so lost, so utterly foolish in my entire life. How am I going to survive being claimed by the crudest, most savage alpha my kind has ever seen? How am I going to subsist on a shattered soul? What's been done to me and my wolf since the Flux...I don't know if there's any coming back from that.

Presley's words ring in my mind, joining with Burke's and the shouts of my old pack. Is it really only a matter of time before I'm just as volatile and vicious as my wolf seems to be?

So many questions pick at me like starving crows at carrion. Yet it doesn't matter how long I sit here and stew, hoping the answers will come to me, none do.

I've spent the last three years being hunted by an alpha, but I never thought through what to do if I was caught by one. I was stupid to think my mother's position would protect me forever. I knew Burke was fucked up, but I couldn't comprehend the lengths he would go to have me. I'm grateful for what my wolf and I did to survive him, regardless of how damaged it has left us. I just wish I could understand what we're supposed to do with this new wolf she's dead set on claiming. She should hate Tyran, should want nothing to do with him. And yet every damn second he's near, she wags her tail like an excited pup and throws my logic and needs right out the window.

With a frustrated sigh, I push up from the shower floor. My leg muscles are shaky and tired, my body in desperate need of food. I'm so hungry I could literally eat a horse right now, and my mouth waters at the thought of gorging myself on meat and blood and bone. Turning the water off, I grab a fluffy towel from a stack on a small table beside the glass shower door. I dry off, hunger suddenly riding me hard.

I find a blow-dryer in a drawer, which makes me smile at the thought of the big bad alpha blow-drying his precious locks in place. I wipe a streak of steam from the mirror so I can see what I'm doing, but the eyes that stare back at me make me flinch in fright. I drop the dryer and step back from the mirror as though a monster is trying to break through from the other side.

"Holy shit."

My hands shoot up to cover my mouth as though I can trap my shock between my cupped palms and then throw it away. My heart gallops through my chest, distress riding it like a jockey. After a minute, I build up enough moxie to slowly approach the mirror and try to make sense of what I see.

I wipe more steam from the mirror, leaning closer to it as I turn my head left and right. My skin is tan, with some light freckles dusting my nose and cheeks. My lips have the same full pout they've always had. But my eyes...the windows to my soul, look like someone took a rock to one of them and smashed it.

My glacier blue hue is normal and untouched in my left eye, but in my right eye, half of my frigid blue iris is cut into with a jagged shard of bright violet. I lean even closer until I'm nearly nose-to-mirror, and realize that no, my left eye isn't unchanged. There's the thinnest ring of brown encasing the pale blue.

"What the hell..."

What's happened to my wolf, to me, is written all over my stare.

No wonder people have been looking at me strangely with a mix of fear and judgment. My wolf is always peering out at them. She's a constant threat, a constant reminder of what we're capable of, staring at them between each blink. I think through the unsettling split-vision that occurs when I'm at my most rabid or vulnerable, and it all makes sense now. My wolf and I are constantly fighting to see out of the same eyes.

There's no gentle back and forth between her and me. We were both crushed together and forged anew by chaos and cruelty, and *this* is the result of our rushed joining, our need for life-or-death savagery. Our accession was so violent that it's visible in the torn half of our irises.

I drop my eyes from the mirror just like so many others that have rushed to look away from me. This physical manifestation of what I am inside makes me feel raw and bare. Once again, I'm divided by how much I hate that my wolf and I have been brought to this, but how proud I am that we've survived.

Trying to get a hold of myself, I pick up the blow-dryer from the floor where I dropped it and turn it on. I stare into my eyes the whole time I dry my hair, forcing myself to get used to them, stomping out any shame and self-consciousness that tries to take root in my chest as I do.

I cannot cower away from who I am.

No, now it's time to find my way.

Once my long brown hair is dried, I pack the dryer away where I found it and tidy up. Tightening the towel around my body, I walk to the closed door that leads to the room I was told I'd find clothes in. It creaks slightly as I crack it open, my breath held in my lungs for safe keeping, but when no one is there waiting for me, I release it, relieved.

I step into the space, and the smell of Tyran wraps around me like a poisonous snake. I'm not sure if his entire home smells like him this strongly or if this is *his* bedroom. Either way, I'm not going to stand here naked and risk him barging in here, frying my ability to think with something other than my vagina.

Looking around, I don't spot a closet door. There's only the doorway I'm standing in and one that I assume leads out into the hallway. There is, however, a large armoire with an equally large dresser taking up one wall. Quietly, like I'm sneaking around instead of doing what I was told, I tiptoe to the dresser and start opening drawers.

I find what looks like hand sewn boxers, socks, pants, shirts and a couple drawers of clean bedding. I try on a pair of boxers, but they slip right off me, so I fold them back up and return them. Moving to the armoire, I pull open the doors and discover animal pelts that have been sewn into coats and shawls, plus some scuffed boots and folded blankets at the bottom.

There's one small cubby that has what looks like smaller versions of the various pants and tops I saw in the dresser, and I even spot a skirt. I pull them out, holding them up, but worry slinks through me when they look too small. There's no underwear of course, which has me setting the tiny skirt aside.

I step one foot and then another into the suede animal hide pants and pull them on. Surprisingly, there's just enough give to the material, and I'm able to pull them all the way up. They're tight, so I sure as hell won't be doing any lunges in these things, but it's better than free lipping it all around this place and hoping Tyran doesn't read into it the wrong way.

I pull the shirt on, expecting it to be smallish too, but to my surprise it's big. It's also white, which doesn't do a whole lot to hide my nipples without a bra. The neck is supposed to tie closed, but the neckline is so damn big it hangs off of one shoulder and the sleeves drape well past my hands. Rolling my sleeves as I go, I move back into the bathroom to have a look. Yep, just like I thought. I look like some braless pirate pilgrim who stole a shirt four sizes too big.

Surveying the state of my outfit in the mirror, I try to come up with a way to fix it. I tuck the front into the ties of the pants which sort of helps, although the Musketeer vibe is undeniable. I snort out a laugh and let go of how ridiculous I look, because it could be worse. I move back to the bedroom to see if there are any shoes to go with this little number. A pair of swashbuckling over-the-knee boots would be in order, but as I root through the armoire, I realize that everything is way too big. Grabbing a pair anyway, just to see if I can make them work, I plop down on the side of the bed to try them on.

Just as I bend down to slip a foot in the buttery looking leather, a distinct scent hits me. It's Tyran's, but there's a layer of something else mingling with it. Boots abandoned, I lean over to smell the bedding. I pull it back and practically shove my face in the pillow. Immediately, an image of Strawberry Bitch waves to focus in my mind. I jerk back sharply as though the bedding just took a swipe at me. Quickly, I reach over and grab the pillow from the other side of the bed.

Maybe I'm mistaken.

Maybe this is a guest room and I'm reading the situation all wrong.

I bring the cotton and downy feathered pillow to my nose and inhale. A deep growl resonates in my chest as my wolf and I find only Tyran's smell here. So this is definitely his room, which means...

I launch to my feet and start to pull at the clothes from my body as though they're infested with fire ants. The shirt, the shoes, the pants, they all come flying off, while my entire body shakes with fury. Did he seriously just give me some other bitch's clothes to wear? Did he honestly have me come into this room so that I'd smell that same bitch all over his goddamn bed?

My vision splits, just like it does every time my wolf and I are set off. But this time, I don't even care that it's further proof of our ruin. I don't try to hold her back. My wolf lends me her claws and her fangs, and in a complete and total rage, I find myself unleashing.

I tear into the bedding like the animal I am. Claws rip through the pillows, the sharp ends raking down the very mattress that sits atop an exquisitely carved arolla pine bed frame. I let my anger loose, let my wolf growl and snap and bite. All we can think about is destroying every single thing in here that was tainted by another female's scent. A female in *our* mate's bedroom.

Feathers explode all around me, raining down like shrapnel as I tear through the bed. My outrage and acrimony are only slightly settled by the satisfying tearing of fabric as I rip Presley from this space. My razor-sharp nails shred her pillow to bits. My teeth snap at the air, as if I can rip out her lingering scent from the very molecules I'm breathing in. Yet the more I decimate, the more I start to uncover.

The deeper I dig and shred, the more I'm able to smell others.

A lot of others.

Other females who've screamed, writhed, and slept beside him in this room. I see red. My wolf refuses to be satisfied until everything is as wrecked and ravaged as we are. She wants to howl with the fury that guides the violence and ferocity of our actions. But when the bed and frame are thoroughly destroyed, it's still not enough.

My gums throb, my enlarged fangs aching, wanting nothing more than to bite into every single one of them. I want to take a bite out of *him* too, and then demolish each and every female that's ever stepped foot in this room. My wolf marks their scents, and my vision teeters between my wolf and me, but determination floods us. We're going to hunt the females down one by one and make them wish they'd never laid down for him.

I rip open the door to the hallway, my wolf's strength almost pulling the thick wood right off its hinges as I go. Latching onto the freshest traces of Tyran's scent, I start to track him through his home. My feet are booming as they race down the stairs, my fangs retracting just so I can bellow at Tyran the way my wolf and I both need, but our claws are still extended and ready.

My split-vision is less disorienting now that I understand what's happening, and instead of fighting it, we work together with pure focus. I dash through the alpha house, past dining rooms, living rooms, and what appears to be another office. I smell Tyran and a few other males behind a door, and I don't hesitate as I burst through it.

Tyran jumps to his feet as though he's expecting danger. The other males—one of them the blond I thought was the alpha—do the same, except more slowly, as though they know better than to get in Tyran's way. The alpha takes one look at me, naked, enraged, with feathers and pieces of wood and bed sheet still tangled in my hair, and his pupils dilate. Every muscle in his body goes taut, and a tic starts in his jaw as he surveys my stance and the rancor coming off me in waves.

"Unless you want to lose your throat, I suggest you look away."

For a moment, I think he's talking to me until every single male in the room immediately drops their eyes to the floor.

They're sitting around a huge oval table like they're having some damn conference, but I'm so mad that I move toward it to rake my nails down that too, ready to destroy some more shit.

"Is there a problem?"

His cool, callous tone has me baring my teeth, fangs threatening to slip down again. "Yeah, there's a *fucking problem*. You sent me up there, knowing full well it's covered in your bitches' smells!" My chest rises and falls, skin gleaming with a sheen that stems from my sweltering anger. "How many of them did you fuck into that mattress?" I demand, taking a step toward him. "Did you want me to go up there and cower beneath their reek? Did you think it would knock me down and put me in my place?"

I don't blink as I stare at him with pure challenge, and he doesn't look away from me either. I don't even care right now that there's a roomful of unknown shifter males witnessing this. I'm too pissed.

Our stare-off makes the room feel tense, nearly claustrophobic, even though the space itself is large, and there's a big bay window to the left overlooking the lake.

"Well? Are you going to say something, or did those bitches fuck you mute?"

Someone in the room whistles low. Someone else makes a coughing noise.

But I only have eyes for Tyran, and a flare of satisfaction goes through me, because that stolid expression on his face finally cracks, letting me see the anger simmering beneath the surface. "I warned you."

My eyes narrow on his low, threatening words. "What?"

His hands drop to his pants, to the leather stays tied between the V of his pelvis. "What did I tell you earlier about walking around naked in front of others when it's not necessary?"

"You think I'm going to wear some other female's clothes?" I demand, seething. "There's no amount of *necessary* that will ever have that happening," I snap tauntingly.

"Then you should have put on mine," he snaps back, his tone gravelly and dripping with warning.

His words clamor in my skull, but my eyes blaze. "You won't fucking *touch* me."

"Wrong." Deft fingers begin to undo the ties at his pants, and my mouth goes dry. But I'm not ready to give up this anger, and I won't just stand here and get punished. I'll get even.

"You fucked all those females, so how about you leave while I fuck all the males in this room? Don't worry, I'll be sure to rub all over the furniture so that when you least expect it, you can catch a whiff."

Tyran goes utterly still.

The ties on his pants undone, the rough fabric hanging off his sharp hips, a hint of dark hair just visible at the top. But the fury that suddenly emanates from him is centered in the growl that rumbles like thunder through the room. The males surrounding us have all gone rigid, and I smirk in satisfaction that my threat has landed its mark, that my words had an effect.

Tyran's eyes glow, the muscles of his chest, arms, and abs jumping, as if he's physically having to restrain his wolf from taking over.

"Get. Out."

I stop myself from flinching at the ferocity of his words, but the other males don't hesitate. Faster than I can track, they all leave through a second door in the back of the room, knocking over chairs in their haste.

And then it's just him and me, my wolf and his.

I launch myself at him.

A curved swipe at his face is deflected before I can land the blow, and my claws catch into the wall instead. I make them retract, replaced by only my fingernails, but he grabs my other arm, wrenching it behind my back and spinning me around until my back is against his chest. "Submit."

"Fuck you!" I spit.

He pulls me against him harder, and I can feel his erection against my ass, but even my wolf doesn't get sidetracked. She's infuriated, nose still clogged with the scents of all the faceless females that he left for us to find.

With my free hand, I reach up and fist his hair, yanking on it as hard as I can.

He growls and shoves me away, and I aim a kick at his balls. Unfortunately, he manages to grab my leg before I can deliver the blow, and he bends back my foot, making me hiss in pain. "You need to calm the fuck down and learn better control. Go for a damn run."

I hear the words, but I don't comprehend their meaning. Instead, my teeth snap at him, hands once more taking swipes. I'm so lost to the rage that my eyes are burning bright, fur popping up along the length of my arms.

"Shift and run," he orders.

I close my eyes as my wolf batters inside of me, trying to break free, but I don't want her to yet. I want to punch and shove and scream at him, I want to fling horrible words, because I feel horrible inside. There's this horrible, gnawing *wrongness* that won't stop screaming in my skull, and I just need...I need...

"Shift!"

My spirit cracks open.

This shift isn't easy. It isn't peaceful. Unlike my mom when her wolf spirit took over, there's certainly no *smiling*.

There is only agony. It's physical, emotional, mental, spiritual. We cry out, my wolf and I, for every hurt that keeps clawing us apart, that's ripped a line down our joining and shoved a jagged fragment in our eyes.

When the shift is complete, my wolf staggers to her feet, feeling bruised and battered all over. But the fury is still there, mouth drooling with the insatiable need to attack, to taste blood. The savagery is all-consuming, just as much as the soul-deep sorrow.

Tyran stands over her, looking not at all concerned by her bared teeth and snarling lips. After a moment of simply watching, he seems to make a decision and shoves off his pants. The next second, he bursts into his huge wolf form as effortlessly as breathing.

It doesn't matter that he's bigger or that alpha power radiates off his dark brown form. Nope, my wolf doesn't give a fuck about anything other than her anger and the need to punish him for disrespecting us. She lunges for him the moment he's fully shifted.

He takes her down in an instant, knocking her feet right out from under her. Before she can even get back up, he turns and runs out of the room. Furious, she bolts after him, following his every step. His longer legs ensure he stays two steps ahead so she can't take a bite out of him.

He leads her directly out of the house through a back door open to the lake and mountains beyond. The fresh air hitting our lungs begins to clear our nose and mouth of the horrible cloying scents of the other females. Our eyes tunnel, legs putting on a burst of speed, as we follow the male taunting us with his *come and get it* look over his shoulder.

And then, we *run*.

FOURTEEN

CRISP MOUNTAIN AIR BREEZES THROUGH OUR FUR AS we fly past trees, over boulders, and skirt tiny streams. All I can hear is the panting of my wolf, our paws as they hit the dirt, and the wrath pounding in our heart. Tyran runs ahead of us, outpacing us no matter how hard we push to catch him.

We're powerful, a force to be reckoned with, and yet we can't seem to sink our teeth into him regardless of how much he deserves it. New smells and sensations dance in our periphery, begging me and my wolf to veer off and check them out. But we can't be swayed, we're single-minded in our need to hunt and hurt the male running two lengths in front of us.

The espresso brown wolf looks over his shoulder, once again checking that we're still on his trail. It's insulting at this point, as though we're too weak to follow where he wants to lead. Every time he looks over at us, it just drives us even harder. We feel like a steam locomotive, but instead of being powered by coal, we're powered by hate and abhorrence and the need for blood.

We chug along after the asshole alpha, unable to catch him but also refusing to stop trying. We fly past the mountain's timber line, the soil lighter and less rich, the air thinner, forcing our lungs and our body to work even harder. We push and pant over rocky terrain, our sights fixed on the pain we want to mete out at the first opportunity.

We run for a long, long time.

I don't know where Tyran's wolf is going, but we chase unwaveringly, our muscles and effort spending our anger faster than we can create it. Then, the brown wolf lifts his nose as though he's chasing a scent, sharply turning left and taking us further up the mountain. We catch the hint of something too, but we can't identify what it is. Excitement for a new hunt moves through us as we carefully pick our way through jagged rocks and outcrops of boulders.

Slowly, one paw forward at a time, our rage starts to peel away like petals falling from a dying flower. My wolf and I physically exert ourselves harder than we ever have before, and it empties our reserves of vengeance and violence so that we can focus on the task at hand instead. But this physical demand, it feels *good*, sating the rabid edges inside of us as we push onward.

Tyran crouches lower as he moves toward a part of the mountain made up of sheer cliffs and sharp ledges. Our footing is becoming more and more precarious, but he doesn't hesitate as he moves, so neither do we. He stops at the top of a bluff, muscles tense and his eyes fixed on something.

By the time we catch up with him, he's leaping over large rocks and darting forward. We hear a snort, as though there's a horse on the other side of the rocky precipice. As my wolf and I crest the large rocks, we see Tyran darting at a herd of mountain goats. My wolf's excitement surges.

Our first hunt.

The herd's white hair is stark against the gray and brown rock of the mountain. The sharp cliffs and narrow footholds signal this as their stomping grounds, but it doesn't stop Tyran from singling out a male on the outskirts of the herd. My wolf and I immediately follow, sizing up our options for how to bring the goat down, for how to work with the alpha to earn the kill. The goat jumps from one rock to another as though there isn't a sheer drop just under its hooves, and we notice that it's not putting all its weight on one front leg.

The goats smell like heaven, and our stomach growls impatiently as we move higher up the mountain to where we think the old, injured goat will run. The wind changes slightly, and the mountain goats finally catch a hint of Tyran's and my smell. They start frantically running, but Tyran is on the injured one, driving him up toward me, as if we planned this ambush in advance.

Adrenaline and need race through my wolf and me as we bolt for the goat, chasing him up the cliff face and teetering dangerously on the edge of a brutal drop off. Tyran and I are one step away from plummeting to what would be a painful and crushing death, but it's as though the danger adds a whole other delicious element to this hunt.

My wolf and I have never done this before, but we move like these mountains have always been our home, like we know this rocky incline wouldn't dare to throw us off. With a powerful leap that has awe flashing through us, Tyran slams into the goat just as we pass a flat ridge in the side of the mountain.

He sinks his teeth into the flanks of our prey, keeping it from moving until I get on even ground with him and take over. I bite into its thick hide, anchoring it in place while Tyran moves up and expertly seizes its throat. He completely avoids any threats from the animal's horns, and we both stay fixed to our spots as the goat slowly suffocates. It isn't a massive animal, not like some of the other healthier beasts in the herd, but it's certainly enough for the two of us, and just as soon as the goat gives up, we tear into it, our wolves gorging themselves.

I take the back end while he starts on the stomach, and we eat, burying our faces in the blood of our kill, snarling and posturing whenever one of us gets too close to what we're gnawing on. I barely have time to be proud of this insanely dangerous feat, too focused on filling our empty belly and trying to ignore what's been left in the wake of my rabid rage.

Eating next to Tyran, sharing our kill, it relaxes my wolf. He's given her something to focus on, and all motions of ripping the goat apart makes her less willing to want to do that to her brown wolf. The other female scents still piss us off, but it feels less pressing with a full belly than it did back at the house.

Tyran was right, running it off helped the savage frenzy, but what's peeled away beneath each layer of temper and mania isn't much better.

Everything I said to him, everything he said to me...

By the time my wolf finishes eating, my chest is aching. It feels like a heavy rock's been dropped in my belly, weighing me down. Tyran's wolf is still eating, but we slink away further up the mountain so my wolf can clean up and clear the evidence of our hunt from her face and paws.

She licks her fur clean as the wind whips around us, the smell of our kill down below. When I ask for control over our body, she doesn't hesitate in giving it back. Bones crack and reform as fur is pulled back inside of me. The wind goes from teasing my fur to lifting the long strands of my hair and tangling them around my face and shoulders.

I stare out at the gorgeous scene in front of me, of rolling mountains as far as I can see. Larger peaks dwarf the one Tyran and I are on, and I can only imagine how high up we are. As I stand there, desolation seeps through me like venom, slowly poisoning our veins, and I move closer to the edge of the cliff, my heart hammering with each inch I take.

My bare toes look so stark against the rock, my body small against the plunge just a step away. I close my eyes against the wind and stare inward at the agony that's been left in the wake of my anger.

I'm rabid because of the constant fury sitting underneath the surface of who my wolf and I are. But we're always a snap away from fury, because of the anguish that sits at the center of it all.

The loss of my dad, my mom, the safe pack I grew up in. I stopped socializing in an effort to avoid Burke and to keep my mother from having to put herself between us all the time. I stopped going to pack hangouts so I could avoid attention or the possibility of being cornered, but it only seemed to make Burke seek me out even more. The harder he pushed, the more I drifted away. In the end, nothing helped me at all.

He killed my mom when he got tired of waiting. Tainted my Flux with his unwelcome bite. Tried to rape me, tormented me, and then threw me away like garbage when he didn't get what he wanted. But what I've realized is that it wasn't just him that broke us. It was my fault too.

It was all the anger I trapped inside. All the times I made myself small, thinking it kept me safer. The submitting to others who were unworthy of the action. Staying quiet when everything inside of me was storming. Holding in the tears instead of letting them flow. Yes, what was done to us shattered our defenses and affected the way we respond to perceived threats. But what I did to myself fractured us just as badly.

I can see it all so clearly, the hurt thrumming at the center of it all. The foundation for this fucked up connection with my wolf, the reason we exist on a hair trigger...it's the *pain,* not the rage, that stokes it all.

"What are you doing?" Tyran asks from somewhere behind me, his voice deep and commanding, but I don't miss the tiny hint of disquiet in it.

I tilt my head back as a cloud moves away from the sun, and light strokes softly against my cheek. It's cold up here, making goose bumps blanket my skin, but I feel like I'm beyond caring.

"Vicious, what are you doing?" Tyran demands again, more dominating this time as he moves closer to me.

Opening my eyes, I shoot out a hand that demands he stop where he is, and inch closer to the edge of the oblivion I'm staring at. "I'm broken," I admit, my words caught by the wind and thrown back at him as if he didn't already know. "I was before my wolf came down to join me, and then after that, they made sure to crush everything else." Pain and memories flash through my mind. "They took my family, my pack, my choice, my future...and I won't let you do the same," I tell him, my throat constricting on the words as grief and hurt spill from my lips.

"You think I'm like your previous alpha?" he asks, derision in his tone.

I turn to look at him over my shoulder, to stare into those tawny eyes and see what my words coax out of him. I expect hurt, maybe outrage, but all I see is stone cold rigor as though he wasn't born, he was forged, and no words or insults I fling his way will make him question what he knows about himself.

"I'm not your old alpha, Vicious," he tells me matter-of-factly, his eyes gleaming. "Like you said, I'm *worse*, right? A savage monster."

I turn around to fully take him in, feeling the drop at my back as I cross my arms in front of me as though it will shield me from his words, protect me from the effect his very presence has on me.

"What am I supposed to think?" I counter. "I don't know you. You just confirmed the rumors I've heard about your pack. You think I'm supposed to be *excited* for my circumstances?"

He laughs humorlessly, running a hand through his messy brown hair. "Right. So you're throwing yourself a pity party? Going to throw yourself off this mountain because life didn't give you what you wanted?" He moves forward, ignoring my demand for space, taking up all of mine as he stands like a chiseled king with corrosive words to disintegrate the rest of my defenses.

"News flash, everyone in Ruin Falls has shit that's happened to them. Maybe instead of listening to gossip and making assumptions, you should *ask* me."

I blink at him. "Ask you what?"

He holds up his arms. "You think you got it so bad being brought here to my pack, that I claimed you? So find out if you're right. You want to know about us, about me, so ask."

It's a challenge, but there's something underlying there, something that makes me fidget on my high horse.

"What...what's your full name?" I ask lamely.

"Tyran Bauer. Age thirty-two. I'm a fucking Leo. No siblings, I've been alpha for ten years, and no, I won't apologize for taking this pack from my old alpha and killing the bastard," he says without hesitation. "You?"

God, we've already fucked and knotted, argued at every turn, and now we're doing this weird *get to know you* talk? Everything is so ass backwards.

"Uhhh, Seneca Rain...and I'm a Pisces?"

He repeats my full name so quietly that I can't even hear it, but my eyes drop to watch his lips as they form the words, and my stomach tightens at just how sensual it seems.

"Tell me who you are, Seneca Rain. Tell me why you're so fucking angry."

My eyes flash with heat for a half-second at his question, but I manage to hold back my wolf. "My pack dumped me here, isn't that enough?"

Tyran tilts his head. "Maybe."

"What about you? Why are *you* angry?" I ask, turning it back around on him.

"Who said I was?" he retorts with a taunt. "Do monsters even feel anything?"

A sigh escapes me, and I run a hand down my face. These boiling emotions keep spitting over the edge, scalding me with every back and forth we hiss at one another. "Fine. No more gossip, no more assumptions. Tell it to me straight. Does Ruin Falls really kidnap shifters and kill their families?"

With twisted nerves, I wait for him to answer, hoping—

"Yes." He answers in an instant, without shame.

My grain of hope is crushed.

"*Why*? How could you do something so horrible?"

The psychopath rolls his eyes, as if I'm overreacting. I take a step back, forgetting for a second that the cliff is behind me, but Tyran lurches forward and grasps my arm, yanking me forward against his chest. "Let go!" I squirm, heart racing from my almost-plummet, while also dealing with the need to get away from him.

"Relax," he snaps, pulling me further away from the cliff before he lets me go. "We kidnap shifters who are being abused."

My body instantly stops fighting him, and I look up at his face. "What?"

He nods. "We keep eyes out on the local shifter packs. If there's an issue and their own packs won't deal with it, we go in. Get them out, bring them here, and then we kill the bastards responsible without mercy."

All I can do is stare at him as this information settles. *Would've been nice if someone had rescued me.*

"What about your pack members? Is it true they mostly live as wolves?"

"You want to judge them for embracing their shifter natures?" he asks with disdain dripping off his tone. "You, Miss Rabid Wolf, think you can look down on them for that?"

Shame and anger claw inside of me. "I'm trying to understand," I snap.

"You have any kin left, Seneca Rain?" he asks instead.

My eyes shutter. "No."

"Me either. My father died when I was young, and I barely remember him. My mother couldn't cope without him and lived the rest of her life as a wolf, because the connection with her animal's spirit was the only thing that kept her going," he says, and my stomach drops at the deadpan way he says it—as if he's learned to be numb to it. "Some pack members stay wolves because they've found peace in that side of their dual spirits. Some do it because they're too afraid, feel too weak in their human bodies. You going to judge them for that? Judge my mother?"

I shake my head. "No, I—"

"You want to stand there like you're so much better than Ruin Falls, even though you don't know shit? You want to walk around like the world should be apologizing to you?" He makes a face of disgust. "Maybe you should take a good look at yourself and stop behaving like you're ashamed of your shifter nature."

"I'm not ashamed!"

His brown eyes level with me. "Oh, really?" He waves a hand in front of my face. "Then why do you flinch every time I look you in the eye?"

My breath catches in my throat, stunned that he noticed something I hadn't even realized I was doing. "Everyone looks at me and sees this," I reply, pointing to my broken iris, the pale blue warring with the gleaming violet of my wolf. "Twin Rivers fucked me up. *I* fucked me up. And now Rabid is all I see."

"So what if you're rabid?" Tyran demands without a hint of sympathy. "You're a fucking *wolf*. Stop thinking like a human. Someone wronged you and your wolf spirit? Then get revenge. Don't walk around battered and bitter. Show them who they should have never fucked with, and be proud of that savage spirit inside of you. Fuck your old pack."

"Oh, like it's so easy to get revenge?" I challenge, my voice irate and yet dripping with desperation.

"You're a wolf, aren't you?" he counters as though that's all there is to it.

"I was *one* wolf," I shout, slamming a fist against my chest, my features bathed in vehemence, my soul drenched in pain. "I could barely stop my alpha from trying to rape me in the middle of my Flux. I couldn't stop him from drugging me and tossing me here to die. I couldn't stop him from murdering my mom or setting up my dad to be killed in the pack war," I seethe at him, voice cracking. "How do I get revenge when I don't even know how to fix myself?" I demand, wishing I knew the answer to that question with every fiber of my being.

"You don't need to be fixed!" Tyran shouts back at me, his eyes livid and his muscles taut with anger. "Accept what you are and use it to strengthen you. The transformation with your wolf is done, it's ancient history. Now change how you're looking at it!" he snarls in my face, his breath hot and his words leaving no space for excuses.

I'm so lost, but I can feel the map in what he's saying.

"*How*?" I ask, despising myself for the weakness spilling out of my mouth.

Tyran presses in against me, my pebbled nipples compressing against the heat of his skin. His body is hard against mine, as unforgiving and rigid as his words, and even though I don't want to admit it, there's a comfort to his presence.

"Stop fighting what you are," he tells me more quietly this time, his deep voice vibrating through me as though it's settling the pieces of myself that I haven't been able to put together. "Stop denying the truth of what you are." Fathomless brown eyes soak me in, hard, honest, reading me as though my story is one he could dive into over and over again. "You are claimed, Vicious."

I open my mouth to argue, but the flint in his eyes shuts me down.

"You participated in the claiming hunt. You might not have had it all spelled out for you, but if you'd listened to your wolf, you'd have known. We're instinctual, and your wolf chose me for a reason."

My face flames with the heated denial, but he doesn't give me room for argument, doesn't give me a moment to turn it around back on him.

"You hate Ruin Falls, when you don't even fucking *know* my pack. You're pissed off at your circumstances, wanting to pretend that you had no choice, but what's your plan when you reject everything that's being offered to you?"

"I'll fucking *leave,* that's my plan," I retort, but the outrage is hollow. Just a mask for the uncertainty I feel, while he shoves reality at me hard enough that I barely feel like I'm hanging on.

"And then what?"

My mouth opens and shuts, mind racing, though I'm unable to form words because...

"You have no idea, do you?" He shakes his head, brown hair mussed in the wind, shoulders bunched with tension. "You were going to just go out and be a lone shifter in some piece of shit town, with your wolf half-rabid and you without any kin or resources?

You'd have gone crazy within a year trying to pass as human, and probably killed some innocent in the process. All because you'd rather run away than face things and be something better than this moping, spoiled little shit you're acting like."

My entire body bristles. "I'm not accepting this claim. I hate you." The venom spat from my mouth doesn't even make him flinch. Instead, my own stomach writhes, because he's right.

He's fucking *right*.

"No, you don't. Who you really hate is yourself, and yeah, your old pack wronged you, but look around. You ever consider that *this* pack might be exactly what you need? All of this could anchor you. My claim could anchor you, if you'd just let it."

All I can do is gape at him because...no. I didn't consider that.

Is he right?

Tyran shakes his head, like he can't contain his disappointment for my own shortcomings.

"You have so much right at your fingertips if you'd just take it. You don't know how to get revenge? You just got fucking claimed by the most ruthless alpha on this continent. Do you think that was by chance? My wolf hasn't ever wanted to claim a female. No one was savage enough for him, until *you*." His eyes bore into me. "Use it."

My breath catches as he suddenly digs his fingers into the bite in my shoulder, pressing right over the punctures. Pain and pleasure shoot down from the marks, and like a dam breaking, my eyes well up with the tears I've been suppressing for far too long.

I can't breathe, can't move as he grounds me in his dominant presence. "My wolf and I saw something in your spirits last night. But we don't want *this*," he says, his arms gesturing to the cliff's edge we're both standing on. "We don't want the shame and the doubt. We don't want your insecure, pitying weakness." The growl in his voice grows rougher with each acidic word. "We *like* your rabid. We *need* it. I want all of what you are and could be if you'd just embrace the broken parts of you and use them to cut down everything that stands in your way. But if you can't do that, if you can't *be* that, then you're right, you're not claimed...because you're not the wolf I thought you were."

Twin streams of anguish fall from the lower lashes of my eyes, but Tyran doesn't soften, doesn't relent. His words storm at me, all vicious lightning and deafening thunder, too potent and powerful to ever be denied.

His hands drop, leaving my claiming marks pulsing with the echoes of loss. "Decide what the fuck you want and who you want to be, and then come find me...or go run away with that tail tucked between your legs. I won't stop you."

He turns and walks away, morphing back into his wolf and taking off down the mountain, leaving me behind in a trail of verbal devastation and heavy truths.

No softness, no sympathy, just face your shit and earn your place here...or leave.

That line drawn in the sand, everything he said, it all bursts from the pent-up emotions I've bottled. Like I've lit the end and thrown a Molotov cocktail, it explodes in a roar of anger from my mouth that echoes from the mountains and then floods from the tears finally broken free as I cry.

And cry.

And cry.

It's not a quiet cry. These tears aren't soft and slow. This is a rending of my soul to expel all the shit I've been harboring. I scream at the mountains, the sky, the rocks, my jagged edges, until my voice is lost and my throat is raw. I gnash and yank and pull as I purge myself of the wrongs, the taint, the loss. I spill my soul on the side of the mountain, desperately needing to get this all out so I can breathe again, so I can rise up and be able to look myself in the eye and be the wolf *and* the woman I can be.

My wolf howls alongside me as we rip our foundation of agony apart. The wind steals my cries, and slowly the tears ebb, the salty tracks of pain drying on my cheeks. Pebbles dig into my knees from where I'm kneeling at the edge of the bluff, but I don't feel the pain. All that's left is me and my wolf, our souls bared, our foundation destroyed, and two choices laid out in front of us: leave or stay.

The question is, which one will we choose?

FIFTEEN

Our heart thunders as we race down the mountain. Rocks break free under our paws, threatening to take us with them, but my wolf and I leap to safety just as they crash down the steep incline. We charge forward, the dangerous terrain under our paws not even a consideration as we run away. Away from the Ruin Falls pack and the wolves that comprise it. Away from the pain and confusion that have consumed us since we were dumped in this place.

The taste of freedom hangs from our lolling tongue as the rabid wolf and I push harder to break away from the last of the chains holding us back. We traverse the dangerous, rocky surface of the mountain, our steps sure and our mind focused on one thing.

Redemption.

Tyran's words ricochet in my head, pinballing around, hitting their mark over and over again. Fear fills our nose as we run, spurring us on and assuring my wolf and me that we're making the right choice. We can do this. We can be everything Tyran said. Not bitter, not ashamed, but strong and proud of what we are. Capable of getting our retribution.

The beast of a mountain goat we're hunting is much bigger than the one Tyran and I caught. It tries to throw us off his trail by moving closer to a wall of loose and hazardous rocks. The path looks like it recently suffered from a rockslide, but my wolf and I can smell the panic that plumes off the frantic animal as it tries to escape, and we will not be deterred.

We've got this. This onyx-horned beast is ours.

The huge male goat slips partially down the incline before it catches its footing again, and luckily, it aims to run further down the mountain instead of up. We're getting closer and closer to the treeline, and the wolf and I can practically taste this kill on our fangs already. We know it's going to be harder to bring down this healthy male than it was to defeat the wounded older goat that Tyran and I hunted, especially alone. We need to avoid the horns and the powerful hooves, but if we can get that neck, this fucker doesn't stand a chance.

My wolf and I spot the perfect in and shove all the energy we have into our legs and paws as we pick up our pace. We aim for a small shelf and leap off of it as though any second we'll sprout wings and fly. Like we knew it would, the lip of the ledge gives us the advantage, and our huge dark gray body aims for the goat's back. Just as we close in, the massive male goat turns and catches us in the chest.

It headbutts us so hard it feels as though we were just clotheslined by a runaway train. We yelp in pain as we go slamming into the mountain behind us. The rocks and shale are unforgiving, and the goat is aiming his horns right for our face as it charges us. My wolf barely has time to scramble up and twist just enough to take the blow on our shoulder. Thankfully, the goat's head is too high, and the point of his horns don't pierce us. He's only able to slam the shaft of his weapons into us, but it's the most painful *dead arm* we've ever experienced.

Our leg goes numb, and we know if we don't stop another hit, our prey's about to take us out. It'll either crush too many bones or knock us off the mountain, and my wolf and I refuse to go out like that. The goat tries to slam into us again, but this time, my wolf and I are ready. We dodge the hit at the last minute and aim a bite at the side of its neck. With all of our might, ignoring the pain now shooting through our battered wolf form, we use our body weight to fling this massive bastard to the side.

We both tumble down the mountain a few times, but my wolf keeps her teeth clenched tightly in the goat's hide as we skid to a stop. The goat is in shock, but we waste no time getting a better hold of our prey's neck. We clamp down on the front of its throat just under its jaws and wait patiently as the mountain goat's struggle starts to wane until it's lifeless on the ground.

My wolf tips her head back and howls in victory, my own chest leaping with the accomplishment. We did it. *We fucking did it!*

We may have only just been joined for a few days and never hunted alone before, but we managed to work together and take down this animal high up on the dangerous cliffs and bluffs of this mountain, with no one to help us but ourselves. It might not seem like a lot, but it proved that we *can* hone our focus, we can use that edge of rabid need to work toward a controlled purpose.

Once we catch our breath, our exerted body cooled by the chilling mountain air, we look down at the impressive kill at our feet. Then, we clamp our jaw down around its neck, and we start to drag the big fucker.

Down the steep mountainside. Past craggy cliff sides and sliding rocks. It's not pretty, but we lug the dead animal behind us like it's all the baggage we're carrying, refusing to give up beneath its staggering weight.

We can do this.

I have the strength to stop complaining and start moving forward, heavy circumstances and all. I have the ability to turn this around. It's a different life than I would've planned, but one my wolf and I can thrive in if we seize it.

Down the mountain we go, nearly falling more times than we'd like to keep track of, until we finally make it to flat ground again. But that's almost harder. Now we have to haul our burden without gravity aiding us, guided only by our sheer determination and need to fix what we can. Every strenuous pull and struggled inch is a living, breathing metaphor, and we need to succeed physically so that we can cross that line mentally.

My wolf is panting, legs shaking, teeth feeling like they're ready to fall out by the time we stop. We drag the mountain goat into the clearing of Ruin Falls pack land, past shifters who stop in their tracks and turn curiously to watch us. We don't stagger beneath the weight of their stares or the animal in our maw. Despite how much our body aches with exhaustion, we don't collapse.

Instead, with our head held high, we drag our offering all the way to the alpha house, where Tyran is standing stock still. Shirt off, pants slung low on his hips, muscled arms crossed in front of his chest. He's wearing a face that's stony and unmoved, though there's a gleam in his eye.

We drop the kill right at his feet and look up at him, unable to hold in our panting, not caring that our fur is covered in dirt and pebbles, teeth soaked in goat's blood from our exertions.

Dusk's descent has curled all around us, hugging the land with gray twilight as a fog threatens to roll in from the hills. I've been gone for hours, practically battered the poor goat's body beyond immediate recognition with the drag, but when we look into Tyran's eyes, it's with the pride of one and a half violet irises...and a jagged glacial blue dissecting the eye on the right.

I feel the rest of the pack watching this exchange as we stand there before him, waiting to see what he'll do, both of us looking out through our eyes at the male my wolf chose.

After what feels like an hour of agonizing wait, Tyran's lips curl into a smile. "*There's* the wolf I claimed."

Pride lifts our chest, and then my wolf settles down while my spirit rises up. I shift, with the taste of mountain goat still in my mouth and its blood caking my chin and chest. Crimson war paint to signal the battle that was fought and won over the sharp rocks of a steep mountain, all to save the jagged shards of my soul.

His deep brown eyes drag over my nudity with heat sparking in their depths. I know I look a mess with scratches, mud stains, and wind-blown hair, but he says, "Savage looks sexy on you, Vicious."

I stomp down on the tentative smile that wants to creep across my face. I don't want him to see just yet what his words, his approval, means to me. I'm not quite ready to hand over those powerful reins just yet. There are things to work out before we're there.

He steps forward, his intense brown eyes drinking me down, but then he smacks the back of my ass *hard*. I hold back the yelp of pain—barely. His smirk widens as he soothes the spot while pushing me toward the deck stairs.

"That hurt, asshole."

"You're lucky it was just one. Every time I turn around, you're naked in front of the whole fucking pack," he counters before leading me to the front door. "Now go get your red ass cleaned up and dressed—in clothes that the other females have *made* but not worn—and then come back. It's nearly time for the reckoning."

He practically shoves me into the house, his large body guarding my back and keeping his pack's eyes off my flesh. The door closes hard behind me, and when I look up and see that I'm alone, I finally release the smile I feel twinkling in my soul. My wolf wags her tail and we both saunter up the stairs.

We did it.

I rub my ass cheek as I head for the bathroom, all kinds of intriguing thoughts filtering through a dirty mind that's once again filled with Tyran's scent. My wolf thinks he's worthy, and although I'm not disagreeing with her instincts or assessment, I think it's time to see what *I* think about this male without the blindfold of anger. I want to find out just how *worthy* he can be.

I LOOK IN THE MIRROR and sigh. He *has* to be doing this on purpose. I don't know Tyran well, but I feel it's safe to say that he has a thing for pirate pilgrims. I adjust the neckline of the cream-colored shirt I'm wearing to try and make it fit normal, but then it just falls off both my shoulders.

With a huff, I pull it back over so only one half of my chest, upper arm, and shoulder is exposed. I leave the two ties at the neck open because putting them in a bow just makes everything look worse. That probably has something to do with the fact that the bow sits eye level with my boobs like it's some game show model just asking people to *check out these prizes*.

Once again, I embrace the Musketeer vibe and tuck the front of the big shirt into suede pants that just so happen to be the exact color of Tyran's wolf—like that's a coincidence. My gaze lands on the door that leads to his room. I haven't had to set foot in it yet, since these clothes were thankfully piled on the bathroom counter.

I'm feeling less volatile about the alpha's past now. Even though I haven't finished the claim by biting him back, he bit *us*, and as far as my wolf is concerned, that makes him ours.

Rationally, I know that Tyran had a sex life before I entered the picture—I did too—so I'm blaming that freak out on the bites both of my shoulders now carry. Newly claimed wolves have done worse things, so I'm giving myself a pass on this one. Still, I have no intention of ever setting foot in that bedroom again. Guess I'll find out how he feels about that soon.

Running my fingers through my hair, I ignore the fact that my top is still a little too see-through, and give myself a small approving nod before dropping my game face in place. It's time to go meet the Ruin Falls pack, and that means I need to radiate nothing but strength and dominance. I can't let myself be thrown by anything that happens tonight. I'm mentally preparing for the worst based on this pack's heinous reputation, but also trying to go into this with an open mind, despite the rumors.

If I want a place here, it's time to show these wolves that I'm worthy of it, no matter what gets tossed my way. Because the truth is, I don't want to live as a lone wolf with humans. Now that I have my other half, I know I could never fit in without a pack, that I'd go just as crazy as Tyran said I would. So I want this to work. For my wolf *and* for myself.

I inhale evenly and turn to leave the bathroom, with my shoulders back and head held high. My bare feet are silent on the stairs as I make my way down. The large house is completely empty, and I see through the large windows that dusk and night are fighting for control over the sky. Speckles of stars watch the battle, twinkling their cheers as night gains the upper hand more and more with each passing minute.

I open the door, expecting to find Ruin Falls all gathered together, but the grounds are empty, and only the chirp of crickets greets me as I step out into the cool kiss of twilight. Before I've made it three steps across the raised deck, I suddenly smell a wolf creeping up behind me. With a snarl, I spin around, ready to fight off whoever is sneaking up on my back.

The male holds his hands up placatingly. I immediately recognize the blond with wavy hair just past his shoulders and deep brown eyes. He was the one I initially thought was this pack's alpha as he stood with Tyran the first time I saw him.

He immediately lifts his chin as I take him in, tilting his head to the side to offer me his neck in a show of respect and submission. My eyes widen at the gesture of the stranger, and we both just stand there for a moment, me staring in surprise, and him waiting to see if I'll accept his action and calm the fuck down.

I straighten up, soothing my wolf and allowing her to settle in my chest as I push away the need to shift, to destroy and defend ourselves.

"I'm sorry, Luna. I didn't mean to startle you. I was coming to get you to take you to Tyran," he explains, and I try not to let my mouth drop open at the title of respect we both know I haven't earned yet.

"I'm not your luna," I correct, ignoring the goose bumps that crawled up my arms when he used the term.

"Yet," he corrects, his gaze assessing and certain.

Feeling awkward, I shake my head, but he simply steps around me and gestures for me to follow. Fires burn low in the scattered pits spread out in front of the houses, and with no idea how to respond to this wolf's confidence in me, I follow him.

"What's your name?" I ask as we approach the treeline that borders the houses.

"Britton. I'm Tyran's Second, Luna," he informs me, and I try really hard not to flick him in the back of the head for once again using a title that I have no claim to.

"Just call me Seneca, please," I encourage, and he gives me a half smile. His eyes, however, look a little wary.

Did Tyran tell him he can't use my name or something? Or maybe he's just worried I'm going to lose my shit like he witnessed earlier.

"How long have you been Second in the Ruin Falls pack?"

"Ten years."

Burke constantly pitted his betas against each other in the hierarchy fights, so the fact that Britton has been Tyran's Second for so long just reminds me how differently this pack is run.

"So that means that you've been Second since Tyran took over as alpha."

He nods, his sun-darkened skin dimming from the shadows of the falling night. "It was his first order. Aside from slaughtering the old loyalists of our former alpha."

My eyes widen at how easily he says that, as if he's talking about throwing away old fruit instead of the killing of his old pack members.

"I know what you're thinking," he says, looking over at me as we walk deeper into the woods, the last of daylight disappearing beneath the canopy. "But this pack...there was a sickness in it. Tyran had to cut away all the rotten parts. I helped him, and we're all better for it."

I'm not sure if I want specifics, but if I'm going to truly stay here, I need to know. "What do you mean exactly?"

"When you have a pack as isolated as ours, it's easy for the crazy to spread. Our alpha became...deranged. Thought he was a god sent down from the moon, meant to cleanse the land." Britton makes a disgusted noise in the back of his throat as he holds back a branch for me to pass in front of. "He was constantly performing crazy ass rituals, fear mongering, spreading these delusions, and getting others in the pack to follow him. But when he started the sacrifices, that's when Tyran knew he had to be stopped."

"Shit," I breathe, shaking my head. "I had no idea."

"Yeah, everyone knows our pack is ruthless enough to kill our own members, but they don't bother to understand *why*. Tyran was completely justified."

Hearing him talk just makes my mind drift to Twin Rivers, to the stark differences between Tyran and Burke. Maybe it's because Britton offered up this information to me, that I feel like repaying the favor, because I say, "The alpha who dumped me here, he killed our prior alpha and a lot of good shifters—including my dad—just because he could. He definitely wasn't doing anything honorable."

Britton grunts. "Yeah, I've heard of that shithead."

I step around a rock, my slightly too big boots squishing as my foot lands in a damp spot. "He killed my mom too. I can't prove it, but...I just know."

A whistle streams through his teeth. "What are you going to do about it, Luna?"

No, *I'm sorry for your loss*. No weird pat on my shoulder. Instead, this shifter just lays it out, and his question repeats in my head. What *am* I going to do about it?

"I'm not sure yet."

He nods, and I notice that the quiet forest is saturated with noises coming from up ahead—voices compounded together with an underlying, steady hum of something else I can't quite identify. "Well, when you figure it out, let me know. I'll watch your back."

His words are so simple, so easily offered with no strings attached that I'm taken aback for a moment. He doesn't even know me, but his blind and complete support calls to something deep in my soul. All at once, the word *pack* lights up in my mind and warms my heart. My throat grows tight with appreciation, and I send the surprising male a small smile. "Thank you," I tell him simply, unable to really communicate what his words mean to me.

We fall quiet the rest of the way, and I can't help but study this unusually loyal male and wonder how much more of this pack is made up of shifters just like him.

I'm figuring out that Ruin Falls is full of surprises.

Night has well and truly fallen when we make it to the gathering. It's not some open fighting field like I expect, though, but the noise is explained the moment I see the massive waterfall crashing down from the cliffside above. It's at least a hundred feet high, with curtains of white crashing into the water below. The river itself isn't very deep—made obvious by Warrik and Reap currently standing in it calf-high, fur covering their legs to insulate from the cold. But what's dangerous is how strong and fast that current looks, as if it would sweep you away the moment you lost your footing.

The rest of the pack is gathered on both sides of the river, and directly to the left, a dawning moon can be seen peeking over the horizon. There are no fires, no flashlights. Just the light of the moon and the churning water, and two shifters waiting in the current.

"This way, Luna." Britton cuts across the space, bringing me past the watchful eyes of the pack.

I set my spine straight and tall, keeping my head raised up with a stoic expression on my face. I have no idea what I'm walking into, but the significance of the night is apparent.

He leads me straight past the gathered shifters this side of the river, where a single tree stump sits. I look over at Britton for confirmation, and he nods silently. The moment I take a seat, everyone's attention seems to settle on me, each pair of eyes lying on me like a brick. There's obviously some importance to me sitting here, because I don't think they're staring just because of my off-the-shoulder Musketeer shirt.

Movement across the river draws my eyes, and I watch as the pack steps aside and Tyran appears with two other betas in tow.

Shirt off, hem of his pants wet and muddy, brown hair disheveled, and muscles tense, he looks untamed and gritty and sexy as hell. I press my thighs together, suddenly glad I'm sitting, even if everyone is standing up. The alpha power roiling off of him seems magnified beneath the first light of the moon and has more than just my wolf perking up.

His eyes collide with mine, and he gives a single obvious nod of his head. A gesture—just like the one Britton gave me. I may not know the ins and outs of the pack, but I know a sign of respect when I see one, and the alpha just recognized me in a moment of honor in front of everyone.

It takes a lot not to fidget on the tree stump, but I manage to dip my head back at him, hoping that it's the right thing to do. He wades into the river, stopping when he reaches the middle, and the glint in his eye I get before he turns to address the rest of the pack allows me to let out a slow breath of relief.

At least I didn't fuck that up.

"Ruin Falls..." he shouts out, his voice commanding, deep, and hypnotic. "Why are we here?" His arms are loose at his side, the question cutting, lacking all fanfare and showmanship. I can tell as I watch him that what he's doing is genuinely about the pack and has nothing to do with needing to defend *his* place in it. Tyran isn't punishing some silly slight. He's not flexing against subordinates to keep a stranglehold on his position or establishing dominance for dominance's sake. Whatever is about to happen is vital and important.

"Betrayal," a male from the gathering crowd yells out.

"Selfishness," someone else declares.

"Trust," a female shouts, and Tyran's tawny gaze jumps to her.

"Trust," he agrees, and Warrik shifts his weight as though that word physically just fell from the sky and pressed down against his shoulders. "Trust and loyalty are the very pillars of our foundation here. If we don't have that, what do we have?"

Murmurs of agreement sound off all around me as the gathering wolves all nod their heads and spill affirmations from their mouths.

There's a heavy tension in the air as Tyran pulls his eyes away from his pack and fixes his stare on Warrik. "You endangered the pack, yourself, and an untested wolf, all because you wanted a shot at claiming something before anyone else could," he accuses.

Warrik growls quietly. "Seems that worked out well for you." His eyes never stray from the fast current of the water he's standing in.

Angry growls rumble through the gathered pack, a thick blanket of unease spreading out all around us with the beta's impertinence. I expect Tyran's body to tighten against the disrespect and for his anger to rise to the surface. I expect Warrik's punishment to turn from bad to worse. But when I look over at the Ruin Falls alpha, all I see is hard disappointment. Warrik is clearly showing that he isn't who Tyran thought he was, and I can practically feel the resignation settling in him as he stares icelike at the beta.

"To me, Beta," Tyran commands, motioning for Warrik to move closer, leaving no room in his tone or body language for argument.

Warrik huffs out a breath and then moves closer to the center of the river where his alpha is standing. There's no explanation of what's going to happen, no declaration of rules, or lecture from the alpha to one of his pack members. Quietly, dangerously, they both start to circle one another, studying, assessing, and cataloging weaknesses.

Everything around us is quiet. It's as though the birds and the insects are watching each step, each twitch of a muscle, as keenly as the rest of us are. The stunning and powerful waterfall at my back is the only thing that dares roar its encouragement for the battle that's about to take place in its waters.

Warrik suddenly charges Tyran, wolf claws extended and intent on doing damage. I hold my breath, every inch of my body tight with worry and the need to keep Tyran from getting hurt. The rabid beast in me starts to rise to the surface, and before I can stop it, a menacing growl vibrates through my body.

People surrounding me are quick to take a step away, and as much as I agree with my wolf's displeasure over what's happening, I tamp down on her and keep my body locked in place.

Warrik swipes at his alpha, and then quicker than my eyes could track if I didn't have my wolf, Tyran reaches out, wraps his large hand around his beta's throat, and lifts him into the air. The snarl he lets out as he brings Warrik's face closer makes my blood run cold. The moon's light spills over everything, dipping the scene before me in a monochromatic hue that makes everything feel more brutal and vicious. Whimpers escape the mouths of the watching pack, and I see several of them lift their chins to expose their necks as though they're submitting from the sidelines, happy to bend a knee or show their alpha their belly from just the sound of his wrath alone.

Pride wells in my chest, and I watch raptly as Tyran drops Warrik's flailing body into the water and then shoves him under the swift rapids. Warrik fights, digging his claws into Tyran's arms as he kicks and struggles to break the hold around his throat.

Tyran yanks him up, allowing Warrik to pull in a desperate breath of air. The beta's face is red, furious, his blond hair plastered against his skin. But Tyran holds him easily, his superior strength no match for Warrik.

"The only way you're getting out of this is if you *trust*, just like you always should have," Tyran tells him, and then quick as a striking whip, he shoves Warrik back under the water.

Warrik battles what's being done to him with every ounce of strength he has. Gouges in Tyran's arms baptize the river with his blood. But Warrik's claws weaken, his hold on the alpha's arm loosening and his splashing kicks in the water less powerful. Just when I think Tyran is going to finish the beta, he pulls him out again. Warrik coughs and hacks, furiously trying to dispel the water in his lungs.

"What will it be?" Tyran demands, his voice even and lethal, every inch of him radiating dominance and raw, pure power.

The beta spits in his face, and with lips pressed together, Tyran shoves Warrik back under the current. The struggle, the fight, the battle for breath is renewed and becomes even more vicious than before. The Ruin Falls alpha stands there, a strand of brown hair plastered to his forehead, holding the betraying beta under the water as though it's nothing. His muscles are rigid from effort, but his face is calm, his eyes fixed on the image of Warrik just under the surface.

The pack continues to watch with anxious intensity, while Reap stands off to the side, face grim and hands trembling at his sides. Above us, the moon seems to watch, her light caught on the torrent of the waterfall as it feeds into the river's merciless hold.

The splashes around the two males get smaller. Warrik's movements slow, becoming jerkier and less purposeful. There's a part of me that feels bad that the beta is enduring this punishment because of me, but just as quickly as that feeling surfaces, another part of me shoves it away.

There's no room in wolf life for empathy when it comes to weakness.

What Warrik did *was* weak. He set me up, tried to use trickery to take me for himself. The result is what it is, but if this beta was willing to do that to me, to break the rules all because he wanted something, what else is he willing to do? Who else would he have betrayed in order to take what he wanted? Like he so disrespectfully pointed out, Warrik's actions may have worked out for Tyran—and admittedly even me—but the root of *why* he did what he did is the real issue here.

I watch with the hard eyes of a dominant female who understands that weakness and cowardice, selfishness and dishonorable intentions, those things can become a plague in a pack. I saw the sickness fester within Twin Rivers, and I understand the need to cut it out like a cancer. I wish someone had stopped Burke—challenged him for his cowardly and selfish acts.

With each passing second, Warrik's movements grow more sluggish. Tyran gives him two more chances to submit, to trust and stop fighting against his alpha, but he refuses. He fights to the end, until his arms and legs are floating unmoving in the current. Until air bubbles stop breaching the surface of the water where his face is submerged. Tyran holds him there for a minute more and then he releases the male and rises to his feet. The greedy grip of the river rapids yanks the body away, and I watch as the beta's lifeless form is carried downriver as though the water itself is banishing him from the pack.

SIXTEEN

Everyone watches his body disappear down the current, the collection of faces looking grim but solidified. Water drips down Tyran's robust frame, outlining the slopes of his muscles as he stands there, breathing evenly. The wildness in his eyes calls to me in a profound and visceral way, and I'm unable to look anywhere else. I just watched him kill someone. I shouldn't be thinking about licking the drops of water from his body. Or what it would feel like to sink to my knees in front of him in that river and taste him root to tip. But heat crawls up the inside of my thighs as I stare at the virile force in front of me, and I'm not even sorry for it.

"Reap," Tyran calls out, and the delta immediately moves closer, despite knowing what's going to happen to him.

Tyran begins to circle him just like he did Warrik, but a flicker of surprise moves through me when Reap gives the alpha his back, refusing to stalk Tyran. At first, I think the delta is giving up, that he's accepting his punishment and refusing to make it harder for Tyran to do what he's about to do. But as I watch Tyran seize him by the neck and repeat what he just did to Warrik, I note that Reap's reaction is totally different.

My wolf wants to snarl at the delta to fight, to value his life enough to battle for it, but Tyran's words are still floating in the air, and I'm trying to wrap them around what I'm seeing.

This is about trust.

I stare at the cogent alpha as he holds the shifter under the water, and it hits me. Reap isn't attacking or struggling because he's not wolf enough, but because he's submitting. He's showing his alpha that he can do what he wants, that he can punish Reap however he sees fit. Whatever Tyran decides to do, Reap will take it. He won't fight, he won't object, he'll give in...because Reap's proving that he *trusts* him.

The lesson Tyran is teaching—not only Reap, but the entire pack—is *trust me, and I'll take care of you. Trust each other, and nothing will dare come for us.*

Emotion swells in my heart as the harsh beauty of it resonates in me. I assumed the reckoning would be some sort of fight, but it's a lesson—a test.

And Warrik failed.

My heart pounds as I watch Tyran continue to hold a capitulated Reap, my entire body stiff with anxiety. Air bubbles slip out of the water, but still, Tyran holds him. Still, Reap doesn't struggle.

He's running out of air...

My nails dig into the wood of the stump, eyes skimming over the pack as they watch just as anxiously.

Finally, Tyran pulls Reap out of the water, and my own relieved breath seems to be yanked out with him. The alpha holds him up, supporting him while he coughs and gasps, working to fill his lungs with precious oxygen.

Tyran's mighty body and presence is like a wall against the brutal current. My chest constricts as I look at the sopping wet delta who's shaking all over, but I feel nothing but respect for him. I can imagine how horribly difficult that must've been, to allow himself to be held under. It goes against every instinct to simply give in like that, but he did it. He proved his trust and submission to his alpha.

With a hand on his shoulder, Tyran moves in and presses his forehead against Reap's. The two of them stand like that for a long moment, as a potent, silent message is communicated back and forth between them. Then, Tyran claps him on the shoulder and helps Reap cross the river, guiding him back up the craggy bank and into the welcome grasp of the rest of the pack. One by one, I watch as the others press their forehead against Reap's and have their own moment with him. It's a powerful and impactful thing to watch, and it begins to alter what I thought about these people.

"If we don't have trust and loyalty, we have nothing," Tyran announces again, but this time as the words leave his mouth, he's staring at me.

His gaze is intense, but I shove everything I'm feeling about what just happened into my expression—respect, admiration, need. I let him see it as I lock eyes with him, refusing to balk or question the inferno rushing through me. Heat swells in his gorgeous brown gaze, and then suddenly, he's stalking toward me.

All at once, I'm prey, and for the first time in my life, I *want* to be.

Tyran doesn't slow as he approaches, and then with one fluid movement, he pulls me from the tree stump and starts rubbing cold water all over me with his soaking wet limbs. I squeal while he does his best to use me as a towel. He chuckles as I squirm and try to get away from him, and the rumbling sound dives straight between my thighs, calling up my desire.

"Go rub against a bush," I gripe, edging around so I can put the tree stump between us.

"That was my plan exactly," he replies with a smirk.

I roll my eyes even as my toes curl. "I mean go dry yourself off on an *actual* plant. Poison ivy preferably."

Another low laugh comes out of his chest, and I note with some trepidation that the entire pack is now looking at us.

"Umm... Just kidding," I say more loudly, throwing in a friendly wave for good measure, just in case any of them think I'm going to come at their alpha with some rash-inducing plants.

Actually, I can't rule out the possibility for the future.

"They're not watching you because of your bad joke," he tells me.

My eyes fly up to his. "It wasn't a bad joke," I defend, and then I stiffen when his words settle. "Wait, why *are* they watching me then?"

"Their alpha claimed a female. You're not fully our luna until that claiming has gone both ways," he says pointedly. "Until then, they'll be watching."

"Well, that's not fucking ominous," I hiss out between clenched teeth, trying to keep my voice down.

He shrugs. "You're an untested, unfamiliar wolf that their alpha suddenly claimed. They'll tolerate your presence out of respect for me and the fact that my wolf and I found you worthy, that I trust you're the wolf for me. But you still have to prove yourself to the pack."

"By biting you," I reply.

"By biting me," he repeats with a nod. "Once you do that, you'll be able to assimilate yourself into the pack and prove that you can look out for them like I do."

I open my mouth to tell him that I *do* want to be here, and that I want to find my footing with Ruin Falls. But when he says it like that, he reminds me that I wouldn't just be accepting a claim. I'd also be accepting responsibility over an entire pack.

Geez, no pressure.

We stare at each other, his brown eyes expectant, ready and waiting for me to give in to what he's saying, but something on the cusp of my own worries holds me back. His gaze shutters at the uncertainty that's written all over my face, and anger flashes through his irises.

"I see."

Guilt and frustration rush through me, crawling up my neck and pressing into my cheeks until it's coloring my skin in a cruel mimicry of embarrassment. Many of the pack turn to leave, their offered backs making it clear what they think about my hesitation to claim their alpha. Tyran steps back from me, and I narrow my eyes at his retreat.

Why does it have to be all or nothing? Why do I have to choose so fast?

"Don't do that," I call to Tyran as he moves to leave. "My hesitation isn't rejection. I'm just..." With an aggravated sigh, I run my hand through my long hair, fingers getting caught in the windblown tangles. "I just need more time. You're asking for too much too soon."

The muscle in his jaw jumps as he clenches his teeth, and all previous heat and playfulness is gone. In its place is the hardened alpha I've heard countless stories about. He looks away from me, his cold eyes watching the rapids of the river, and I suddenly wonder if it's *my* face he wants to hold beneath that water.

Would I trust him enough not to fight?

The question sours everything, only made more bitter when Tyran turns and stalks away from me without another word. My stomach churns like the water behind me, the falls looking eerily similar to the white rabid froth that I've tasted in my own mouth. I try to swallow down the discomfiture and resentment on my tongue as Tyran and the pack abandon me to be alone with the moonlit river.

I know they're loyal to him, but they take his side without even trying to understand mine. Alpha or not, Tyran is being unreasonable. I've only just met him. He can't expect me to decide that fast, to just...

You're a fucking wolf. Stop acting like a human.

His previous words ring in my mind, making it clear exactly what his frustration is with my hesitation. But the thing is, I'm not *just* a fucking wolf, none of us are, so why does that seem to be such a bad thing here?

I get that my wolf likes him, but what about *me*?

For the last three years, I've done everything possible to avoid being forced into a claim, and now here I am being pressured into another one. These alphas act like it's all no big deal, but it *is*.

With an irritated huff, I take one last look at the river and the falls and then start to walk back. I pick my way through the shadows of the tall trees, stewing on what just happened. The reality is that we don't even know each other. Our wolves like the other's smell, and he fucks like a god. That's a *yay* for my vagina, but not exactly a solid foundation for a mate-for-life situation. I don't care what he says about trusting my instincts, because I'm scared of what will happen if I choose wrong.

I take my time as I stomp through the underbrush, scraping a clawed hand against the trees as I go and trying to work through my thoughts. Annoyance and outrage settle in my limbs because these fucking *trees* know more about this guy than I do. His scent covers them, as though he personally marks each one every morning.

I tip my head back and take in the canopy of pine needles and leaves. "Do you know if Tyran is going to treat me right?" I ask, as though the vegetation will lean over and whisper all their secrets. "Will he respect me, hear what I have to say, care about my opinions?" Unsurprisingly, the foliage doesn't answer. "Yeah, that's what I thought," I grumble, just as peals of pup laughter and hearty conversations reach me from where the pack is gathered around their fires.

Stopping at the treeline, I stand there, painfully aware that I'm always on the outside looking in. The pack mingles, laughing and teasing, eating and bonding, and something like longing fills my chest. My irritable gaze finds Tyran easily, his large, hard body moving from one group to another. He checks on them, pausing to talk or tease or chuckle. His eyes are bright and comforting, his smile jovial and warm. Gone is the icy castigation that was just aimed at me. I survey him as he brushes hair from his face with a hand and chortles deeply at something another male says.

As I watch, he saunters over to a fire that has a few cuddling couples surrounding it. I study them and huff incredulously; I don't even know if the alpha is a cuddler, since he's always leaving. Yet I'm expected to bite the impatient bastard just because he bit me first.

Please, I snort.

A figure stands and offers him their seat, and I realize it's a female when the light of the flickering flames catches her profile just right. Tyran sits, a wide smile on his face, and then my mouth drops open with utter shock when the female moves to sit in his lap...*and he allows her to.*

Red slams down over my vision, and rage curdles my blood as

Tyran's hands go to the female's waist. She wraps an arm around the back of his shoulders, and the group collectively laughs about something. But from the outskirts of their camp, all I can see is anger, all I can taste is the salty call for blood, the demand for death skittering up my spine as I fight to keep my fur and fangs inside.

Hurt and disrespect rocket through me like bombs, and before I even know that I've taken a step in their direction, I'm suddenly standing outside of the group, staring at Tyran and Presley like I'm going to destroy them. My wolf is snarling inside my chest, demanding that I take what's mine, but I shut that all down.

A feral, spine tingling growl crawls up my throat and spills from my lips like oil from a wrecked tanker, and all the laughter, teasing, and friendly exchanges drift away. The happy sounds die, my presence serving as an off switch.

Tyran's eyes narrow on mine, and there's something in them that I'm too pissed to read. But he does nothing. Just sits there with a bitch in his lap, after all the bullshit he just spewed at the reckoning, after everything he just made me believe.

"Trust and loyalty, huh?" I snarl, raking my gaze over the two of them like they're the piss puddle a scared dog leaves behind when it smells our kind. "And here I was thinking those words actually meant something to you and your people. Good to know they're just your nicknames for this bitch's tits," I snap, turning my glare to Presley, who bristles at my words.

"What's the problem, Vicious?" Tyran asks with faux confusion. "You're not interested in claiming me, right?"

Presley leans back against his chest, and everything inside of me howls and rages. "Why are you pushing so fucking hard?" I snap at him, my yell carrying through the clearing and silencing all conversation. "I asked for time, not for you to act like a little bitch and start playing games," I seethe.

"Who's playing?" he growls back, and it's all I can do not to scream.

I'm seconds away from losing it and attacking anything and everything around me. I hate that I feel this way, and worse, I hate that it's over some prick who clearly isn't worth my time. I rake my eyes over Tyran, disgust and ire etched on my face. He looks back at me just as angry.

"If you would just listen to your wolf..." he starts, but I'm not going to sit through one more useless lecture from this asshole.

"Oh, fuck you and your *the wolf is always right* bullshit."

I swear the pack sucks in a shocked breath of air, and I want to turn and glare at them all.

Tyran's eyes burn as he takes me in. "I feel sorry for your beast," he snaps at me, and his words feel like a dagger to the chest. "I can't even imagine how many years she's suffered from you second-guessing her all the time," he accuses.

Pain slices through me, and I laugh hollowly at how ridiculous he is.

Some fucking mate.

How the hell did I think, even for a second, that this pack would be right for me?

"Years?" I taunt. "You're such an idiot, *Alpha*. You haven't listened to a damn thing I've told you. What day is it?" I snap.

"Friday," Tyran answers just as brusquely.

My head shakes as I let out a derisive laugh. "My Flux was *four* days ago, asshole. But tell me more about how I should listen to my wolf all the time. A wolf whose chances were fucked from the get-go. You want me to listen to my instincts, Tyran? Should I start ripping your pack apart and piss on their dismembered bodies before rolling around in their blood? Because *that's* what my rabid wolf wants me to do right now!"

A shiver runs through me as I work to stifle my shift, and a collective gasp sounds off around the pack as tension fills the air like cloying, oppressive humidity. The blood drains from Tyran's face, and he stares at me completely stunned.

"*What*?" he demands, standing up and shoving Presley to the ground.

She lands hard on her ass and grumbles in protest. "Hey!"

My eyes snap to her. "I will rip off your fucking arms and beat the shit out of you with them if I hear another peep out of you," I seethe at her, but Tyran steps in the way, cutting off my line of sight and snapping my fury onto him.

"Your Flux was four days ago?" Tyran asks hollowly, once again proving that the douche needs a damn hearing aid.

"You're pathetic. You want to be my mate, but you don't hear shit I have to say!" I bark at him. "Yes, four days ago, I got my wolf. Do I need to go back through what else I got that day?" I hold up my fingers and start ticking them off. "I got attacked, drugged, beaten, starved, and dropped off on your land, where I was locked up, then let loose, all to be claimed by a bastard alpha who's clearly just as unworthy of the title as the rest of them."

I grab my too big shirt and whip it off, my pants coming next. *I'm so out of here.* Tyran growls, but the entire pack is silent as I toss the clothing in the fire. They land with a satisfying *thwap* that sends a plume of embers toward the shifters gathered around. I turn and stomp toward the woods, ready to let my wolf loose and get the fuck away from this place once and for all, just as soon as we're a safe enough distance away that we don't go rabid on their asses.

"Seneca!" Tyran calls out to me, but I don't give two fucks what he has to say. "Wolf!" he shouts, like I'm no longer even worthy of my name. Ignoring him, my mind churns with thoughts of where to go. Maybe Hess's brother will take me in now that Burke dumped me. Hopefully, he'll offer me sanctuary after what Burke did to Hess.

Heavy footfall sounds behind me, and I can feel the moment Tyran reaches out to stop me from taking another step. I immediately drop to the ground, my instincts guiding my body like I've handed control of it to violence itself, and I kick out. Tyran tries to dodge the strike, but he's a second too slow, and I manage to sweep his legs out from underneath him. I leap back as he goes down hard, ready for him to roar up and meet my fight head-on.

He doesn't disappoint, but I'm on him before he can even spring to his feet. He lets me get a solid hit in, no question that he allows my fist to connect with his jaw, but it doesn't strip the satisfaction I feel as his face snaps to the right from my blow.

Thank you, wolf strength.

I leap to the left as he tries to wrap his big hands around my waist, and my body shifts seamlessly. In less time than it takes to breathe, my wolf is standing in my place, her lips pulled back and her snarl aimed at the male who claimed her. Tyran looks pissed, but I don't care. He did this to himself. He wants to see me trust my wolf more? Fine. I'll trust her to fuck him up just like she wants to right now.

"Shift," he growls, wiping at the blood seeping out from the split he's now sporting in his bottom lip. My wolf growls her objection, and it lights a fire in Tyran's eyes. "I said *shift*," he bellows, only this time, the command is laced with so much power that my wolf can't hold out against it.

Shock ripples through me as my body starts to pull the fur and fangs back in despite our efforts to resist. We've been here before, up against Tyran and his commands. My wolf and I thought our power was close to equal, but as he releases the full force of his unwavering authority, I'm stunned by how all-consuming it really is.

No sooner has my wolf retreated inside of me than I'm being thrown over Tyran's shoulder and carried away. He lopes through the center of the pack's gathering area, like what's happening is no big deal, but the motion, the movement, the theft of my will, it sets off an explosion of memories in me.

Suddenly, I'm not in the middle of Ruin Falls pack land. I'm not safe, having some ridiculous shifter domestic dispute with an asshole alpha. I'm back in Twin Rivers. I'm chained, weak, and vulnerable, slung over the shoulder of a beta as Burke walks behind me, his eyes trained on parts of me I'd rather die than let him touch.

My breathing changes, and a panicked snarl rips itself from my throat as a new, desperate, and terrified fight consumes me. "Put me down!" I demand, but when he keeps walking, my panic spreads. Claws tear out of the tips of my fingers, my blood pounding in my ears. "Put me down now!" I repeat shrilly, and this time, Tyran detects the alarm and distress boiling over in my tone, telling him that I'm not fucking around.

He drops me back to my feet immediately, dipping down until his eyes are level with mine. His gaze searches, looking for hints in my eyes about whatever just happened. Tears come for me, but I give them the fight I never could give to Burke's betas that day. I stomp out their existence, refusing to let the pain take root. Memories swirl in my mind of the brutality, the taunting, the drugging, the sound of my old pack as they blamed me for all of it.

"I didn't know, Seneca," Tyran offers, worried eyes surveying the dead, broken mien that's dripped down over me and stalled my emotions, cracking my ability to cope. "I didn't know that you'd just had your Flux," he tells me. "I heard what you said about what happened to you and how you ended up here. I thought it happened over time, I didn't realize..."

"They carried me like that, slung over their shoulders," I blurt, ignoring his words and hating how hollow my voice sounds. "They chained me, locked me up. I was naked and defenseless, and they carried me like that," I say again, as though I'm reminding myself that it's not happening now. I look down at my hands, claws still out and ready like I wish they could've been then.

"My pack threw things at me, screamed for me to be put down, that I was a traitor, a rabid bitch. They just let them... They always just let Burke..." My eyes find Tyran's, spilling with pain and questions and anger.

In response, understanding and fury flash in his eyes. "Never again. I promise," he declares to me, as though he alone holds the power to ensure that.

Tears once again well in my eyes against my will, and their presence does more to unsettle Tyran than anything I've ever seen.

"Never again?" I ask him quietly, distrust hammering through every word. "You dangle the pack in front of me like a carrot. Promise me I can find my place here, that this"—I gesture between the two of us—"is meant to be. You claim that I can have everything I've always wanted, and then you rip it all away from me when I don't do what you want, *when* you want. What kind of life is that?" I demand, my voice pinched with hurt and fury as hot acidic tears spill down my cheeks, burning away the hope and safety I thought I could find here.

"I fucked up," Tyran concedes, worry paling his face. "I made some bullshit assumptions, and I fucked up beyond belief. It will *never* happen again. You were right to take your time. I should've never pushed you. I'm so fucking sorry, Seneca."

As much as I want his admissions and apologies to pierce the armor that now has a stranglehold on my heart, they don't. I shake my head, and dismay filters through his features, his eyes begging mine not to give up, not to walk away just yet.

"Never again," he repeats, still dipped down so that his face is even with mine. There's no escaping the beseeching way he's looking at me, his tawny brown eyes petitioning that I hear him out. "I won't push you. I'll let you lead, help you learn. No one will ever hurt you again...including me."

Covered in the shadows of night with the fires behind me, I close my eyes against what he's saying, wishing I wasn't so desperate for all of that. Wishing I didn't feel the pack's attention still at my back.

"Can we talk?" he asks. "No bullshit, no games, just talk like we should have done from the beginning."

I open my eyes and look at him, survey the appeal and apology swimming in his beautiful brown gaze. I observe the way he's brought himself down to my level as though I'm finally someone important enough to reach and treat like an equal. His full lips are parted with anticipation, his body tight, waiting to see what I'll say. As though he's willing to fight for what he's asking for—to fight for *me*.

"Fine," I relent, taking a step back from him, needing more space between everything that just happened and the hurt still swimming in my veins. I try to dive back into the ever-present anger always just below my skin, to not feel the pain that's wrapped itself like tentacles around my chest. But the anger is too far away, and I'm left tired and reeling in its absence.

It figures that the rage and fury would abandon me when I want their fiery protection to cocoon me. I can overreact and lose it over a smell on some asshole's bed, but when I'm drowning in hopeless agony, I'm left to navigate it all on my own.

I start to walk toward the alpha house, Tyran at my back as though he's both herding me and protecting me, and all I can think is...

Where's the rabid bitch when you need her?

SEVENTEEN

Tyran and I walk upstairs together.

My chest feels tight from all of the emotional cacophony that's erupted, and I realize just how nervous I am.

Arguing, lashing out, that's all easy. With my wolf's rabid temper, it comes second nature. But it's taken its toll. And now, talking, trying to connect emotionally, to deal with the truth of what's simmering inside...that fucking scares me.

I follow Tyran's steps as he leads me up the wooden stairs, but instead of turning toward the bedroom where I know I'm going to be surrounded by those countless females' scents, he leads me in another direction.

"We aren't going to your bedroom?" I ask with confusion as he moves through the house, aided by the light of the moon shining in through the windows.

He passes me a look of reluctance. "That wasn't my bedroom. That was where..." he trails off guiltily.

"Ah. That was where you just had sex...sex with females like Presley." Nausea rolls through my stomach like dice. I don't want to know what numbers come up on his sexual tally.

"Yeah," he admits, not denying it. "I lost it a bit when you didn't claim me back right away. I didn't realize how much it was going to bother me."

His words are casual, but there's something in the slight tic of his jaw that he just bit down against that tells me there's more here. My eyes flit back and forth between his until I realize what it is I'm looking at.

Hurt.

I hurt him too.

There's a vulnerability that blooms in the space between us. It's as fragile as gossamer, and I worry if I don't tread carefully, that I'll crush it beneath insensitivity like he did to me with this whole claim bullshit.

Tyran watches me, waiting for me to say something, and I try to put myself in his shoes instead of just stewing in my own hurt and frustration.

"Why didn't you just tell me that I was hurting you?" I ask, searching his expression for answers I'm not sure he'll allow himself to be unguarded enough to share. "Why fuck with me, especially after everything you said at the reckoning about the foundation of this pack, and then go and pull this shit?"

"I was trying to get you out of your head. I was aiming for an instinctual reaction," he admits, running one hand through his shoulder-length hair. "But..." He lets out a breath as we stop in the hall, the planes of his face bathed by shadows as he turns to me. "I realize that was wrong, because this is all new to you and your wolf. I should have picked up on that. I'm sorry that I didn't."

"You should be."

He doesn't get pissed at my condemnation, but nods, as if he really does understand where I'm coming from now. "I have a past, and I shoved it in your face to play on your wolf's possessive nature. But I swear to you, the moment my teeth sunk into your skin, everything changed for me. I'm sorry if I was pressuring you too fast. The unfinished mate bond is driving me hard. You're all I want, Seneca. My wolf and I have been waiting a long time for you."

I forget how to breathe for a moment, able to do nothing but look at the sincerity in his expression and the magnitude of his tone.

You're all I want.

My heart squeezes in my chest, and my wolf watches him, hears the gentle murmur of his voice. Her need for her mate grows in intensity, with an all too present urge to rub her scent all over him and erase any other female he's ever touched.

Gently, Tyran takes my hand and pulls me forward, toward another set of stairs I haven't been to yet. He opens a door and lets me in, and I step into a massive bedroom. My eyes widen as he steps inside and closes the door behind us.

The interior walls are rounded and stacked, like this part of the house is more log cabin than the rest. The wood has been painted a charcoal gray that's just a shade darker than the fur of my wolf. To the right, there's a platform bed with a waist-high headboard that's entirely made of dark leather, and the bedding looks soft, its ash-gray color going nicely with the walls.

To the left, there's a sitting area with an L-shaped couch, a cream rug splashed with gray covering the hardwood, and a hanging fur hammock suspended from the ceiling.

I wander over to the hammock, letting my fingers brush over the dark fur as I take in the wall of windows and glass doors behind it. The balcony outside overlooks the lake, and from here, I can see the dark water reflected by the gentle lights of the starred sky, framed by the silhouettes of the mountains behind it.

It's the most breathtaking view I've ever seen.

Tyran clears his throat, and I glance over my shoulder, finding him scratching the back of his neck as he looks around. "So, this is my bedroom. Bathroom is right through there," he gestures to a second door.

I'm surprised to realize that he's...nervous.

He catches my curious look and shrugs. "I've never brought anyone up here before."

Surprise fills my features. "Why not?"

"I was waiting for my mate."

My throat tightens at the implication of that and the gesture, but I don't know what to say. He walks over to a dresser and pulls out a dark shirt with buttons down the front, holding it out to me. I take it gratefully and slip the shirt on, tugging the front closed before I sit in the couch's corner seat.

I find myself tipping my head up and scenting the air, but Tyran is telling the truth. There are no other smells in here other than his, and it settles my wolf.

"So..." Tyran begins, taking a seat on the other end of the L so he can face me. "All of this wolf shit is pretty fucking new to you then."

I snort. "Very."

Tyran watches me for a moment. "I would've done things differently if I'd known."

"You mean things like *not* claim me?"

His brown eyes caress over my face. "You and I are fated, Vicious," he says quietly. "My wolf picked up on your scent during the claiming hunt, and it was all he could concentrate on. We just had to get to you. To prove ourselves so that you and your wolf would have us. So no, I'd have still run like hell to find you. But I wouldn't have been so angry at you for fighting your wolf nature, for taking your time, because I would've understood instead of thinking it was a rejection."

The raw honesty in his face makes my stomach dip. "You really think we're fated?"

"I do." He nods, his expression growing grim. "I'm sorry about Presley. I was thinking like an alpha and not a mate, trying to push my pack member into trusting her animal nature. It's no excuse, but I really didn't want to hurt you. I wanted you to see plain as day what your wolf wanted so you could follow her lead."

I don't sense any dishonesty from him, but it still pisses me off.

"She wants you," I admit. "She wants you *too* much. But don't play games, Tyran. I'm overwhelmed enough as it is with her volatile emotions and instincts, *and* with mine. I'm overwhelmed all the time, actually."

He leans forward, his bent elbow propped against his knees, like he wants to get closer but he's trying to respect the space I might want. My eyes drop to the leather of the couch as I curl my knees beneath me, as if I can curl up against the frenzy going on inside my mind.

"I feel like ever since the night of my Flux, I've been in survival mode. The need to fight is always right there under the surface, and then *you* happened, and..." I shake my head, trying to find the right words as I sift through my jumbled emotions. "She wants you so intensely, and you keep telling me to trust her, but this is all so new. She's either rabid and wants to attack, or she's possessive and jealous, pushing me to claim you. I'm dealing with all the newness of being joined with a wolf. Navigating instinctual pulls that *I* don't understand, in addition to my own shit. It's so much to sort through. My mom just died, Tyran. And the betrayal and hate toward my old alpha and pack rides me every second of every day just on the coat-tails of my grief."

Regret and guilt flashes past the murky depths of his gaze as he runs a hand down his face. "You and your wolf have been fucking amazing. You've had a lot of shit to deal with in the last several days—shit I had no idea about. That's on me, but I'm fucking proud of you for being so strong." My wolf preens at the pride in his voice while the human in me appreciates his contrition. "I wish I'd known. I wish I'd slowed down and just *asked* instead of assuming I knew what I was up against. I'm a fucking asshole, and I'm sorry, Vicious. I couldn't understand why you refused to listen to your wolf. I thought you were just lashing out at me and Ruin Falls instead of seeing the potential here and rejecting me because of rumors started by wolves who would never understand what we're about."

The stark honesty in his voice quiets my turmoil. "Well, I *was* lashing out, but only because I was scared and hurt. I ran from Burke so I wouldn't be claimed, only to dive headfirst into you," I remind him. "I thought my wolf trapped me with an even *worse* alpha, with a worse pack."

His head bows beneath the weight of my words. "I didn't help my case."

My lips twitch slightly at his understatement. "No, you didn't."

"I guess your wolf didn't either. It's a fuck ton for you to process."

He's not wrong. "Yeah, I was angry and confused at her, plus dealing with her extreme reaction to every perceived threat. Meanwhile, she's also pushing me every second of the day to claim you. Even right now, she's *right here*, flooding me with her intensity and her...needs." A blush heats my cheeks, and the marks on my shoulders seem to flush too, as if me admitting to the constant physical draw toward him has made the claiming marks perk up with want.

Across from me, Tyran's eyes flash with hunger, his wolf rising up to the surface. But he takes a deep breath, suppressing whatever shot of desire I just caused. "I'm not saying this to rush or sway you in any way," Tyran begins. "But some of that will settle, *she* will settle, if you decide to finish the claiming."

My wolf shoves up against me so hard that my arms prickle with her fur.

Claim him, she persists, her whine making my chest grow tight.

"Right now, your wolf is even more volatile because you haven't bitten me back," Tyran explains. "I think she might have wanted us to become mates right away that night because she senses that you both need it. Your rabid nature needs an anchor, and she marked me as what you both need."

I nod slowly, thinking through his words before peering at him from under my lashes. "But will you?" I counter. "Anchor us? Be what we need instead of pulling shit like you did tonight? Can I trust you, Tyran?"

As if my words stoke a small spark of hope, he slides forward on the couch until he's close enough to take my hand in both of his, stilling it between his touch. I hadn't even realized I was fidgeting, my nervousness creeping into my movements.

He looks me right in the eye. He doesn't flinch away, doesn't waver like so many others have when they see the indisputable evidence of my unhinged and fractured soul. I realize that Tyran has never looked at me with a grimace or hesitation, despite the violent presence and constant threat apparent in my gaze. And right now, he's stripped off his own alpha mask to let me see the honesty of the male beneath. "I swear to you, Vicious. I'll be the monster your savage side needs. The safe place all of you deserves. I'll be the male that grounds you always. I *will* be worthy of your claim, and you can trust me implicitly. Just give me another chance to prove it."

I didn't realize until right now just how much I needed to hear that from him. My wolf whines again, her desperate noises making my eyes prickle. Tyran's touch is a balm that soothes my hurts, and his words quiet the raging, rabid pain inside of me.

Mate, my wolf says. *Claim. Trust.*

I let out a shaky breath. "I'm glad to hear that."

Mustering up my courage, stepping out on a fragile limb, I scoot forward until my knees press against his thigh. He looks down at the contact and then back to my face, swallowing hard as I lean in closer. His entire body goes tense, as if he's physically holding himself back from moving or touching me. He's letting me choose, letting me come to him.

I don't stop until our faces are just inches away, until we're sharing air, the heat of our breaths mingling against parted lips. My claiming bites are pulsing against my skin, spreading heat and need everywhere. My nose is consumed with his perfect scent, the earthen amber and woodsy cedar a path I always hope will lead me home.

"Don't mess this up, Tyran Bauer."

"I won't," he vows, his tone low but sincere, eyes dipping to watch my lips as they move.

"Good. Because right now, what I *need*, what my wolf needs, is for you to ground us. Because I don't want to spiral anymore. Show me what it will be like to be your true mate," I whisper, watching his throat bob. "And Alpha?"

His eyes drag back up to mine, voice gone rough. "Yeah?"

"*Earn it.*"

I fuse my lips against his a second later, stealing the surprised breath he sucks in. I kiss him like I'm diving straight into the deep end, trusting that even though I can't see the bottom, he'll be there to guide me just like he's promised.

Tyran pulls back, cradling my face with his hands. "Tell me what you want, Vicious."

"You and me," I answer without hesitation, trusting in the instinctual pull I feel between us, and hoping like hell this is right. "I want it to be you and me."

He seems to understand what I mean, because Tyran wraps his arms around me and pulls me into his lap until we're pressed together as close as two people can be. And then he kisses me like there's only us in the entire world and nothing else. He kisses me like a male starved for his mate, like a male as desperate for connection as I am.

I writhe on top of his lap as he takes my mouth. His cock hardens beneath me, and I grind down, stealing a groan from his throat as his shoulder muscles bunch beneath my fingers. My body is a lit match slowly being consumed by the fire inch by inch. My stomach flutters with hope and yearning, and every part of me feels like it's falling into every part of him.

We had sex during the claiming hunt of course, but we were complete strangers then, driven by the instincts of our wolves. Now, we're connecting on a deeper level, and I want him not because my wolf does, but because I feel this intrinsic bond too.

Somehow, in this short amount of time, I've found a male who feels like he could be steady ground beneath my feet—if only I stop running and he stops trying to topple me. When all of the complications are stripped away, I feel *him* and I feel *me*, and this feels *right*.

His tongue delves in deeper, one hand combing between the open shirt I'm wearing so he can skim his touch up my stomach. My breath catches when he cups my breast, and I find myself arching into his touch.

"More." I reach back and pull the shirt from my shoulders, letting it drop until the fabric just barely hangs on by the points of my pebbled nipples.

Tyran pulls back, biting his bottom lip as his dark eyes devour me. "You're fucking gorgeous."

With his tousled hair, fuck-me face, and hardened body built solely for sin, I couldn't agree more. My hands drop to the ties of his pants, but one lightning-fast hand traps my fingers, making my eyes flick up to his. "Are you sure about this? Because I want you to be sure, Seneca."

I feel the weight of his words, but instead of being heavy, oppressive, they solidify his anchoring presence. "I'm sure."

He moves so fast, I squeal in surprise as I'm suddenly lifted up in the air. He takes three steps, and then my bare ass hits the hammock, my borrowed shirt puddling to the floor. "I have thought about fucking you on this since I took you against the hard wall of the cave," Tyran says, the rumble of his voice doing delicious things to me.

"This *is* much more comfortable." I spread my thighs boldly, inviting him to step between them as I untie the laces of his pants and push them down. His hard, delicious cock feels so good in my waiting hand, and I squeeze him in my fist. "Perfect height too."

"Harder," he grinds out, jerking his hips into my hold.

I do what he wants, squeezing harder, but he reaches down and curls his own fist around mine and says again, "Harder."

Using his touch as my guide, I grip him like he needs. His head tips back as I clutch his cock, and every time he makes another one of his sexy groans, it makes heat bank between my thighs.

Tyran lowers his head, eyes gleaming with hunger, his nostrils flared. "I can smell my female's needy cunt."

Without warning, he drops to his knees, and I make a noise of protest at losing the feel of him in my hand, but he shoves his head between my thighs and starts to *devour* me.

"Holy shit..." My eyes roll back, hair tickling my ass as I arc backwards.

Tyran doesn't ease into pussy eating. He doesn't try some fancy moves or polite licks. He fucking eats me out like it's the last goddamn meal he's ever going to have, and he wants to taste me on his tongue for the rest of his days.

My fingers fall into his hair, and I pull at the strands, not to direct him where to go, because he is one male who does *not* need to stop for directions. He slurps me up and sucks my clit, making my nerves light with electric bolts of pleasure. And when he shoves a finger up my pussy and curls it against my G-spot, I tip backwards until the hammock is cradling my back, my head hanging off the other side.

"Fuck, fuck, I'm going to—" I come so fast and so intense that my entire lower half ripples with the aftershocks, and a gush of wetness lets me know that I squirted, marking my male and this place with my pleasure.

When I'm able to open my eyes again, I lift my head to look between my legs, but Tyran isn't there anymore.

"Drop your head again and open that pretty little mouth."

Eyes widening, my head hangs down again, finding Tyran standing right in front of me, his cock at the perfect level with my lips. My mouth waters. It actually *waters* at the sight of him.

I part my lips, opening my jaw wide, and he wastes no time stuffing his cock into my mouth. He goes too far, and I panic a little when my breath gets cut off, especially at this angle, but Tyran threads his hands in my hair. "I got you. Breathe through your nose."

Breathing in as he pulls out, I do what he says, exhaling as he pushes back in. "Good girl," he croons sexily. "Now widen your jaw. I'm going to teach you to swallow my cock."

God, those filthy words of his make my pussy clench, make desire rush up in me. I want to please him the way he pleased me, I want to make him lose control and to be the sole reason for his every blinding pleasure.

He pulls almost all the way out of my mouth, and I look up at him, my gaze gleaming with encouragement. He flashes me a sexy grin before thrusting back into my mouth. He doesn't hold back, hitting the back of my throat and immediately making me gag. My eyes widen with alarm. "Shh, it's alright. I got you. Swallow."

I gag again, tears building in my eyes, but I'm fucking determined, so against my body's natural reflexes, I swallow him. The response I get is instantaneous. A groan rumbles through Tyran, and his fingers tighten in my hair. "Fuck, just like that, Vicious. Swallow my cock down, choke on it."

He gets his wish, because it is wet and sloppy and not at all dignified, but it drives him wild. Tyran starts fucking my mouth like he can't help himself, and an electric pleasure zings through me because *I'm* doing this to him. I let my tongue lather around him, open up my jaw as wide as it can go. I don't let myself feel embarrassed when I choke or gasp for breath, lips dripping with wetness, because he fucking *loves* it, which makes me love it even more.

Just when I feel his cock thicken, and I think he's about to explode, Tyran wrenches out of me. "You're a cock sucking goddess, you know that?"

I laugh a little, wiping my mouth with the back of my hand, just as he lifts me up like I weigh nothing and repositions me into a sitting position in front of him.

Pressing in against my dripping pussy, his brown eyes latch onto mine. "I'm going to fuck you now, Seneca Rain." His tone is just shy of a rumble that rivals the depths found only in a volatile volcano.

My lips pass a breath of relief. *"Yes."*

Tyran thrusts into me so hard I cry out.

The intensity of his invasion stalls my lungs and spikes such intense pleasure in me. I wrap my legs around his hips and dig him in deeper, relishing the feel of him.

He starts fucking me, every thrust making the hammock swing backwards so that when gravity brings me back, it's in perfect time with his next thrust. His dick is deeper than it's ever been before, making me pant and moan approvingly of this perfectly ruthless pace.

"Faster," I demand, my nails dragging down his chest, drawing blood. My wolf salivates at the sight, so much so that I feel my eyes burning with her presence, and I jolt forward, dragging my tongue against his chest. "Fuck me harder!"

Tyran grips my hips and pounds into me so hard I can't take a full breath. "You're a demanding, vicious little thing, aren't you? You want me to fuck you on every surface of this room? Not stop until your pussy is sore and throbbing?"

He poses the question at the same time that he lifts me up in his arms and spins me around until my back is pinned against the cool glass of the window. *Fuck, he's hot.* "Yes!"

"I'll give you whatever you want," he tells me, lips skating over my neck, fingers pressing into my mating bites. My pussy clamps down on his cock with his touch, and Tyran growls against my ear. "You. Gorgeous. Sexy. Fucking. Beast." Every word is a thrust, his dick pistoning into me so powerfully that the window rattles against my skin.

I want him everywhere, all over, I want him in every part of me. My wolf howls beneath my skin in agreement, and I feel my fangs drop, and all I can think is *yes*.

This is right. This is what we want.

I don't hold back, don't second-guess. I don't let my humanity get in the way of my instincts. Instead, I give in to the need to claim. The need that's been riding my wolf and me since we first smelled this male. The never-ending drive to give into the promise that's right there in Tyran's eyes.

His eyes widen and I hear him suck in a shocked breath, and then my wolf's fangs pierce his shoulder, the copper tang of blood immediately filling my half-shifted mouth.

The moment it happens, it's like a million live wires hit water.

White-blue light floods my vision, jolting from my body to his as our bond snaps into place.

The claim is so intense, his cock so fucking deep, that an orgasm explodes through my entire body, until I'm clamping down on him so hard that he roars his release in me.

I must black out for a second, because when I blink, he's staggering us both toward the bed and setting me down tenderly. My teeth are still buried in his shoulder, but I retract my fangs, pulling in the partial shift I needed in order to claim him.

As soon as it's my mouth and teeth again, Tyran hovers over my body, pressing his forehead against mine, his gaze so intense, so filled with both surprise and awe. "I'm fucking yours now, Seneca. And I *will* earn it."

A smile creeps up my lips. No trepidation fills me. I'm not immediately regretting what I did at the height of our passion.

Instead, I feel...*settled*.

Like finally, all the pieces of me are right where they should be.

"You're mine, and I'm yours," I agree, my voice husky.

Tyran groans as if he loves hearing me say that. He grinds his hips against mine, and I realize that he's still inside of me, his knot fusing the two of us together. Blood drips from his wound, and I lean up to lick another drop, making him groan again.

"Fucking Christ, that shouldn't be so sexy, but it is."

I giggle, and I have no idea the last time I felt this light, this *happy*.

"I can feel you," he says, his lips coming down to place a kiss over my own claiming bites. "I can feel your emotions."

Inside my own chest, there's a swirl of something sturdy and dominant, completely satiated with the feeling of his own wolf basking in his mate's presence.

"I can feel yours too."

Our bodies have clicked together like two clocks in sync, our panted breaths are echoes of the other's, and I can feel his deep-rooted happiness that our joining is complete.

He turns us over so that he's on his back and I'm lying right on top of him, our bodies still fused with the pressure of his growing knot that somehow makes everything so much more erotic.

Tyran's warm eyes are hooded as he looks at me like he wants to drink me in and never stop. "You and me, Vicious," he says with a low murmur, reciting my earlier words back to me. But this time, it's not a request.

It's a promise, dipped in our blood and guarded by our wolves. One that he intends to keep.

Just like he keeps the other one, because for the rest of the night, he does fuck me on every surface of this bedroom, until I'm boneless and at peace, sinking beneath the depths of sleep, knowing my anchor won't let me drift away.

EIGHTEEN

"MATE."

I bat something away from my face.

"Vicious."

Something else drags against my hip, and I groan and turn from it.

"Seneca."

"What!" I snap, rolling over.

I turn to find Tyran smirking over me. Daylight is streaming through the huge windows and balcony, making me squint. His bedroom is a bit of a mess with the evidence of our nightly activities. Which are apparent with my body prints on the windows, the scrunched-up rug, and the coffee table shoved out of place.

I sit up, rubbing the sleep from my eyes and wincing at the bit of soreness present between my legs. "You're already dressed," I whine slightly, seeing his loose tunic rolled up against his strong forearms and a pair of pants hanging on his hips.

Tyran's smirk widens into a full-blown grin. "Are you pouting because you wanted me to fuck you? *Again*? You're getting a little greedy now, don't you think?"

"No," I rush to say, though I feel my cheeks going pink.

He chuckles with a shake of his head. "Don't worry, Mate. I'll see to your needs later, but I figured you'd like to come have something to eat. You've been sleeping for a good fifteen hours."

"I have?" I ask in surprise. "Damn. I must've needed it."

"I wore you out," he replies cockily before he drags a tray from the nightstand to set it next to me on the bed.

The moment the scent of food hits my nose, I salivate and dig in. Tender, rare meat melts in my mouth, making me moan in appreciation.

"And here I was, thinking you only made that noise for me," he quips as he watches me from the foot of the bed.

"You have lots to learn about me."

His eyes smolder with something both hungry and affectionate, and it makes my stomach flitter. "I'm looking forward to it."

Once I've eaten every bite of meat, potatoes, and fruit, I feel renewed and so much better than I have in such a long time.

"Well?" I ask with a wag of my brows. "You fed me, are you going to *see to my needs* now?"

He responds to my playful flirting with a crooked smile. "We could... Or I could give you a tour of the pack, show you around properly."

Excitement fills my chest, and I'm up and out of bed in an instant, hurrying over to his dresser as his laughter follows me. "Should I be offended that you chose the tour? And with such enthusiasm?"

"Maybe," I tease as I riffle through his drawers, suddenly very thankful that our last foray was in the shower last night. Then something dawns on me. "Oh, *shit*."

He must feel the flood of unease that washes over me, because Tyran is at my side in an instant. "What? What's wrong?"

"I claimed you," I remind him, dropping my wide eyes to his shoulders—both of them, since I gave him twin bites just like he did to me.

"Yes, I know…" He trails off with a hint of guarded wariness, and I realize it's because he thinks I regret it.

I immediately shake my head and explain. "That means I'm the luna."

Relief settles through him, passing over the bond. "Yes, it does."

"I'm going to be meeting the pack as the new luna. That's a big fucking deal. I've only been a wolf for like four seconds, and now I have an alpha mate, and I'm a damn luna over an entire pack!" The anxiousness in my tone accompanies a slight nausea that rises in my stomach.

Before I can spiral, Tyran grips my arms and lowers his face to mine. "Hey, don't do that. Don't feel like you can't handle this. You're a strong ass wolf, the pack saw that last night just as clearly as I did. They're ready to embrace you as their luna."

Heat crawls up my neck at the thought of the fight Tyran and I had in front of everyone. I look at him skeptically. "I didn't freak them out with my threats of pissing on their dead bodies and rolling in their blood?" I question, unconvinced about just how ready they are to embrace me as their luna. I know for sure there has to be a certain strawberry blonde who's not so psyched about it.

Tyran chuckles and brings my face to his for a quick kiss. When he pulls away, my lips follow him of their own volition, not at all satisfied with the brief taste of him. "They were just as surprised as I was that you've had your wolf for such a short amount of time. It took great strength to hold back and show the restraint you did," he tells me, and I snort, shocked by the compliment.

Leave it to Ruin Falls to think that threatening them all with death and dismemberment last night was a show of restraint.

"I've heard quite the earful this morning about the stunt I pulled. Many of them are not at all happy about the way I treated you. Trust me, Vicious, they're ready for you. You're one of us now."

A smile tilts my lips, and an appreciative warmth washes over me at the thought of pack members taking Tyran to task for what happened last night. Aside from my mother, no one has ever stood up for me. I don't know if this pack can understand what it means to me that they did.

Tyran's eyes fill with understanding, and his smile grows even warmer. "Go out there and be yourself, get to know the Ruin Falls pack, and everything will be fine. It's you and me, remember?"

He pulls me in for a fortifying hug and kisses the top of my head, his declaration wrapping around me like a protective shield. His presence reassures and calms me, and when he releases me, I have a big smile on my face. "Okay," I agree, unsure of what I'll be facing but ready for it all the same. "If you say so."

He chuckles and places a kiss against the bite on my shoulder. "I do," he replies, nipping my skin and making a thrill of heat dip from my mark down to between my thighs. He digs his hand into my still-damp sex hair and gives it a tug. "Just trust yourself. You'll find your feet in the pack." His mouth comes down to mine, and he reaches back and squeezes my ass, pressing me in against his semi-hard length.

"Mmm, maybe we should continue this instead," I say against his lips.

"Later," he promises with a smirk as he pulls back. "It can be your reward."

I roll my eyes and try to smack his chest, but he moves away too quickly and walks over to a second dresser I recall being bent over and fucked deliciously hard against last night, and tosses some clothes at me. I yank the too-big shirt on with a sigh. "I think I need to take up sewing," I say with a frown.

"No, these clothes are good." He saunters over, deft fingers working the laces at the front of my shirt. He pulls them as tight as they'll go, until not even a centimeter of cleavage is visible.

"*Good*?" I ask like he's crazy. "This is a muumuu for pioneers."

"Yep, nice and loose on your body, and for once...*covered*," he says pointedly.

I grin and then head for the door, but he stops me before I can even grip the handle, shoving more clothes at me. "Pants."

My brows pull together, and I look down at my legs. "This *shirt* is a dress on me, Tyran. It goes down to the middle of my thighs!"

"Yeah, and the only thing I'll be able to think about is slowly pulling the hem of that shirt up higher until I can see that sweet, wet, little pussy. Then I'll have to find the nearest place where I can bury my face in it and then fuck it until you're squirting all over me," he says roughly, lips against my ear before he pulls back and levels me with a look. "So put some damn pants on."

Tantalizing heat pulses between my thighs at his dirty words. "Shit, this mating claim is intense," I say, fanning my suddenly hot face. I untie the neck of the shirt that was made for a man four times my size, and Tyran eyes it like he wants to pin me down and cinch it back up.

I'm game for the pin me down part, but the clothes have to go. I pull the neck to the side so that one of my claiming bites is on full display, and his eyes heat with approval. Pulling up the pants, I make a plan to find the pack tailor and sort out something that fits and leaves all traces of pirate-pilgrim-muumuus in the past where they should have always stayed.

As soon as I'm settled, Tyran grabs my hand and pulls me from the sanctuary of his room, *our* room, and I suddenly feel like we didn't spend quite enough time holed up in there. We need more time screaming and moaning, talking and teasing, while we trace every inch of each other over and over again with our tongues.

Tyran stops and shoots me a warning look over his shoulder, but there's no missing the hunger in it or the fact that he quickly adjusts his pants. "Vicious, you have to cut that out, or we're going to give the pack a whole other kind of show than what they're expecting," he teases, and it coaxes a salacious smile from me.

We march down the stairs, and he slaps my ass hard when we get down to the bottom and head for the front door. I bite back a groan from the yummy sting that moves through me, while Tyran *does* groan, feeling exactly what I am through our marks.

I'm going to have so much fun with this.

The sun is high as we step out of the alpha house, and I squint against its too bright greeting. I'm guided down the deck as chirping birds and a warm breeze tease my senses. It hits me just how much has changed since the first time I stomped up the wood planks of this pathway. Tyran squeezes my hand and then calls out a greeting to Britton and Harlan, who are both waiting at the bottom of the stairs.

"Seneca, you know Britton is my Second in command, but allow me to formally introduce Harlan, my Third," he declares, and the warm smile I'm offering Britton is suddenly joined by wide eyes as I turn to the tall, lean female I met earlier with hair and eyes the color of light oak and a massive scar on her throat.

I'm surprised that she's Tyran's Third. Not that she doesn't look formidable, just that most packs are sexist as fuck and don't have a lot of women in positions of power—unless they're attached to a powerful mate. Harlan chuckles and gives me a knowing smile before stepping closer to me and pressing her forehead against mine.

Surprise freezes me for a second, but then I relax and close my eyes, realizing that she's offering a gesture of respect, a greeting meant for the dominant mated pair in a pack. "Well fucking done, Third," I tell her when we pull apart, proud to be part of a pack that sees both sexes as valuable.

Harlan shoots me a wink before the serious veil she's always draped in drops back down over her face. She looks around us as though she's watching for danger even in her own pack, and a sense of safety and confidence fills me.

Britton steps toward me next, and I turn to him as he too presses his forehead to mine. "Congratulations," he offers wholeheartedly. "Tyran's been parading those bites around all morning like a proud peacock. I've never seen the bastard so happy," he teases, stepping back and shooting a sly smile to his alpha. "We all thank you for that by the way," Britton teases. "There's been a sudden rush in meeting requests over the last twenty-four hours. I'm sure that's not related though."

Tyran laughs, and it moves through me like the rumble of a geyser on the edge of erupting, which only makes me want to do a little erupting of my own in the near future. His chuckle is punctuated by a low groan, and a flash of satisfaction strikes through me as he shoots me a look.

Britton clears his throat, pulling our attention back. "I thought we'd stop by the ceremonial grounds and make sure everything is in order for tomorrow, and then we can circle around the territory," he declares. Tyran nods and gestures for him to lead the way, and I fall into step next to him as Britton pops on his tour guide hat and starts showing me the ins and outs of Ruin Falls.

"Ceremony?" I ask as we wind past the alpha house in the direction of the sparkling lake. I can picture just how much fun it will be to play and swim in there when the days are sweltering and muggy like they're bound to become in a couple months.

A hint of worry coalesces in my chest that doesn't belong to me, and I turn to look at Tyran. He runs his fingers through his dark and shiny hair and looks around before fixing his gaze on me. "We have a Flux planned for tomorrow," he explains, and a trill of alarm rings in my mind. Tyran presses his lips together in understanding, while I try to push the rush of emotions away, ignoring the consternation they stir up in me.

I've witnessed dozens upon dozens of ceremonies in my life. One bad one shouldn't spoil them all, even if it did happen to be mine.

"You don't have to attend. No one will pressure you or be offended if you don't," Tyran tells me, his hand firm and ardent where it's clasped around mine. "But I do want you to know that we do things very differently here, and it might be good for you and your wolf to see that."

Nodding, I do my best to stave off memories of Spirit Weaver Yaromir standing by while Burke tore into my arm. I can still smell herbs and lust tinging the air, tainting what should have been sacrosanct and hallowed.

"How is your Flux different?" I ask, as I banish all thoughts of what happened to me and focus on the here and now.

"We stick closer to what the ritual used to be, before it became convoluted and more about the pomp and circumstance that some packs now embrace," Britton tells me over his shoulder as he leads us through the trees, the sun sneaking past the tall tops and dappling us with its warm blessing.

His explanation makes me think about Twin Rivers and the gifts and competing that always surrounds the Flux there.

"Here, it's more wholesome, more rooted in tradition and the old ways. Every year, when there are enough ready members of the pack, we get together and invite the spirits down. We gather on a blessed piece of land, and the participants choose who they want to blood them—usually a family member or close friend. Once they shift, they run with pack members who've been chosen and tasked with guiding them and teaching them the ways of their wolf and our pack. We all get together for a pack meal afterwards. Enjoying what the kappas have been hunting for the past couple of days," Britton explains, the last bit clearly his favorite.

Tyran looks over at me with a warm smile, and I offer him one back. It definitely sounds more low-key than the Fluxes I've attended my whole life.

"It's sacred, but it's simple. It's *us*," Harlan offers from behind me, and it's clear by the look on her face that *us* now includes me, and the sentiment warms me from the inside out.

The trees end abruptly, and Britton guides us out into a clearing that looks perfectly round. I can see the lake not too far off between the trees, and just outside the hard-packed circle, there's an interesting table that's made out of perfectly positioned boulders.

I step into the circle that's empty of all vegetation, not a single stray leaf or twig in sight. Without them having to tell me, my spirit seems to recognize that *this* is the sacred ground they were talking about. I can feel it.

As I look around, a playful breeze twirls around my legs and sends the ends of my hair dancing around me, and I swear I can hear the whimsical yip of wolves playing in the wind. A shiver moves through me, and I gasp, looking around and finding the knowing smiles on the others' faces. A giggle slips out of my lips as I spin slowly to take it all in, feeling the connection to the land.

"What was that?" I ask, wide-eyed and thunderstruck, as Tyran pulls me closer and kisses my lips softly.

"*That* was one of the eager spirits who's ready for tomorrow," he declares, his beautiful eyes alight with excitement.

I can't help the smile that stretches over my face before I plant my lips on his, needing to taste the happiness I see on his face. Reluctantly, I pull away, all too aware that we're not alone. With a chuckle,

Tyran brings our entwined hands up to his lips and kisses my knuckles. The gesture is sweet and intimate, but when I catch a flash of the scar on my arm—the one that every Totemic shifter carries, indicating that they've been blooded and joined by a wolf—my smile falls.

I look at the marks in my skin, and something heavy and hated sinks into my depths. Burke did that to me. As grateful as I am for my wolf, I want to cut the skin from my arm, suddenly unwilling to bear Burke's mark for another second. I start to run my fingers over it, as if I can simply smooth it away, but the more I touch them, the more I hate it.

Off. I want Burke's mark *off*.

My nails start dragging down my skin as I try to scratch the marks, clawing them out of existence, and my mate bond spikes with concern. I know Tyran can feel the disgust and anger coursing through me, because he asks Britton and Harlan to give us a minute.

The next thing I know, he grabs my arm and tugs it around him, away from my nails, and then I'm being pulled down into his lap. "Breathe," he murmurs, cradling my face. But a wall of red has slammed down over me, the untamable rabidness rearing its head and demanding blood and vengeance. "Just breathe, Vicious. If you need to shift, we can. We can run it off. You just tell me what you want to do," he encourages softly, raw power running like an electric current through every word.

"I want to rip this off," I declare, my voice more a frantic snarl than anything else. I call on my wolf's claws, determined to scratch Burke's bite from my body.

Tyran tugs my arm forward to look at it, and understanding darkens his gaze as he bites back a menacing growl. He stares at my arm as though the mark is now the most offensive thing he's ever seen. That makes two of us.

When he glances up at me again, his eyes are angry, but it's on my behalf, not aimed at me. "May I?" he asks, and it takes me a moment to understand what he's asking. His mouth slowly morphs into the half-shift of his wolf's muzzle, and it dawns on me what he wants to do.

My throat grows tight with emotion, and I nod, unable to speak.

I watch with bated breath as Tyran aligns his teeth with the marks. I feel the passion and affection he has for me swelling in his chest as he does what he can to right this wrong. I gasp as his sharp teeth sink into my arm, then throw my head back when I'm suddenly flooded by sensation as a rush of wind whirls around us.

My wolf howls inside of me, the sound both a celebration and a lament. Tyran holds us tightly against him, his fangs digging in deeper, ensuring that everything he is replaces what was forcibly taken from us before. Images fill my mind of flashes of my wolf, but I'm not looking out through *her* eyes, I'm seeing her through Tyran's and his wolf's perspective.

I see her standing strong, formidable, a force to be reckoned with. Then suddenly she's running, her eyes glowing violet, beauty and strength pouring off her in waves. And then out of nowhere, there's me, staring up with savage fury in my shattered eyes, desire dripping from the snarl on my face.

I can feel what Tyran felt the first time he saw me. Feel the awe and need that coursed through him as I fought the rabid parts of me and saw the salvation in him. Devotion and hunger pound through him as he watches me throw my head back and shout out my release, our bodies fused together while my claws rake up his back. He craved me more than his next breath. Through his eyes, we've never been anything but pure beauty and raw power personified.

The moment Tyran's fangs retract, the connection snaps, and I'm back in my body, sitting in Tyran's lap, tears dripping silently down my cheeks. His warm tongue laps up the blood until my wolf healing kicks in and stops the flow.

"Did you see that?" I ask, my voice barely above a whisper.

A stunning smile crawls across his face before he nuzzles his new mark on my arm. "I didn't need to see it, Vicious. I lived it," he tells me, voice laced with all the emotions swirling inside of me and calling to our bond, strengthening it, deepening it, until it feels infinite and invincible.

"Better?" he asks, his eyes jumping from mine to my arm and back again.

I lean in to claim his mouth, letting him feel my *thank you* and just how much what he did means to me. "The best," I tell him against his lips before I move to get up. "Now, show me the rest of our pack, Alpha," I declare, helping him up from the ground. "And hurry, because I really need to get back so I can fuck my mate until he can't walk." A laugh spills out of me when he groans and tries to pull me back.

"One extra-quick tour coming right up," he announces, grabbing my hand and dragging me out of the circle. My laughter bounces off the large tree trunks like it's wrapping around me and filling in the last of the cracks in my soul.

And just like that, rabid or not, every part of me feels like it's starting to fit together perfectly, jagged pieces and all.

A KNOWING SMILE FLITS ACROSS Tyran's face as I eye fuck him from afar. I see a chuckle vibrate through his chest before he focuses back on the group of males who cornered him to discuss pack matters. I've been trying to steal him away for the past two hours, but the pack is not having it.

It's not even just him they're intent on holding hostage. He's tried to extract me a few times too. But every time, he's shooed away by pack members who are clearly displeased by the showdown that went down and their alpha's role in it all. I have to admit, I kind of love how they defend me, even if it has kept us from sneaking off like I'm so desperate for.

A huge plate of food is jutted toward me, and I tear my gaze away from my mate. "Eat, my luna," a sweet female named Jenny says. She's only a handful of years older than I am, with a soft voice and a ready smile. "I made it especially for you. Used my mother's favorite rub," she tells me, her gaze bright and eager.

I give her a smile and happily dig into what I think might be my fifth plate of food. I shove a massive piece of meat into my mouth, savoring the juices that explode and awaken my tastebuds. "Mmmmm," I moan shamelessly, and Jenny swells with pride.

I chew the almost raw meat, ready to shovel in another bite, when suddenly, heat engulfs my mouth so quickly that I feel as though I'm about to breathe fire. *Holy shit.*

"Jenny, would you fix Alpha a plate? He was just talking about your secret recipe earlier, and I know he'd never forgive me if he didn't get one," Harlan says. Jenny practically melts into a puddle of excitement and immediately rushes back to her fire to get more food. "Hurry, dump it in here before she gets back," Harlan orders.

I have to blink back the water in my eyes several times before I can see the animal skin bag Harlan is pointing to on the ground between us. I dump the plate of meat into it, almost sad that something that started out so amazing could turn on me so quickly. But sweat has broken out over the back of my neck and my upper lip.

"Damn, that rub is no joke," I wheeze out with a cough.

"Here," Harlan offers, handing me a large cup made out of an animal horn. "It's goat's milk. It will help with the burn."

I take the offered drink greedily and throw it back as quickly as I can. My mouth feels like it's melting, but the milk helps stop the inferno building, so that's something at least.

"Thank you," I tell her, my voice huskier than that of a smoker of fifty years. "Pretty sure that sweet, innocent female just tried to kill me," I add, a small laugh bubbling out of me, as I debate whether or not it's appropriate to lick the log Harlan and I are sitting on. Maybe the bark will scrape off the top layers of my tongue that are still on fire.

Harlan laughs and cinches the bag of meat closed, moving it discreetly behind us with her feet. "Her mother's secret rub is our healer's cure for most common illnesses. That stuff will burn the nastiest of germs from the body. You should pretty much be immune to everything for the next year," she teases, making me crack up.

"I owe you one."

She waves me off. "Name your pup after me or something, and we'll be even," she jokes with a laugh.

"Done," I happily concede.

"The whole pack has a bet that the day a new wolf can stomach Jenny's food will be the day she finds her mate," Harlan chuckles. "Or at least, we all hope he'll be able to handle the heat. Otherwise, the dude is screwed."

I smile and look out at the pack all eating and mingling and enjoying each other's company. There are no fights or tension, no omegas walking on eggshells, or females trying to lurk under the radar. It's all so easy and free and comfortable.

Wolves lie sleeping and relaxing at our feet, but instead of being disturbed by it or scorning that many members of the pack prefer their wolf form, I'm embracing the freedom they have. Who am I to judge how they prefer to live?

"So, Harlan..." I start, returning my attention to the pack's Third. "Tell me about you."

I spent the day with her while I toured the pack lands and met the other members of Ruin Falls. I've discovered that Harlan is dry, funny, and serious about her duties. She's quickly become my new second-favorite member of the pack.

"There's not a lot to tell, really," she counters casually.

I snort out an incredulous laugh. "The scar on your neck screams otherwise."

Her lips tip up. "Well done, Luna. Most wolves stare at it for ages before ever growing the balls to ask."

"I blame Jenny. Her meat's clearly burned away all my manners and ability to small talk."

"Then you're better for it, I say," Harlan declares, a playful hint in her tone. "I'll take balls and honesty over awkward staring any day of the week."

"I'll just take the balls," I counter, and Harlan groans and drops a hand down her face.

"Just go fuck already," she encourages with a chortle. "I'm pretty sure the pack have bets going to see how long they can keep the two of you apart before you guys lose it and tell everyone to fuck off and then disappear for a week."

I throw my head back and laugh, my heated face having nothing to do with the fire and everything to do with wanting to do just that. I catch Tyran watching me hungrily before someone demands his attention and he looks away again. "Place my bet on another half an hour," I quip, making Harlan chuckle.

My fingers come down to trace over the new marks Tyran placed on my arm. They've already healed, and not just from the outside. They healed something on the inside of me too.

"My scar is courtesy of my brother," Harlan says quietly, pulling me from my thoughts, her dark eyes on my arm. "He attacked me when I unknowingly claimed a wolf he didn't approve of. I didn't know who he was, just that my wolf wanted him, but I found out soon enough that I wasn't allowed to make that choice. I have no idea how I survived, to be honest. When I woke up, I wished I hadn't, because my brother killed my mate right after he thought he'd killed me."

I'm stunned silent by the violence of her past and the almost casual way she describes something so brutal and wrong.

"An older couple in my pack hid me until I was strong enough to run. News of Tyran taking over this pack was just starting to spread, so I took a chance that I might be able to join since they were half a pack short. I've been here ever since."

I blow out a breath as she looks me in the eye. "If your brother's not dead, I'll help you kill him," I offer in place of platitudes and useless sympathy.

She bumps her shoulder against mine, a smile on her face. "You're alright, Luna. I couldn't imagine a more perfect fit for Tyran—and I don't say that lightly," she tells me, and I'm humbled by her sentiment. "Alpha helped me hunt my brother down a while ago, but thank you for the offer."

A group of pups run past us, playing tag and laughing, and I watch them go, their happy squeals painting the dusky night with euphoria.

"Incoming," Harlan announces quietly, her body tensing ever so slightly, and I look up to track what it is that's unsettled her.

I expect to see a female with strawberry blonde hair coming our way, but when my searching gaze lands on ash-brown hair and wide hazel eyes, I realize it's Reap who's making a beeline for us. The pack members nearby go quiet, their gazes judgmental, and I can see how self-conscious that makes Reap as the skin around his eyes tighten.

I thought the reckoning and his proving that he trusted Tyran at the river would've mended things with the rest of the pack, but from the look of it, it's going to take more time for this wound to heal.

Reap reaches me and Harlan like a charging bull, and just when I'm convinced it's time to call on my wolf to deal with him, he drops to a knee in front of me and tilts his head to the side, giving me easy access to his neck. "Luna, I just wanted to tell you how sorry I am for what happened. Regardless of whether or not you were pack, I should've watched out for you. I hope someday you can find it in your heart to forgive me."

Taken aback by the delta's show of submission, I study him, not sure what to say. My thoughts drift back to how scared I was in the shed and to Warrik's words. I can still recall the relief and then the horror that overtook me after I peeled the boards back and escaped, only to realize I'd been set up to be claimed.

A cyclone of different emotions whir through me as I stare at Reap before my gaze skitters over to Tyran's. He watches intently, as though he's curious about how I'm going to handle this. Debate filters through me for a moment, but Reap doesn't move from his kneeling position, patiently awaiting whatever it is that I'm going to do. I can tell by the resigned look in his eyes and the apprehension tainting the air that he's not sure how I'm going to react.

I rise from the log Harlan and I are sitting on and stand in front of the repentant delta. I wait until a hint of edginess and uncertainty moves through the pack, and then I lean down to Reap.

"If anything like this ever happens again, it will be a very different kind of hunt that goes down between you and me," I tell him evenly, letting a trickle of my rabid bleed into the warning. He nods stiffly, understanding passing between us, and then I grab his arm and help him get to his feet. Reap stares at me with sorrow-filled hazel eyes, while I make mine as warm as I possibly can. Then I reach up to grab his face and guide his forehead down to mine.

I've been greeting pack members exactly like this all day, but the moment our foreheads touch, signaling that I accept Reap as part of my pack, every rigid muscle in his body relaxes, and I can feel the wash of relief and gratitude as it moves through him. We stand like that for a bit, me radiating my acceptance and forgiveness, while Reap soaks it up and lets it fortify him.

Tyran comes over and pats Reap on the shoulder when we separate, offering him an approving nod. Then without warning, he scoops me up in his arms bridal style. I squeal as he whips me off my feet so fast it makes my head spin, and starts to carry me off toward the alpha house.

My laugh accompanies the whoops of the pack, but I find Harlan over Tyran's shoulder. "Well?" I call out.

She looks up at the rising moon as though it's a floating clock face in the sky, and then back at me with a sly grin, shaking her head. "That was only twenty minutes, Luna. Better luck next time!" she shouts after me, and I raise a fist in faux outrage.

Dammit, sooo close!

NINETEEN

I DREAM I'M RUNNING.

I know it's a dream because my wolf and I are sprinting side by side through a meadow of knee-high grass that's soft as silk and smells like lavender. There are wildflowers in all kinds of colors sprinkled throughout the meadow around us, and it feels like we could run forever in this perfect place, without our body getting tired, or ever tiring of our surroundings.

Laughter overflows out of me, and my wolf turns her happy face to mine, tongue hanging out of the side of her mouth in a wolfish grin that makes my soul soar. We're so free and happy, and just as I think it can't get any better, I feel *him*. The smell of amber, cashmere, and cedar inundate me, and I lose myself on their current as Tyran's hands circle my waist from behind, pulling us to a stop.

I'm naked, just like I always seem to be since my Flux. But as rough palms move up my torso, Tyran's fingertips teasing the undersides of my breasts, I could care less that I spend more time out of clothes than I do in them.

I arch my back as he grips my heavy, full breasts, pushing my ass against his already hard cock.

He groans and nips at my neck, and I lift an arm and wrap it behind me, threading my fingers through the thick dark brown waves at the back of his head.

Tyran's lips drop to the claiming bite on my right shoulder, while he pinches my nipple between his fingers. His other hand drops lower and lower down my stomach until he's spreading my folds and running his digits through my wetness.

"Fuck, you're so ready for me, Vicious," he purrs in my ear, and I moan in agreement, rolling my hips against the hand, while also teasing the erection pressed against my ass.

The meadow around me starts to blur, the images growing fuzzier and less sharp, as though we're surrounded by a watercolor of blue skies, tall grass, and flowers, instead of a real place. I watch as colors bleed into one another, melting and mixing, just like the desire pooling between my legs that's coating Tyran's fingers.

He pulls me back tight against his chest, one breast held firmly in his grip, while he slips two fingers inside of me. I rest my head on his shoulder, reveling in the way he plays my body. Fingers slip in and out of me, the palm of his hand rhythmically pressing against my clit, and Tyran's needy pants in my ear have me on the cusp of exploding.

I moan and mewl as he licks up my neck and starts murmuring dark and dirty things that make me even more wanton and wet. "You ready for me to fuck this pussy, my mate?" he asks, his voice deep and husky, riding the edge of his own hunger and need. "Want me to bend you over and bury myself deep inside? Or maybe I should flip you and let you choke on my cock while I mouth fuck your cunt until you squirt all over me."

Slick with my ardor and want, his fingers pull out and skim back between the cheeks of my ass. Tyran groans as he spreads my wetness there, circling my asshole slowly while he pinches my other nipple between his fingers and sucks on my shoulder.

"Are you ready for me to take you here, Vicious?" he rasps, pressing ever so slightly and making me whimper with need. He applies pressure but doesn't push past the ring of muscles fighting against the press of his finger. "Should I get you ready?" His hand drops from my breast and moves down to circle my clit instead.

I grab onto his neck from behind and arch, giving him all the access I can as one hand rubs my clit and the other steals more from my wet folds and redirects the liquid desire back to my ass. I've never been played with *there*, but the way Tyran is softly pushing and teasing, circling and lubricating, it's a whole new flood of sensations that I can't seem to get enough of.

"Tyran." His fingers start to move faster around my clit. "Tyran, please," I plead, my body on the cusp of an intense orgasm but still desperate for more.

"Bend over for me, Seneca," he orders, his gruff tone dripping with power and avidity.

Eagerly, I press forward just as Tyran lines up the tip of his cock with my pussy. I can already feel my inner walls starting to tighten as I approach the crest of the orgasm still building in me, and I groan at how good he's going to feel...

He thrusts into me deeply, and I shatter as I'm rocked by the explosive release that yanks me from the watercolor dream world. Instead of a melting meadow, I wake up to find my fists gripping bed sheets, my face pressed against a pillow, and Tyran's hands holding my hips as he fucks into me hard from behind. Every thrust shoves my whole body forward toward the tan leather headboard, his dominant control of my body lighting me up with pleasure.

I cry out at how good he feels, shoving my body back against him as he pistons in deeper and faster. I thought my dream was good, but knowing it was real is so much better. Pushing up onto my hands and knees, my mate adjusts to the new angle and fucks me savagely into the arms of another orgasm.

Shouting through my second release, I meet him thrust for thrust as he pounds into me, deep and punishing, and exactly what I need. He slaps my ass, eliciting a yelp as the sting pushes everything to that line of pleasure and pain that I know we'll start to edge around just as soon as his knot embeds in my pussy.

I drop my chest to the bed, ass still in the air, and beg for more. "Harder," I snap, challenge and need spilling out of my demanding tone.

He growls and gives me what I ask for, and I feel his hand move from where it's holding my hip to drop back to my ass.

My body practically hums as he fucks me ruthlessly. "Yes, right fucking there!" I scream when he slams against the perfect spot, and I feel a finger press in against my ass. He breaches the tight ring of muscle just as my third orgasm rips through me like a tidal wave. He impales into me again and again until he goes still and bellows out his release, cumming inside of me, his knot already expanding to lock every drop in place.

I ride the last waves of ecstasy while he stretches my pussy and presses in, trying to get deeper than he already is. His thumb rotates inside of my ass, his hips and stomach applying even more pressure to what he's doing as he rocks against me from behind.

"Good morning," he rumbles before he pitches me forward again, and I laugh airily, floating in a warm pool of bliss.

"Good fucking morning to you too," I pant, my body jellied and fuzzy and sated in every possible way. "You might be my new favorite alarm clock."

"*Might*?" he teases, hips driving into me again, eliciting a gasp when he pulls his thumb out of my ass and rubs his palms tenderly over my butt cheeks.

"Definitely," I correct with a euphoric giggle as Tyran drops his weight down on me and then rolls us to our sides as we ride out his knot.

He kisses my shoulder, and I look back to steal his lips before we both relax into each other. "Have you decided if you want to come today?" he asks before he nuzzles my neck, tickling my skin with the scruff on his face.

"I mean, maybe I didn't scream loud enough, but I just did… three times," I tease, and he nips my earlobe, his deep laugh resonating through me.

"Come *to the Flux*," he reminds me, and the word steals some of my afterglow.

I try to shake it off and remind myself of what Britton and the others explained about how it's different here. Then I remind myself that I'm now the luna, and at some point, I'll have to stop running from these things regardless of how triggering they might be. I sigh, and Tyran brushes strands of hair from my face.

"I'll go on one condition," I declare.

His eyes are patient and molten, and I can feel tenderness and excitement filter through him. "And what might that be?"

"Shower sex," I announce shamelessly with a mischievous smirk.

"You're insatiable," he groans, but he's already picking me up—carefully, so as not to jostle where we're still connected—and carrying me into the bathroom. "I suppose a mate's gotta do what a mate's gotta do." I laugh until he turns on the shower and plunges us both beneath the freezing water.

I DO MY BEST TO ignore the stirring apprehension in my chest as I follow Britton through the trees to the sacred grounds they showed me yesterday. The smell of familiar herbs in the air causes anxiety to pool in my gut, flashbacks flickering through my mind of what happened during my Flux. I try to shake the trepidation away, but my wolf is pacing inside of me as though we're expecting the worst.

"You okay?" Britton asks as he surveys me from the side.

"Yeah, I'm good. I'll feel better when I see Tyran and my brain can stop convincing my body that we're reliving something fucked up," I confess, probably a little too candidly, but I don't think Britton is going to look at me like I'm a lesser wolf because of it. He nods, his eyes kind and filled with empathy, which only confirms his character.

The trees thin out, and I can smell and hear the pack just ahead as we get closer to the sacred circle set to the side of Ruin Falls territory. My wolf whines, as though she's trying to comfort me while fighting her own restless unease. I do what I can to reassure her that everything is going to be fine, just as Britton and I step out of the woods. I look around at the large round piece of land currently containing what looks to be at least half the pack.

A small group still in their human form is split apart, making way for the pack's Second in command and me. I spot Tyran off to the side doing something at the long table made up of boulders. Bowls of herbs are set on the flat top of the rock formation, smoke rising out of them and producing the smoke I'm used to smelling at this ceremony. There's no massive bonfire anywhere, and instead, there's a large cast iron bowl—one that oddly resembles an oversized wok—containing a small fire within its black edges.

Britton moves to the side, and with his large back no longer blocking my view, I see that there are shifted wolves of all sizes gathered around too. They make up shades of gray, white, brown, black, in all kinds of combinations, and they've formed a perfect circle, each of them facing inward.

I frown in confusion. "What are they doing?" I ask Britton before he moves too far away.

"They're encircling the Flux participants."

My feet skid to a stop as I take in the scene before me, and shock crashes over my body and cements me in place. Because standing in the middle of the circle are a bunch of kids.

Kids.

The youngest looks like she can't be more than eight, and the oldest participant is maybe thirteen. It's a mix of boys and girls, and they're wearing the rustic wear of animal skins and linen like the rest of the pack. I look around as though I'm waiting for someone to come explain to me what the hell is going on, but no one does. Britton doesn't even seem to realize that I'm planted, unmoving and stunned.

"What the hell, Britton?" I hiss.

He stops and turns to me, his blond brows lowering in a frown. "What?"

I stare at him incredulously but manage to swallow down the rising anger. Instead, I veer off and head straight for the boulder table where Tyran is working. When I'm two steps behind him, he says, "Why are you pissed, Vicious?"

My steps stop short, and he turns his head to look at me, tapping the bite on his shoulder. "I can feel you, remember?"

I sidle up next to him, careful to keep my voice low. "Can I talk to you for a second?"

"Of course, Mate."

"Seriously, what the hell is going on?" I say, not to be thwarted by his use of my title.

He continues grinding herbs before tossing them into the cast iron fire. "You're going to have to be more specific."

My eyes skate over to the circle of wolves again. Each and every one of them looks like sentinels in a ring, while the children stand inside, seeming nervous beneath their still and watchful presence. "This is..." I blow out a breath and shake my head, feeling claws start to press through the tips of my fingers. Because this...this isn't *right*.

In a blink, Tyran's dropped what he's doing and has turned me to face him fully, blocking me from the rest of the pack. "What's wrong?" he demands.

"They're *kids*, Tyran. The Flux can *kill* us. It can give us wolves that call to a mate. Not to mention the pain of shifting and managing the wild it unleashes, and your pack is forcing kids to go through this?" My voice cracks at the end, and I take a steadying breath. Everything Britton told me to put me at ease has gone right out the window as I think about those pups.

"First of all, it's *our* pack," Tyran says sternly.

A crooked finger comes up to lift my chin, and I look at him with a sheen of red over my eyes. "Our pups are not in danger, Seneca," he says with a hint of impatience, like I'm just overreacting.

"Don't," I tell him, knocking his hand away. "This *is* dangerous. How can you expect children to handle this? It's too soon. Way too soon. What if they get a spirit that overwhelms them, or what if the shift goes wrong, or—"

"Our pups are raised knowing that when they're ready, they will earn their wolf spirit. Their parents, our healer, and me as their alpha watch them to ensure they're ready."

"But—"

He cuts me off. "Your old pack may have made you wait until you were older, but to us, *that's* cruel."

"No, it makes sense," I argue. "We have to be older so we can handle this shit."

Tyran shakes his head and gives me a pointed look as if to say, *and how'd that work out for you?* "Wolf spirits choose us, Seneca. They wouldn't choose a host if the connection weren't there, and sometimes, they don't, and our pups have to wait and try again later. But that shit you're insinuating about our other wolves trying to mate them right away? I don't fucking appreciate it," he says, eyes hardened.

I lean away from his anger, but it's feeding into me through the bond, his face as stony as the table pressed against my back.

"The Flux for us has nothing to do with taking mates. It's a sacred rite of passage. These pups will finish growing up *with* their wolf spirits, learning and growing together. To us, *that's* how it should be as a Totemic shifter, and they become stronger and more in tune with their animal because of it. Mating comes much, much later, and that too is aided by following the instinct of their wolf. Which you would know if you'd watch and learn instead of jumping to fucked up conclusions."

His words fall one by one like rocks to rattle against my skull and then weigh me down with contrition. Through our mate bond, I can feel just how offended he is by what I'm saying, how much he believes in his pack and these children waiting for their wolves. I grab on to his words and examine them, trying to see how they fit in what I thought I knew as I look over at the wolves and the way they're guarding the pack's young. There's no doubt in my mind that they would never let something bad happen to their pups.

It makes me reevaluate, because the more I think about it, the more I realize that the things he's saying...*they* make sense. Guilt fastens around me like too-tight buttons all the way up my throat.

I didn't realize how narrow-minded I've been behaving until just now. Up on the mountain, I figured out how to drop the guilt and judgment I was harboring about myself and my wolf, but right now, I realize that I walked into this pack thinking they were feral beasts, and I've unknowingly been clinging to that prejudice ever since.

That is...until now.

"I'm sorry." The whisper falls from my lips, the shame making my eyes drop down. "I didn't mean to accuse you or your—*our*—pack of doing anything horrible. I was just shocked and worried, and...I'm sorry," I say again. "I never understood how different things could be."

Tyran sighs, and his hands come up to settle on my hips. "Different doesn't always mean bad, Vicious."

"I know. I'm getting it. Slowly, but I'm starting to understand." I peek up at him through my lashes. "They really will be okay?"

"I swear it. I would never let any harm come to the pups of our pack," he promises, one hand moving to press against my belly button. "And one day, when we have pups of our own, you'll see how much care we take in raising them to be strong and respectful of the spirits they're trying to earn."

"Our own?" The words fall out unbidden, because...I never really thought about having pups before. I didn't even expect to take a mate I'd ever want to breed with. But the moment Tyran said it, I find that it's not a horrible thought.

One side of his lips crook up. "Yep," he says, voice dropping an octave. "I'm going to fuck you again and again and again...and then one day soon, I'll plant a pup in your belly, and you'll swell with the life *we* made."

I find myself growing teary-eyed, because as unexpected and terrifying as that sounds, there's no denying how badly my wolf and I want that.

"Okay," I say a little breathlessly. "Can we stop talking about this for now? Because I can't be weepy *or* horny during my first Ruin Falls Flux."

He chuckles and nips my lips before pulling away. "Alright, I'm set up here. You ready?"

"I don't know what to do."

"I'll walk you through it."

Tyran grabs a bowl and motions for me to pick up the other one. I follow his lead as he walks to the fire and tosses in the herbs. The second I do it too, the smoke goes from light and wispy, to dark and thick, like stirring clouds of thunder.

When we turn around, I note an older female with graying hair standing off to the side, her hands clasped in front of her, and a twine of herbs hanging off her neck. Tyran and I walk nearer to her where she stands just behind the circle of wolves, and the moment I get close, I sense a familiar power that brings both a sense of comfort and a rush of devastation.

Healer.

Hazel eyes flit to me, and the woman smiles, face crinkling as she nods to me. "Luna. Alpha."

"Seneca, this is Healer Vorria. She'll make sure the pups transition well," Tyran tells me.

I clear my suddenly tight throat. "My mother was a healer," I say, and the woman seems to glean a lot from that simple sentence, because sympathy fills her expression.

"Then I am blessed to know that our new luna has been raised beneath such a caring nature," she says kindly, but that just makes my eyes burn more. All I can manage is to smile and turn away, hoping everyone will think it's the smoke that's getting to me.

Tyran holds out his hand to me, and I take it immediately. Two wolves move over to let us through, and then we're standing in the middle of the circle, a half dozen children in front of us. "You six have proved yourself ready to invite a wolf spirit down," he says, looking each one of them in their hopeful eyes. "It's time to choose the wolf you'd like to be your spirit guide."

All at once, the pups move. Four of them find wolves in the circle that they go to, and I realize they must be their parents. The oldest boy marches straight up to Tyran, chin held high, gangly shoulders thrown back with pride. "Alpha, will you honor me?"

My mate nods, and I smile, but then I feel a tug on my shirt. I turn around in surprise, finding a little girl standing there looking at me like I hung the moon. "Miss Luna? Will you...uhh...spirit guide me?"

My eyes widen, flashing up to the healer first and then Tyran for help, but he winks at me and nods in encouragement.

Shit.

I have no idea how to spirit guide, let alone if I'm even deserving of such a thing. But the little girl is looking at me with big brown eyes, and I just can't find it in me to gracefully decline. Besides, how would that look to the rest of the pack? I don't want to disappoint anyone, especially not her.

"What's your name?" I ask the brown-haired girl.

"Briar."

"I'd be honored, Briar," I say, and the beaming smile she sends me melts me so much I'm surprised I don't turn into a puddle at her feet.

Outside of the circle, Healer Vorria begins to sing an old song, her voice mingling with the smoke-filled air. I sidle up next to Tyran, not just for emotional support, but so I can copy his every move and hopefully keep myself from fucking this up.

One by one, the shifters chosen to act as the spirit guides for the pups kneel down. I drop to my knees in front of the girl, and she offers her hand. Vorria's voice is soft and lyrical, so different and *calm* compared to the intense chanting and drums that surrounded my own Flux.

"Take her hand," Tyran instructs, nodding to me.

I repress the urge to wipe my sweaty palm on my pants. I can't let on how nervous I am, not when the little girl is depending on me, and not when she looks so sure and steady herself; there's not an ounce of worry in her innocent face.

Taking the girl's hand in mine, I hold steady and watch Tyran as he does the same for the boy in front of him. Behind us, I can hear more exchanges happening, but I focus on my mate. He looks at the boy and says, "May a wolf spirit bless you."

Then, in a half-shifted mouth, he bites down gently on the inside of the boy's wrist. He winces, though he suppresses any noise, and then Tyran steps away, mouth already shifted back and smiling.

I turn back to the girl and give her a warm grin. "Ready?"

She nods enthusiastically. "My wolf is up there waiting for me."

"You can sense her?" I ask with surprise.

"Yep. She's ready."

"Well, alright then, let's not keep her waiting."

I call on my wolf, and she washes over me in a half-shift. I bite the girl as gently as possible, just enough to let her blood tease the air so her wolf will recognize her scent and latch onto her spirit.

The moment I'm done, two tawny wolves come forward, and the girl grips their fur. Her eyes light up like she's just seen something, and I move out of the way instinctually. I can't see what she's seeing, but I feel something as a loud wind brushes up against me. The girl's eyes suddenly roll into the back of her head, and she goes falling back. With a cry of alarm, I try to catch her, but the other wolves are already there, helping her weight to settle onto the ground. I spin around in a circle, seeing that *all* of the kids are sprawled out, some of them shaking, some of them looking like they aren't even *breathing*.

"Tyran..." Panic jumps from my throat and curdles my stomach. I search for Tyran's calm excitement in my soul, and I tug at it and wrap it all around me like it's the coziest of blankets. He reaches out and takes my hand, squeezing hard.

"It's alright. Watch."

With anxiety banging against my heart like a snare drum, I watch as Healer Vorria comes into the circle and begins to check on the pups one by one. The rest of the wolves are still fully shifted other than Tyran and me, two or more of them waiting patiently beside the kids. Vorria continues to sing quietly, a soft hum not to compete with the wind of the spirits, but one that complements it.

There's no violence, no pressure, no ritual with blood symbols marked on skin in the dead of night. It's simple, comforting, *right*.

It takes a few minutes, but the boy that Tyran bit is the first to begin to shudder. With a painful grunt, fur sprouts along his limbs, and the protective wolf circle seems to close, watching with excited pride.

Before he's finished, two more start to do the same, and then all of their bodies are shifting for the first time, the little girl included.

Tyran comes over, a huge grin on his face. "Every single one of them received a wolf spirit," he says, looking so damn proud. A grin splits my face, my heart still pounding wildly. I look around and see the young wolves finish their first shifts, tails shaking, tongues lolling. They crouch and lick at the muzzles of the wolves all around them, paws dancing over the ground.

He was right. The spirits didn't force these pups to grow up or push them to take on roles they might not be ready for. They wiggle with adolescence and juvenile excitement, and as shocking as it is to see, it's also beautiful and incredibly humbling.

I watch the pack eagerly greeting the newest wolf members, and I wonder, what would life have been like if this is how *I* grew up?

Tyran sidles up to me, wrapping his strong arms around my waist and nuzzling my neck. "You ready to run, Vicious? Ready to show these wolves what yours can do?"

My eyes widen with surprise, and I turn in Tyran's arms. "Me?" I ask, my eyes searching his for answers.

"You," he answers with a sexy smile that makes me want to do all kinds of naughty things to him. An excited yip comes from one of the new wolves like they're trying to hurry us along, and Tyran chuckles.

"Okay," I say with nervous excitement.

With a grin, he backs away and starts to rip his clothes off to ready for the shift. I turn around and do the same, because ogling him in front of the new pups probably wouldn't be the best idea. When I glance over my shoulder to see if he's watching me, he shoots me a wink before effortlessly melting into his massive brown wolf.

I join him a second later, paws steady beneath me. For a split second, I worry that my wolf will freak out around all these strange wolves she hasn't met yet and that I'll have to fight her for control in front of the pups. But as soon as the worry crosses my mind, it's eased just as quickly. Because the little girl wolf, all shiny brown fur, comes right over and licks my wolf on her neck. Instead of growling or getting territorial, my wolf's lips pull back into some semblance of a playful grin.

Tyran's wolf comes over and hip-checks us, and then with a howl, he darts away, leading the run. The new little ones bound after him with excited yips, while the older wolves move to encircle them, ensuring the pups are protected from every possible angle at all times. I join the protective circle and take up position on the left. We all span out so the little ones can get their legs under them with plenty of space to amble and frolic and race as they learn what it is to be a wolf.

I realize as my paws fly through the forest, that this is what taking a wolf spirit *should* be like. This is what being a Totemic shifter is all about. As we run together as a pack, protecting the pups and letting them smell and pounce and pant and wag, I see just how beautiful it all is.

This pack doesn't sexualize shifting like Twin Rivers did, doesn't force the females to experience the Flux at the same time so the stronger males can choose them. This pack doesn't make their members wait until they're adults so the claiming can happen. This pack has it right. It's sacred, it's about a true joining with your wolf, and just letting two innocent spirits connect.

I have no idea how long we run together, but it's so incredibly *freeing*. For the first time since I got my wolf spirit, she's shifted because it's *fun*. Not to attack, not for survival, not even for the baser instincts driving her. She just...gets to be a wolf playing in the woods with the pack.

With our new pack.

After a while, when the pups have become used to their new spirits and the wolves have gotten to run to their heart's content, Tyran starts teaching them how to hunt. The pups break off into groupings with the adults. Tyran's wolf goes around to all of them, watching over, helping to teach.

I take the opportunity to let my wolf get better at it too. The mountain goat was our only experience so far, and that was about a lot more than just the thrill of a hard hunt.

Tyran's wolf watches me as I dart off to chase the scent trail of a bunny, and I can sense the amused pride in him. My wolf plays around for a bit, not hunting too seriously, more just enjoying the chase. The sun warms our fur as we lope to catch up with the scattered rabbit.

It's so bright and beautiful all around us, and my wolf comes up with big plans that involve lying around and sunning ourselves for the rest of the afternoon. We've never been able to do that, and I can't deny it sounds like heaven. That is, *after* Tyran and I sneak off to a cave or two so I can ride that dick and sink a few more marks into his skin first. I'll *really* give him a reason to strut around the pack shirtless.

Giddy glee fills our paws at the thought of our mate, and we pick up the pace, ready to catch our prey, but my wolf skids to a stop when a distinct and familiar smell fills our nose.

Presley.

TWENTY

The trail of Presley's scent tells me exactly where to find her, but I'm not sure what I want to do about it. I didn't realize she was here running with us, but now that I know, it feels ordained, like this is the perfect time to set some things straight.

Strawberry doesn't like us. I get that, and honestly, the feeling is pretty fucking mutual.

But...after what my wolf and I have experienced the past few days with the pack, and with witnessing the Flux today, it's changed me. All of this bonding and running with the pups brings everything into perspective. It makes what's happened between me and Presley feel petty and pointless.

I want to solidify my place here in Ruin Falls, and to do that,

I need to confront every piece that feels like it's keeping me from doing that. And one of those major pieces comes in a boobalicious, Presley-shaped package.

It's time to talk to her one-on-one, female to female.

At my urging, my wolf abandons the trail of her rabbit and redirects her focus on Presley's scent instead.

This probably won't be a very easy talk, but it needs to happen. Now that I've claimed Tyran and am Ruin Falls' official luna, I have to sort things out, regardless of the fact that she sat on my male's lap. My wolf growls at the memory, but I tell her to knock it off. *We're not approaching Presley to start shit*, I remind her, hoping she'll keep her rabid feelings in check.

I mean, if Presley comes for us, we'll do what we've gotta do...

I shake away that thought and side-eye my wolf who's almost *hoping* that will happen. But I'm genuinely not wanting to cause trouble. I want to clear some things up so we can move on. I've claimed Tyran now, our bond is settled, so she needs to respect that.

Presley's trail grows stronger, and when we round a hill, we find her tearing apart what I think used to be a badger.

Well, crap. Feeding wolves are always bitchier than they are without a kill to protect. Being that Presley is already a cunt, I have no idea what I'll be up against with this shit. I debate turning around and leaving her to it, but I know she'll smell me here, and I don't want her to think I tucked tail and ran.

I ask my wolf for control so I can talk to her and hopefully defuse what could otherwise be a very volatile situation. Begrudgingly, she gives it to me. We watch Presley intently, trying to work through what to say to her as fur recedes inside skin, sharp teeth disappear, and we move from four legs to two.

I don't know what it says about Strawberry Presley and her white and red wolf, but neither notice that I'm standing here watching them until I start to step down the hill and purposely snap a twig under my feet. Her wolf snarls, moving to stand over their kill, bright angry eyes now trained on me.

"I don't want your...whatever that is." I look down at the ripped up carcass between her paws. "I'm not here to fight, I just want to talk," I explain, my arms up in a gesture of goodwill as I continue to advance on her.

A warning growl rumbles from her chest when I get about ten feet away, but there's not a chance in hell I'm going to let her tell me where to stand, so I walk another two feet closer before I stop.

She's a white wolf with a dusting of red on her muzzle, ears, and flank. She'd be pretty if her ears weren't pinned to her head and lips lifted in a snarl. Her wolf looks up at me like she wants to rip me apart. The threat in her stance sends the hairs on the back of my neck standing up, and I drop my hands and stare down at her with every ounce of *you do not want to fuck with me* I can muster.

"Shift," I snarl, not interested in the slightest at having a one-sided conversation. I intend for the bark of my order to make it clear that I'm not going to put up with disrespect. But there's a layer of power to my command that I've only felt once before, and that was when Tyran forced a shift on *me*.

The wolf instantly folds in on herself, revealing a huddling Presley in a matter of seconds. She looks down at her hands like she's shocked her fur disappeared, and lifts that same surprised gaze up to me. Her expression quickly morphs to outrage as she rises onto her feet, placing her hands on her hips and pursing her lips. "You had no right!"

"The fact that you just shifted would say otherwise," I counter and then tell myself, if we're going to get anywhere, I should probably lay off the snark.

Her eyes flash. "That's just Tyran's alpha showing up in you because you're fucking him. You're not my luna, and if you ever force a shift on me again—"

"You'll what?" I challenge, taking a step forward and a page out of Tyran's playbook. He's firm, he's honest, and he takes no shit from anyone. "I told you I wanted to talk, but you and your wolf want to get disrespectful—big surprise there. I'm not here to have a pissing contest with you. I'm genuinely here to talk, to see if that bad foot we got started on and that whole *your ass in my mate's lap* thing can be worked out."

She glares at me but doesn't go for a hit, so I guess there's that. Crossing her arms over her chest, her eyes widen as if to say, *well, talk then*.

Which is great if I had any idea what to actually say. Maybe I should've planned this better, but oh well. "I'm sorry Tyran did that to you the other night. You didn't deserve to be played with just to get a rise out of me. It was mean, and I'll...uhh...punch him in the dick for you," I offer.

Presley's green eyes widen slightly, clearly not seeing that angle coming, and I tamp down on my own surprise, because I hadn't planned on saying it either. We're both quiet as my words fall slowly like feathers to the ground. The air between us is taut and apprehensive, and even though I'm a little shocked that this is what I led with instead of the tried and true, *Bitch, if you touch my man again, I will fuck you up*, there's a heavy truth in what I just told her.

A ray of sun catches her hair, making it glimmer like rose gold in the beam of light. She shifts from one foot to the other, like she's not sure what to say.

"I'm also sorry for the meat my wolf stole. I didn't mean it as a sign of disrespect, and to make it up to you, I'd be happy to hunt with you until you feel like I've paid an adequate price."

"I don't need your apologies," she snaps at me with a glare that clearly communicates that she thinks I'm beneath her.

"That's fine. You'll get them all the same," I counter.

"What do you want?" she demands, clearly not trusting this exchange in the slightest. I don't know if I can blame her, I have daydreamed about ripping her apart a lot in the last twenty-four hours.

"I want there not to be any animosity between us. I'm not saying we have to love each other or even be friends, but I feel like a mutual respect is in order, especially since neither of us are going anywhere and I *am* the luna."

"Oh, I'm not good enough to be your friend now?" she accuses, and I reel for a beat.

Is that what she got from what I just said?

My brows pull together. "Umm, that's not... Do you *want* to be my friend?"

"No," she clips irritably, and I look around us as though the trees can fill me in on what the hell just happened.

"*Oookay,*" I respond, not sure what else to say to that. "So, not friends, but not enemies?" I honestly don't know if we've made any progress here.

"He didn't play me," she lobs at me, and it's as though she tossed a ball, but instead of catching it, I just watch it bounce to the ground. I have no idea what she means, and I'm starting to wonder if she's nuttier than a fruitcake.

"Tyran," she announces with a roll of her eyes. "He didn't play me. He asked me if I wanted to mess with you. I said yes. He would never fuck with pack just to get back at someone. That's not how he works," she explains, her tone going a little more judgy with her last statement.

I ignore the *if you knew him like I know him* jab and instead nod my head in understanding. "Okay, noted. No dick punching on your behalf then." *I might punch him there on behalf of myself though.*

"Are we done now? My beaver is getting cold."

I blink, fighting with everything inside of me not to look at her crotch. *What the fuck is wrong with this girl?*

"My wolf hates it when the blood gets cold," she adds, and I realize she's talking about the carcass still positioned between her feet. Beaver, badger, pretty close.

A laugh escapes me, and I'm about to tell her what I thought she just meant when something bites me in the back. A flash of pain radiates through my shoulder blade, but when I whirl around, there's nothing there. I reach around behind me to feel for whatever fucked up bug just took a bite out of me, but my blood runs cold when I wrap my fingers around a dart.

I yank it out, whipping back around, yelling, "Presley, run!" My voice fills with every ounce of command I can manage.

Terror and rage rise inside of me, both battling for control over my body. A whimper escapes her as she morphs into her wolf, but the fog is already creeping into my head, the effects of the dart horrifyingly familiar.

"Run! Now! Get Tyran!" I scream at her, and relief flashes through me as she disappears into the brush a second before a dart hits the spot she was just standing in.

I attempt to call my wolf, to shift and give myself some weapons to try and hold them off, but I can't connect. Staggering away as best I can, I continue to call to the beast inside of me as though I can click over to the right channel and everything will align inside of us. I stumble through the woods, refusing to be a sitting duck for the Twin Rivers bitches who just started a war.

I can smell Conrad and Saul, and I think Ryden too, all of them closing in on me. I push my leaden legs harder, desperate to get away. Rage the likes of which I've never felt before explodes inside of me like an atomic bomb, and I don't know if it's coming from Tyran or me or a combination of us both. I hope Presley catches up with him soon and that he can get here fast enough.

"Where's the wolf we were supposed to meet? Burke said he'd be here with her and to bring him too. That was the agreement," I hear Saul ask stupidly as I try to duck behind a tree and hide.

His words don't make sense to my muddled mind. Is Burke here? I sniff for the cowardly piece of shit, but his scent isn't anywhere on the wind.

"Who fucking cares? He's not here, and we're not going to sit here all day waiting for him. Go get her, she should be down by now," Conrad orders, and I debate playing dead and trying to attack them by surprise, but I worry if I lie down, I'll never get back up again.

I lean against the bark, trying to stay upright. The tranquilizer is deadening my senses and slowing my reaction time, but I wonder if you can build up a tolerance to this stuff, because even though I feel its effects, I'm sure as fuck not down like they think I should be.

I pray to the moon and all the stars that Tyran is close and on his way with help. I even crack a smile at the thought of what he's going to do to these fuckers when he finds them. Suddenly, Saul's big ass face pops up in front of me, and all thoughts of Tyran and help disappear as I try to tap into my rabid and fuck him up.

I'm slower than I should be, but when he tries to pull me away from the tree, I launch my hands forward and dig my thumbs into his eye sockets, pressing as hard as I can. I bellow in rage as he stumbles back with a scream, tripping on a bush behind him. I fall with him, determined to blind the bastard and take him out of the equation. He shouts and claws at my hands as I try to crush his eyeballs. I feel one give with a sickening *pop*, but before I apply more pressure to the other, I'm yanked off of him and slammed to the ground.

My lungs empty completely, and I can't scramble away before Conrad's on me. He presses his knee into my chest, pulling a long knife from his belt. I try to scream to force him off of me so that my lungs can expand, but he presses the blade to my neck and gets in my face. When his weight shifts, I gasp in a desperate breath of oxygen, then try to push at his hand to move the knife from my neck. But the brute is huge, and the drugs have suppressed my wolf and her strength.

"Don't move, Seneca, or I'll fuck that pretty little face up," he threatens, pressing into me harder. A whimper forms in my throat, but I shove it down. No, these bastards won't get a peep of weakness or fear out of me. "Burke can't wait to see you again," he taunts, the blade of the knife slowly moving from my throat down my chest, a stinging trail left in its wake. "When a wolf called three days ago and informed Burke that a certain little pet had it too good here, he happily traded that wolf a place in our pack to get you back. Now you can get the punishment you deserve since Ruin Falls turned out to be so disappointing."

Conrad's words spiral around me and leave me reeling. *Did Presley set me up? Did she do this?*

Threateningly, his knife dips past my belly button, down to between my thighs. I suck in a breath as he twines the sharp tip of it through my curls and then lowers it to my seam. The disgusting smell of lust permeates the air, and I try to struggle out from underneath him again until he presses the blade to the inside of my thigh. I go still. My mother taught me all about anatomy, and I know if he cuts me deep enough, he could slice right through my artery, and I would bleed to death in minutes.

"Stop fucking around. Let's go," Ryden barks, fear dripping from his voice as he looks around wildly. He picks Saul up from the ground, who's now bleeding from both eyes. "We still need to get back to the car, and you know a sentry or something heard this little bitch screaming," he declares, shaking Saul for good measure and eliciting a whimper in return. How that pisser ever became a beta, I'll never know.

My hands start to go numb from the drug, and I can practically feel it moving up my arms and legs, deadening everything in its path.

"Coming," Conrad says, a sinister smile on his face. "I just want to give Rabid here a little taste of what she has to look forward to." I feel him flip the knife in his hand and press the handle of it to my opening.

I snarl and fight to get away, panic and a zing of pain shooting through me. But out of nowhere, a wolf leaps from the surrounding bushes and barrels into Conrad. A menacing snarl roars through the air all around me, and Conrad slams back from the impact, his knife flying out of his hands. The white and red wolf rips into the bastard beta's arm and thrashes as hard as she can, opening deep wounds that have Conrad screaming for help.

Presley lets go of his arm and snaps for his face, but Conrad flips her off of him. I struggle with everything I have to roll over, the sounds of Conrad shifting into his wolf spurring me on. I look to see if Tyran is with her, but no other wolves join in on the fight, and I lurch to my feet with a growl of effort, turning around as Presley attacks Conrad.

The sound of a vicious fight is all I can hear as my vision starts to blur and my limbs grow even heavier. I pitch forward, trying to focus, and see that Ryden has put Saul down and is instead scrabbling to grab Conrad's knife so he can attack. I beg my body for just a little more as Ryden grips the handle and picks it up.

Presley forces Conrad back, and even though his wolf has to have a solid fifty pounds on hers, she fights ruthlessly and tirelessly to get the upper hand. Ryden jabs at the white and red wolf, going for her throat, but I lurch forward, stepping between them at the perfect time. The knife sinks into my stomach instead, and I gasp at the burning sensation and the pain that hammers through me.

I look down at the blade sunk into my skin, blood dripping from the metal. The drug has disconnected me, or maybe it's the shock, because even though I feel the pain, it's sluggish, almost separated from the rest of me. I want to rip the blade out and slit the throat of the spineless piece of shit in front of me, but I can't feel my hands, and my legs give out beneath me, sending me crashing to the ground. A high-pitched yelp assaults the forest, and I look to see Conrad back in his skin, and Presley struggling in his chokehold.

"No, don't fucking hurt her," I yell at him, but the order lacks all power and sounds more like a croak as pain slurs my heavy tongue.

"Let's go!" Conrad shouts at Ryden, picking Presley up and carrying her with him, keeping a hand on her muzzle and legs pinned. "Leave Saul," the beta barks, and Ryden scoops me up from the ground and starts running behind Conrad.

Fear and fury crash inside of me, but I think it might be Tyran's emotions, because all I feel right now is resounding pain. Ryden runs clumsily through the trees and foliage, jostling me with every step and leaving a trail of blood in our wake. At least Tyran won't have to track my scent to find me.

Conrad runs hard, Presley's wolf still gripped in his hands, and Ryden falls further and further behind. I work to keep my eyes open, but they keep trying to shut. I think I hear a snarl coming from the woods.

Tyran.

"Fuck this shit, you're not worth it!" Ryden growls, and suddenly, he throws my body to the ground before he takes off after Conrad, my weight no longer slowing him down and allowing him to shift.

I slam against the unforgiving earth, my momentum rolling me, making the handle of the knife catch the ground and slice sideways before it's torn from my abdomen. Agony explodes through me, and this time, I do scream from the pain, but all that comes out is a sick mewling sound as my body hits a tree and stops rolling. I gasp for air, but the world spins and my vision curdles, my body not sure if it wants to vomit or pass out. My hands press to my stomach, and I look down at the puddled ground. So much blood.

The world goes quiet.

For one heartbeat.

Then two.

Three.

More blood gushes, my body shaking with tremors, my vision spinning and dotting with black, and I realize. I'm...*dying.*

Dread and horror agitate through me as anguish settles in my belly, and I feel tears stroke down my cheeks. My wolf whines inside of me while my heartbeat seems to slow. Just when I was settling into my new life, Burke had to rip it away. I don't want to die, not now when I'm right on the cusp of having so much happiness. My eyes sting with gut-wrenching sadness at the unfairness of it all.

But then I hear Tyran's ferocious snarl, and for a millisecond, my heart leaps, knowing he's here. That he came for me.

"Vicious!" he yells just as he pulls my face away from the dirt, rotating me onto my back. His gaze widening on the wound. "Fuck!" He presses hard against my abdomen, making a scream tear from between clenched teeth. "Vorria!" Tyran shouts, and I hate the panic I hear just under the rage.

"Presley," I grit out, my tone imploring. "They took Presley."

But Tyran isn't listening. He's staring down at his hands, where my blood is still flooding from my body. Fear charges through me, and I look up at Tyran, realization washing the rest of my strength away, because it's *his* fear. And somehow, that makes it so much worse.

"This is not fucking happening!" His eyes latch onto my face. "You fucking fight it right now, or so help me, I will follow you into the afterlife and drag you back here kicking and snarling," he threatens, and despite the terror working its way through my veins, I crack a smile at him, because I don't like seeing him hurting.

Unfortunately, my smile just seems to make more panic flare inside of him. "Vorria!" he shouts again, and I swear his command shakes the very mountains around us, but maybe that's just his trembling hands.

The sound of heavy paws hitting the ground is coming from somewhere I don't have the strength to track, but suddenly, there's a light gray wolf skidding to a stop next to Tyran. The wolf's fathomless brown eyes bore into me.

Britton.

He whines as he takes me in and Tyran's hands pressed brutally against the knife wound, trying but failing to staunch the bleeding.

"I've got her," Tyran snaps at him. "She said they got Presley. They must be parked at the northern service road; that'd be the closest access point by car."

Britton doesn't even yip in understanding, he just tears off in the direction I last saw Conrad and Ryden. I send all my hope with him that he catches them and rips them apart. Another wolf bounds out of the bushes, and oddly, it's carrying a little pack in its mouth. Bright hazel eyes meet mine, and the brown and white wolf morphs into the Healer Vorria.

I forgot she'd been with them on their Flux run, and hope flares through me as she completes her shift and kneels down next to me, assessing the damage. She lifts Tyran's hand and then slams it back down against my stomach.

"*Fuck,*" the old lady snaps, turning to pull something out of her bag. I would laugh at how funny it is to hear this tiny little thing go full foul-mouth, but I can't feel my body anymore, and I don't know if that's from the drug or the damage.

"Shot me...with a dart," I pant out, my voice barely above a whisper.

"Of course they did, honey. Cockless pissants like that could never take one of us head-on," she reassures me, and I again want to smile at what comes pouring out of her mouth. If I survive this, we're totally becoming besties.

I look up to find Tyran staring down at me, his eyes hard and determined. "If you think you're ever getting out of my sight after this, think again. I've never leashed a wolf before, but I think it's in your best interest if I just attach you to me at all times."

Vorria starts to chant, and despite my inability to really feel my body, the telltale cool feel of healing magic washes over me.

"You're the one who keeps...leaving me," I accuse playfully, my words partly slurred and clumsy as they tumble out of my mouth. "I just wanted...to stay in bed," I add, giving Tyran my best *you should have listened to me* look. "I mean, what's a girl gotta do to get a cuddle?"

"Stay here, Mate, and I'll cuddle you all you like." When I cough, Tyran's throat bobs and his eyes go pained. He leans in, pressing his fingers into my claiming mark, like he wants to remind me of our connection, anchor me to this world even though my body is trying to slip away. "You hear me? You're not going anywhere, Seneca."

"Bitch ass, leg humping *fuckers*," Vorria barks out, and Tyran looks over at her with concern. "There's a lot of damage, Alpha," she tells him plainly.

His lips pull back from his teeth. If he were in wolf form right now, he would be snapping and growling at her. "*Fix it*," he bites out, and just those two words fill me with horrifying sorrow at his desperation to keep me alive, to keep me with him.

I didn't get enough time, I think, as teardrops flow from my eyes. Not nearly enough time with this pack, with him. My wolf whines inside of me, the wound paining her, our shared spirits cracking.

Vorria shoots him a sympathetic look. "I could drain myself dry, and I will, Alpha, but it might not be enough," she tells him matter-of-factly, and I blanch at the truth I hear ringing in her words as fear soaks my cheeks.

Tyran looks like all the breath was stolen from his lungs in a brutal hit, like he'll never be able to breathe again. "You're fucking *strong*, Seneca, so I want you to fight, you hear me?" he says, hands cupping my cheeks and holding me firm. "I just got you, and I refuse to let you go."

My eyes are pulled away from his beautiful brown ones when Vorria presses down brutally against my wound, making me see stars and let out a gargled scream. I look down, watching as she presses harder against my stomach and shoves her magic forcefully into me. I gasp at the sensation that starts to spread, feeling the cool flood of her power. I immediately close my eyes and do something my mother and I used to do. I visualize the blood stopping and the layers of muscle, fat, and skin starting to knit back together.

Leading the magic, my mom used to say.

I focus as much of my energy as I can on getting better in hopes that it helps to save Vorria. I don't want her being drained to death—not even for me. Vorria gasps, and I open my eyes to try and see what happened. Her hazel gaze is fixed on me, and there's a gleam there now that wasn't there before.

"What?" Tyran demands.

"She has a spark," she declares, a palpable relief washing through her.

"What does that mean?" Tyran demands, and I'm grateful he does because I want to know the same damn thing.

"Luna, you said your mother was a healer?"

"Yes," I croak out. "But...I didn't...get...the gift," I add, struggling to form words even though it feels like thick cotton is being stuffed in my head, making it hard to think.

"You may not have gotten a strong enough spark of magic to become a healer, but you have a spark, honey, and you can use it to help me."

I try to nod, but I think I mostly look like I'm losing muscle control of my head and neck.

"Just focus, Luna. Focus just like you were. Shove everything you can at what's happening inside of you, and maybe we can do this together," she instructs, not wasting another second as she begins the cool rush of magic again, a soothing balm against my worried soul.

"Push," the healer demands, and I close my eyes, once again focusing all my energy just like my mother always taught me.

She never mentioned a spark, but she always made me do this when she used her magic on me. It happened less than a handful of times, a broken arm here, or when I fell out of a tree and cracked my head open, and then there was that time I accidentally sliced my hand with a knife while trying to peel a potato. Each healing moment stands out in my mind like a beacon guiding my way.

"Come on, Seneca. *Fight.* Give it everything you have. That's a fucking order from your alpha," Tyran yells at me, that raw, dominating power lacing his voice and demanding more than I ever thought I had to give.

The order stirs my wolf, his power reaching her even past the drug that's keeping us apart. Heat eddies inside of me, my stomach suddenly feeling like a whirlpool of hot and cold. My wolf and I fight, fight harder than we ever have, to stay here, to heal, to keep Vorria from draining herself dry.

I give my all, the effort so exhausting that I can't even open my eyes. My mind spins, my stomach rolls, and I shake all over and fight to stay conscious. Numbness spreads, and I don't know if that's a good or a bad thing, but I'm unable to ask. The vortex in my body slows, and tides of magic suddenly begin to recede.

"Was it enough?" Tyran asks, his voice desperate. "*Was it enough?*" he bellows when only silence answers his pleading question.

I want to reach up and stroke his face, to tell him how thankful I am that he was the wolf to claim me. But I can't feel my hand, can't even blink open my eyes. All I can do is float in some weird space between sleep and consciousness.

"Alpha," Vorria whispers feebly, her voice barely audible.

"Please, is she going to be okay? Was the spark enough?" Tyran pleads, and his pain, his vulnerability, it breaks my heart and sends my wolf into a howled lament.

Before Vorria can answer him, unconsciousness rears up and pulls me down into the darkness against my will, and then there's nothing.

TWENTY-ONE

"MATE."

Something presses against my face, and I bat it away.

"Vicious."

Another annoying touch at my stomach makes me groan out a protest, because dammit, all I want to do is *sleep*.

"Seneca."

A sense of deja vu washes over me, even though I feel disoriented and groggy. Through a raspy throat, I grumble, "I really prefer your other ways of waking me up." I drag my eyes open so I can blink up at the sexy, shirtless shifter looming over me.

Stark relief washes over Tyran's expression, and he settles next to me and cups my cheeks in his hands. "Don't you fucking *ever* try to die on me again."

His face is lined with weariness, dark circles beneath his brown eyes revealing his worry, the bond pulsing between us telling me the same thing.

Everything that happened rushes back in. The pain, the fear, the smell of blood leaking out of me dangerously fast, and Tyran as he begged and ordered me to fight, to live.

He releases me as I lift the sheet to look down at my stomach. There's an angry red puckered scar there and some healing herbs mashed over it in a sticky paste. I'm shocked that it looks as good as it does. "How long have I been out?"

"Two days," Tyran tells me, scooting in beside me with his back propped against the headboard as though he needs to be close but doesn't want to jostle me. "Vorria was just here again a couple hours ago with the salve." Relief washes over me to hear that the healer is okay. I test the spot gently and then sit up, only wincing slightly. "Don't try to move," he admonishes, but I ignore him and wiggle up until I'm leaning against his chest.

The second my head rests against his shoulder, he wraps his arms around me, careful not to touch my stomach. "How's the pain?" he rumbles, mouth against my hair as he lays a kiss on the top of my head.

"It's not bad at all," I reply honestly. "Whatever Vorria did, it worked."

"What you *both* did," he tells me, reminding me of what happened before I blacked out. "Your mom must've been one hell of a healer, because you had enough in you to save yourself *and* keep Vorria from draining dry."

The pride I hear in his voice, and his mention of my mom, make a tear leak from the corner of my eye. I don't know if he can sense it through the bond or he scented the brine in the air, but he shifts us until I'm pulled onto his lap and he can look at my face. A calloused thumb brushes against my cheek before he presses his lips against the spot.

"You're okay," he murmurs, knowing exactly what I need to hear. "You're so fucking strong, and I'm so damn proud of you." He buries his nose against my neck to breathe me in, and I feel a shudder go through him, emotion vibrating down the bond.

After all of the fighting, all of the fear, my mind is catching up with my healing body, and my wolf and I both seem to let out a shaky sigh at just how close that was. Somehow, we survived. I sit for a moment, safe in Tyran's arms, his strength and his scent surrounding me, anchoring me, fortifying me for the battle that I know is coming.

"Presley?" I ask, her name an aching question in my heart and on my lips.

I know the answer before he speaks. I can feel it in the tensing of his muscles, the pulse of anger down the bond. "They took her."

Despite my healing and fragile state, I want to rage, to rip into something, to howl until the pain that statement causes me subsides. I breathe through the need for vengeance, bottling it up so I can release it later. My chest tightens with the drive to do something to make them pay, and I look at Tyran and see and feel that he's experiencing that same overwhelming force.

"What's the plan?" I ask, knowing that there has to be one in that beautiful and ruthless head of his just waiting to be executed.

His eyes gleam mercilessly, but his hold around me tightens, as if he's afraid to let me go. "Britton's been tracking them. He stayed shifted, but he lost them a few times, took him a while to track them back to their territory. He was just able to get away to call me to let me know where they have her. He can't get to her alone. There are dozens of betas surrounding the place and even more patrolling."

Thoughts race through my mind of all the things they could

be doing to her right now...of all the things they wanted to do to me. My stomach roils, and my skin heats with fury. "We have to get her out."

Tyran nods in agreement. "We're leaving in an hour."

I'm pushing out of his hold and getting to my feet in an instant. "Vicious," he sighs. "You aren't going."

"The fuck I'm not," I snap back, walking—albeit tenderly—toward the dresser to get clothes.

Tyran opens his mouth to argue, but a knock sounds at the door. He pushes out of the bed and stalks over to it, exchanging some low words before he shuts it again, and then the smell of food fills the air, making my stomach growl longingly.

I manage to slip on some pants and socks, but when I try to lift a shirt over my head, my stomach screams in protest. "Fuck."

Large hands come around me, and I turn to face Tyran as he helps me thread my head through the neck of the shirt and then slips my arms through the sleeves. He does up the laces at the front gently, his worried brown gaze surveying every inch of me as though he's reassuring himself that I'm okay and that what he's doing isn't hurting me.

"Eat," he says when he's done, gesturing toward the wooden tray he's placed on the bed.

I give him a look but walk over and sit on the edge of the bed, trying to hide the sigh of relief from my aching wound. The food is barely cooked meat, both warm and tender, that practically melts in my mouth, and a huge helping of mashed potatoes. I shovel it down a bit faster than I can taste, and all the while, Tyran leans against the wall next to me with his arms crossed in front of his chest and an unreadable look on his face.

After I gulp down the cup of water, I wipe my mouth, already feeling better, stronger. I look over at him, silence stretching between us.

"I'm going," I finally say.

"No."

I get to my feet, proud of myself when I suppress the grimace, but Tyran cocks a brow. "You think I'm going to let my mate go into a dangerous situation when she *literally* just got up from her deathbed?" he demands.

"Okay, firstly, it was more like my healing bed, because I didn't die, I *healed*. Secondly, you're not going to *let* me do anything. Mate or not, I'll do whatever the fuck I want. I'm the reason that Presley was taken in the first place. So yeah, I'm going, and it's going to be fine."

"How?" he shouts, his sudden raised voice making me jump a little as I come to a stop in front of him. His face looks ragged, his expression crazed with worry. "How the hell can you say it's all going to be fine when you almost just fucking *died*, Seneca?"

I think he expects me to shout right back at him, but instead, my face softens. Because beneath the shouted anger, that fear I felt before I blacked out is still there, tormenting him. We haven't known each other for long in human standards, but we're wolves, and that connection is implicit.

My hands come up to lie against his chest, my palms feeling the race of his heartbeat. "I know it's all going to be okay, because *you'll* be with me," I tell him softly with an underlying edge of conviction. "I may be a little slow on the uptake sometimes," I confess, "but it hasn't taken me long to understand that when you're with me, everything is always exactly as it should be. I trust you."

A ragged breath comes out of him, and then he drops his forehead to mine. I feel all of the potent worry and suffocating fear that's been tightening around him since the moment he found out Twin Rivers wolves snuck onto his territory.

"I'd tie you to this bed, but I have a feeling you'd somehow get out and come on your own anyway, and then my wolf would go crazy and not be able to concentrate," he says on a growl.

"A fair prediction," I nod against him, a small smirk playing on the corner of my lips.

He sighs and pulls away to look me in the eye. "You have to promise you'll stay by my fucking side at *all* times, Seneca."

"I promise."

Tyran grumbles but relents. "Fine. But I swear to *fuck* if you do anything to put yourself in danger—"

"Yeah, yeah, you'll spank my ass red," I finish for him before standing up on my tiptoes to nibble just beneath his ear. "I'm still waiting for that, by the way," I tease.

A pained groan escapes him as heat simmers in the depths of his eyes. "I'm still pissed you're asking me to be okay with this. Don't try to distract me with sex."

I smile. "Why? Is it working?"

"A little, yeah," he admits grudgingly.

When I laugh, Tyran shakes his head and then grabs my face, fusing his lips to mine.

He devours my mouth, sweeping his tongue inside and turning my head just the way he wants me. Heat floods the juncture of my thighs, and a moan slips from my throat, but just when it's getting hot and heavy, he pulls away.

At my noise of protest, he smirks. "You'll get the rest of that *after* we get back safe and sound."

"It's a date," I reply. "Now let's go get Presley. And Tyran..." I start, my eyes hardening and the blood in my body heating with wrath. "I won't be happy until Burke's pieces are spread out on every corner of that territory, and his betas are nothing more than puddles of blood and pulp on the ground."

He shakes his head as I turn to head for the bathroom. "You're a savage little thing."

"You like it," I toss back over my shoulder.

Just before I close the door, I hear, "Yeah, I really fucking do."

I HANDLE MY BUSINESS IN the bathroom and wash up, pull back my hair, and wrap my stomach to help support the still healing muscles and dull the sensitivity of my skin there. I peek quickly at my reflection in the mirror, the sectoral heterochromia of my eyes no longer a shock or cause for alarm. The first time I looked into my eyes, I thought they were a reflection of just how fucked up I was. Like they were a warning to everyone else around me of what I was capable of.

Now, I don't see a warning, I see a promise. A promise of what I will do and the lengths I will go to protect myself and my new pack. My eyes *are* a reflection of how fucked up I am inside, but I no longer think that's a bad thing. I'm rabid, and there's not a damn thing wrong with that.

In such a short amount of time, Tyran and Ruin Falls have shown me a different way. And now it's time to show our enemies what happens when you fuck with us. It's time to make Burke pay and then burn his legacy to the ground.

When I leave the room, I find Harlan waiting for me just outside. "Luna, Tyran is in the meeting room," she tells me as we hurry down the stairs, and I follow her to the same place that I stormed into after I discovered Tyran's sex den.

I push the door open, and Tyran and the other betas look over. Just like before, all the males rise to their feet, and I nod at them in greeting and move to the empty chair next to Tyran, taking in the maps spread out on the table with positioning markers placed throughout.

"We were just finalizing our plans," Tyran tells me as I sit down, and I wait in silence for them to continue. "Britton gave us some information, but can you look these over?"

With a nod, I quickly check over all the maps, filling in the gaps, moving things around until it's just right and everyone has a clear picture of Twin Rivers' territory. The betas study it, talking through the plans.

"He knows we'll be coming, but Twin Rivers has never clashed with us in the past, so he'll have no idea what he's up against. Britton said they were moving Presley again, but if he can pinpoint exactly where she is, we'll go in hard and overwhelm them, and we can be in and out with minimal casualties," a beta named Darren states.

"That's assuming you want a quick in and out plan, Alpha. If you'd prefer to tear down Twin Rivers in its entirety, really set an example, then I'd send a team to extract Presley, while the rest of the pack focuses on cutting the hierarchy down," another beta chimes in.

Tyran nods, his eyes far away as though he's playing different scenarios out in his head. A knock at the door pulls the room's attention to it, and Harlan steps inside.

"They're here," she declares evenly, and everyone at the table pushes to their feet.

I follow suit, turning a questioning gaze to Tyran, who gestures for me to follow him. "I called in reinforcements," he explains. "We have allies with Plummet Lake pack, and I invited them here to join in on the fun."

I nod, my brow furrowing as I try to think through why the pack name sounds so familiar. Or maybe it's the word *allies* that's giving me pause. My mind tries to work through whatever it is that's bothering me about the situation as I follow Tyran and the pack betas out of the house.

And then it hits me.

Saul's voice rings in my mind clear as day, as the memory rushes through me of what the Twin Rivers' betas were discussing as they were searching for me.

Where's the other wolf? Burke said he'd be here with her and to bring him too. That was the agreement.

I turn to Tyran, pulling him to a stop, and the other pack members immediately do the same. "We have a traitor," I announce, and the males and females go eerily silent as my declaration sinks in.

"What makes you say that?" Tyran asks carefully, his eyes flashing with anger as a tic forms in his jaw.

"When Twin Rivers attacked me, they were talking about working with another wolf. That wolf was supposed to be there when they took me. They traded me for a place in Burke's pack."

The betas go tense, shooting looks between them, but it's nothing compared to the rigidity now coursing through Tyran.

"At first, I thought they might be talking about Presley," I admit with a bit of a wince. "She was the only one I could think of who really doesn't seem to like me and might have the right motivation, but she attacked them. She didn't leave me to fight them off alone, even though I ordered her to."

"Did they say who it was, give any more hints other than they were supposed to be there when you were attacked?" Tyran asks, his expression deathly cold and detached.

"No, but I'm pretty sure it was a male, they said *him*," I answer, frustration and regret marring my thoughts. I try to play back what happened. But between my panic and fear, my body's reaction to the dart they shot me with, and the emotions filtering through the bond, Saul's words are all I can pick out of my memories.

"I'm sorry," I offer Tyran and the betas, but his eyes soften for me, and he kisses me, his lips dismissing my apology.

"Nothing to be sorry for. You did good, and now we can all be sure to watch our backs until we can narrow down who it might be." Tyran turns back to his betas. "Travis, get with Link. He ran his nose over every inch of the attack area. Make a list of every wolf he picked up; we'll start there."

Travis salutes Tyran and immediately jogs off.

"Brody," Tyran barks out. "Get what you can from the male that was left behind, then kill him."

"Wait, you have Saul, Burke's beta?" I ask, surprised.

"We do, do you want to speak with him?" Tyran asks gruffly as though he doesn't like the idea of me being in the same place as one of the males who tried to take me.

I shake my head. "No, but, Brody? When you kill him, make it hurt...*a lot*," I instruct, and with a wicked smile, Brody salutes me and lopes away.

"Harlan," Tyran asks, "are they at the meeting point on our territory?"

She nods. "Yes, at the falls where you instructed."

"Load everybody up, we'll be leaving immediately after the meeting," Tyran commands, and three betas break away to follow his orders.

We walk quickly to the treeline, and Tyran reaches over and takes my hand as we make our way through the woods. He pops off orders about protective formations and the possible traps Burke may throw at us while we go, and I watch my mate, in complete awe of his confidence and control. It's easy to see why he's so formidable, and my wolf and I revel in this dominant vengeful side of him. He's just as savage as us. Perfect fucking mate.

Tyran orders his Third in command to stay by my side. The *no matter what* part of his order to Harlan makes me and my wolf bristle. But then it hits me just how awful the last two days must've been for Tyran as he watched me fight to heal and come back from what was done to me. Just the thought of anything happening to him overwhelms my wolf and me, and a new kind of rage begins to simmer inside of us.

Half of the betas with us shift and then span out in different directions. I breathe through the small twinges of pain that prick my stomach as we hurry, ignoring Tyran's probing eyes when he looks over at me as we go.

A little pain never hurt anyone. He'll just have to get over it.

Quickly, we climb up a steep hill to get to where Tyran's allies are waiting, volatile restlessness settling within our group. I can feel the need for blood moving through the pack, and I know that the time to leave, the time to *fight*, is getting closer.

Soon, the sound of water as it plummets off a cliff and falls recklessly to the ground pounds in my ears. It's a steady, immutable white noise that serves as the perfect background to the rhythm of the heartbeat in my ears and the contention thumping through my veins.

Then I come face-to-face with three consecutive waterfalls falling from a sheer cliff. They bathe us in their mist as we move closer, the water in the air like an eerie fog that's cloaking us from danger. The falls feed into a churning river that's sporting sharp stones jutting up every few feet and several downed trees that were caught in its wrath. Ruin Falls suddenly seems aptly named, the water willing and capable of utter destruction.

We step out of the milky haze of water and find several pack sentries guarding four males who look patient but alert and ready for anything that may come their way.

I study Tyran's allies with guarded curiosity, but when my eyes land on one of the males, my heart stops and anguish rips through me. The memory of Hess's bruised, battered, and bloody face pops up in my mind, followed by Burke's callous tone as he told me he was dead. I suddenly realize why the pack name Plummet Lake sounded so familiar, my mind jumping back to the night after my mother's funeral when Hess and I sat and drank a beer.

He told me then that his brother is the alpha of the Plummet Lake pack. What he didn't tell me is that his brother was his damn twin. Anger and sorrow curdle my thoughts as I take in the alpha.

They look exactly the same in every way, same blue-gray eyes, same round face, same color and style to their hair. I know it's not Hess solely because the scent is different, barely, but enough to confirm that I'm looking at a genetic replica and not my mother's best friend.

Unabashedly, I stare at the unknown male, only able to see his brother, and it sends a pang of misery and regret through me.

Does he hate me? Does he know I'm the reason his brother is dead?

"Thank you for answering our call, Kier," Tyran offers in place of a greeting.

"The pleasure is mine, Tyran. When I heard Twin Rivers was the target, I wouldn't have missed it for the world. My brother has been trying to leave the pack for years, and it's high time I help make that happen."

Tyran smiles, but there's nothing kind or warm about it. It's the smile of a savage beast when it knows it has cornered prey. But horror catapults through me at Kier's words, and I stare wide-eyed at the alpha.

Oh God, Kier doesn't know.

Tyran's head snaps to me as my feelings rush through him. He puts his back to the visiting envoy, and two wolves step between the groups, guarding their alpha's back as Tyran dips down until our eyes are level, his gaze burning to understand the panic and anguish now crashing through me.

"Vicious, talk to me," he murmurs, reaching out to hold me as though he's trying to anchor me and bring me back to the here and now.

"He's dead," I whisper, my voice hollow and worried.

"Who, Vicious?" he asks, clearly confused, but I look around him and fix my gaze on Kier.

My throat tightens, but I swallow past it, dismissing the sadness that I don't have time to focus on right now. I don't know what he'll do when I tell him the truth. Maybe he'll still help us, his mission turning to one of revenge instead of rescue, but I have to tell him what Burke did to his brother.

"Hess is dead," I call out hollowly, squaring my shoulders and readying myself for what will probably be a violent reaction. However, instead of rage or agony crumpling the alpha's face, he suddenly looks as confused as Tyran does.

Keir shakes his head, and my heart breaks a little at the gesture of denial. "No...my brother's alive," he replies slowly. I open my mouth to contradict his words, but he keeps going. "He's currently locked up in the Twin Rivers pack cells, but I assure you, he's still breathing."

Now it's my turn to shake my head, the gesture a rejection of his statement. "Burke beat him to force *me* to go through with the Flux. I saw it with my own eyes," I explain, hating that I'm the one who has to tell him this. It's bad enough that what happened was my fault. But now I have to shatter Hess's brother as badly as knowing *me* shattered Hess in the end. "I was trying to run, to get away, but Burke caught me and he... he killed Hess. He told me himself when he left me here," I explain, my eyes bleeding sorrow, my heart aching.

Kier looks at me more intensely, as though he's trying to figure out what's going on. I watch as something dawns in his eyes, and he takes a step closer, making the Ruin Falls wolves standing between us growl in warning. The Plummet Lake alpha raises his hands in apology and steps back before settling his stare back on me.

"You're Seneca? Seneca Rain?" he asks. His tone is perplexed, as though he's expecting me to say yes, but there's just a hint of doubt that maybe he's got this wrong.

"Yes," I answer simply, guilt weighing down my shoulders as Kier makes the connection.

Surprisingly, the alpha's eyes warm slightly. "Hess told me about you and your mom. I didn't realize you were here."

"This is where Burke dumped me after..." I trail off, not wanting to get into it, but I gesture to my eyes, and the males surrounding Kier fidget and go taut as though just the gesture was a threat against their alpha.

"Well, that piece of shit lied to you," Kier declares, not an ounce of doubt in his words and his tone brooking no room for argument. "Hess is hurt, but he's alive. I would know if that weren't the case," he tells me, his fist bouncing on his chest and indicating what has to be a connection between him and his twin brother.

A small spark of hope ignites in my soul, and I stare at Kier as though I'm trying to peel him open and spot any signs that he could be wrong. He looks back at me, his countenance certain, his eyes filled with steely conviction. The spark in my soul morphs into an inferno, and I tilt my head back to the sky and breathe out a sigh of relief.

Hess is alive.

Happiness hums through me. Even though Hess and I were never close, I'm grateful to know that Burke lied. I should've known he was full of shit. I should've questioned it, made sure. I just took what he said at face value because it seemed exactly like something he would do.

Tyran squeezes my shoulders and then turns back to the other pack. "I assume you've brought more than a couple betas as back up?" he asks the other alpha.

"I have every warrior, hunter, sentry, and beta I could spare, while still keeping my pack protected."

Tyran nods and gestures for Kier and his males to follow us. "Perfect, you can ride with us, and we'll pick up your pack as we head out. Claw Ridge will be joining us too, but they'll take a little time reaching Twin Rivers. We'll work everything out on the way."

Kier smiles coldly, his eyes alight with promises of retribution and pain. "Let's go rip those cowards limb from limb."

TWENTY-TWO

"He should be here."

I look at the frown marring my mate's face, the only outward sign of the worry I feel churning beneath his hardened exterior.

"Let's give him a few more minutes," I suggest, though anxiety is starting to spike in my stomach too. Luckily, my wound there is feeling so much better and hardly hurting at all anymore, like my wolf helped heal it in double time so we'd be ready for tonight.

But Britton was supposed to meet us here so he could confirm how many wolves are guarding Presley and show us where she's being kept. Tyran spoke to him just four hours ago, and we've been at our meet point now for almost thirty minutes, but...no Britton.

The woods are quiet, the canopy of trees covering us beneath the moonlit night, though the still shadows do nothing to ease my worry. If anything, the woods sound *too* quiet. My wolf doesn't like the smell of it either. She likes the scent of *her* woods, back at Ruin Falls. This place, this land, it's been tainted by Burke's presence, as if even the mulch in the dirt and the leaves in the trees have been altered and poisoned by him. I grew up in these woods, spent most of my life wandering between these trees, but there's absolutely nothing about this place that feels like home anymore.

A Ruin Falls wolf moves through the shadows to approach us. I watch until the moonlight highlights his face and recognize Brody.

"Any news?" Tyran asks him quietly.

"Alpha, the leak was *Warrik*," Brody says with an irate expression on his face. "It seems before the reckoning, he was making some moves. He was trying to leave and join Twin Rivers pack, and to earn his spot, he was supposed to hand over information...and Luna."

Rage heats my blood and makes me snarl. I wish there was a way to bring the betraying wolf back from the dead just so I could rip him apart and kill him all over again. I can feel the same fury bleeding through my mate bond, and Tyran's eyes are hard, the tic in his jaw working overtime.

"He died too easily," he seethes, and I nod, breathing through the haze of red that's trying to drop over my vision.

"At least he's dead. That's one less problem we have to worry about now," I remind him.

Tyran nods, dismissing his beta with a wave, and returns his angry gaze on our surroundings.

"You're sure this is east of the main pack house?" he asks me.

I nod, and even though I'm basked in darkness, I know he and Kier can see me. "Positive."

He lifts his nose to the air again, and I do the same on instinct, but there's no sense of Britton anywhere. He never came this way.

The wind is on our side, blowing at us and the wolves below. It's just Tyran, myself, Kier, and his Second up here for now. As a precaution, Tyran and Kier had the rest of their pack members spread out below us. The betas are so well-trained that I can't sense them at all, even though I know wolves are crawling over this forest behind us, split up in groups as they keep watch and wait for signals.

"We need to move in, Tyran," Kier says from where he and his Second are crouched to our left. "We can't afford to waste time. The longer we sit here with our thumbs up our asses, the more chance Twin Rivers has to pick up our scent."

"Burke's betas don't come out this far to do their territory checks," I say quietly.

Kier shoots me a disbelieving look, eyes flashing in the dark. "This is his land, isn't it? Why wouldn't he have his wolves check it and mark it?"

"He's cocky," I explain. "Not to mention lazy. He doesn't run perimeter checks himself, and his betas know they can get away with not crossing the river every day. They all think the water is a deterrent and only check up to one side of it."

Tyran moves from his crouched position beside me and stares off between the thick trees. At first, I think he's listening for something, but when he runs his hand through his shoulder-length brown hair and frustration flows into me from our bond, I understand what's up. "I don't understand. Britton should be here. Something's wrong, I can fucking tell."

I grab his chin and turn his troubled eyes on me. "Britton is your Second, so he knows what he's doing," I say, because there's no way anyone is ready to consider the alternative, that he was somehow killed by Burke or his betas. "If he's not here, then it's because he couldn't make it safely without being followed. So, what do you want to do?" I ask, looking at him steadily, hoping that my calm determination will ease him.

He's been on a razor's edge of madness since the moment he found me stabbed, and the hits have kept on coming. Presley being taken, Britton alone, the only one that could follow her. And now his pack, his *family*, is here, putting themselves in danger. But I know that my presence is making things even worse. I sense that furious anxiety in him like an exposed live wire, which is why I'm making sure to keep my promise and stay glued to his side.

Tyran looks at me, and after a second, he lets out a breath and nods. "Alright. We move forward," he says to Kier.

A resolute demeanor settles over him. "Vicious, do you think you can get us to the same place Burke held you at after you attacked him?"

A flash of the cold concrete cell and the dented metal door shiver through me. My memories of that night are hazy from the damn tranquilizers, but I force myself to look through them step-by-step to try and pick up on any hints of where it might have been.

It was definitely underground and close to the main pack houses. I was out of it, but they carried me for a bit before the pack was suddenly there hurling things at me until they shoved me into the van. I certainly never knew about any concrete holding cells being built on pack land, but I think I can figure out the general location based on what I remember.

"Yes," I tell him with a determined nod.

I start to track silently through enemy territory, leading us up to the thinnest part of the river where we cross.

Tyran and Kier said that Burke will be expecting us and that he'll have tricks up his sleeve, and I find myself holding my breath as I wait for him and a flood of warriors to come pouring out of the darkness at any moment.

My wolf is practically keening inside of me, begging to be let out, but it's not time yet.

We seep into Twin Rivers territory, making our way past through the shallow parts of the river until we get to the other side. I'm shocked by how well the packs move, as though all we are is shadow. It makes pride and goose bumps crawl all over my skin, and my wolf's savage need begins to warm my blood as we get closer and closer.

"I know what that look means," Tyran declares quietly as we move like wraiths over the flat land.

"What look?" I deflect as I stop and suck in a deep lungful of air, looking for the scent of Burke, betas, fear, and me all in one place.

"You're getting amped about going a little feral on your old pack."

"Whaaaat?" I say in false shock. "That doesn't sound like me at all."

My sardonic voice earns me a grudging smirk, while Kier and his Second chuckle a little behind us. "Just remember what we talked about, Vicious."

Meaning, I'm still healing. Meaning, I better not fucking need *more* healing, or Tyran might lose his ever-loving mind.

"I'll be fine, and I'll be right by your side the whole time, Alpha," I say, leaning up to plant a kiss on his delicious lips. "Now hurry up," I whisper into his ear so only he can hear. "The quicker we get our pack safely home, the quicker we can get to the victory sex."

I don't hear the growl he gives me, but I feel its vibrations pressed against my side. He reaches around and squeezes my ass, mouthing, "Perfect fucking mate," against my lips.

I smile and pull away, again focusing on where we need to go.

"Damn, I've been claimed for twenty years, but half a day around you two has me wishing my mate was here right now," Kier says behind us, and Tyran shoots him a cocky smile and an eyebrow wag.

I lead the way, Tyran at my side, giving quiet bird calls or mouse chirps to guide the rest of the pack at our heels. Kier and his Second keep pace with us, and I start to pick my way through the woods with honed focus. I can't think about how much everyone is depending on me to get us where we need to go. That's a lot of pressure riding on the shoulders of a wolf that was starved, drugged, and half mad when she was carried out of where we're trying to find.

But I'm not just Seneca Rain, ex-pack member turned rabid anymore. I'm the motherfucking luna of Ruin Falls, and I will not crumble under the pressure.

I stop at a treeline through the woods with a clearing just ahead, and a sense of familiarity hits me.

We're here.

Certainty moves through the bond to Tyran, and he surveys me. "You're sure?" he whispers, his voice barely more than a breath.

Half of my right eye glows violet in the dark, the presence of my wolf pressing up against my control as we share our vision. I tip my head up, and she scents the air around us, picking up on even the most underlying and diluted of smells.

There, beneath dozens of Twin Rivers pack members, is my own scent...and Presley's.

"I'm sure," I reply decisively.

We're not far from the main pack house where Twin Rivers held the Flux ceremony. From where I was attacked and then later chained and slung over Conrad's back while my pack threw insults and rocks.

"Looks like a damn woodpile," Kier murmurs from his spot by a tree to our left.

He's not wrong. The place I've led us to looks completely inconspicuous. Just a huge dumping pile of chopped wood for fires and scrap pieces from fences. We're a good distance away, but even with the cover of night and low brush, my shifter vision identifies everything with perfect clarity.

It makes sense the cells are hidden. I never knew the pack had anything like it before they tossed me in there. There was no light, no sound, not even any scents other than the overwhelming stench of bleach and my fury. The fact that it was underground doesn't surprise me in the slightest.

When Tyran doesn't say anything, I glance over at him, but he's facing the woodpile with flared nostrils, the glow of his wolf's eyes flashing through the dark. I reach down and grip his hand. "What is it?"

He blinks and looks over, but the anger doesn't leave his face. "I just picked up your scent. I can smell your rage. Your *fear*, like it's stamped into the earth itself," he growls. "It's making my wolf go fucking crazy."

Fur erupts down the length of his forearms, claws threatening to descend, so I squeeze his hand tighter. "Hey. If you go savage, I go savage with you," I tell him with a small smile. "Soon, but not yet. Come on, my alpha. What's the plan?"

Like those words flipped a switch, Tyran seems to snap back into leader mode. "I don't like how quiet it is," he says with a shake of his head as he surveys the area again. "Burke will know we're coming for Presley, and I still haven't caught a whiff of Britton."

"I don't scent Hess either," Kier adds.

They're right, I can't smell the two males at all. "Maybe they're keeping them somewhere different?" I offer.

"Is there anywhere else you know about?" Tyran asks me.

"No, but I didn't know about this place before either."

Tyran considers this for a moment, his focus on the huge woodpile that's got to be hiding some sort of bunker doorway somewhere, while my ears are perked to focus on the sounds behind us, to stay alert on our pack that's spread out amongst the trees and cloaked by night.

"Regardless if we smell the males or not, Presley's scent is here—faint, but it's here," Tyran declares, as though he's talking to himself more than anyone else. He looks around as though he's sorting through our options.

"There should be betas crawling all over this place," Kier points out, and Tyran nods as though the other alpha is confirming his suspicions.

"So if this is trap one, what domino effect is it going to set off?" Tyran asks.

I chew on my bottom lip, trying to think through the options. "Burke isn't a fighter, not a very good one at least, but he is calculating. I don't know if it really matters which trap we spring first," I tell them as I survey the innocent looking wood pile. "He knows we'll be here for our people, and from what I know about Burke, he'll use one of them as bait and the others as leverage, just in case. He doesn't fight fair. He'll make it almost impossible to walk away from this unscathed and feeling like we won."

Tyran nods, clearly contemplating what I've said. "Okay, how do we want to spring this trap then?"

For some reason, his confident, unruffled answer about willingly walking into a trap makes heat spread through me. I adjust my legs ever so slightly, but of course, he picks up on it anyway and sends me an incredulous look. "Really? *That* got you going?"

My shoulder lifts in a shrug, because I'm just as surprised as he is, considering the inappropriate timing. "Look, I don't know what to tell you. The new mate bond is really intense," I whisper, hoping like hell that the others can't hear.

Tyran shakes his head, but a smirk crooks the side of his mouth before he clears his throat. "Alright," he says, looking to Kier. "Two betas to check it out. One of mine, one of yours? And then the three layer approach we discussed on the way here."

The Plummet Lake alpha nods and then lets out a soft trill that resembles a cricket.

Within seconds, two wolves emerge from the shadows, both as black as night and easily blending in. Tyran and Kier both quietly issue orders, and I hold my breath as I watch the two betas stealthily walk out of the treeline and head for the stacks of loose, forgotten wood.

Several other wolves move up alongside us, but I don't turn to take them in. In my crouched position on the forest floor, I watch, not even allowing myself to blink as the two black wolves dip their noses to the ground. Together, they start to sniff the perimeter, going in opposite directions as they attempt to find an entry point into the underground space.

The two of them round the massive wood pile at about the same time, disappearing from our view. Beside me, Tyran is tense, head cocked, eyes glowing as we watch, neither of us even seeming to breathe.

Seconds pass. *Too many* seconds.

There isn't a sound. Not a single fucking sound. And still, our betas don't reappear.

"Where are they?" I ask, desperately scanning, my heart pounding in my chest. Next to me, Tyran curses. "They can't just have...we would have heard something. Seen something..."

All of a sudden, the sharp scent of blood hits the air. And then, my stomach drops with the sight that spills out. Twin Rivers betas start *pouring* out of a gap in the wood pile on the left side. They shoot out of the bunker like bullets, heading right for us.

Tyran shouts out a warning call for our pack, but it gets drowned out with the sound of wolves attacking us from behind.

They're coming at us from both sides.

I hear Kier curse before he and his Second fold into their shifted wolves. Terror flashes through me with the realization that I led us right to Burke's perfectly planned slaughter, even though we anticipated a trap. I still feel responsible. Bile rises up in my throat, and rage pounds in my pulse as time seems to slow down, and I watch enemy wolves racing toward me.

Before my emotions can totally override my much-needed focus, Tyran grips my arm, forcing me to look at him. "Don't leave my side." Fur is already sprouting all over his body. "Let her out, Vicious," he encourages calmly. "Let her rip through you and show these wolves what you're fucking made of."

A heartbeat later, his shift is complete. His words wash over me, heating my blood and calling to the savage beast I've always been. I drop into myself without hesitation, and my wolf bursts through me, all claws, fangs, and fury. A Twin Rivers wolf leaps at us, but Tyran is ready for them. He unleashes in a way I've never seen before.

That scrapple during the claiming hunt, the way his power forced me to shift, his prowess and unwavering focus when he hunted, when he claimed, all of it is *nothing* compared to the wolf before me now. This is the ruthless alpha of Ruin Falls. Tyran's brown wolf tears through the first Twin Rivers pack member while it's still leaping through the air. One second, the attacking male has a throat, and the next, he doesn't.

The body falls at my feet just as my wolf shakes out her shift, and a second wolf barrels into Tyran, hoping to knock him off his feet. This one is smaller than my alpha, though he makes up for it with quick snaps of his teeth and a dodgy trick of his feet.

Tyran misses his throat by an inch, the male managing to leap backward out of range. Unfortunately, he didn't count on me. The moment he's near enough, my wolf lunges, teeth sinking into the back of his neck. He panics, trying to get out of my hold, but my wolf digs in harder and jerks his head up, forcing him to bare his throat. Tyran rips into it a second later, and the male goes limp.

Before my wolf even drops him to the ground, another is already on top of Tyran. Snarls tear from their throats as the Twin Rivers male attacks from the side and drags claws down my mate's flank. My wolf bares her teeth in vicious anger, and then she's on the male, tackling him to the ground and tearing into his exposed belly. All she feels is the need to attack, to maim, to wound. Within seconds, her mouth is dripping with blood, and spilled guts pepper the ground around our feet.

Sharp teeth dig into her flank, the scent of our blood mixing with the others already permeating the air. A howl of surprised pain escapes us, and she spins her body around in hopes of throwing the new wolf off. But there's no need. My mate lunges, jaw clamping down on the attacker's skull, and then he bites down.

Bone shatters between his powerful jaws, the wolf unable to even whine in pain before it's dead. The body is just another heap on the ground, further proof of the devastation of our savagery. Glowing brown eyes lock with ours, and the bond between Tyran and me pulses in proud satisfaction at how well we work together to take down our enemies.

All around us are the sounds of ferocious battles encircling and trapping us in their brutality. For a moment, my wolf's senses become overwhelmed by the snarls, howls, and cries of pain. All she can think of is her pack being hurt, being slaughtered by the sheer numbers of Twin Rivers, but Tyran's massive brown wolf rubs against us, drawing our attention to where he's pointing his muzzle.

I see two Ruin Falls wolves battling side by side, each of them watching the other's backs and fighting off the wolves darting at them. They defend themselves with fierce precision, taking advantage of the openings the Twin Rivers create in their haste to attack.

We may be outnumbered, but Tyran shows me that our pack is better prepared, better trained, and far more effective in battle than I realized. Bloodlust pumps through our veins as I turn back to him. With a happy yip, he jerks his head to the left and starts racing that way with a clear direction to follow him.

My wolf takes off after him, her violet eyes scanning the dark grounds as Tyran heads for the pile of wood. Wolves split off from the fight and move to surround us, and the familiar smell of Ruin Falls fills our nose as the formation Tyran designed tightens in against us and we move toward the underground cells.

The doorway is half-hidden beneath a strategically placed pile of logs, creating an overhang above the cellar-style entry. Tyran's wolf looks at us over his shoulder as if to remind us to stick close to him before he heads inside behind several of our wolves.

We don't hesitate to follow him, our paws racing down the surprisingly wide set of stairs. We hit the bottom a second after Tyran, staying so close that we can feel every swish of his tail against our front legs.

The space is a plain square room covered in Twin Rivers' scents. There are pinpricks of light feeding from the ceiling that make it look like someone poked holes into the top, like feeding air to a bug in a jar. If it weren't for my wolf's superior senses, I wouldn't be able to see much of anything.

Both my wolf and Tyran's stop to take it all in as Kier comes up behind us and does the same. Anxiety pulses through me at the dead silence in the room, but my wolf is focused as she allows herself a moment to take in her senses, determining what she can pick up. With so much of Twin Rivers polluting the air, it's difficult to pick up anything else other than the scent of bleach, as if they mopped this place floor to ceiling in the caustic stuff.

In front of us is a hallway, a claustrophobic expanse of concrete walls and floor. But my wolf's lips peel back, nose tilted in the air, because she smells *us*, and right next to it is Presley's scent, thicker and filled with fear and blood.

Tyran's wolf lets out a low growl, and then he creeps forward, pausing once to look back at us. I'm confused for a second, but then realize he doesn't want us walking behind him. My wolf steps up to him, and only when we're side-by-side does he start forward again. Kier takes up the rear with two layers of wolves behind him, just like two layers of wolves are in front of us. Our paws silently tread forward, noses trained and ears perked for the slightest sound.

My mate's side presses against mine, muscles tense as we walk. Lights hang uselessly from the short ceiling above us. The bare bulbs are turned off, the depleting light making the darkness close in on us more and more, like the hallway might just swallow us down at any moment.

It's why we don't see the attack before it's right on top of us.

The *pop pop pop* of an all-too familiar tranq gun goes off at the same time that five wolves burst through a doorway to our right. The front layer of wolves dive in front of the darts, taking them full-on, but still fighting the intruders mercilessly as the drugs start to kick in. Screams and yelps bounce off the cinder block walls, but we rush forward in search of Presley.

An overwhelming scent of fear and desolation makes my wolf want to sneeze in order to dispel it. We smell other females down here, females that felt debilitating fear. With a snarl from Kier, someone behind us shifts and starts opening doors.

Terrified screams pierce the quiet as we go, but Tyran and I are focused on one thing only, rescuing our pack member.

Halfway through the cells, we smell her again. An impatient whine escapes my lips as we wait for someone with hands to open the latch on the door. There are no locks that we can see, only old industrial freezer-like handles that automatically lock once they've clicked in place.

An arm reaches through the cluster of wolves, the hand yanking on the latch and swinging the door open. More pops fill the air, and another layer of wolves in front of us take several darts with growls and well-timed leaps to ensure their alpha and luna aren't hit. We rush into the room, making short work of the two Twin Rivers betas who were lying in wait with their tranquilizers.

We spin, looking for any more threats, and that's when we see her.

Lying on the ground in her human form, beaten almost beyond recognition, is Presley. The smell of blood, hate, and terror float in the room, and my wolf and I can't help but see ourselves in the broken female that's sprawled out on the cold concrete floor. Tyran moves to approach her, but I cut him off. If her time was anything like mine was down here, a female's touch and comfort might be less alarming at first than a male's.

My wolf and I smell Conrad on her skin as we move closer, and visible handprints have been bruised into her arms and thighs. She whimpers as she senses our approach, and my wolf immediately pulls back, giving me control. Our fur falls away, our jaw cracking into place as I step forward and put myself in Presley's line of sight. Her eyes are squeezed closed, but I notice a fresh bite is marked into her shoulder, and my wolf and I rage at what's been done to her.

"Presley," I whisper, trying to choke down the horror tightening my throat as I take her in. I'm careful not to touch her, not to trigger her in any way, and I wait until my voice registers and she hopefully opens her eyes. "Presley, it's me, Seneca. We're here to get you out," I reassure her, but she's lost in her mind, her body trembling violently against the fear I can smell rolling off of her in waves.

Tears drip down my cheeks as I look up at Tyran, the brown eyes of his wolf staring at me while we trade agony back and forth through our bond. I pull in a shuddering breath, my wolf losing it inside of me, needing to destroy the males who did this to our pack.

The sounds of battle reach down to us from the cells, and I know we need to get Presley out of here and find the others. I'm terrified I'll traumatize her even more by just picking her up and carrying her away.

So instead, I bite back a sob and move across the room to palm a dart gun that's resting on the floor. I hate what I know I have to do, hate that it's what they've done to her *and* to me. But if she's unconscious, we can get her home, get her somewhere safe and familiar, and then try to help her work through the horrors that happened in this room.

With quick succession, I send two darts into the meat of her outer thigh, and my heart breaks when she doesn't even cry out from the pain. It's as though she's locked down tight in her mind, and I worry if we'll ever be able to coax her back out again. Tyran growls deeply, and two wolves from our group immediately shift and bend to pick Presley up.

Agony rips through me as I give myself back to my wolf, and as soon as we're on our paws again, a fire and furor like we've never felt before consumes us. We look over at Tyran, and we can feel the same resolution pulsing out from him.

It's time to make the fuckers pay.

TWENTY-THREE

TYRAN AND I TEAR OUT OF THE CELLS LIKE VENGEANCE made corporeal.

The cries of abused and newly freed females fall away in our wake. Kier's voice echoes behind us as he arranges extraction for each and every one of the ten wolves that we found down in the bunker. Disgust and horror provoke a merciless response from us as we start to tear through Twin Rivers wolves like vengeful tornadoes, leaving only destruction in our wake.

We hunt for Britton, Hess, and Burke as we purge a path of destruction through the land I once called home. I revel in the blood spilled by our teeth and claws every time my wolf and I take another enemy down.

Plummet Lake and Ruin Falls destroy Twin Rivers wolf by wolf, and it's music to my ears.

While Tyran and I continue to fight together, taking down anyone who comes for us, a huge black wolf leaps at me. At first, I think it might be Burke, and my wolf snarls in anticipation of taking the fucker down, but it becomes clear that it's not him when we don't smell his sickly-sweet scent of rotting fruit. Tyran and I quickly destroy our attacker, and the taste of his blood keeps us hungry for the hunt of the alpha.

Howls fill the night air all around us with calls of retribution and declarations of fear as Ruin Falls and our allies purge this pack. While Tyran and I dispatch another beta, I smell him...Conrad. Burke's beta calls to me like a beacon, demanding justice for his sickening scent being all over Presley, for the stench he left behind in the cells, for what he wanted to do to me.

Ferocious focus fills both my wolf and me, and we nip at Tyran, who's finishing off another attacker, to tell him to come with us. We follow the scent my wolf has latched onto, dodging fighting wolves and dead bodies strewn across the ground. Twin Rivers is suffering mass casualties, but I can't find it in my heart to care. Not when their scents cover that bunker. Not when they all helped to run this pack with fear and force.

Burke and his boys systematically destroyed everything that this pack, our people, were supposed to stand for. Too much of this pack let a monster call to their own, while the rest of them turned a blind eye, thinking the depravity and destruction wouldn't come for them.

They were wrong.

I can see the realization on the faces of the people and wolves huddled off to the side in fear as they take in the carnage and our demand for retribution. My wolf and I fly past them, past the alpha house, with Tyran on our heels right as we spot Burke, Conrad, and several other betas throwing bags into a van. *Kill kill kill,* my rabid beast bays.

The males' eyes are frantic and wild, their movements hurried and reeking of cowardice. They brought all of this down upon them, and now they're going to run? He doesn't deserve to call himself an alpha.

I'm sure Burke thought he had the upper hand, had the numbers. It's clear by how he and his sycophants are scrambling that they've quickly learned that one wolf with heart, one beast fighting for who they love, for what they believe in, *that's* worth more than a whole pack of honorless animals.

As we race forward, I suddenly smell Hess and Britton, but I don't see them anywhere.

My wolf throws her head back and howls out a declaration to our packs that I've picked up the scents. Answering howls reach us on the wind, and then Tyran and I are purely speed and power as we leap at the Twin Rivers' hierarchy. We slam into them, sending them toppling over like bowling pins.

Some of them try to shift, try to put up a fight, but by the time they can even call to their wolves, Tyran has ripped their throats out. Conrad steps in front of Burke to shield him, but that's fine by me. I've already shown Burke that I can best him, and I have no doubt I'll do it again. But first, it's time to bathe in the blood of the fucking scumbag beta who hurt Presley.

I snap at him, but his brutish arms shove my wolf and I away, our teeth unable to tear into him like we want. We redirect our efforts and feign a leap, but instead of putting all our power in it, we turn it into a small hop and snap at Conrad's legs. Blood explodes into our mouth as we sink our fangs into his meaty thigh, and we start to snarl and shake our head, ripping away at the muscle and skin as he screams and tries to pry us off.

Conrad lands blows to our head and body, one slamming into us so viciously that it disorients my wolf and me. We're forced to let go and back up to shake off the haze. Tyran darts for Burke, but the gutless weakling pulls a gun from behind him and aims it at my mate.

Everything slows.

My wolf's howl is my inner scream. We know judging by the distance that we'll never be able to reach them in time, but we try anyway. Tyran's eyes narrow with rage, a threatening snarl tearing from him as he stares Burke down. Time seems to speed up again as soon as our paws pummel against the ground, but Burke squeezes the trigger.

A bang pierces the night and my soul, simultaneously.

But faster than a blink, a light brown wolf appears out of nowhere, and the bullet meant for Tyran tears into her instead.

Harlan and her wolf slam to the ground, a crimson blossom blooming quickly out of the wound in her side. Another howl tears from my wolf, but huge, angry hands clamp down on my neck, cutting the sound short. Our focus is ripped away from my mate and his wounded Third as Conrad yanks my wolf off the ground, mercilessly crushing her throat. He leers at us, blood splattered across his face and eyes, reveling in the pain he's causing and the control he has over us.

We claw at him, but our paws aren't capable of peeling his fingers from around our neck. Our most lethal weapon, our teeth, are at this monster's mercy. If we stay a wolf, we're going to die, but if we shift back into my body, we're even more defenseless.

Rabid rage beats through our body as we wiggle and thrash, doing everything we can to break Conrad's hold, but nothing works. We fight against succumbing to the panic and fear trying to pull us under as black spots start to taint our fractured vision. My wolf and

I both stare out of the same eyes at the ruthless beta who's trying to kill us. I wonder how many vulnerable wolves are out there with this face haunting their nightmares, and just like that, a strange calm washes over us.

I scream inside, because I know my mate won't get here in time. We've already been out of breath for too long, and Tyran is too far away. I stare into hate-filled, murky green eyes and scream at myself that this is not how it ends.

My wolf and I were forged from violence and survival. So much so that we fractured ourselves to become what we needed in order to survive. And that's when it hits me. I know what to do.

I call on my wolf, begging her to pull back and to let me through. It's not a shift that I'm after though. The shattered pieces of our souls come together, the thin veil separating our jagged halves making a new joining possible. I wind myself around my wolf's essence, feeding everything I am into her, while demanding everything she is in return. I feel her give in to what I'm trying to do, morphing us into an in-between state where we're neither wolf nor person, but both at the same time.

Like our cursed Lycan cousins, my body twists and breaks to make room for something new, something we shouldn't be able to do. Both wolf and woman, possessing the same body at exactly the same time, just like we can do with our eyes. Our fractured pieces coalesce into something so much *more*.

Our limbs and torso elongate, our paws stretching into savagely sharp claw-tipped fingers. Our face morphs, and we see a flash of uncertainty, a flicker of fear, blaze through Conrad's eyes. That's the only reaction he has time for.

My wolf and I use every ounce of strength we possess in our new form to shove a hand straight into the bastard's chest.

Bones shatter with the impact, and our claws pierce the vital organ keeping this cruel, lecherous piece of shit alive. We stare into his eyes mercilessly, death drenching our gaze, as the red veil of rage we normally see through darkens to black.

The grip around our throat weakens just a second before Conrad crumples to the ground, the last of the air in his lungs bursting out of him like it too can't wait to abandon this monster. Gore drips from my hand and arm as I tip my head back and roar out my victory.

A car engine starts, and I snap my head in the direction of the van that's peeling away. I see Burke in the driver's seat as he cuts the wheel, desperate for escape, running over his own pack members in the process as he charges through the melee. I snarl in outrage and charge after him, refusing to let him get away and not have to answer for his crimes, for everything he's done over the past three years. My wolf and I sprint, giving it everything we have, our legs pumping, our breaths heaving.

With elongated strides, we catch up with the back bumper.

Then, we're even with the rear wheel.

Our glowing eyes reflect in the back window.

Driving ourselves even harder, we come up even with the driver's side.

Our lungs pull in great gulps of air, our body primed to hunt and kill the alpha who's haunted our waking steps from the minute my wolf and I became one. Terrified black eyes jump from the road in front of him to where I'm running alongside the van. Burke screams and yells for the van to go faster, and violent satisfaction fills me as the smell of his fear makes our blood sing.

A howl erupts from behind me, and I can feel Tyran's worry and anger as he calls out into the night again. His need beckons me, and I snarl, knowing what it means. A frustrated, screaming growl vibrates through my chest, but when it comes to choosing between vengeance against Burke or answering the call of my mate, my mate will win every time.

I slam a clawed fist against the driver side window, and it shatters under the force of my vehemence as Burke screams. I look him in the eye, my rabid stare vowing that he'll see me again, and then I slow my pace, letting the van race away from me as I turn to answer Tyran's howl for help.

Sprinting back the way I came, I race past the pack house. Part of me is demanding that I turn and finish off the threat to our pack, to destroy the reason why we're even here, but our pack needs us. Twin Rivers wolves yip in fear as they part and make way for me, quickly backing away as I approach the gathering in the heart of their territory. Just behind the pack house, surrounded by a protective circle of our wolves, I find Tyran, Kier, Vorria, and another male. I don't know him, but he smells like magic, so I assume he's Plummet Lake's healer. Just past them, with a wicked scowl, bruises all over his face, and a makeshift sling on his arm, is Britton. *Thank the moon our pack's Second is okay.*

As soon as we're close enough, Tyran comes over to rub against me and my wolf, not even bothered in the slightest by our new form. His response warms us, and I run my claws through his fur, beyond grateful to have found such a worthy male who understands and accepts everything we are no matter what.

Vorria's gaze snaps to me. "Luna, we need you," she barks, her thoughts and actions firmly planted in healer mode. I recognize the strong countenance. I've seen it many times from my mother over the years when situations were dire and there was no time to waste. My wolf releases her hold on our form, and our souls drift apart as her wolfish features pull away, leaving only me in possession of our body.

I rush forward and bite back a gasp as I see Harlan and Hess lying before me, both healers scrambling to save them. Harlan's wolf whines, quietly snapping my attention back to her, and I kneel down and shove my hands in her bloodied fur, knowing healers need contact to do what they do.

Vorria places a hand on my arm and the other against the bleeding hole in Harlan's side. I keep replaying the image of her jumping in the path of a bullet that could have killed my mate. My eyes burn, and I beg the spark of magic that exists inside of me to help her. The Ruin Falls' healer chants something so quietly that I can't make it out. Instead of focusing on the words, I allow the rhythm of how she's saying them to wash through me, while I try to lend her everything I can to help the wolf beneath our touch.

The telltale coolness of healing magic seeps out from Vorria's hands, coating Harlan's body. I add that same heady warmth I felt when Vorria asked me to help with the knife wound in my stomach, hoping I'm actually doing something. The third healer presses sharp looking tongs into Harlan's wound at the same time, and I can't help the warning growl that spills out of my lips when he twists them, causing Harlan to yelp in pain.

Tyran steps up, shifted back to his human form as he presses a hand against my back to calm my growl. "It's okay, Vicious. He has to get the bullet out, or we'll never be able to heal her completely," he assures me, and I do my best to swallow down my warning.

With another twist, the other healer pulls the mouth of the tongs out, which are now clamped around a small piece of metal. I stare at the bullet, hating how something so small could cause so much damage. The healer drops it into a pad of gauze, and I focus all my attention back on the she-wolf, making sure we fix her up and get her back on her feet in no time.

Harlan's bleeding slows, and I watch in awe as the wound slowly knits back together. Her uneven pants begin to even out into steady breaths, and relief hammers through me when Vorria pulls her hands back and nods.

Howls of relief and happiness fill the sky, and my own heart leaps with it too, until the healer redirects my attention to Hess. Vorria pulls me closer to him, his face almost unrecognizable, breaths labored, pallor sickly. Guilt and heartbreak swarm me like wasps, and a hitch in my throat stifles the emotion I feel building in my eyes.

What have they done to him?

A renewed rage sets my insides alight, and I suddenly wish I'd ripped Burke from the van and shredded him when I had the chance. Tyran fits a shirt over my head, and I look behind me, offering him a warm, sad smile before threading my arms through the sleeves. I lean over Hess, placing my hands on his shoulder, terrified that even my light touch could be hurting him. Kier is kneeling by his head, whispering soothing things to his twin, while Vorria and the other healer take their place at Hess's sides.

The rush of magic that I feel shoved into his body makes even me gasp. It's less as though the healers are feeding into the male, and more like he's syphoning it out of them, his body in desperate need of help. I believed Hess was dead, so it kills me to think of what he's gone through this entire time, all because I didn't think to come back for him.

Trying to feed my spark into him, I close my eyes, blocking out the view of his beaten face. Instead, I think of Hess laughing with my mom, or the times he just sat quietly next to her as she cried. I think of the moments where he tried to get close to me, and all the times I shut it down. At first, I think I did it out of loyalty to my father. Later, I pushed him away because I was worried what Burke would do to him if he thought we were close, and I didn't want my mom to lose him. Now, here I am, kneeling next to the male and hoping with everything I have that I can help save his life.

Bones crack brutally into place as the healers' magic washes through him. It's a painful, agonizing process, every broken bit of him needing repair. The healers work meticulously to right the wrongs done to his body, and I add my searing heat to their balmy cold. The healers look worn out, their expressions determined but strained, so even though I myself start to feel tired, I keep pushing, keep trying.

Slowly, Hess's skin grows less clammy and gray, and starts to turn back to a healthy hue as bruises disappear from his body. The Plummet Lake healer next to me crumples over in exhaustion, and a female wolf rushes to check on him.

"He's okay," she announces quietly, and two wolves bring a stretcher for the healer and lay him out on it.

Vorria is still focused and stern as she works on Hess, but I don't miss the bead of sweat forming on her brow. She's been healing our pack when she could ever since the fight first broke out. I can only imagine how drained her reserves must be right now. I try to pour more of my spark into her, because even though I still have no idea how it works or why my mother never mentioned anything to me, I'm grateful I can at least try to help. It's so much better than the feeling of helpless frustration that's radiating off of Tyran right now.

Suddenly, Hess gasps and his eyes fly open, making me flinch in surprise. He sits up with a rush, his face panicked and pained. "Run, Seneca...run!" he shouts, as though he's still trapped back on the night of my Flux. His words rush through me like a torrent, the plea from him to save myself like a brand to my soul.

How many times did I wish that someone would stand up for me against Burke? There were far too many moments where I hoped someone, anyone, would help pull me from the abyss. To hear Hess try, like it was his dying wish... It feels like something just healed inside of *me*.

"I'm okay. You're okay too," I reassure him, and my steady, quiet voice instantly makes him sag back in relief.

Hess blinks up at me, and then with a grimace, digs into his pocket and holds out his hand. I look down, my eyes widening when

I see the broken pieces of my mom's hair clip in his palm. With choked tears, I pick up the cracked wooden pin, my thumb brushing over the rose blossom top. Then I curl Hess's fingers over the rest of the pieces for him to keep. "Thank you," I whisper, feeling more gratitude than I could ever express.

He lets out a shaky breath, and then Kier pulls him into his arms and hugs him with all his might. "You're alright, brother."

I grip my mom's pin before my eyes land on Tyran's tawny brown gaze where I see pride and love radiating from his stare. A smile crawls across my face, and I move toward him so he can wrap me up in his strong arms.

We did it.

We got our family back.

We cut out the cancer.

Even though Burke got away, there's only so far he can run before we find him, and we *will* find him. I don't doubt it for a second.

Tilting my head back, I kiss my mate's lips and hold him close. All I want to do is get lost in him, to leave this place behind and truly start our life together, never to look back again.

"You are the most beautifully savage thing I've ever seen in my life," he whispers against my lips.

"Takes one to know one, Mate," I purr, pulling back from him and surveying the damage all around us. "Did we lose anyone?" I ask quietly, almost afraid of the answer.

But to my surprise, Tyran releases an incredulous snort. "We had some bad injuries that Vorria had to sort out, including the two betas who first approached the woodpile, but this pack didn't have it in them to truly stand up to us. It was like slaughtering drunk frat boys. They didn't stand a chance."

A voice cuts through the air. "Thank you, Alpha," a Twin Rivers male offers, stepping out from the crowd. There are a group of Twin Rivers' wolves huddled together, just set apart from the rest of the packs and being guarded by our betas, including Britton. "Thank you for rescuing us," he adds, straightening his spine and pressing his shoulders back.

Tyran snarls at him ruthlessly, his eyes flashing. "I am not *your* alpha. I would never degrade my name or my pack by claiming the weak wolves in this one," he bites out, and the male flinches and hurries back to the others. "You should all be ashamed of yourselves. Ashamed of what you allowed to happen here, especially to your own females," he bellows, his voice like a brutal hit against the gathered survivors of those who surrendered in the Twin Rivers pack.

I can smell the fear and see submission quaking through them, but it disgusts me as much as it does Tyran.

"I will be back here in three weeks," Tyran barks. "If you don't have a worthy alpha by then, if you haven't cleaned up the mess you let Burke make, I'll cull the rest of you. None of you are worthy of what we are, so you better work hard and fast to prove that there's hope for you."

Gasps and cries ring out from them, and someone shouts to me from the crowd. "Seneca, stop him! Don't let him do that to us!" I can't see who, but a feral growl rips out of my chest.

Tyran's alpha power pulses, muscles bunching as he stands before them like an immovable force. "Do *not* ask my mate for mercy!" he yells, each word laced with power and dominance as he stands proudly, hair windblown, expression brutal. "Where was *your* mercy when she needed it? You dare to even speak my luna's name as though you have the right? You have nothing, you are nothing, in her eyes, and in mine. Don't ever speak her name again in my presence!" he snarls, body shaking with protective ire.

It does all kinds of things to me to see him stand up for me, to see the fury aimed at the people who spat on me, threw things at me, shouted for Burke to put me down like a dying dog.

I move closer, pressing a hand to his cheek and pulling his rage-filled gaze to mine. "Let's go home," I tell him softly. The word *home* wraps around me like a warm blanket, burying me in its security and familiarity in a way I never could feel or recognize until now.

Tyran's eyes flit back and forth in my gaze, softening only for me. I don't know what he's looking for or what he ends up finding, but he nods, leaning down to kiss me briefly before pulling me to his side and setting his arm around my shoulders. As one, we turn away from the remnants of Twin Rivers, done with the battle and the threats for now.

We move to join the rest of our pack, and Tyran presses his nose to my hair and pulls in a deep breath. "Best idea ever, my mate. Home it is."

And just like that, my past is left behind, and the future is bright, with my mate by my side and a new pack to belong to.

Home it is.

EPILOGUE

Six Months Later

THE EDGE OF THE LAKE IS LITTERED WITH SHE-WOLVES. The water glitters in the afternoon light, and the sun pours down its blessing, warming us despite autumn's languid approach. The sound of happy squeals tickles my ears as wolves play. Some of them are wrestling, their mouths and feet kicking up water and splashing anyone who gets too close, some of them race to swim across the large expanse, and some wolves are lying next to me on the bank, like Harlan, Presley, Trinity, and Daisy.

Discreetly, I watch the two former members of the Twin Rivers pack as they relax and unwind, two things that haven't been easy for either of them since they arrived here. I look to see where they're touching. They always are, a hand, a foot, an arm pressed against another arm. No matter what's happening around them, or what they're doing, the two of them are always connected physically. It's as though they need it so they can remember they're not down in those cells anymore, they're here now, and they're safe.

We took in all the females that we found shattered and abused that night. It was weird at first to have familiar faces around, faces I grew up with and didn't have the best opinion of, but the reality of it is that none of those girls are the same, not after what was done to them. Slowly, with a lot of help from the pack, they're starting to open up again, starting to believe that the worst just might be behind them.

"Are you going to shift back anytime soon?"

The sound of Tyran's voice has my wolf perking up, tail thudding against the ground where she's lazing on her side. The four females next to me do nothing more than cast Tyran an impassive glance. Even Trinity and Daisy, who used to go as still as statues and bare their necks in fear every time Tyran came near. It's nice to see them realize that while my mate *is* a savage beast, he's also a good male and nothing like Burke.

Tyran snorts at the sight of us. "Look at you, spending most of your day on paws instead of feet. Ruin Falls rubbed off on you."

My wolf looks up at him with bright violet eyes, tongue lolling, gray fur warmed, with an expression like, *yeah, and?*

"Oh, don't give your luna such a hard time," Healer Vorria calls from where she's sitting in a wooden porch swing against the back of the house behind us. "She was busy working with me all morning, flexing that spark of hers. She managed to help Ash during labor. Fucking brilliant, that. Your mate is getting stronger."

I laugh at the old woman's foul mouth, while a flash of pride crosses Tyran's face. "Is that right?" He kneels down beside my wolf, his hand coming up to stroke her gray fur. She instantly rolls over onto her back so he can scratch her belly, and a deep chuckle comes out of him. "Belly rubs and sunning herself. Just look at our rabid luna now," he teases.

My wolf halfheartedly attempts to nip at his fingers, and he shakes his head at her. "Attacking your alpha? That's not very nice."

He stands up again, and when he blocks the sun's rays for too long, she kicks out her back leg at his ankle in a playful reprimand. He knows these lazy sunning moments are quickly tapering off as the cold threatens to set in.

Tyran dodges her kick. "Shift, you vicious thing."

It's not a command, but I'm eager to talk to him for myself, so I give my wolf a little nudge. She huffs at me but lets herself fold in as my body takes over. In a few seconds, the fur and tail are gone, and I grin up at my mate as I stand.

Of course, he already has his shirt whipped off and is tugging it down around my head. "Ow," I grumble before slipping my arms through the sleeves.

"Don't pout," he laughs, pushing my hair away from my face and tucking a dark strand behind my ear. "You get naked often enough that you know the drill." His brown eyes scan the lake, as if he's cataloging exactly which males might've seen me, not that any of them would ever disrespect their luna by ogling. "Besides, I've come to the conclusion that you must do it because you like wearing my shirts."

My lips curl into a grin. He's not entirely wrong. Wearing his shirts means I'm surrounded by his delicious scent. It also means that *he* ends up shirtless, which never fails to make my mouth water. The fact that my nudity in front of the pack sets off his wolf's possessive nature is an added bonus. It makes the sex even more off-the-charts.

"I missed you," I say, even though I saw him when he left at dawn. "How did the hunting lesson go?"

"Terrible," a male voice cuts in.

I look over and find Terris, the older, battle-scarred male with the missing eye. He walks up with his rough-voiced mate beside him—the female who cared more about me tainting the deer they caught than the fact that they found *me* on their pack land. I've learned that these two live on the outskirts of pack land for a reason. And that reason is, well...they're assholes.

But they're loyal assholes, at least. Not that they've apologized for dragging me to their house and putting me in the shed until they could alert Tyran of a strange wolf on their land. I don't take it personally anymore though. I've learned that they just don't know any better.

"*Not* terrible," Tyran sternly corrects, shooting Terris a look as he and his mate keep walking, heading for the lake with fishing poles. These two might be unpleasant, but they hunt and fish tirelessly to make sure the pack is fed.

Shaking his head at their backs, Tyran then looks back at me. "The pups are getting better. Some of them will make excellent kappas."

I look over my shoulder. "Hear that, Presley? You're going to have new blood to boss around soon. I know how much you love to do that," I tease.

Presley's white and red wolf pauses from licking her paws. She shoots me a glare, lifting one side of her lips to flash a fang. It's basically the equivalent of a wolf middle finger. I laugh and stick out my tongue at her, and her wolf chuffs before going right back to the meticulous grooming.

"How's everyone doing?" Tyran whispers in my ear.

I smile at the warm concern in his tone. "Good," I whisper back. "Harlan said Presley is still having nightmares. I talked with Vorria about this tea my mother used to make that might help. We're going to see if we can track the ingredients down tomorrow."

Tyran nods and surveys the red and white wolf. She's come a long way, fought hard to make the progress that she has, but PTSD is not an easy fix or quick battle. Far too many survivors of Twin Rivers understand that all too well. Presley's more subdued now, but I can almost say we're...friends. What happened during that attack when I was almost killed and she was taken changed things between us, bonded us in a way. And Trinity and Daisy seem to be good for her. All of the females have been able to help each other actually, as they work through their shared experiences with Twin Rivers' toxic abuse.

I only wish that I could serve them all Burke's head on a silver platter. It still sends my wolf snarling every time we think about how he got away. But at least we're all here, healing and happy, and we stripped him of his power and pack. Twin Rivers is now nothing more than a miniature pack, run by a she-wolf who Tyran is keeping his eye on. They know that they're under scrutiny and they better not step out of line, or they'll have Ruin Falls to face, and they won't be spared again.

"So, you helped Ash give birth to her pup?" Tyran asks me, drawing my attention back to him.

"I didn't do much," I admit. "Ash did all the work, and Vorria was amazing as always."

The old healer arches a gray brow. "Don't sell your shit short, Luna," she barks, though her face is the picture of calm contentment as she continues to rock on her swing overlooking the lake. "You gave me a hell of a boost."

I give a little smile, shaking my head at her. "Fine," I relent grudgingly. "I helped. A little. Ash and her pup are healthy and resting."

When I'm not helping to merge the two packs together, making sure everyone feels like they have a place and a purpose, settling disputes, or generally watching over everything, I also help Vorria. Ever since I was able to use it to help Harlan and Hess, the crass healer has been having me practice to draw out my spark more and more.

Admittedly, I can't do very much. But...the magic, as small as it may be, makes me feel closer to my mom. It makes my grief for her a little sweeter and a little less bitter, like she left a piece of her with me.

"My spark is getting easier to use," I tell my mate. "And I can use it for longer."

Tyran wraps a hand around my jaw, his brown eyes glinting. "You're a fierce warrior *and* a gentle healer. Perfect fucking mate," he murmurs, lips skimming against mine.

I nip his bottom lip, enjoying the heat that banks in his eyes from that tiny gesture. "Right back at you," I say, before kissing him deeper, pressing my body right up against his.

He lets out a groan and pulls back with a shake of his head. "Alright, gotta fuck you now."

"Tyran!" My eyes bug out at his declaration that was *way* too loud, but he simply pulls me away by the hand, not caring who hears or sees. "I was going to go swimming," I grouse.

He looks over at me as he leads me toward the pack houses. "If my mate wants to go swimming, then we'll go swimming."

Butterflies take off in my stomach as Tyran changes trajectory and heads for the woods, taking me up a narrow path.

As we get deeper into the woods, my eyes land on a familiar sight.

Our cave. He brought me back to where it all started.

This is where our wolves came together. Where he chased and I dodged, where we ran together, tested each other, fought each other, took in every movement, sight, and smell, before ending up right here.

My wolf latched onto his scent that night, and she's never let go. It took me a little bit to catch up with what she already knew during that claiming hunt. That Tyran is our match in every way. He's the monster to my rabid, the anchor to my spiral.

The perfect fucking mate.

My eyes latch onto the mouth of the cave, the shadowed entrance of the shallow space somehow still smelling like us. So much has changed since he sunk his teeth into my shoulders and claimed me. Even then, before we knew each other, he grounded me. Looked me in the eye and didn't recoil at what he saw. From the very beginning, he accepted *everything* about us.

Tyran looks at me over his shoulder, curiosity in his face. "I'm picking up some very interesting things through the bond right now."

Despite my attempt to tamp it down, a blush reaches up and pinches my cheeks. "Oh yeah?" I ask airily. "My wolf must still be happy over that squirrel she caught earlier."

He sends me an amused look, looking so damn sexy with his chiseled body and his gorgeous smile, it's almost impossible not to stare. "*Right*," he taunts, "because your wolf is always feeling very loving toward whatever she viciously hunts."

"Uh, yeah." My heartbeat goes double time.

Loving.

Is that what he was picking up from the bond?

Tyran suddenly turns and picks me up by my ass, my thighs wrapping around him immediately. "How loving, exactly?" he asks, his brown gaze boring into me.

It's no secret how well matched we are in every way, how well connected. But this is the first time the word *love* has come up. It's just something that's there, grown into our mating bond. Something I know we both feel, maybe even deeper than the word itself.

"Completely and intrinsically," I answer without hesitation, my hands curled around the twin claiming marks on both of his shoulders.

Happiness pours through the bond, and he groans, either because of my admission or my possessive touch on his sensitive marks. "How set are you on this whole swimming thing? Because now I just want to fuck you up against the first tree I reach and show you how *loving* I can be."

I laugh and bury my nose against his neck, licking a trail up to the underside of his ear. "I'm *very* set on it, unfortunately. Better hurry."

He curses when I end my reply by leaning down and biting his claiming mark. "Fuck, Vicious, you're playing dirty."

Tyran squeezes my ass and starts to walk down the hill with me pressed against him, while I continue to nip and lick and kiss his neck and shoulder. When my eyes catch onto the body of water, I gasp at how picturesque it is. It's more of a pond than a lake, totally secluded with tall trees standing guard, and chutes of sunlight streaming into it.

"I *knew* there was some damn water near the cave," I say, poking at my wolf, though she pretends not to hear me. This bitch took us all the way to the pack's stronghold pretending like it was the only water available. I roll my eyes at her, and she just chuffs shamelessly inside of me.

Tyran strides straight for the pond and stops at the edge, and then without warning, tosses me in.

I gasp at the shock of freezing cold water as it engulfs me, the middle of the pond just a foot too deep for me to stand up in. "You asshole!" I shout as I come up splashing and sputtering.

I shove the wet hair out of my face and swim closer so I can stand up and glare at him. Blinking the water out of my eyes, I look up to see a smirking Tyran drop his pants, his cock already thick and hard. "What? You said you wanted to swim," he says with a grin, fisting his dick as he strides into the pond at a nice, leisurely pace.

"Prick," I grumble as I wipe water from my eyes.

Tyran wags his eyebrows at me. "Yeah, what about it? My mate enjoys a good prick on the nightly."

I roll my eyes, ignoring the thrum of approval that floods me. "I wanted to go swimming, not become a popsicle after getting dumped in a freezing cold pond."

He wades over to me, hands gripping my waist as he spins me around until my ass is wedged against his length. I'm covered in chills from the icy water, but the moment his body presses against mine, the heat of his skin sinks into me, turning those chills into something much more sensual. The shirt I'm wearing is clinging to my body like a second skin, the cream fabric gone completely see-through.

"I just wanted to get you wet," he says with a playful nip against my shoulder before his hand delves between my legs. His fingers immediately go for my clit, pulling a gasp from me. "Mmm, but I see you already were."

Of course I am. My body is in a constant state of arousal when he's around, and the slightest thing can set me off.

I shove my ass further into him, teeth chattering. "Make it up to me by warming me up."

His hand moves, coming up to cup my breast instead, plucking at my poor, frozen nipple through the shirt. "Love these tits, love seeing your nipples hard and wanting my hot mouth."

I moan at the promise of that, and Tyran turns me in his arms and lifts me again, water streaming down my body as I'm held halfway out of the water. He places my breasts directly in front of his mouth, arm muscles bunching as he holds me up.

His lips close over one nipple, and my hands come up to dig into his thick brown hair, my eyes fluttering closed. His mouth is even hotter than I anticipated, and that fire when I'm surrounded by such coldness sets my nerves alight, the abrasion of the fabric against my sensitive skin making it even more intense.

He takes his time with one nipple and then the other, laving, nipping, making me ache. "Take this shirt off," I plead, but he just skims his teeth over my pebbled skin before popping off.

"You're not in charge right now, Vicious," he says, his voice low enough to rumble against me, his dominance making my pussy throb.

With my thighs straddling his torso, he slides me down the front of his rock-hard body, lining himself up perfectly as I go, and then impales me fully in one hard swoop.

"Fuck!" I moan appreciatively as my head falls back, my breath stolen from the sudden intrusion.

He groans, holding me down, making me squirm. "There's where I like my horny little mate. Right here against me, my arms cradling her sexy body, while her cunt squeezes my cock."

I roll up my hips, trying to get him to move, but he holds me there, making me take all of him, making me feel every inch of him buried inside.

"Looks like my mate is the impatient one now."

"Tyran," I growl.

The noise gets cut off as he lifts me by the thighs and then drags me back down, slow, so slow that it makes me burn with need, the shirt and the cold forgotten. Again and again, he slides me up and down his cock, until I'm so crazed with need that all I can do is wriggle while unintelligible noises spill from my lips.

"My luna wants to come, doesn't she?"

I nod, my face buried against the crook of his neck, and feel him cutting through the water before pinning me to a sun-soaked boulder, the water now only calf deep.

"Brace your hands behind you," he orders.

I'm quick to do what he says, my body begging for release. As soon as I'm in position, his hungry eyes skate over my form, and I look down to see what he sees. My body is arched toward him, his sopping wet shirt clinging to my curves, my still hard brown nipples visible. The fabric is bunched around my waist, his thick cock buried in my pussy.

"You are the sexiest fucking thing to ever walk these lands." His declaration is more growl than anything else, and I feel his dick pulse inside of me. He leans forward to take my mouth, tongue thrusting in, teeth biting, demanding that he get to taste every sound I make. "Gonna fuck you hard and fast now, Vicious, because we have somewhere to be."

I'm too needy to have the wherewithal to ask where, and in the next second, it doesn't matter anyway. Because before I can even blink, Tyran unleashes. He fucks me on that rock without restraint, like a beast possessed, and I fucking *love* it.

"Arch up more," he demands. "Feed me those pretty tits."

I bow my back as far as I can, and his devilish mouth descends on my breasts again, at the same time that one hand comes to my clit. He owns my body, every part of me, and the bond throbs with pleasure both ways as I reach higher and higher to my peak.

"Come, Mate. I want your pussy squeezing me, and then you're going to take me in your hands and open that vicious mouth of yours."

My pussy gushes at his filthy order, and that's all it takes for me to explode. The release is intense and fiery, flushing me head to toe in heat.

"Fuck, yes," Tyran grounds out. "Christ, you're sexy when you come."

I blink up at him, my body shaking as it falls back down from that epic plummet. His teeth are gritted, eyes locked on mine, doing everything he can to hold back his release. "I want to watch you work my knot until you're bathed in my cum."

God, I could come from his dirty talk alone.

I reach down and finally rip off the shirt, sending it slapping on the ground somewhere behind me. Then I scoot back until his cock slips out onto my hand, my juices coating it.

"Squeeze hard, Vicious. You know how I like it."

Instead of listening, I scoot closer and then lift my breasts up, squeezing his cock between them. I'm rewarded by a sexy groan. "Fuck, yes, let me fuck those tits."

He reaches down to take control of my breasts, pressing them together as he thrusts his hips forward again and again. "Open that mouth, tongue out," Tyran rasps.

I stick my tongue out as far as it'll go, my eyes locked on his face as he comes. The first ropes of his release hit my collarbone, more shooting up over my cheek and tongue.

"Fucking gorgeous."

The second his release stops, I wrap my fingers around him and start to stroke his still hard length. I use my other hand to wrap around the base, right where his knot is expanding. I fist him tightly as I jerk him, squeezing as hard as I can.

Tyran loses control. He starts thrusting into my hands, while letting out incomprehensible curses and growls. He comes again, more ropes of his release splattering over my breasts, marking me all over, bathing me in his seed and desire.

"I need one more inside that cunt."

He drags me forward, back into the water, shoving into me so hard I scream, his knot immediately expanding and tying us together. But his hand is there, plucking and rubbing my swollen bundle of nerves. Even without the mobility to thrust, my pussy flutters, and he plays with my hyper-sensitive clit, wrenching another orgasm out of me.

My pussy clenches around his knot, milking everything we can out of him, and then we're panting against one another, totally spent, my body clinging to his. We stay like that for a while, just breathing each other in, floating in the water and enjoying the peace as his knot deflates and he slips out of me.

"You were right," he says, still a little out of breath. "Swimming was a good idea."

I laugh and lean back, wiggling out of his hold until I can dunk under the water. When I come back up, washing the cum off my body, Tyran frowns. "I preferred that stayed on you."

My eyes roll, but I lean forward and give him a kiss. "I love you, but I'm not walking around the pack covered in your cum. Not again, anyway."

The smile falls from his face, and instead, intensity overtakes his expression. He reaches for me, cupping my face in his hands. "You said it."

"Were you waiting for me to?" At his nod, my heart melts and my eyes soften. "You know I do. And you love me," I say, because I feel it. Every day we're together, I feel it. "It's you and me."

"You and me," Tyran repeats, voice dropping before he plants a gentle kiss on my lips. But when he pulls away, there's a sly glint in his eye and a savage smile on his face.

I look at him warily. "I know that look."

"What look?" he says with a smirk as he starts to walk us out of the pond.

"The look that says you're about to go all savage."

He laughs. "*Someone* is going to go savage, but it's not going to be me." My wolf sits up in curiosity when he adds, "I have a surprise for you."

TYRAN SINGS LOUDLY OFF-KEY TO some country song I've never heard before. I laugh as he commits fully to a twang he doesn't have, lamenting long and hard about a road to hell and I think something about a red baseball cap and beer. We bounce down a dirt road in his truck, and I look around at the unfamiliar foothills, trying to figure out what we're doing here. I've given up on asking at this point. Not even a little road head pried his delectable full lips open.

We round a corner, and I spot another truck parked just up ahead, with two tall familiar males leaning against the side of it. I turn to Tyran, a wide smile on my face, and unbuckle my seat belt to slide next to him. I kiss his cheek and nuzzle his neck, excitement zipping through me at the sight of Hess and Kier.

Hess and I have been talking every week since he settled down in his brother's pack. It's been amazing to get to know him and forge the friendship we should have always had. We're the only two people left who really knew my mom. It's been special and cathartic to keep her memory alive through our chats and for me to understand why she loved Hess as a friend so much.

The truck's barely rolled to a stop before I'm flying out of the door, a giggle following in my wake as happiness buzzes around me like bees to new spring flowers.

"Hess!" I shout, as though the male doesn't know his own name. "You look so good!" I observe as we close the distance between each other. We take a quick moment to press our foreheads together, and then he lifts me off my feet and twirls me around.

"Seneca, it's been too long," he rumbles, squeezing me tightly against him as Tyran and Kier chuckle and greet each other with alpha handshakes and back slaps.

"Did you bring Pru?" I ask Kier, looking around to see if his mate made the trip, but he smiles sheepishly and shakes his head no as Hess sets me back down on my feet.

The alpha and I press our foreheads together in greeting, and there's an electric excitement to the air that has me feeling like I'm on cloud nine. It's so good to see them. Our packs have grown a lot closer since the battle that demolished Burke and his crew. We get together as often as we can, but it never feels like it's enough.

"Do you know what we're doing here?" Hess asks me, shooting his brother a look as though he's been about as forthcoming with info as Tyran. My brow furrows, because I thought Hess and Kier were the surprise, but now that he mentions it, Tyran wouldn't have brought us to the middle of nowhere for a get-together.

I look over at Tyran, a giddy shiver working its way up my spine. "There's more?"

He shoots me a devilishly handsome grin and wags his eyebrows. "I thought we could get up to some hunting. I've heard the elk are particularly huge and ruthless in these parts."

My smile grows even wider, and it's all I can do not to jump up and down and clap with excitement. I bound over to him and wrap my arms around his neck, kissing him deeply. "Fuck the elk, let's find some mountain lions or something," I suggest, and Tyran's deep laugh works me over in all the best ways.

"There's my vicious mate," he teases, and then he threads his hand in mine and starts leading me to the trees.

Hess and Kier are on our heels, and I'm just about to ask what's new in their pack when a breeze rushes through the trees. With it comes the smell of fruit on the cusp of going rotten.

Burke.

I stop in my tracks, every hair on my body rising, my vision fracturing as I search the surrounding woods. A menacing growl tears out of my throat, and fur starts to sprout out of Hess's arm as he scans our surroundings too.

Tyran steps in front of me, dominance radiating off of him. "Seneca, it's okay. Come with me," he instructs, and although everything inside of me doesn't want to move, my wolf and I primed to shift and deal with the threat, we trust our mate and do exactly as he asks.

I hear Kier guiding Hess in the same way that Tyran is guiding me, but I don't understand why until we crest a hill, and it all clicks.

Hanging from a tree, his ankle wrapped brutally in a snare, is none other than Burke. He looks over to see me and starts wiggling and flailing frantically, which only causes the snare to bite into his flesh deeper. The smell of his fear permeates the land like a thick fog, and I close my eyes and let all the rabid parts of me revel in it.

"You found him," I say, satisfaction pouring through the bond both ways.

"I found him," Tyran confirms with a nod.

Seeing the ex-alpha like this feeds the rabid beast inside of me.

"Happy hunting, Vicious," Tyran whispers in my ear, nipping my earlobe before he pulls back. With wide eyes, I turn to him, completely shocked and overwhelmed by what he's done. Tears well in my eyes as I kiss him deeply, taking my time to show him what this means to me.

"I love you," I whisper against his lips as we pull apart.

"I love you," he answers back simply, moving his mouth to my shoulder and biting his mark there.

I shake my head, still completely in shock, and then move down the hill to our prey. "Best. Fucking. Mate. Ever," I call over my shoulder.

"You know it," he calls back from the top of the hill.

I chuckle and reach over and squeeze Hess's shoulder as we get ready for the best hunt of our lives. "You want to run him down first, or should I?" I ask.

A savage smile tilts his lips. "The lead is all yours, Luna," he tells me, wicked excitement in his voice mixed with pride that Burke will *finally* get what he deserves.

I walk over to the base of the tree and spot the cable of the snare looped around the trunk of the tree.

"Don't do this," Burke starts to plead. "You don't have to do this. You can be better than I was," he begs. "Take the pack! I won't come for them. You did me a favor, actually, I was ready to be done. There's a lot of money and power in that pack, it's all yours," he declares, trying to trade things he no longer owns and make promises that we all know he'd never keep.

Hess and I look at each other, half offended that this idiot thinks he's going to talk his way out of the *very* painful death that he's earned.

Burke swings slightly, making it so he can't see us, and when it's clear his begging is going to get him nowhere, the threats start. "You're fucking cowards, stringing me up like this. Couldn't fight me properly, so this is what you resort to? You'd both be nothing without me, and this is the thanks I get? Cut me down, and I'll fuck you both up! And when I'm done, I'm going to destroy everything you ever cared about. You're going to wish you never fucked with me, Seneca!"

His body rotates enough that his malicious black eyes once again land on me. "I should have taken you the first time I saw you. I should have fucked that virgin pussy and licked up your tears when I had the chance. I should have slit your fucking throat and cum down it while you bled to death," he snarls, spit flying out of his mouth as though the venom of his words is poisoning even him.

A low growl starts in Hess's chest, but I pat his arm to tell him I'm okay. Nothing this foul monster can say or do penetrates my armor.

"Shoulda, coulda, woulda, Burke, but thanks for the ideas of what we can have done to you before you die," I tell him casually, and I watch his face pale as he slowly spins away from us.

He puts everything he has into trying to free himself one last time, but when he can't, when the begging doesn't work, and the threats and taunts fall on deaf ears, he goes quiet. I watch as he spins another full rotation and I pull in a deep fortifying breath.

"I'll give you a choice, Burke," I tell him, and his eyes narrow at my words. I'm not surprised. For someone who's lived their life stealing the choices of others, I'm sure it's alarming that he's now being offered one. "Tell me how you killed my mother, and I'll make this quicker and so much less painful than it could be."

Hess tenses next to me and silence falls around us like delicate snowflakes.

I can practically hear the calculation going on in Burke's mind. I know he's looking at all angles, trying to gauge whether or not he can lie, barter, gaslight, or deny his way out of this. I wait patiently, giving him all the time he needs to see clearly exactly what I see. That there's no way out of what's coming.

Burke's black gaze falls on Tyran and Kier up on the hill behind us, and then he looks at me. Anger shines in his eyes, but it's slowly drowned out by the desperation that once again creeps in. He's cornered prey and he knows it.

"I've been rehoming females to some of the southern packs who needed them," he starts, and I have to work hard to school my features.

I tamp down hard on the emotion that wants to surge through me as I recall the females we found in the cells from Twin Rivers, and the ones we discovered from other packs. I thought he was hurting them, and that was bad enough, but I had no idea he was selling our kind too.

"Some of the boys got a little too rough with a couple that were already paid for. I had no choice but to bring your mother in," he goes on, and anger roils through me.

I know all too well the disgust and horror that must have gone through her at witnessing what was happening in those cursed concrete prisons. I'm sure she quickly realized the minute Burke showed her his dirty little secret that he was never going to let her leave knowing it.

Was she scared?

Did she try to convince him to let her go, or did she know she was doomed?

"The girls needed a lot of healing, and she was getting drained..." He spins slowly around, pausing as though he's searching for some formation of words that will make what he's about to say less repulsive, less triggering, so that I'll keep my promise of *quick* and *less painful*. "When she tried to stop, I forced her to keep going." No one speaks for a long moment as Burke's words settle heavily around Hess and me.

I can feel Hess fighting through the rage and sorrow now pumping through him. There's a slight hitch to his breathing, like he's swallowing a sob down over and over, refusing to let it go. Burke's back is turned towards us as he completes another spin and I close my eyes, fighting not to picture what my mom's last moments must have been like.

I want to ask Burke what her last words were, because maybe she asked him to pass along a message to me, but I choke the questions down. I know she would've never let his presence or even his voice taint a loving message between us. She would have known there was nothing she could say that I didn't already know.

Her loss was devastating, but I knew she loved me. There was no doubt in my mind about what I meant to her. I saw time and time again as she put herself in harm's way for me, how she'd pick herself up from grief, from hardship and struggle, and then she'd lift *me* higher, in a way only a loving mother can.

Pain and loss swell in my chest, but I know I'll have to make time for them later. Because right now, it's about justice. It's about retribution and repairing what we can. We'll be looking into the southern packs, we'll right what wrongs we can, and it will all start with Burke.

My wolf and I shift my hand into claws, and the sight of it makes Burke piss his pants. I slash out at the snare wire, and the pitiful former alpha drops hard to the ground. He scrambles back away from Hess and me, and I tilt my head and watch him go.

"You said you'd make it quick!" he yelps as he struggles to get to his feet.

"I lied," I answer simply, as I think back to what he said to me the day he dumped me on Ruin Falls land. I sift through the memories until I find his exact words, and then a vicious smile spreads across my face, his terrified stare solely focus on my rabid eyes.

"*I'd start running if I were you,*" I call out in a cruel mockery of what he said to me the day he thought he was leaving me for dead or worse.

Just like I hoped he would, with the blood draining from his face as brutal reality stares him down, he gets to his feet, and with a limp, he bolts. Dirt and leaves kick up behind him as he tries to flee, cursing me as he goes.

I smile as my wolf and I shift, and then just as soon as Hess is covered in fur and ready to go too, we start hunting Burke like the animal he is. I may be rabid, but *he's* the beast who deserves to be put down.

My wolf howls out her ferocity, the need for vengeance driving us forward, the call for death and vengeance right at our claw tips. For all the people Burke hurt. For my old alpha, my dad, my mom, Hess, all the females back in Ruin Falls.

For *me*.

This fucker is mine.

IVY ASHER is addicted to chai, swearing, and laughing a lot—but not in a creepy, laughing alone kind of way. She loves the snow, books, and her family of two humans, and three fur-babies. She has worlds and characters just floating around in her head, and she's lucky enough to be surrounded by amazing people who support that kind of crazy.

WWW.IVYASHER.COM

@ivy.asher

@IvyAsherBooks

@ivy.asher

RAVEN KENNEDY has two beautiful daughters plus a very supportive husband, and she's lucky enough to have her dream job. She's a California girl born and raised, whose love for books pushed her into creating her own worlds. The Plated Prisoner Series, a dark fantasy romance, has already sold in over a dozen countries and is a #1 international bestseller with over a million copies sold. It was inspired by the myth of King Midas and a woman's journey with finding her own strength. Her debut series was a romcom fantasy about a cupid looking for love of her own. No matter the genre, whether she makes you laugh or cry, or whether the series is about a cupid or a gold-touched woman living in King Midas's gilded castle, she hopes to create characters that readers can root for.

WWW.RAVENKENNEDYBOOKS.COM

@ravenkennedybooks

@ravenkennedybooks

@ravenkennedybooks

@18343962.Raven_Kennedy

www.ingramcontent.com/pod-product-compliance
Lightning Source LLC
Chambersburg PA
CBHW020456310726
48979CB00016B/2675/J

* 9 7 8 1 9 5 9 5 3 7 0 1 4 *